WHISPERS OF THE CROOKED MAN

BLOODLINES

RYAN HOLDEN

RYAN HOLDEN BOOKS

Copyright © 2024] by Ryan Holden

All rights reserved.

No part of this publication may be reproduced, distributed, or transmitted in any form or by any means, including photocopying, recording, or other electronic or mechanical methods, without the prior written permission of the publisher, except as permitted by U.S. or UK copyright law. For permission requests, contact www.RyanHoldenBooks.co.uk

The story, all names, characters, and incidents portrayed in this production are fictitious. No identification with actual persons (living or deceased), places, buildings, and products is intended or should be inferred.

Edition Number: One/2024

About the Author

I fell in love with the idea of writing many years ago. Then I grew up, fell in love with many other things, and had to learn how to be an adult with responsibilities. Two teenage sons later, things didn't turn out too bad, and now I have a little more free time to reunite with my first love... I want to create a world that readers sink deep in and never want to get out. A supernatural detectiverse with intriguing cases and loveable characters. Join me on this rollercoaster.

Contents

Prologue 'One week ago,'	IX
Epigraph Haunted by the Crooked Man	1
Chapter 1 'Gerald - December 1987'	3
Chapter 2 'Gerald'	12
Chapter 3 'Gerald – Home - présent Day,'	21
Chapter 4 'Frank Ecklestone One Week Ago,'	25
Chapter 5 'Gerald-Présent Day,'	28
Chapter 6 'Gerald-The Next Morning,'	32
Chapter 7 'Détective Reynolds,'	38
Chapter 8 'Killer,'	45

Chapter 9 'Gerald–Library,'	50
Chapter 10 'Gerald,'	55
Chapter 11 'Détective Reynolds,'	60
Chapter 12 'Gerald,'	64
Chapter 13 'Gerald,'	68
Chapter 14 'Détective Reynolds - Morgue,'	73
Chapter 15 'Gerald,'	80
Chapter 16 'Detective Reynolds,'	84
Chapter 17 'Dr Thornton,'	90
Chapter 18 'Détective Reynolds,'	95
Chapter 19 'Gerald,'	100
Chapter 20 'Détective Reynolds,'	105
Chapter 21 'Gerald,'	111
Chapter 22 'Détective Reynolds,'	116
Chapter 23 ' Gerald - Melwood 8 PM,'	123

Chapter 24 'Gerald,'	133
Chapter 25 'Gerald,'	138
Chapter 26 'Détective Reynolds,'	142
Chapter 27 'Detective Reynolds,'	148
Chapter 28 'Détective Reynolds,'	156
Chapter 29 'Détective Reynolds,'	162
Chapter 30 'Gerald,'	171
Chapter 31 'Gerald,'	180
Chapter 32 'Détective Reynolds—Back to my worst moment,'	187
Chapter 33 'Gerald,'	195
Chapter 34 'Gerald'	201
Chapter 35 'Gerald.'	207
Chapter 36 'Gerald'	211
Chapter 37 'Détective Reynolds,'	216
Chapter 38 'Gerald,'	224

Chapter 39 'Detective Reynolds'	228
Chapter 40 'Gerald'	235
Acknowledgements	244

Prologue

'One week ago,'

It looked like a war zone. Except the dead were the ones rampaging through the streets. We were driving painstakingly slow, zig-zagging hundreds of the undead staggering across the middle of the road and any sidewalk. We passed at least two cemeteries where my stomach churned, watching decomposed bodies punching out the ground. Some had flesh peeling from their bones, oozing black fluid. While others were a little fresher. None of it will leave me for a while.

I was in awe and terrified by how it had happened. Were those creeps in suits that powerful? In that vision through the killer's eyes, he taunted Nathan's father about the gates of hell. George described those guys as demonic knights; could they tap into the underworld? Give the dead a little wake-up call. How else is it possible? The more I thought, the more my brain hurt. None of this should be possible, let alone be my reality. Did my father know how bad things could get? Nathan's father mentioned a plan B. I hoped we would find it at this place marked by a little square on their flesh.

It makes me wish there was a 'do-over' button, rewind to before the accidents, and warn Charlotte and her father to avoid certain things. Maybe ask Father more questions and take an interest. Perhaps I'd be more prepared and, in exchange, warn him about what's to come. I know that's all pie in the sky, and I must start facing what's happening to me. My bloodline is cursed; if I let the darkness in, I'd be the same as the killer. Maybe even do exactly what he is. Was this what I had to come? The reason I keep seeing through his eyes. Or were we connected in some other way?

We neared the end of Wickham Street and exited the village of Billing, Which, much like ours, Maplewood, Melwood and Filton, was drenched in darkness. Not a light in sight. I'd be bold enough to say the power had been cut off on purpose, leaving these villages isolated. This game was getting old. Those fuckers knew what they were doing. Creating distractions and vulnerability, letting the undead terrorise normal life.

This leaves me with the question: Can the undead turn humans? I get they can kill, but what if it's a scratch or a bite? Would that do? I still don't know how that happened when Nathan's father grabbed onto my wrist. It had to be the bloodlines; we're connected like in that photograph. All of them together. It must've been as we swung into another bend; I bumped against the armrest, and a thought came to me. A sickly, stomach-churning thought that I didn't know what to do with.

I'm back at the bar, the two polaroids slide out, and I see that symbol, the moment I'd absentmindedly carved into a coaster moments earlier. The devil star in a circle. Except this was blood on the sidewalk next to my father's body. It couldn't be, not when we'd asked for help. It's not like Nathan was in the right state or frame of mind for me to bother him on this. Besides, it made no sense anyway. Not that it stopped the tired cogs in my brain from turning.

Our wheels rumbled over another cattle grid into an even darker country lane. We continued slow, not thinking there'd be any traffic, and I heard Gerald mention we could end up mowing down some of the dead if they'd made it this far. I could see the logic.

Nathan was slumped as far into the corner of his seat as possible. His expression was pale and vacant. Not the usual happy-go-lucky friend I was used to. Death does that. I would know. I sensed that Detective Reynolds knew that, too. He didn't say anything but empathises and goes out of his way to help while not pushing Nathan or me. I reckon he's been through some version of hell himself. Damn, that word, 'Hell', to think that's what we were trying to stop, the real thing. The detectives had mapped out that weird yet spooky diagram that was somehow printed on Nathan's parents' backs. Fuck, I haven't even thought about how I'm going to handle that. Do I plead ignorance? What good was the truth right now anyway?

Headlights beamed against a black-and-white sign as we swept around another bend, with the sore growing on my elbow feeling like the hundredth one we'd taken. 'Kingsley' was three miles out. Behind that sign, the view would otherwise look picturesque, with trees as far as the eyes could see and hilltops kissing a slightly lighter purple of the sky. Peaceful, that's how it looked, moments that have been few and far between. Reminded me of the girls, praying to god they were safe.

Mother didn't tell me where they were headed; safer that way. It's not knowing if they're okay that worries me. I feel they are, though; I can't say why; it's just a flutter in my stomach when I think of them accompanied by that thought. Hoping they were obliviously sleeping while the world went to shit. This part of it, anyway. Mother would undoubtedly have heard the news; she has 'Radio Two' on twenty-four seven. No sooner had I been comforted by that image. Another came flying in like an express train, the father's head.

Before and after shots. The pleading and a final chuckle of defiance. Then, the yawning, chomping, mindless view rocking in a pool of blood on the table.

I'm looking at Nathan, worried as you'd expect. His world had been smooth sailing as far as he knew. He had a wealthy family, and he got to run around Willowbrook or wherever playing private investigator. Everything he knew had imploded, but that was without the truth. The look on his face now was a man in need of alcohol; boy, could I join him. All of this feels like a never-ending nightmare we can't wake from. We're rolling into 'Kingsley' I'm wondering what's waiting. Nathan is twitching and seems edgy and aggravated. Perhaps his father was lying, hoping to throw the killer off balance. Soon, his father's bloodline will sink its claws in, and all of this dark stuff going on with me will take root. It seems odd he hasn't asked, 'When does this happen to me?'.Does he know something I don't?

I'm looking out the windshield into the darkness, like the black growing within. I see Detective Reynolds's hand change out of the corner of my eye. Dark fur grew thick and bushy; his hand doubled, maybe tripled in size, with his flesh becoming shades of brown. Seeing all this in a surreal, slow motion was scary and remarkable. Then came the claws. Menacingly long, thick, stretching to thin with sharp tips. They were as black as the night around us and just as daunting. I wouldn't want to be on the wrong end of them. Why? That's what I asked myself. The little I knew of this world, I mean their world. It had to mean something, voluntarily changing like that. It feels weird, with the inclination to respect their job as Detectives, but easier when it's less formal. So, I'll call it that way. After all, nothing about this felt 'Law' related. Not no more.

Michael did the same; his hair was lighter, longer, and thinner. No, so werewolf, but more akin to a feral animal. A fox. I'd say. Maybe it's more obvious to obvious, but these moments of the calm before the storm. I was learning as much as I could. Anything to take my mind off what's bothering me the most. Secrets. I don't like them; I was never good at keeping them, and in the last months, I've made it my job, much like Nathan, to uncover the reality behind them.

Look where it got us. George and Michael, though, were bothered right now. I was busy craning my neck and looking for the obvious when something weird happened to me. That bar is uniquely high for me, but this... I was propelled back through the eyes of the killer. Not literally, but those heightened feelings and senses. I could hear heartbeats. That might sound like my stress was getting to me, and it was my hearing. It wasn't. I could hear the double pacing of our supernatural friends in the front. Nathan's was steady, low, almost a sleeping rhythm; he'd withdrawn far into himself and his dark thoughts. Just like I experienced in that vision, George rolled his window down; I watched his head tilt, inhaling to catch a scent. I hate to be rude, but I'd only seen that with a dog. Thank god these were no dogs. His ears twitched, too. My nose began going, too; I picked up on it all. Overwhelming in all its stinking glory. The toxic diesel spewed from our car, a dampness showing rain coming.

That shudder came again; I drifted back in my seat as I felt it. Death. That's what it was. The long, bony hand of death stroking my grave. Vibrant and deadly, it came in ferocious waves carried on the bitter breeze. Death blended with sulphur was travelling toward us, which had George alert. Michael was slower to it, I noticed. Again, why? I asked myself, why was I experiencing this? I shook off the chill in time for another wave. Chills, that is. This was different; I knew what came next. Seems the pre-cursor to our dark standoff.

A finger-like brush of my cheek, then with the usual cold, melancholy, *'Are you ready, Gerald, ready to finally give in? Embrace it because what's coming? You'll need me. Now...Let...me...in. Let the darkness in and own your bloodline and its burden. No crosses need bearing. A curse doesn't need to mean a curse.'*

"I can't; I'm not evil. I've seen evil, and that's not me if I let the darkness in. I become the one killing and looking to turn this world on its head." I whispered but caught George's eyes staring at me in the rearview. Not once have I said yes or embraced it. I came close in the basement, but I didn't. So why am I experiencing what I am? Why did the darkness help me at the farm and the basement, teasing me with all the heightened nonsense?

There's no manual for it, and my father ran from it. Nathan's parents, too. The more I dwelled on that puzzle and startling reality, with that melancholic calling hitching a ride with that ever-present terror bobbing on the tiny boat through my sanity. The river had become a tumultuous sea rife with monsters. All waiting to devour the boat, its passengers become captive to them, beasts.

A world of eat or be eaten. Kill or be killed. To compound my impossible choice in this 'most dangerous game', the boat had lost its steering rudder long ago. Broke loose when I watched Nathan's mother have her jugular cut through and his father, a sword clean through his heart. I guess what I'm saying is that at least two of the four bloodlines have run or attempted to hide from this, and they've ended up dead. Would doing the opposite have the same outcome? That's not me deciding to give in, more 'devil's advocate' playing 'blackjack with a losing hand, deciding whether to stick or twist.

I'm sure this all seems like the rambling of a man who's finally lost his mind, having skirted close for a while. Perhaps that's why the call came at this moment, when morale is low, heading into the unknown, surrounded by the 'undead' staggering through the streets, dripping their decomposing flesh all over the place.

'Why such one-dimensional thinking? If a mundane is inherently evil, it is in their nature that when the opportunity is within their grasp, they will become evil. If a mundane is inherently good, trod a righteous path all of their life, even when opportunities have presented themselves so willingly and that mundane still chooses to walk that righteous path. It will be their nature to be good.'

"So what are you saying?" I said. It was probably my tired brain. I thought I understood the basics and the point, but then I kept looking for hidden meanings. When is evil ever truthful, I asked myself. Nathan continued twitching. I still heard his ultra-calm heart while Michael and George sounded as though readying for that deathly sulphur stench.

'If a mundane is naturally good, like yourself. Look at this crusade for the truth you've been on. I've watched it all; I hear your thoughts, and I know your doubts. I also tantalisingly know your potential. A mundane in pursuit of good. So, why would you think evil would be your path?'

Was I being reeled in? While something approached that I sensed was nothing good, the darkness whispered a sales pitch that made me think. "Are you implying that just because I embrace the darkness, that sounds very much hauntingly evil? I mean, the clue in the word, 'darkness', speaks volumes. It doesn't mean I will become some crazed killer like the other guy. I mean, what the hell is he?"

'Finally, the penny drops. I knew mundanes were sometimes slow, but with you, I had hope. As for him, he has become one of the fallen Knights; there are many other names or titles, but those like him have fallen from the cause, much like the two that hold your detective friend's girl. They were The Knights Templar at one point, until they became Baphoments chosen or the Eternal vigil

because at any one time there's two Knights watching over, creating chaos and evil in the world.-' I butted in as the last sentence hit me hard.

"What? What do you mean watching over and creating chaos?" I said, forming a picture that these Knights have been the spark for many a conflict that blights our world.

'You see, there's always been that hope, that quest to resurrect all the Knights slain centuries ago when their allegiance to Baphomet was leaked to the King of France. Who ordered them located at eradicated? Including their General Francois, Louis Philip the second. As evil as they come before embracing the devil. There was a belief that one day, the required relics would surface, and one day, a bloodline would give in to the power. Or they will go mad as so many over the years have. Now, there's a hungry killer playing puppet. While thinking he's playing chess. For the most part, in your life, he has. Suppose those Templars are broken out of hell with the demons. There will be an unstoppable army of undead led by some of the fiercest soldiers ever to walk your earth. To answer your question, the Knights need the right environment; they feed off it. You mundanes are easy to manipulate, and by them creating a world ripe with evil, it's like a drug. A highly intoxicating drug that fuels them.' I was stunned into silence. Although I had been whispering, I knew George was listening.

"What would that make me?" I asked. They say curiosity killed the cat. Well, I say better the devil, you know. Corny, right?

'That's one of life's mysteries, I told you; if you let me in, you will experience all the power you can imagine. But... that doesn't mean you have to fall, too. Could well be a true Knights Templar, one to restore faith and order.'

"But in the beginning, you made it seem you wanted me to kill and do bad. What happened?" I asked, thinking back to when the haunting began.

'What's one of those four-legged beasts in the wild? Oh, a LEOPARD. That's right. A leopard has spots. Those spots cannot change—you mundanes and your humanity, those inclinations, mostly to do bad. So, in general terms, you are all leopards, too. I thrived off your anger, pain, and hatred. So, to me, you were just another leopard with power within reach. There is no use in trying to make spots or stripes. Since then, I've watched and listened as you've strived against the pain and adversity. You can be what you want to be. Until then, I would be on guard; something is coming.'

The whispers stopped abruptly, and the chill was gone, but I could still feel that presence this time. I say darkness because it feels that way. If what it alluded to was true, I had hope, and the girls were swaying me. I could never forgive myself if it went wrong and they came to harm. The reality is, I've been a kite dancing in a hurricane, and lighting was stoking the skies with all its terrifying, strobing might.

Those heightened senses had stayed, too; the nearer we got to Kingsley, the death felt. My ears twitched, which was odd. Getting a taste of what the detectives go through. For good reason, though.

'BOOM, BOOM, BOOM'

My hand tingled; I looked, and I could see real close as the tiny black hairs ruffled to attention, like wind through fields of straw or a forest of trees. Tiny pimples popped across my flesh beneath; My heart was flying, causing my throat to tighten, and Fear was taking over to the tune of a beating drum. That's how loud and what I heard first before each one thinned out. They were wings flapping. Hundreds of them building to a deafening crescendo. Much like the layby, I saw the piercing blue next. It was bloody scary. A horizon was becoming a nightmare. Except for Nathan, who'd stayed oblivious, we all knew what was coming without uttering a word. More importantly, how? Were they following from afar, or did they know much more about this game than we realised?

With everything the darkness preached, I couldn't help but feel disheartened. The lengths to which these evil bastards go to. Manipulating us mundanes, as we're called. Stirring the pot, creating a world ready for them to enjoy. Sure, there's a lot of evil to go around in various forms. What scared me more was letting loose all those Templars and their General. Nowhere would be the same.

George rolls the car to a stop at least two hundred feet from the road sign 'Welcome to Kingsley'. The horde of deathly ravens swooped toward them, their beady eyes glowing brightly before they seamlessly moved, becoming one of those creepy Knights. His face rippled in the moonlight, looking more like a walking corpse. Patches of flesh had long since decayed, allowing his skull bone to show through. I could feel the hatred dripping from his. Stepping slowly, the heavy heels of his shiny shoes clapping against the empty road, echoing a sinister tune.

"What are we doing, Georgie?" Michael says, glancing anxiously toward his friend.

"Fucked if I know. How did they even find us?" George says, thinking like I had while checking on us in the rearview.

'We can end this now. Hand him over with the puzzle piece and the box. He joins us and you lot can go on your merry way. The lovely Ellena included.' The creep spoke as though he were sitting with us in the car; his voice sounded that close. I shuddered again, shaking through the chill. Everything about this morbid freakshow curdles my blood. I had no intention of going anywhere and hoped George was on the same page.

"I trust you can hear me, so hear this. No way in 'hell'." George said. I couldn't resist a chuckle—a poignant choice of words.

"Ooh, nice use of the word Georgie." Michael quipped.

"Why, thank you, I thought you'd approve."

'You think you're so clever. This ends one way, with your death, and the same goes for everyone around you."It may have been a trick of the moonlight or the car headlights capturing in front of us: the street sign, the scenic view of endless trees and the creepy Knight. I could've sworn his eyes changed; pearlescent black became blood red.

"Hey guys, not to rush you or anything? But do you have a plan for dealing with something centuries hellbent on killing us?" I said, noticing George look at Michael as they exchanged smirks as if sharing some inside joke I wasn't a part of.

"Well, we've had a little experience with old things. Michael experiences it every Saturday night down the YMCA chatting up the elderly."

"Hey, you dick. That was one night I volunteered to help run the bar for a friend." Michael said, laughing. I'm looking at these two, so calm and cracking jokes in the face of all this danger. How do they do it? It must be bloody hard on their families. The Knight widened his stance, braced to charge at us; what he thought he would achieve was anyone's guess. His right foot dug into the gravel, twisted, and he powered forward.

"Georgie... erm Georgie. In case you missed it theres a scary looking Knight charging at us, you may want to do something." Michael said, eyes raised, waiting for an answer.

George jammed the car in gear, and with the handbrake on, he throttled the life out of the engine. The car was rocking and vibrating; I shuffled backwards in my seat, feeling the rumbles beneath me; loud wheel spinning filled the air. His claws gripped the wheel tightly. "Fuck it," George says, "Let's go through him." Michael frantically grabbed at his seatbelt, checking he was strapped in. Still, Nathan was oblivious, the three litre engine rocked the chasis some more, I toyed with being brave. There's nothing brave about crashing through a windshield if everything goes wrong.

I'm fighting against the tension to the best of my ability. My eyes dart to the front, the Knight is picking up speed, his coat flails wide, his deathly hand breezes to the butt of a sword. My eyes flick to my belt as I struggle, George unleashes the handbrake and hi BMW beast. The chasis twists and turns against the torque, burnt rubber teases my senses. My eyes dart to the front again, we're flying, the Knight is too.

Finally, the tension releases, and I yank the belt into its lock. I'm looking on in fear and awe that this creepy Knight was taking on a car now doing fifty miles per hour. Bizarrely, the Knight seemed just as fast. Then... everything slowed. Or looked that way. The front of our car connects painfully with the Knight as he draws his sword. A loud banshee shriek rocks the air; thunder claps in the sky. What happened next scared the living daylights out of me. As we plough into the Knight, he crumbles, not into Ravens, but more like decayed pieces of his body. Each part phases ghostly through our vehicle.

His horrifying face was full, gritted teeth, blood red eyes, his sword comes through as the rest of his body is still in pieces. Then I feel it, the darkness rapidly forms a barrier around me, all those gruesome body parts richochet off me. The sword wooshes past, and the scary part is that the Knight smiles as he blazes through, phasing through the rear of our vehicle. George slams on the brakes, screeching tyres roar in the night, and the chassis sways side to side until we stop. My hands immediately pat over my body, checking for wounds while struggling to rationalise what just happened. There's nothing. The detectives swivel in theirs looking shocked, I look out the rear, the Knight is now fully formed, sliding his sword away. Everything went silent.

'Blood...'

I could smell blood—and death and sulphur. But the blood was closer, a lot closer.

"Cuh...Cuh." What just happened, Gerald, I hear beside me. I turned slowly, realising where the blood was coming from. Nathan had a puncture wound to his stomach, his white t-shirt swelling with red and then black. I didn't understand. Judging by their faces, the detectives didn't either. There was another smell, poison I assumed, it smelt rancidly toxic.

'Your friend has twenty-four hours before the poison reaches his heart. Find the box and surrender yourself to the puzzle piece and the box, and we'll let your friend live. You have my word as a Knight.'

"what about your murdering friend?"

'That fool has another quest to fulfil. Don't worry; we'll allow you to uncover who they are. It's only fair to know who has tormented your family after all. Tik Tok.' Before I got to respond, the Knight crumbled into the blanket of Ravens filling the sky. I'm staring at Nathan, watching black track lines spread through his skin as his wound wreaked of the toxin. Twenty-four hours, that's all we had to decide the world's fate. What do I do?

Epigraph

Haunted by the Crooked Man

Crooked trees creaked and groaned like the creepy, crooked man in the early dawn. Deep in the heart of darkness, raging red eyes glared through the inky veil. My pulse trembled in the face of death as wisps of charcoal flesh peeled from his bones. Casting long, bony shadows along the ground, dirty grit kicked up clouds while stone crumbled beneath each haunting step. Winds whipped and snarled coldly as it rattled through the ravages of twisted metal and shattered glass. His cloak tails flailed in the wake of each heavy boot as evil stalked his prey.

Rusted hulks of abandoned cars carrying the scent of decay mingled with the sharp tang of blood as streaks of crimson marred the thick, chalky gravel path. Streetlights swayed gently, their flickering silhouettes blending with the pale moonlight. It was swift, almost graceful in its horror—a sinister prelude to an imminent, chilling death. Anticipation of the worst tasted sickly sour yet with distinctive, vibrant and coppery undertones, blood. My stomach churned violently, yet no vomit came—only dry heaves that left me feeling hollow.

His arm sliced through the breathy white clouds as diesel engines rumbled in the hissing air. Chains rattled, their metallic clinks choking out the silent night before painful wails, gargled and bloody, erupted around me. The poor man's body was gruesomely torn to shreds; limbs and flesh lay in a bloodied heap apart in a sick display of violence. And then, nothing but silence and darkness, a cruel emptiness, until my eyes bolt open.

Chapter 1

'Gerald - December 1987'

'My fragile sanity weaves through terror. A tiny paper boat floating down the 'blood swollen' Willen river. Fighting bravely to right itself against the treacherous, murky current and never-ending whirlpools. Whose frothing jaws hunger to drag the tiny boat to the river's darkest depths.'

Deep in the heart of darkness, raging red eyes glared through the inky veil. Another sleepless night had been and gone, another blood-filled bad dream. It's always him—the crooked man. I woke gasping for air, my vest clinging to my clammy skin. I couldn't stop shaking. The nightmare terror, much like my flimsy nightwear, still clung to me, a persistent echo of dread that refused to fade.

Fear is a curious thing. Whether we like to admit it, we all have a little something tucked away in the deep recesses of our consciousness that scares us. He is my deeply disturbing something. Fumbling for the lamp beside a half-drunk glass of water, I tried to shake it off. His presence has become my constant companion, a shadow I couldn't escape. My hand lingered over the creased space beside me, looking longingly, lost in a daydream. As much as it still hurt, I knew it would be empty, as it had been for a while now. Leaving me to choke back the tears; Charlotte was no longer there. God, I miss her so, and part of the reason I can't let it drop. The details matter, and they don't add up.

My chest was tight; everything about the dream felt so awfully real, as if I saw it through his eyes. Every gust of wind, every particle of dust mingled with blood—I could smell it all, the iron tang heavy in the muggy village air. This was all I could think about as I sat at the bar, waiting patiently for my guest. The terror that had gripped me for the second night in a row had me paranoid, unable to sit still. Was it his torment or this place that was driving me mad? The omnipresent gloom of Willowbrook seemed to seep into everything that made me... well, me.

South of the unashamedly picturesque Pennines, where wanton winds howl through the oppressive shadows of the Yorkshire Dales, lays our Hellscape. Nestled among rapturous hills, it exists under a near-constant, haunting cloud. Winter lingers here nearly three-quarters of the year, but this season feels colder and more sinister. Each drift of the tavern door brings an icy gust that slices through to my pimpled flesh.

Fog has swept in early tonight, a ravenous beast devouring the dim glow of village streetlights under its bloodthirsty blanket of grey, gnawing at my fear, the dread that I won't see what's coming—the crooked man—until it's too late. Darkness surrounds us, and nobody seems to care. A sinister veil conceals the truth from the mundanes in this inconsequential village. Nightmares and evil lay in wait, and I straddle both sides of that elusive curtain, never feeling as if I belong to either.

For most of my life, I've felt I'm meant for something more, but what? Even the ironic, crusty village welcome sign, with its lopsided haunches and faded green boarding, now bore the words 'Welcome to Hell' sprayed over the loose white lettering. It kind of suits, actually, but the cheeky bastards missed a trick; they should've used red instead of blue. You know, for impact. That little extra menace to go with the vandalism.

Before you call me crazy, you need to know the full story, the good and the bad, probably mostly bad. But as the saying goes, never judge a book by its cover. Besides, haven't you heard? Crazy seems to be the new normal. Crap, I lost my thread. Where was I? Ah, yes. From what I've said, the only person deserving my blame is dead. It's hard to believe a year has passed, yet it feels like yesterday.

It's an incessant weeping wound. Festering. An itch I long to scratch, knowing full well it does me no good. But I can't move on. I must know what's wrong with me. Perhaps I'm defective. Not in a broken toaster kind of way, but wrong, made weird or different.

It's hard to explain and has worsened since Father died. It scares the crap out of me. Many things have happened, and I struggle to explain what I've been seeing. Let alone hearing, wait... Fuck, it's suddenly got cold in here. Or is it me? Brrr... goose pimples shuffle across my neck...The sort that makes you shudder and twist your body like some bloody contortionist.

'Hush, little baby, don't say a word. Mamma's gonna buy you a mockingbird, and if that mockingbird don't sing, Mamma's gonna buy you a diamond ring.'

Fuck... Charlotte? Is that... No, it can't be. Just breathe, Gerald, breathe. Right. Where was I? Again!

Ah, that's it—the things I'm seeing, the recent nightmares, and like then, the teeth-jarring voices. Even before him, there have been moments. Always when I least expect it, fleeting. A passing mundane in the street. I see their faces. For a moment, it takes my breath away—a shimmer or a ripple, and what should be a normal, glum face is death or the dead walking. Pale flesh changes to mottled, grotesque grey, decaying, oozing old, toxic blood. There's a rotten meat smell.

My mind gets foggy, like a slow-motion haze. I try to get attention, but no words come. I hear the shrills of a pain-riddled yawn without their mouth moving, aside from spewing blood, and their cloudy stare focuses on me. I look behind to be sure, hoping they're seeking someone else. They're not, and a horrible, churning grimace comes with that haunting stare. When any of it fully registers, or I realise it's not a hallucination, the mundane paleness returns.

At the age of somewhere between eight and ten, I don't know exactly how old I was when the darkness first revealed itself to me. Plenty of nightmares came with them, too, as you'd expect. My mother, even then, may have been playing games, toying with the truth and my sanity. She would roll her eyes before I'd dared utter the first words, displaying a wry smile without trying to be condescending, as mothers do and say, "Now, now, Gerald, I'm sure it's your childish imagination. Next week, it'll be dinosaurs." It's the heavy exhale of relief at the end that tells more.

I didn't argue because, eventually, they stopped—until my late teens, that is. That's when they evolved. They were not just dead faces anymore but scenarios—remnants. I ended up calling them. Each one depicted somebody dying—sometimes more than one—before fading into a spooky cloud.

Then, at the beginning of this year, life got turned on its head. And the rest? Well, you'll find out soon enough. Since then, I've been sliding, mentally and physically. A smouldering ember of darkness is held within, growing with an evocative sense of déjà vu. I'm not even sure this moment hasn't happened, and I'm simply reliving the memory. No, it has to be real. The pub door drifts open, but nobody's there. A chill floats through it, biting, prickling my flesh. I'm awake in the now, waiting and hoping my time isn't being wasted. I need the impending medical report to get answers, good or bad.

'Hush, little baby, don't say a word. Mamma's gonna buy you a mockingbird.' For god's sake, not again, please stop. Please stop. Breathe, not much longer now.

I'm struggling to handle all these things. I have so many questions and crazy threads to pull on in my search for the truth. The most burning question is why they left me stuck somewhere wicked that the world would sooner forget and so unprepared.

Why didn't Father tell me the truth about all those haunting experiences or that my life would be pummelled until I hit rock bottom and changed forever? There's a neat yet poignant turn of phrase: what is it... Oh, that's it. "The sins of the father are to be laid upon his son." Poetic, right? In a nightmare-on-Elm-Street kind of way.

'Let me in, Gerald, and we'll eat those sins together. And you, listening... Will you walk into my parlour, said the spider to the fly. Utter a word, and I shall peel your flesh as though it were wings. In case you think I misspoke, I'm talking to the one shaking; for hell's sake, are all you mundanes made so weak and desperate? Heed my warning. After all, 'tis the prettiest little parlour that ever you spy.'

There he goes again. I try pretending I hear nothing, but it's damn near impossible. It's as if all these noises and voices are competing for space in my brain. So hard to know if what I hear is real or if you could hear him a moment ago. If you couldn't, well, you're lucky.

If you only understood how bad it is here. I know experiences sway me, but it's different, darker. Even old maps have us and the surrounding five villages clustered together, representing the "devil's pentagram." Now, if that isn't painting a bloody weird picture, I don't know what will. For now, I'll park that there and leave it to your imagination. Believe me, this place isn't right. All you have to do is look around and watch the other mundanes going about life, pretending. I can't anymore.

You could say I refuse to lie to myself anymore, not since the noise. It's all of it, everything that Willowbrook encompasses. I'm bloody scared.

'Awww, poor little Gerald, you know there's no need to be. Although that fear is so intoxicating... Sniff. And you there, yes you, I see you continue listening to this weakling. Tut, tut... Come now, Gerald, let me in.'

Oh god. You heard it this time, right? Please tell me you heard him. I... I don't know how much more of this I can take. I need to know I'm not alone. If I see behind the veil, surely others can. They have to. I need them to. The nightmares we kid ourselves aren't real. We hide from the secrets sewn into its dirty fabric. Since he appeared, I have struggled, like moments ago, to discern reality from illusion, nightmare torment from a mental breakdown. Why can't I escape?

He haunts me. His eerie whispers saturate our cobbled streets, their sinister melancholy swallowed by the cruel darkness. A shiver coils down my spine at the thought of what's lurking.

'I'm not going away, Gerald, so why don't you let me in?'

Shut up... Leave me alone. He doesn't stop calling. Well, it's more of a wail. Every word is as though he's weeping, yet low and slightly hushed. That may not make sense to you, and in truth, it's hard to describe other than it's so cold.

'All you have to do is open up and let me in.'

The mere thought of his bony fingers, covered in decaying grey flesh and tipped with razor-sharp nails. His demonic eyes pierce with a deep, garish red vibrancy, framed by the unusual yet intimidating attire of a dirty, bloodstained trilby that's caught the chaotic splatter from what I dread to think—previously murdered mundanes.

I know... I sound a few sandwiches short of a picnic; mock me at your peril. Then I hear the desperation as he calls out, 'If I let the evil in, my pain will stop.' I don't want to give in. But since Father died, I no longer want to endure the pain; I'm weak, and he knows it.

His cloak flutters like torn wings, whipping into a menacing symphony against the empty night. **'Let me in, and the pain fades,'** he continues toying with that 'tiny paper boat', appearing briefly in the shadows—a fleetingness in the still air, a ghostly figure in reflections when no one else can see the torment that plagues me. In the cold, the unforgiving night that smothers our mundane little village is a faded blot on a map, easily overlooked.

What gets me is this place would seem appealing to outsiders. Other mundanes who didn't have to endure 'weeping willow'. Shrouded in all the traditional charms of thatched-roof homes from yesteryear and quaint shops. Even uncannier is that it never harbours over 1,500 souls. It doesn't dare, as though that's a magic number, and no one seems to question it or leave unless it's in a pine box. Surely you're getting what I'm saying now?

Charlotte and I dreamt of escaping, taking the twins and exiling ourselves somewhere far away and warmer. But the grip of this cruel place and Charlotte's sudden death kept those dreams forever out of reach. Damn, see, my head is a mess. I forgot to mention that I lost my wife just six months after my father. Perhaps now you'll understand why I hold such disdain for 'Willow' and why I'm barely holding my shit together.

There are various reasons bounded around for our meagre populous by those who dare to see beyond their blinkers. Some say it's because of a hex or dooming omen dating back to the Domesday Book, brought on by bedraggled travellers or AWOL knights running from their troubles, seeking refuge. Only their sins came with them and never left. In some weird way, I can imagine the 'knight' one fitting for this place.

Others whisper that deep within the hallowed halls of the less-than-'godly' ruins of St. Peter's church (trust me, the rumours are about what went on), there's an unspoken rule etched in blood, a pact that binds the village to some exaggerated dark omen, one scribed by Satan himself.

Personally, I believe most of that is nonsense, but the way my life has spiralled, I'm mindful that in every embellished tall tale, there's an element of truth. What our village lacks in its ability to attract fantastic tourism, it compensates with a dark and rather morbid statistic.

It has one of the highest mortality rates in mainland U.K., especially from murder. It's been like that for centuries and does little to ease my terror. Whether any were because of a curse, evil nonsense, or something more sinister in this godforsaken village remains a mystery. Still, its dark legacy has earned this drearily quaint place the apt nickname 'Weeping Willow.' And the black cloud above.

A wise person might say it's merely a village leaning towards what will garner the most attention. Mark my words; those numbers will grow, i can feel it with every glimpse of him.

It was nearly 7:30 p.m., and I was still waiting for the report to arrive. A man by the name of Colin Milton was due to bring it—a friend of a friend. Colin was the type who could pass for a librarian or an undertaker: weird and gangly, the quiet sort probably bullied in school. Sketchy, yes, but I hoped he could clarify my nagging doubts about my father's death, his health, and the rumours of his drinking. However, Colin had been reluctant to get involved, fearing for his job at the hospital and wary of the local gossip.

In Willowbrook, the mundanes clung to rumours like flies to dung. I knew little about Colin, and whether he could be trusted was up for debate. If he were shady, surely there would be stories? But then, the absence of rumours was in itself suspicious in such a small town. Everything about him was a blank, squeaky-clean slate—perhaps too squeaky. Only time will tell.

I took another swig of whiskey, contemplating a refill as pieces of my beer coaster accumulated beside the bar.

"Another one, luv?" The question snapped me out of my thoughts, a husky voice tinged with a northern accent cutting through my melancholy. I saw a tall, curvy, smiling brunette in her thirties approaching. Her heels clicked unevenly on the floor—one slightly more worn than the other—creating an uneven rhythm.

For a moment, my mind blanked. I struggled to recall her name, muttering under my breath, "Shit, what's her name? Oh, wait… It's Janice." I gasp as I glanced back at my glass and then up again.

When will this torment stop? Her face had changed. Janice's face was horribly corpse-mottled grey, with gory, blackened blood oozing from her eye sockets and mouth. It had happened again, flipping unnerving.

"S… s… sorry, what?" I stammer, recoiling into my seat, fingernails digging into the wooden armrests as I struggled with the horrific vision. Was this a deranged hallucination?

"**I… said… When the gates of hell erupt, Solomon will bring forth the 72 that will usher in the Apocalypse, and the dead shall rule…**" I was stunned, expecting the usual call. Instead, I'm left puzzled. Janice's voice became a curdled, agonizing wail, blood spewing endlessly from her mouth. I clenched my eyes shut, then snapped them open again, not daring to breathe.

"Hey… you okay? Fancy another one, luv?" Her voice was back to normal. I cautiously met her gaze; she looked just as she had before—no blood, no deathly pallor.

"Um, yes, please, Janice," I croaked, the smoke and nicotine roughening my voice. Unfortunately, I'd taken up smoking again after a decade. I needed something—anything—to keep my nerves at bay.

Janice placed a drink on a fresh coaster, glancing at the mess I'd made with the previous one. "So, your day was that bad?" she probed, sensing my discomfort.

"Er… Sorry, what did you say?" I forced a tight-lipped smile, avoiding her gaze. I noticed

I'd made a strange pentagram coaster, much the same as our little village cluster on the maps I mentioned already—a design I didn't remember making. Confused, I sank deeper into my seat.

A breeze brushed my cheek, unsettling me further. I shook it off as if it were just a draft. "I said your day was that bad? Isn't this one of those religious star things, you know, what those devil-worshipping freaks are into? You come here every night; this is the most I've seen you do. We exchange small talk, and you keep to yourself, clutching that newspaper. You always look so lost in thought. So, what's going on with you? Especially with this masterpiece?" Janice inquired, pointing at the pentagram.

Again, I shifted uncomfortably, knowing I needed to consider something suitable to deflect further probing. My eyes darted to a rowdy crowd, struggling for the right words. The back of my neck trembled with a constant coat of gooseflesh, feeling that featherlight graze again—this time from below my hairline to the edge of my collar. Doing my best to shake it off, I tucked my shoulder tight as if to make a shield or something. Pointless, I knew that, more a reflex than anything else.

"Uh, I do not know why I did that. I must've seen it somewhere; besides, I like it here. It's your whiskey. You don't water it down," I stammer, wracking my fragile brain to recall anything.

"Water it down? Who on earth would do that?" Janice's disbelief hung in the air. She inspected my newspaper, pointing out that I always have it with me.

"That newspaper you're holding, it's the same one you had yesterday. It's been about six-"

That haunting whisper buzzed past its venomous plea. **"Let me in,"** pierced the silence. My pulse thumped beneath my skin.

My head darted from left to right, looking for 'him,' only seeing oblivious customers happily drinking. "Y ... Yes, it's all about the gossip pages and the crossword inside. I've been enjoying revisiting them. I'm a little stuck on a few words, so I take my time. It's my little haven to juice up the brain matter when I'm here." I continue twitching, my right hand trembling slightly.

"But that's a six-month-old newspaper, and I can't recall you opening it once. Not at all."

'Let me in; you got to let me in.' The Crooked man's icy call grated across my earlobe, inducing a temporary numbness. I was unravelling. If there was anything I could take from this moment, the whispers were different tonight, and it had me spooked. There was a purpose to it. How else can I explain it? My eyes lurched at the door, seeing it glide closed with no one there. Then to Janice, who appeared normal.

With an awkward smile, my throat tightened as I struggled for words. Janice's probing was relentless, believing there was more to the story. A glance at the newspaper revealed lines familiar to me and could be recited by heart:

'A tragic accident on the M1 occurred just before midnight; a silver Ford Granada was slammed into the concrete bridge support and divider from the slip road. The casualty, a twenty-seven-year-old woman, a mother and a wife, died at the scene, leaving behind two young daughters in the car, unhurt. And a caring husband. A passer-by states a swerving lorry that had nearly caused several accidents along the stretch rammed her vehicle sideways. Believed the driver may have been drunk or under the influence of drugs,'

'Let … me…in…and…the…pain…will…fade.'

The crooked man cut through again. Stomach churning, a shiver stood my arm hairs on end as a trickle of panic sweat drifted from my uneven sideburns. Darkness will not leave me be, and I can't say how much longer I can resist.

Chapter 2

'Gerald'

'Gerald'

Janice looked around, noticing an empty glass, and an abandoned newspaper far newer than the tattered rag I clung to. She slid it over, trying to give me something fresher to read, perhaps to distract me from destroying more of her coasters. Little did she know, I held on to it as a 'carrot,' something to drive me on in my search for answers, even if it felt haunting. When she glanced at the front page, her expression darkened to match the cloud above. Janice stared at the main article.

"A 59-year-old man found hanging at 3 a.m. in his home is being treated as suspicious after signs of foul play were discovered," Janice read aloud in a morbid, droning tone. "Police found the full-time scrapyard worker, a father of three and grandfather of two after neighbours complained about a strange smell coming from his first-floor apartment."

Janice paused, her smooth, lightly blushed face reflecting concern and curiosity. "Do you remember him?" she asks, tapping the photograph on the article under my nose.

Feigning vagueness and slightly irritated by the grimy, potent ink's stink, I reply, "Not really, no. Why?"

"You must. He borrowed your bloody lighter before the two of you talked like nattering old hens for forty minutes. Near the end, you exchanged a whisper, and he was soon gone. Come to think of it, his face looked a little shocked. What did you do? Dare him to ask me out?" Janice explains, attempting a little humour, tapping the photo again. Her eyes widened, trying to force me to recall a memory I didn't want to. Not my finest hour. The longer I didn't answer, I noticed the quiver of her bottom lip. Building anxiety mixed with fear.

Playing along, I concealed the true nature of the encounter. "Ah, yes. He seemed okay, maybe a little on edge. I can't think why."

'Oh, come now, we both know that's not true.'

The Crooked man cooed again, grazing my ear, forcing me sideways, releasing a shudder, my eyeballs bouncing as I searched for the voice, hoping he wasn't loitering nearby.

Janice nodded, her face troubled by the news of the man's death. "I know. What a small world. He'd been in a few times before and always seemed nice. Now we know why."

"A small world indeed," I mumble, diverting my attention back to my glass before taking a large sip, scorched by the sharp burning down my throat. It was a momentary respite, but I couldn't decide what I was washing away—the grief or the awkward article.

'That won't help. Look at the servant and then your hands; you did that. Look, they're covered. Drenched in blood,'

My tormenter teases, his tone dripping with melancholy. Making me twitch, I looked at Janice and gasped. A wisp of black cloud drifted and scooped a small knife from a lemon board. It encircled her throat but never touched. Janice's flesh peeled open like slicing butter, allowing a river of blood to flow, the colour draining from her skin.

I looked at my hands. They were covered in blood; my throat dries with shock; no end to my torment tonight. A quick blink and everything returned to normal. The blood disappeared. Relieved but confused, I lurched for another shaky sip of my drink, this time smaller. My throat felt shrivelled.

That tiny boat was spinning in the river like a kite caught in a hurricane. Janice drifted to attend to another customer. Still puzzled and unnerved, I slid my watch from beneath my jacket cuff, admiring it momentarily. It was my dad's, an old silver Rolex with an ivory face, worn with age but with a newer, replaced underbelly. The clasp was sticky, but that didn't bother me. Dad had worn it for five years before that fateful night.

On Halloween last year, at a family gathering, he called me into his study to give me the watch. I thought little of it other than being happy and honoured. Yet Dad was restless, peering out the study window several times after handing the watch over. Besides that moment and work stress, Dad seemed in good spirits, at least as far as I saw, so there was no need to question why. Years had taught me not to pry too much into my father's business.

We didn't know Father would be gone a year later. A bizarre accident while walking home from the pub. A reason for meeting Colin. Father was said to have stumbled drunk, crashing into some scaffolding, forcing it to collapse. Which was bullshit; none of us had seen him drunk, ever. It wasn't his way. Sure, some wine or a glass of whiskey here and there, but that's it. So, I figured it would be good to get my hands on the real toxicology reports and hope they explain how such a sturdy structure collapses after a collision with one man. The details didn't add up, not that anyone would listen except for a friend who reached out to Colin for me.

'Awe, poor Gerald, if you can't handle the pain, just let … me…in before it's too late,' each tormenting whisper became more haunting. The relentless shivers continued to ripple over my shoulders.

I remained fixated on the watch in a hazy daydream, fighting to ignore the Crooked man's haunting noise. Weary of the time to get home, I didn't want to be late. Colin was due with the report any moment now. Assuming he had the guts to show up, I trusted Nathan to mediate, and when he said, 'It's in hand,' I believed him.

'Don't pretend, just … let…me…in, let… me… in,' wailed the voice, tempering my anxiety, merging with the surrounding chatter. The noise became a disheartening background hum. Massaging my neck to soothe the pressure, I stowed away the watch, squeezing my eyes shut for a moment, praying for peace that had been elusive. The anticipation for Colin's arrival added to the unrest. Reflecting on the events of last week, the hours leading to the ' hanging,' the timeline was unsettling if Janice could link the victim to me. How challenging would it be for the police? Lost in that morbid daydream, the haunting whispers broke through.

'Don't fight it; let … me…in, and let's make the Willows weep. Be on the right side of what's coming.'

My head dropped, running a hand through my hair, grappling with the struggle against the relentless calls. If it's not the remnants, the Crooked man is messing with my 'Tiny' boat with unrelenting ease while the swollen river thrashes against the bankside. And now that river flows with blood.

The pub door drifted open, and an icy gust ghosted in. I jumped, reaching for the shiver down my neck, hoping it wasn't the Crooked man. Shock soon turned to relief when I saw who it was. The clock ticked to 8:10 pm as Colin shuffled in, head bowed and shoulders hunched. He looked sheepish as he made his way to the bar.

His anaemic, gaunt figure was enveloped in a dull brown tweed suit, its drabness only emphasised by the dark, almost ominous overcoat draped over his shoulders like a modern-day reaper's cloak. He adjusted the spectacles perched on his nose, briefly scanning the other customers before finally making his way to the bar.

Colin's hands trembled as he gripped the newspaper Janice had shown me—the mysterious death of a 59-year-old scrapyard worker. I tried looking away, motioning for Janice to bring another round of drinks to calm my nerves about the news.

Colin sipped his whiskey, his eyes meeting mine with newfound confidence. He opened his satchel, revealing a weathered, light brown folder with reddish-brown hues that grabbed my attention. Swiftly, Colin removed the folder and slid it in front of me—a well-organised stack of papers that spoke of Colin's precision and dedication—that or some OCD.

"Have you read it?" I raised a curious eyebrow, knowing how limited scientific knowledge was and how it might hinder my understanding of technical jargon.

"I have," Colin replies, his voice no louder than a whisper.

"And?" My curiosity danced with dread, their intertwined waltz teetering on the precipice of knowing.

"Would it surprise you if I told you that your father had next to no alcohol in his system?" Colin's revelation hit me like a sledgehammer.

My head tilted, a mix of shock and confusion swirling. "For heaven's sake, you're saying he wasn't drunk?"

Colin nodded, confirming my suspicions. "He sipped what's left in your glass."

"And he bloody well didn't stagger about in a drunken stupor." I could feel my blood boiling, knowing the situation wasn't right. Colin helped prove it.

"No, but something else is happening, and it gives me the creeps. His veins were coursing with adrenaline. I mean, off the charts high. It was as though he experienced the rush of an exhilarating climax; this was the epitome of fear, Gerald. Your father's dopamine, adrenaline, and glutamate levels were through the roof."

My face churned as the horrifying details settled like a suffocating fog. My father, who lost his life because of an alcohol-induced mishap, had fled the pub in sheer terror.

While grappling with the implications, the recent newspaper article, with its ominous headline, seeped into my thoughts. How did a "Hanging Man" earn a front-page feature? I needed the truth and to clear my father's name.

With a last gulp, I drained the remnants of my whiskey, the amber liquid offering some clarity to my fragmented world, just in time to catch the trailing words of Colin's warning.

"Be careful if I were you, Gerald. There may be some truth to the stories of 'enemies'; otherwise, how else do you explain the fear?" Colin's once-pallid face now seemed drained of all colour—an unnerving sight for a man who already looked anaemic.

I shuffled the papers, patting one end on the bar, when two small square pieces of card dropped, smooth with a slight polythene coating. I knew what they were—Polaroids. No sooner had I flipped them open than I got the shock of my life. Jabbing them at Colin, I reeled in disgust.

"What the hell are these? Why? What on earth is going on?" The Polaroids depicted a small pentagram-like symbol inside two circles, drawn in blood beside my dead father's trapped, outstretched leg—the scaffold accident. The same I carved in the coaster and another coincidence for the position of our village.

Colin gulped as a bead of sweat dribbled from his brow. "Shit, I'm sorry, that slipped my mind. I found them by chance with the paramedics' papers from the scene that night. I wondered if you knew about them. If not, then that little creepy thing adds to the mystery of your father's terror." Colin settled into his words as he spoke. Yet, seemed a little too quickly.

'**Why is it I get bound to you? Your eyes may fail you, but common sense should not.** Do you mundanes believe every fanciful tale spoke?' The voice hissed around me, speaking sense, yet I couldn't be certain whose sense it was. Mine, or was I insane?

"Beats me. It wouldn't seem so obvious, but it's made in blood and crazy enough for photographs to be taken. Yet my father gets branded a drunk and up to no good." My anxiety continues to build, glancing at my watch on edge.

"I know. But make no mistake. Be bloody careful; this is just the beginning, and I fear if that symbol holds any meaning, darkness lays ahead," Colin's disquiet wasn't reassuring with the Polaroids and what Colin knew now. If there was more to my father's terrifying experience, I understood the warning in blooding—it seemed I'd opened a can of worms, adding another layer of danger to an already fraught journey.

Our conversation drifted into a sea of whiskey meant to steady rattled nerves. An abrupt chill pierced the air, and a whisper brushed against my neck, teasing. I scanned the unaware pub crowd, but everything appeared normal.

That was until I noticed him in the corner. Hidden amidst the clouds of cigarette smoke, tall and gaunt, clad in that black coat draped over his frame. The wide, dirt-stained trilby made his presence far more sinister. The Crooked man sat in chilling stillness, holding a pint of Guinness with elongated fingers, frozen in a picture of mystery and menace. I didn't need this now. The noise and whispers were one thing, but with him sitting there, taunting, while unravelled, it was too much. Or was it another illusion?

Sparks tingled the back of my neck. I recalled another time, a passing moment when life... well... was less unhinged. It was from the hospital—the birth of the twins. It was a weird but happy day, although I almost missed the birth because I'd gone to the canteen for coffee. While in the hallway, I crossed paths with a stranger. I remember his words clear as day. 'Any change for the phone?' the guy says. A chill rushed through my body as if it was happening now.

I was busy stirring my coffee when those words echoed a few feet away. I turned to see a tall man wearing a grubby black canvas hooded raincoat and an unusual-looking dirty black trilby pulled down to conceal his face, leaving only a menacing chin visible.

The man's voice had blood-twisting gravel that would've usually bothered me were it not for the special day. In haste, I scooped a handful of change from my pocket and handed it to the man, who grabbed it with black leather-clad hands. Unlike now, the leather did little to pad out the bony surface or disguise how unusually long the man's fingers were. He'd held my hand for under five seconds, but the impression lasted. Little did I realise I'd crossed paths with the Crooked man.

"What are you looking at? Shit, is anyone watching? Did anyone see?" Colin interrupts, riddled with anxiety.

"A guy in the corner at your six o'clock. He's dressed in all dark clothing and wearing a funky-looking hat." Colin turned his head left, almost giving himself whiplash. His confused expression made me seem like I was going mad, which would've been understandable. I still saw him clear as day. Was it only me? Was I alone, after all?

"Are you messing with me? There's no one there. The symbol may have been a tipping point for you," Colin's words were emphatic, causing an awkward shuffle in my chair.

My heart thumped against my ribcage. Reliving every vivid detail of that hospital scenario and any fleeting glimpse since, I could taste the sterile, metallic tang in the air, making it difficult to dismiss it as a hallucination.

Moving closer to Colin, I whispered. "Colin, I'm telling you the truth. He was there, you know. The hooded raincoat, the trilby hat—it's too weird to be a coincidence." I stopped short of muttering, 'the Crooked man.'

Colin's scepticism wavered, and he glanced toward the empty corner where I'd mentioned. To him, the place remained empty. He picked his words, sounding worried. "Gerald," he says, "I understand the stress you've been under. Our minds can play tricks on us in times of great turmoil. Hallucinations and delusions aren't uncommon."

That part, I understood; as I said before, I call them remnants, and they centre on death, except for tall and scary. My frustration was bubbling, a mix of anxiety and terror. My fists squeezed so tight that my knuckles turned white. "I'm not going crazy, Colin. I can't be. I know what I bloody saw, and I'm not one to be taken by delusions. That guy is genuine. You can call me paranoid or whatever you want, but I swear, I saw him." I was trying to convince myself more than Colin, at least for now, to get through this meeting and resume 'abnormal' service.

Colin's gaze shifted between me and the empty corner, torn between rationality and fear for my well-being. His analytical mind struggled with the inexplicable, but his empathy drove him to acknowledge the profound anguish I'd experienced.

"We should wrap things up and go," Colin suggests, uneasy. You need to take it easy, and let's talk somewhere safer and more private—you know, just in case."

I agree, though I wasn't too happy about it. As we finished, I couldn't help but worry that I was the only one who could see the Crooked man. I was determined to dig deeper, no matter how insane I looked or how far it took me into the darkness.

"24 Hours Earlier in Rugby," Moonlight shone through the curtains, unveiling a shocking crime scene. A blue and white strip of crime scene tape was draped across door number 17, with silver-plated embellishments and signs of a violent break-in. Forensics moved about detachedly. The constant clicks of the camera reverberated through the room, capturing the brutal details from many angles. A horrid stench of death filled the air. Gagging could be heard around the place. In the background, police radios hummed and fizzed.

DS Michael Dalton and I stood dejected, thinking, why the hell us again? The old boy, unable to bear the overpowering stink, smothered Vaseline under his nostrils. No matter how much death he'd come across, he was still uncomfortable whenever he got a whiff of a ripe corpse: that and the fact our sense of smell was far too attuned for this line of work.

The scene was a confusing puzzle, and I bloody hate puzzles. A ladder was strung up against the ceiling, a decaying corpse was suspended, and the chaos was caused by messing up the lounge. We gawked at the disturbing sight. There were too many perplexing threads to untangle that linked the man's life and who may have wanted him dead.

We were supposed to be recovering from our not-so-relaxing break in Scotland, only to be summoned for another favour. The tab is getting high, and I still need a quiet little chat with our Mr Locke. DI Bainton, the man in charge of this constabulary, had an eerie feeling about this murder. With all his wealth of experience, nothing he came across stood out like this. He feared there was more to it. Bainton was right.

The double-locked front door was the first alarming detail. This confounding factor made it impossible for anyone normal to leave—arrive, yes, but not leave. The ladder was hooked through the gap in the bannisters, but not attached to anything. It defied the laws of physics and reasoning, spanning the ceiling with a noose dangling from it—a horrific call to the now motionless victim. DI Bainton was left wondering, grappling with a mystery that worried him.

Michael led the way for a change. I wasn't in the mood, not so soon. The tough rope fashioned into a noose was thick and strong. It encircled the victim's neck like a squeezing boa constrictor, painting a horrific picture.

Michael whispered as he drew near. "Georgie, do you see what I do?"

"I do, Michael. It's a freaky one."

Michael moved his flashlight across my face, creating eerie shadows as he spoke. "Locke's bill keeps getting bigger. How long do you think?"

I looked at the sick mosaic of death and suffering before us, attempting to understand the nightmarish tale imprinted in anguish and blood. "Judging from the body's condition, I would guess it has been here for about a week. The flies buzzing around the ruptured blood vessels and the bloated tongue that's been partially chewed off—it's fucking awful. This could be personal, Michael. It's possible the killer stayed to watch the life drain from the victim's eyes. And it truly reeks."

Michael's face furrowed, looking the body up and down. "But, George, how? How could the killer do this? I mean, leave it like this? And why do you think they 'hung around' to watch? Know what I mean? Hung?"

I couldn't stop myself from letting out a low laugh at Michael's morbid humour. His words lingered. "I'm not sure. It's all too weird, and there is no evidence of a fight."

"I noticed that too. The whole thing is bloody ominous, matey, and we're being screwed. So, be careful, Georgie," Michael says, his voice tinged with concern.

My ears twitched, my eyes changing. Fortunately, I stopped before my red grew brighter, feeling something was amiss. "Shit... they haven't left... we are not alone,

Michael. I sense it, or them. Something dark, evil, and pissed. I don't know why I'm picking up on it, but I am. The anger... it's terrifying, Michael... There's going to be another victim soon if there isn't one already."

As Michael's jaw dropped, we held our breath with dread as we continued our investigation. My hackles were going haywire, and I kept looking over my shoulder, expecting to see somebody there. As sure as the devil's death knell tolled its haunting chorus, there will be another, maybe many.

Chapter 3

'Gerald – Home - prEsent Day,'

The house was quiet, disrupted only by the 9 o'clock news. Cigarette smoke meandered through the hallway, searching for the draft that ushered it through. I slung my coat on the hook, and keys clattered into a multicoloured dish on the side table that Charlotte dared to make in one of the few pottery classes she stuck to before realising how boring it was. My footsteps betrayed any attempt at sneaking in, creaking floorboards wailing through the hall.

It was 9:01 p.m., a minute past the childish deadline, and I knew judgment would follow soon. Mother's words, "Your priority should be the girls," tormented every step, a reminder of where my obligations lay as a single parent. I couldn't help but feel a little patronised. I'm the only one who hasn't given up the search for the truth while juggling everything. And the constant, nagging noise in my head.

"Is that you, Gerald?" Mother's voice, half-engrossed in the flickering television, called out.

"Yes, Mum, it's me. Who else would it be?" I reply, weary from a long day and no closer to the truth. I knew what would come next: the well-meaning but stifling advice. The kind I wasn't in the mood for. My experience at the pub went a step further than what's gone on lately. Those photos, I can't believe it. Why weren't we shown them at the time? Bloody sick. I walked slowly, delaying as long as possible.

"**Oh, I don't know, Gerald. Why don't you fucking let me in, and let's find out.**" Mother's voice was different and cold, like the whispers and Janice at the pub. I stopped dead. My throat dried up; I struggled to respond. A dribble of sweat bobbled on my brow.

"Wh... What? What did you say, Mum?" I could barely talk; fear and confusion had set in. Okay, it was more like it had returned home like me, having moved in a while now.

"I said...Your priority should be the girls, not chasing shadows. Christ, are you okay, Gerald? See, I knew all the extra strain you've piled on would get to you." Mother's words echoed, all back to normal but full of worry. The mention of shadows sent an involuntary shiver down my spine, forcing a glance over my shoulder and questioning if I'd heard the different voice at all or whether it was in my head.

I kicked off my shoes. Oooh, that immediate feeling of shoeless feet, curling the toes in freedom. It's so soothing, especially after another shit day. A pile of mail on the table beckoned; there was a small, unassuming yellow 'jiffy' package, no larger than an A5 sheet and two inches thick. My name was stuck across the front, a pre-typed label. The imprint around the package resembled a cassette tape, filling me with dread. Who would send a tape? My head was racing, seeking answers where there were none.

"Oh yes, that came around 3 o'clock," Mother says. "I was just returning from the baker's with the girls when I caught a Royal Mail delivery guy about to leave a card. It needed signing for."

Turning the package over, I heard a faint rattle from within. My heart quickened, and I glanced up at the mirror, catching a fleeting glimpse of a dark shadow darting past.

"Did Dad ever mention attending any... private parties or meetings?" I ask, hesitating, afraid of what might be revealed. The package in hand rattled again, and a sense of impending doom settled in.

"Well, he had his nights out," Mother began, her voice carrying the tone of reminiscing, "like anyone else. We weren't joined at the ship just because we were married. But as far as I know, nothing out of the ordinary. No secret swingers' clubs or anything."

Her words made me recoil at the thought, but I had to ask to delve into my father's past, even if it meant confronting uncomfortable truths.

"Oh, come off it!" Mother retorts, unable to hide her amusement. "We were young once, too, you know. Did you think your generation invented the seedy stuff like sex, drugs, and rock and roll?"

"Again, with the sex stuff, Mum," I mutter, thoughts consumed by the mysterious package. "Seriously, though, has Dad ever seemed worried about anything? Anything at all that struck you as odd?"

Mother didn't respond. She stood by the kettle, her hand poised over the switch, her face a mask of contemplation. Her hand trembled, mirroring the unease that I had sensed.

My fingers gripped an open edge of the package, ready to tear into it when I remembered Frank's ominous warning: "There are things in this world you don't want to mess with." I had ordered nothing, but my gut told me I had to continue.

The sound of a spoon clinking against a teacup filled the air as Mother refocused on the clock. She took a deep breath and carried my coffee into the lounge before grabbing her handbag and keys.

"Right, I'm off," Mother announced, her smile forced as she came over to kiss me. I looked up from the package to see Mother... I jumped back, my hand shaking... I nearly dropped what was in my hands. Mother's face had changed. Like Janice, mottled grey flesh, blood oozed from her eyes and mouth. She looked dead, and I was terrified. Not only about what I was seeing, but about everything.

My mind was cracking. Or felt so. Mother breezed closer. I could smell the overwhelming stench of decomposing flesh, blood, and, oddly but no less scary, the sweet toxicity of embalming fluid. I clenched my eyes tight. My feet wouldn't move, and I couldn't seem to tilt my head further away. It's cold, oh so cold...

"Oi... Come here, you daft sod... You're never too old for a kiss from your mum." My eyes bolted open. Mother was back to normal. My heart couldn't stop thumping. "Now. Remember to drop the girls off on your way to work and ensure you go. I hear the new boss isn't as friendly as the old one."

I smiled and nodded, shaking off the endless nightmare. My attention went back to the package. Mother noticed and rolled her eyes before heading for the door.

"It's probably just a video Charlotte ordered for the girls," Mother suggests, her voice fading as she left. "Don't stress too much about it."

Of course, I knew she was right, but I couldn't shake an odd feeling. I tore the cassette tape open with trembling hands and stepped into the lounge. My eyes widened, staring at an ordinary cassette tape with a white sticky label—one of those you buy to record a show or movie you might miss. But it was the red felt-tip handwriting that left me stunned.

"Things you need to know–Tape One," the words taunted. It was in my father's handwriting. "What the hell?" I mutter, trying to understand how it was possible.

The mention of "Tape One" had me wondering if more tapes were coming, but my thoughts kept returning to Frank, his ominous warning, and what was so bad that he hung himself, assuming that's how it played out. Not that anything is as it seems these days.

Chapter 4

'Frank Ecklestone One Week Ago,'

Frank Ecklestone finally made it home in the dead of night, fear gnawing at his sanity. His white Capris roared into Berkley Square, Rugby, its engine growling like a beast through the stillness, spewing exhaust fumes into the cold air. Frank swung his door open, fingers trembling as he fumbled with the keys before flicking the engine off. Eventually, he summoned the energy to stumble from his seat, drenched in panic sweat, eyes darting left to right, probing the shadows.

The harsh streetlight glow revealed his pale, terror-stricken face, eaten alive by paranoia. The confrontation with the stranger at the bar replayed in his mind, a grim reminder of everything he'd been running from, the secrets he dreaded being uncovered, and what he'd had to do.

Little did he know, the killer was waiting, concealed in the inky darkness of the far-right corner just behind unkempt bushes. Their head tilted, a wicked smile dancing at the corners of their lips. The killer relished Frank's palpable terror, savouring every cloudy, rasping breath escaping his frightened mouth. Frank, scrambling and muttering, **"I said nothing; nobody knows anything. He knows nothing. Just thinks he does."** His voice quivered like a leaf in the wind. The car door slammed shut, echoing through the quiet cul-de-sac. Frank stumbled over the curb leading to the communal door of Berkley

House. His frantic pace outwitted the sturdiness of his feet, moving as if his life depended on it, still looking behind and seeing nothing.

Inside, Frank made a beeline for his second-floor apartment, number 17. His shaking hands fumbled with his keys, casting nervous glances over his shoulder. Unbeknownst to him, the killer followed, slithering silently at an ominous distance. Frank hesitated at his doorway, eyes scanning the dim corridor behind him. Shielded in the shadows, the killer slipped stealthily along the darkened walls, drifting up the stairs with eerie grace once Frank was inside.

His coat was thrown onto a chair, keys tossed onto a cluttered table, and Frank's trembling fingers reached for a beer to soothe his nerves. He glanced at the ladder and the old gym rope propped against the wall beside the silver fridge, remembering another job he hadn't got around to yet. For the first time in a while, he felt safe—until now. Its presence served as a stark reminder of his constant need to be ready to escape. The end window offered a route down to a flat-roofed bin shed, but he hadn't figured out the logistics beyond tying the rope around the nearest supporting pillar and hoping for the best with the ladder. Handy work like this was never Frank's forte.

He'd managed eighteen months in this place, the longest so far, yet it was his fourth move in five years, as the shadows of his past sins still clung to him. His mind was a breeding ground for ghosts, regrets, and unrelenting torment. The killer understood this all too well, revelling in Frank's plight. With some false reassurance, Frank moved around his flat, checking the place over, muttering like a madman, "Just a passing phase," whispers that lacked the courage of their conviction. Deep down, he knew the stranger's prodding was much more than that. "He'll get bored and go away ... just clutching at straws, he knows fuck all."

Frank finally settled into his worn recliner, hoping to relax with any old crap on TV. Suddenly, a loud clap shattered the silence like a balloon popping, plunging the room into darkness. Frank fumbled his beer, spilling it onto the floor. Each drop echoed creepily, teasing the last of Frank's intact nerves. The situation worsened when the fleeting headlights of a passing car cast obscure shadows across the room, briefly revealing the killer's menacing silhouette.

His hand spasmed open in fear, and the beer bottle slipped from Frank's already shaky grasp, shattering into a million pieces. Frank froze. His throat tightened, and his breath became shallow. The ladder he had planned to use for escape was miraculously gone. All Frank could do was mutter, **"I'm fucked,"** a grim truth that the killer savoured.

The killer knew they had plenty of time, remaining in the shadows, relishing Frank's rabbit-in-headlights terror.

The silence was broken only by the erratic rhythm of Frank's frantic, wheezy breathing. His eyes darted around the room, clinging to the irrational hope that the ladder had somehow moved itself to the window, ready to save him. His pulse pounded in his ears, and cold sweat streamed down his forehead. Frank desperately needed to scream for help, hoping a neighbour would hear, but his vocal cords were paralyzed with fear, rendering him a silent, terrified mute.

Amidst his desperation, Frank did the only thing that came to mind. Using a frayed fingernail, he began carving into his arm. Blood oozed from each slice, dripping quicker with each stroke. Finally, he spelled out the word, **"B ... O...O...K,"** his vision blurred with pain. He was too disoriented to notice the gym rope slithering on the floor, manipulated by the killer like a sinister snake charmer.

Frank stayed frozen, helpless, resigned to his fate or perhaps too exhausted from years of running to fight. In the looming darkness, he trembled in the face of the unspeakable horror that awaited. The rope continued its eerie dance, its rough twine brushing against Frank's arm before coiling itself around his neck, not once but twice. It tightened with a relentless grip, choking the life out of him. Frank's mouth gaped open, his swollen tongue turning a shade of purple, his eyes bulging with terror. He dangled in the air, suspended by the merciless twine, his life slipping away.

The killer remained unmoved, an embodiment of evil, as they watched Frank's futile struggle. Moonlight filtered through the window, casting irregular ripples of light across the room, revealing a shadowy figure steeped in darkness, focused on their grotesque work. Blood seeped from Frank's mouth, eye sockets, and the gash on his arm, yet no one could witness his agony.

No front door slammed shut, and no cries for help echoed through the neighbouring apartments. The killer faded into the night, leaving behind only Frank's lifeless body, swaying in the moonlight like a puppet of horror. Blood dribbled from his pale, swollen face. He'd met a gruesome end, with one last message carved into his flesh. But who was it for?

Chapter 5

'Gerald-Présent Day,'

My hands shook as I held the tape. Hypnotised, drawn in by my father's vivid handwriting, I didn't know what to think or feel at that moment other than dread. The room seemed to shrink, shadows crawling from every recess as I grappled with the cassette.

With the waning echoes of the news, the onrushing radiance of Halloween III - Season of the Witch cast an eerie, shifting light across the room. Much to Charlotte's irritation, I had a penchant for horror and gore. No matter how often I'd seen them, my morbid fascination persisted. Given how weird my life has been, you'd think I'd be put off by that stuff. Not in the slightest. The urge to immerse myself in the mindless violence of a movie tugged at me. A chance to escape, even for a few minutes. Life had become a nightmarish, low-budget flick, with the mysterious tape occupying the spotlight as a messed-up, ill-timed prop.

Why now? Why would I be sent such a thing a year after my father's death? There were no doubts. It was his handwriting, so how was it possible? This played on my mind as I begrudgingly sipped tepid coffee, unwilling to let my mother's efforts go to waste. Not that she'd know, but I would feel bad. It took all of five minutes before I eventually decided there was only one thing to do if I wanted to know. Abandoning my seat, gliding across the cold, unyielding hardwood floor, I reached the VCR with a shaking hand.

An adrenaline surge coursed through me as I struggled with the unfamiliar tremors ripping through my body. After all, the situation was hardly normal. I continued, eager to uncover the significance behind my father's decision to make a tape. With the cassette in place, I retreated to the safety of the sofa, fingers wrapped around the remote. Caution to the wind, I mutter, "Fuck it." With an unsteady finger pressing play, the VCR whirred to life, emitting a clunky hum. Unless the recorder's settings were off, Father had recorded this tape a year before he'd died. Making the situation more bizarre than I realised.

The black screen morphed into a fierce, grainy grey, showing Father looking messy. His once crisp blue-and-white striped shirt was now loose, and a dark blue tie hung slack around his neck. His shirt's top button was undone, and his usual slicked-back hair was dishevelled.

"Can you hear me? Can you see me?" Father's eyes darted above the screen, and it appeared he was talking with someone just off-camera. With a forced smile, Father was uneasy as he spoke. Perched on the edge of my seat, my shaking hand urged me to switch drinks for something stronger.

Pausing the tape, I reached for a hidden whiskey bottle buried under a stack of magazines. It was a reflex, a habit I couldn't let go of. Mother had been pouring any bottles she found down the drain, but I kept a few stashed away for a rainy day or a shit one like today. Finding comfort in lingering memories of Charlotte and Father, I poured a shot into my coffee, prepared myself for what would be revealed, and hit play again.

"Hey Gerald, it's your dear old dad. Shit, how stupid of me; of course, you can see me," Father's voice quivered. "I imagine a million thoughts racing through your mind, questioning why I sent you a bloody tape. If you're watching this, I'm gone, and it's down to you, I'm afraid."

The tears were coming. I paused again, mirroring how Father looked. I wanted to savour Father's weathered image, still finding it hard to believe, when I noticed an unsettling presence lurking in the periphery. At first, it appeared to be a shadow, but it didn't seem right. Though no other voices were heard, the image was faint but detailed enough to resemble a human figure. Hesitating, wiping my face, legs shaking with stomach-churning anxiety before the tape restarted.

The unsettling shadow held my attention now. The harder I looked, leaning as far forward as possible without falling off my seat, the air filled with bone-chilling fear. Common sense said to stop, but I couldn't. Maybe there were 'answers I needed,' I thought, hand trembling a little more. Before realising it, it was the same as I've been seeing. 'Him'… Yet, I couldn't figure out why it was on the tape.

Father continues, heavily laden with remorse, "…We tried our best to shield you all, but it wasn't enough. I inherited something from my father when he passed; sadly, it wasn't anything good. Your Nana has all those crazy stories about ghosts and things, but it has been her way of coping with reality. Then there's you. I'm aware of the other stuff you can see, the weird and 'dead' ones. For the most part, there's a simple answer. We are fucking cursed, son. If that can be called simple, there's a lot more to it, connected to some knights centuries ago, from what I gather." Father muttered. His voice grew shakier the more he spoke. Wide-eyed with shock, nausea slowly welling up as those words sank in. 'We are fucking cursed.' Stunned, remembering the village gossip, it now didn't sound so far-fetched.

"There's an old book, a grimoire, and so much more I don't understand—even talk of fucked-up demonic shit. The mere idea of it terrifies the heck out of me. Thanks to our ancestors, we were expected to carry out unimaginable acts, but I can't … I cannot… I… I… I'll stop babbling until I know more. I need you to keep you and your family bloody safe; I love you, son."

The tape ended, leaving me in creepy silence, dropping the remote. How could such a dark secret have been kept for so long? Frank's words of caution haunted my thoughts. And now this. 'Did my father know Frank or of him?' Piecing together a nightmarish puzzle, and it terrified me. No matter how freaked out I was, my eyes stayed fixated on the now black screen. With each sip of coffee, the room seemed to grow colder. I briskly rubbed my arms as a shiver rumbled through me. A coat of goose pimples erupted over my skin while I was unnerved by the feeling that someone other than my father was looking back at him through the TV.

My haze drifted deep in thought, only to be abruptly snapped back by a jarring noise—a loud clap. It echoed through the air. Eyes fixed ahead, frozen. The shadow thumped against the TV like a scene from a horror movie; then came its bone-chilling laughter, curdling through my ears. My temporary paralysis subsided, throwing myself backward onto the sofa. My reflection appeared on the screen, too, warped amidst the shadowy outline.

' **C o m e … o n … G e r - ald…I'm…right…here…all…you…have…to…do…is…let…me…in. Henry wouldn't want you to be lonely. Let the darkness in, and you will never be alone again.**'

It was him again, the 'Whispering Man,' but how? How did he fit into my father's narrative? Weeping, mournful cries surfaced, this time rumbling with a crackle through the aged television speakers. Searing heat tormented my eyes at the sight of me in the hood. The surrounding air had turned icy now, and my breath hung like a mist.

'What the fuck is going on?' I gasp, my breath catching in my throat. It seemed my father and I may have shared a common torment.

Chapter 6

'Gerald-The Next Morning,'

With a heavy head and the regular rumbling of anxiety, especially in light of last night, I made it to Mother's, dropping the girls as usual. Only to find the atmosphere mirroring everything I was feeling. Mother was acting strange. Okay, stranger than normal. The bar can be quite high, but this morning felt different. Among a line of rum bottles, and one looking freshly opened, I spotted an envelope. It had been ripped recently and bore a peculiar crimson wax seal with a mysterious symbol. Another of those pentagrams etched with the goat's head.

Everything about it seemed eerie. Judging by the smudged lipstick on the glass, the contents weren't much better. It was early, and Mother had already started drinking. That wasn't like her; she'd lectured me enough lately. For her to crack open the rum was bad.

A loud clanking broke my stare. Mother returned to the table with two cups of coffee. She'd seen me looking at the symbol, causing her lips to tremble. She went to speak but paused, taking a deep breath. "You might as well see for yourself," she says, slowly sipping her coffee. Her cheeks were flustered.

I quickly grabbed the envelope. Its texture beneath my trembling fingers had a certain elegance, a sophistication absent from the typical cheap ones from the post office. The symbol on the seal caught the sunlight, its design eerily captivating. A goat's head was nestled within a five-pointed star in the centre of a double-lined circle. Perhaps there was some truth to his theories on occultism. The inner and outer rings were filled with mysterious glyphs and symbols, adding an air of mysticism. My eyes darted to Mother, seeking any signs of recognition or understanding in her expression.

Mother's voice shuddered as she finally spoke up. "It's not what you think," she gushes, her eyes filled with a haunting sadness that lingered.

My finger delicately traced the seal's smooth contours, savouring the anticipation before cautiously opening the envelope. Inside, there was a slender slip of paper, and then I found what caused Mother's need to drink. Gruesome was an understatement and defied belief—a two-inch by two-inch piece of flesh scarred with the same sinister symbol—bloody human flesh.

"Goddamn," I choked out, reeling at the horror. The raised lines formed a grotesque pattern that left me at a loss. 'What the hell were my parents into? And why now?' That was all I could think about. I turned to Mother, looking for answers.

"I wouldn't call it 'godly.' But you're not far off," she whispers, her voice heavy with emotion. I could see tears bubbling at the corners of her eyes. "I'm so sorry, Gerald. We didn't want this for you. All of those things you told me you could see, it's real and now the 'why' is coming home to roost and I'm scared. I'm bloody terrified, to be honest."

"Are you serious? Why all the lies and secrets? Do you not understand how messed up I am because of it? And whose bloody flesh is this? How did this happen? Why?" The questions poured out, each more bewildering than the last.

Mother struggled to find words, her voice barely a whisper. "While I may not have all the answers, I know that mole. It was on his lower back. Your father shielded us from so many things for our well-being. He'd been better prepared for this world than you before his father's passing. With a deep loathing, he grappled with the idea of this legacy becoming your responsibility, striving to break the curse that had haunted his ancestors. And others shortly before his death, he mentioned a searing, burning sensation in his back. Still, he refused to let me or anyone look at it. Now we know why," she says, her voice cracking, holding back the urge to break down completely.

My mind spun, thoughts shifting towards the safety of Olivia and Lacey. They, too, could be at risk.

"I've got to protect my daughters. If all of this is true, I can't allow the same darkness that consumed my father's life to threaten what's left of my family."

Mother retrieved a newspaper hidden in a drawer and placed it before me. The headline rocked me backward in my seat: "A Serial Killer Stalks Willowbrook?" it read. The article detailed a second gruesome death in less than two weeks—a trucker with ties to Willowbrook was torn apart.

My heart thumped as I saw the truck fronts in the accompanying photograph. It was one of the rowdy group from the pub, one I'd suspected of being involved in Charlotte's accident.

"Gerald … Did you go out last night?" Mother asked softly, her voice sounding worried.

"No, never. Why are you asking and showing me this?" I reply, unease deepening. Not that I could remember after the horrifying tape. "Do you know what's really going on?" I ask, thinking over everything. Then back to the newspaper again.

"There are a lot of possibilities, but I fear it's the curse and the bloodlines being driven into the open. Are you sure you didn't go anywhere at all?" Mother asked again, her voice quivering. I didn't understand why she'd ask.

Feeling confused, I reply, "I'm bloody sure. Why the hell are you asking that? You don't seriously think I could do that? What do you mean, driven into the open?" Did my mother suddenly think I was a killer? She'd never questioned me before. Why now? Whether it was because emotions were running high or she was holding something back, I found her behaviour odd and slightly unnerving. Considering I held an envelope containing human flesh, that said a lot.

"Well, descendants from knights, being pulled into the open for a purpose I'm unsure of. It's odd timing though, and the little I knew from your father goes way back. I can't bear the thought of anything happening to you and the girls. This family has already endured too much loss," Mother gushes, refusing to make eye contact. There was more, but I didn't push. The idea of my father and tales of knights didn't ring true, and how did the chaos in my head fit, or the whispering man? What became clear, there was more to father and this mess than I'd realised. It had to be dangerous if father could keep these secrets for so long. A curse and a strange wax symbol. What's next?

She continues, "Gerald, there are things in this world we don't understand. Your father was always secretive, but he did it to protect us. He didn't want you to inherit this curse, even if you'd always seen the world differently."

I sigh, feeling the weight of my family's darkness pressing down on me. "I need to figure this out, for the sake of my daughters. I can't let these secrets consume them, too."

Mother nodded, her eyes filled with worry. "Be careful, Gerald. This feels like only the beginning, and I don't want to lose you, too."

I promise to be careful, but I knew deep down I had no control, not with the voices and hallucinations. The answers lay hidden in the shadows of my father's past, and I had to uncover them if I wanted to have a future.

"*Gerald,*"

I stared into the mirror, hands trembling. Cold water gushed from the tap, its rhythm a haunting melody that splashed against my palms. Lost in the maze of my thoughts, I watched with dread as beads of condensation raced down the spout.

My reflection, drained of colour and contorted with fear, stared back at me from the foggy glass. The whirlwind of the morning merged with the night's terrifying revelations, weaving a nightmare I was desperate to escape. The memory of Father's severed flesh, wrapped in the envelope with a bizarre wax seal left in the kitchen, weighed heavily. It was a puzzle piece more unsettling than the tape, gnawing at my sanity like a starved rat.

Why didn't Colin mention the missing patch of flesh during Father's autopsy? That's all I kept thinking about. Surely, he would've noticed. The air in the bathroom was thick with tension, made eerier by the low hum of the fan, casting long shadows that danced in the corners of the room. Life had taken a nightmarish turn, thrusting me into a world for which I was ill-prepared, burdened not only by my father's ominous legacy but also by the haunting whispers that coincided with the presence of whispering man stalking my every move, especially earlier.

The image of the black cloud wielding a sharp, gleaming knife against Janice's throat sent a chill crawling down my spine. The atmosphere of the bathroom was getting too much; every breath created white plumes in the soapy air. I twisted the tap shut, still shaken.

Suddenly, a strange sound sliced through the silence. My heart thumped hard. I knew the sound, and what followed had me frozen in place. Lines slowly etched themselves into the condensation-covered mirror, gradually speeding up with creepy intent. Each stroke deepened my apprehension as they formed the very symbol I'd just been thinking about: a double-lined circle with a five-pointed star. The dreaded goat's head was the only element missing, leaving me struggling to understand what the hell was going on and how it was possible.

Terror tore through my veins. I wanted to run but couldn't, so I remained rooted to the spot. Making matters worse, an invisible presence drew nearer, smothering the air behind me. Cold brushed my earlobes and cheek, pimples rippling over my flesh as a heavy breath whispered close.

I could feel someone close, yet no one could be seen. My stomach churned, and a faint tug at the front of my shirt brought my neck hair to attention. **'Hush, little baby, don't say a word. Mamma's gonna buy you a mockingbird, and if that mockingbird don't sing, Mamma's gonna buy you a diamond ring.'** a grating, melancholy voice sings that rhyme again. It's the girl's favourite and sung by one person only. My Charlotte. It cut through the silence like a hot blade through flesh. I spun frantically, desperate to see where it came from.

Sweat trickled over my temples, and my eyes darted to the mirror's reflection as a blast of wind swept past. My gaze followed as streaks materialised with dread and fascination until three ominous words stared back.

"Kill... For... Me."

"Do that for me, Gerald. I need you to do that for me."

There was no doubt it was Charlotte's voice. Yet, the undeniable truth lingered—she was gone. Recent talk of demonic curses had screwed with my faith in what was possible and rational.

"It's alright, Gerald. It's me. You can trust me. It's your Charlotte," she whispers soothingly in my ear. Was this happening? How?

I wanted to talk to her so badly. To tell her what I didn't get to before she died. I yearned to apologise for not standing up to my boss that fateful night. I should have been in the car with her, and Charlotte wouldn't have been driving so late. And maybe, just maybe, that lorry wouldn't have smashed her off the road. More than that, though, I was sorry for the crazy that's been in my life, the times I've told her what I saw. And the strange look I'd get before a reassuring smile.

I wanted to share the bizarre, harrowing strange that had unfolded since her death, the revelation that my family was cursed, possibly linked to 'knights'. Strangely, perhaps Charlotte had been lucky to escape from the spiralling madness that now consumes me.

Staring into the mirror, Charlotte's voice echoed in my ears. My heart was pounding against my chest, throat parched with terror. Because the painful truth remained—I couldn't have those conversations I yearned for. Charlotte... was... dead. It wasn't her speaking.

I was soon wide-eyed with dread as reality drenched itself in this unsettling truth that rapidly twisted and warped hauntingly. Looking back from the mirror was the imposing, cloaked figure, its dirty hood concealing any view of its face. An enormous hat cast a shadow that added to the horror.

"Gerald, if you loved me, you would seek revenge upon those responsible. Let the darkness in. Your father would agree—they deserve punishment, all of them. Baphomet demands that you paint the streets with their blood, and the pain will fade like the dead leaves in autumn." Charlotte's voice reverberated chillingly from the looming figure. Rigid, unable to do anything except mutter, "Baphomet demands it," as my blood curdled with fear. I tried blinking repeatedly, hoping to clear the horrifying illusion, but the steam persisted, as did the disturbing symbol.

"Gerald, are you alright? I know this is all so overwhelming," Mother called out, concerned yet tinged with a curiosity that left me questioning how much she truly knew. Her shrill voice was enough to shatter the surreal trance I was in. Left with a bewildering question: "What the bloody hell is happening?"

"I... erm, yeah, I think so," I stammer, throat dry and gravelly, unable to understand the reality that had just unfolded. The steam quickly dissipated, and the messages ceased haunting me, but the sinister symbol remained etched into my mind, compelling a need for answers about so many things. For now, I'd settle for the unique wax symbol.

Chapter 7

'Détective Reynolds,'

If there's one constant in my life, it's murder. I needed time before dealing with more of it. My head was still in Scotland, grappling with vampires. How that ended has left me in limbo, and I fear they're not done with us. All I wanted was to go home, invite Ellena over, and lock ourselves away for at least a week. Seems the moment we get close, death pulls us apart. There's no escaping it. Now was no different.

Our unmarked car rumbled through the rugged, twisting streets of Newport's industrial estate, tires thudding against the pavement. The atmosphere in the car was tense as Michael and I exchanged worried glances. We were on our way to O'Hanlon's Haulage, a well-known company in the village and the transportation industry.

Our arrival in the small village had so far been met with cautious silence, the lingering unease of the first murder casting a shadow over the community. The local folks were left bewildered by the murder, unable to grasp its bizarre nature, as a growing dread filled the air.

As we approached O'Hanlon's, there was no hiding our apprehension. It was already 1 in the morning. When security patrolled, they saw the company gates wide open. In the cold, unforgiving night, the security team stumbled upon the lifeless body of a forty-five-year-old man. He was torn in two, his lifeless limbs bound to the merciless grills of two massive lorries.

I gazed at the path, my thoughts consumed by fear and curiosity. I questioned whether we were walking into a nightmare from which there was no escape. For such a small place, it's attracting a hell of a lot of trouble, and I fear a repeat of Scotland. Not that I'm telling Michael that. This case was already pushing me to my breaking point.

The silver spikes, resembling skeletal fingers, cast eerie shadows as we loomed closer to the gates. I rolled down my window, picking up on the putrid odour that overwhelmed my senses. It was the smell of blood, thick and cloying, saturating the air.

"You getting that, Georgie?" Michael asks, his voice tense, his nostrils twitching as he revelled in the stink.

"Afraid so. Lots of it, too," I reply, unable to hide the strain in my voice.

"You sensed anyone or anything else yet?" Michael inquired, his eyes scanning our surroundings.

"Sadly, Michael," I sigh, "this is strikingly similar to the previous one. Aside from the chaotic chemo signals standing around waiting for the miracle of a body reattaching itself, I haven't picked up on anything else. Not even faint."

I was tense and full of frustration. My unique abilities have been a double-edged sword, captivating and tormenting me simultaneously. Sensing things that others can't isn't always a good thing. However, this gift has become a burden of late, darker since all the bone-crunching I had to do. Michael and I made unique partners in our fight against all that goes bump in the night. If only we could catch a break.

"You're making it sound like the victim strapped himself to both trucks, and the lorries magically reversed on their own." Michael's skepticism was clear, but he was also in denial. Scotland got to him, too.

I smirked at Michael's comment, even allowing a sly smile, but my eyes betrayed a lack of joy. It wasn't only the vampires that raised the bar; it was Ruth and the magic she could do, which meant the lorries magically assisting wouldn't seem so far-fetched. Only I wasn't so sure Willowbrook wanted their supernatural sins laid bare.

When we arrived, the coroner's van was already on the scene, casting a long shadow over the gruesome picture. A short man with a slightly larger build, the coroner appeared uneasy, his face reflecting the horror before him, looking anxious. He, no doubt, had seen many things in his line of work, but this was different.

Stepping out of the vehicle, Michael and I swiftly flashed our warrant cards at the police officer managing the scene cordon. The blue-white tape parted, and we slinked forward, our senses on guard for a repeat of the last scene being watched. Something evil drenched the ground we walked upon in blood.

I whisper to Michael as we approached the body, "Nothing yet." But then, an involuntary shudder coursed through me, and I reached for the back of my neck. Michael experienced it, too, a disquieting sensation that made his skin prickle.

"That was strange," he says, his eyebrows furrowing in confusion. "Wait up, check out your 9 o'clock." Michael whispers, his eyes darting around the scene as he noticed the two guys in black suits and ties who did not look like detectives.

I followed his gaze and saw two mid-thirties men dressed impeccably in dark suits, their polished shoes clicking on the pavement. They stood out, and their presence was strange, considering the morbid scene. I couldn't shake the unsettling sensation that something was off about them, Michael too, causing a chill to creep down our spines.

A distance away, the two men watched the unfolding scene with fixed eyes, acting as if they were mere onlookers, rather than the feeling I was getting. One held onto a small black book with obsessive enthusiasm, while the other jotted down notes in a black pocket-sized notebook.

I ask, whispering, "Are they watching us?"

"Yeah, but trying not to be obvious," Michael replies, his voice filled with caution. "But it begs the question, how long they've been here, watching the body? It doesn't seem to faze or concern them."

My unease was growing, the hairs on the back of my neck standing on end. "I don't like this, Michael. I don't like this at all. We are missing some big 'dots.' This village isn't as innocent as it appears. I need to check whether there is a heat path around the cabs and body."

To most, the yard appeared indistinguishable from its gravelly surface, marked by the haphazard footprints of officers and onlookers. As I looked around, I could see the heat signatures left behind by others, giving me an insight into what was fresh and what was not.

"Hurry," the old git whispers, his eyes flickering to the watchful, unknown figures. "Photographs are being taken, and the flash is dancing like a playful toy."

Crouching down, I shuddered at the chill of the cold ground against my fingertips. My eyes flashed blood red, and I could suddenly see the hidden world beyond the perception of anyone else. This was one trick I was glad to have in my supernatural arsenal. Heat streaks marked the raised layers of crumbled stone, a haunting reminder of the violence and brutality unfolding. I could see the power, the force that had torn a man in two, and it churned my stomach.

While investigating the scene, I wondered, 'What will it be this time? The Kanaima was dangerous, the vampires, I thought. They're the deadliest, and I still think the big battle is yet to come.'

Michael was about to turn back to me, thinking he had given me enough time when I saw him check out those two guys. He'd noticed movement. One of them adjusted his suit jacket collar, causing his shirt cuff to slide forward. Unusual cufflinks were unveiled, showcasing a round symbol depicting two knights on black horses, each carrying shields decorated with crosses.

However, what stood out was the circular black pin or badge discreetly tucked under the collar lapel of a particular man. The emblem, an old-style Red Cross, mirrored the design on the cufflinks.

Watching Michael's face, deep in thought (that's when his forehead wrinkles clap together), he thought they were familiar but couldn't recall its meaning. Michael leaned close to me and whispered, "Georgie, have you finished?"

Still crouched, I reply, "Yeah, still nothing, and it's getting annoying ... wait... the blood splatter, the pattern changes. Fuck, it's everywhere because the killer wanted it to be. The blood is in a symbol, the five-point star in a circle. Satan." My voice stretched an octave in shock.

"You've got to be kidding me ... and as if things couldn't become any stranger or worse... there's another factor we may need to explore," Michael remarked, his voice low and tinged with exasperation. "If that's about the devil, do you know anything in that encyclopaedia brain of yours, on the intricacies of religious beliefs?"

I shrugged, but was intrigued. The cross, Christ, and the church. Why does it seem like this case has taken a strange and unexpected detour? I wondered to myself.

Michael subtly gestured towards the two mysterious men, their presence cloaked in an unsettling veil of curiosity. At least one of those guys has knights, shields, and a cross as hidden emblems on his cufflinks and lapel.

With a frown, my instincts were on high alert. "Should we say hello?"

"It would be rude not to. I speak, and you listen. We can start deciphering their symbols once we're back at Willowbrook station. They could tell us something, especially about this crap on the ground. I can't believe we came so close to missing it."

His eyes locked onto the two men. Michael's suspicion grew stronger with each passing moment. He sensed something was awry with them, and they had secrets much darker than the night enveloping them. Willowbrook's secrets were about to unfold, taking us on another journey, as long as it's not like the last one.

As we cautiously approached the mysterious figures, Michael tightly gripped his leather warrant card wallet. He caught their unsettling gaze and spoke without hesitation, "Excuse me, do you have a minute?"

The two men shifted their gaze towards him, their faces calm, but their eyes said otherwise.

Every facet of their appearance radiated menace, casting eerie shadows over the scene. The man's shoes, gleaming with military precision, told a story of discipline and order. Layers of ash and charcoal clung to the soles, hinting at an affinity for contemplation by open fireplaces. The faint scent of tobacco, not from common cigarettes or cigars but from a pipe, suggested a certain importance, though not necessarily from a legal standpoint.

My thoughts raced back to Michael's cryptic mention of knights and crosses and the blood-dripped 'devil' symbol across the gravel by the body, which made me think of religion. A gold ring on the man's pinkie finger, subtly concealed, bore a raised logo, and his tie, fashioned like a sword with a small black emblem at its centre, added another layer to the mysterious puzzle.

As I took in these eerie details, a shiver rippled through my hackles, causing the fine hairs on my neck to stand on end. They might appear to be churchgoers, but I didn't like what I was reading. Unsettling dots connected in my mind, setting off alarm bells that reverberated between my ears. Why would representatives of the church be present at a crime scene?

The man on the right, shorter and leaner with sharp facial features, echoed the meticulously cataloged details. But it was his accent that intrigued me the most. A twang, perhaps French or Italian, concealed beneath a veneer of something other than English. Each word was spoken with measured precision, a deliberate effort to mask their origins. Michael's ears pricked at the peculiar intonations, too. The wily git was never slow on the uptake.

Neither of us suffered fools or lies, but when Michael's 'gut' tells him something is wrong, he listens and wastes no time cutting to the core. "What's your interest in the crime scene?" Michael demands, his voice laced with a hint of venom.

The man's response, a claim that the deceased was a loyal parishioner, did little to sway my skepticism. His heart remained eerily steady, starkly contrasting with the lies in the air. Since when did the church send representatives to pay respects to the deceased?

Michael, not mincing his words, covered his nose to shield himself from the stench that clung to the scene. His gruff, Cockney-inflected tone dripped with cynicism as he probed for answers. "Is that right now? Excuse me for a minute as I digest the thick stench that wafted up. What's his name?"

The man's response veered further into deception as he painted a portrait of Mr Patrick Sheh as a troubled disciple, often expelled from casinos because of his mingling with the wrong crowd. It was a story that didn't align with the facts, and my intuition refused to accept it. Why, if Sheh was such a nuisance, would these guys come to view his body? Their eloquence and intelligence suggested a deeper layer of deception.

My patience was wearing thin. I took a bold step forward. "And you appear under the impression we were born yesterday. As you called him, Patrick Sheh meant more than that to you. Otherwise, you wouldn't be here. Now, respectfully, I would like to see some identification, please."

Tension drifted between us as we faced off, eyes darting like shadows in the moonlight. I knew that the answers I sought wouldn't come easily. Then, the man on the left, his smile chillingly unnerving, produced a white business card from a Bible. Its thick, textured paper exuded an air of luxury; on it, a cross was inscribed unlike any seen in typical churches. Below, a phone number, "913, 0309," stood without an area code.

I exchanged a perplexed glance with Michael, who wore a furrowed brow. A gust of wind, laden with the scent of blood, swept through the night, causing both of us to tip our heads instinctively. I wondered if the card was some twisted form of humour, a way to throw us off track.

Suddenly, as moonlight washed over their faces, my heart quickened. I stepped back, muttering, "Just when I thought it couldn't get weirder." I caught an unsettling image—a distortion. No trick of light but a nightmarish shift that rippled across their features. Their skin withered, like that of a long-buried corpse, only to revert to its smooth, living state in the blink of an eye.

My heart raced, and a sickly sensation settled in my gut. Something darker and far more ominous was at play in the quiet town of Willowbrook, and it had little regard for the trappings of the church. The two mysterious men who had taken an interest in the crime scene harboured secrets that didn't bode well for the murky road ahead.

Before we could probe further, a voice called out from behind, startling us. Our eyes darted briefly, a natural reaction. By the time we looked back, the mysterious duo had vanished. A sinking weight settled in my chest, adding another layer of strangeness to an already crazy night.

We approached a nearby Portakabin, where a uniformed officer awaited. Michael dwelled on the sudden disappearance of the two men, causing him to reflect on Scotland again. I knew that was the case because I'd done the same. Now I grappled with the darkness that entrenched my life. The involvement of 'the Church' only deepened the riddle, leaving us with more questions than answers.

A simple business card, an unusual cross, and a phone number devoid of an area code—details that seemed ominous were leading them down a twisted path of the unknown. All the details bothered me; the cogs spun in my mind, piecing everything together, wondering if Willowbrook's constabulary was corrupt or just blind to everything happening. I knew there was no way in hell some random dead guy would get a visit from the church, except the Pope, of course.

"Hey, detectives, it's not much, but it's enough to confirm something fucking strange. They realised the concealed camera, and it went off," the officer called out, holding the cabin door open for the detectives.

I paused at the threshold, my gaze lingering on the carefully recovered sections of Mr Sheh. The wind whistled through the yard, carrying an eerie chorus that seemed to echo through the pipes and barrels. A tingle prickled at the nape of my neck. It was happening again; we were being watched. Had the two men merely strayed further out of sight? Even up close, the trouble was that neither I nor Michael read anything from them other than a heartbeat, and that didn't sit right.

Inside, the tape played on a grainy black screen, revealing tantalising fragments of a sinister image. Two looming lorries flanked a stricken man on the ground, caught in the throes of an unnatural spectacle. A hooded figure materialised, their arms weaving intricate patterns as chains slithered from the lorries to ensnare Mr Sheh. The realisation that nobody touched those chains churned my blood, and no one appeared to be driving the lorries.

The hooded figure turned toward the camera, a veil of darkness concealing their face, and with a deliberate movement of their arm, the camera abruptly ceased its recording. We were left in stunned silence, senses overwhelmed by the puzzle we had just witnessed.

Chapter 8

'Killer,'

'Killer,'

The killer waited patiently for the right moment to choose their prey in the crowded, dirty tavern. The rest of the group had called it a night and hopped into a shared taxi, leaving only the middle-aged man standing by the door. His bald head shone in the dim light, and he was dressed in faded blue denim jeans, a worn Michael Jackson T-shirt, and a navy blue parka casually draped over his arm. His shirt inched upward as he grappled with the rebellious parka, exposing a protruding gut and a symbol etched upon his flesh, sending icy tendrils of dread through the killer's veins.

An insatiable thirst for the unholy consumed the killer's vengeful mind as the cryptic and foreboding emblem resonated deeply. After draining the last of his drink, the man staggered out of the Bull and Barrow, clumsily crashing through the rickety door and shattering the previously calm atmosphere. The night had reached its conclusion for his friends, but for the hunter, it marked the start of an exciting journey.

The killer loomed in the night's darkness, their intent solely focused on one singular purpose. Deep down, they knew certain souls would never find redemption, no matter how hard they tried or how much they wished for it in the eyes of a god. The killer's faith was of a peculiar kind, one that had been forged in the fiery pits of hell and yearned relentlessly for vengeance.

While the man was stumbling forward, the killer silently pursued him, concealing themselves in darkness. The man was headed towards a sprawling car park filled with the sights of cars, a blue van, and his white truck without its trailer. Completely oblivious to everything except his erratic thoughts, the trucker desperately held onto the frigid silver handrail, his foot stumbling awkwardly on the unforgiving metal step.

Overwhelmed by the weight of his past, his face flushed with guilt and intoxication. With a sudden, ungainly leap, he lifted his cumbersome body upright as he forcefully yanked open the door of the cab. Whether driven by stubbornness, lack of care, or being drunk off his ass that clouded his judgment, the man's intent was clear, and the killer revelled in the certainty of it.

A pregnant pause filled the air, creating a temporary veil of apprehension that caused the windows to mist. It made little difference to the killer. The man's fate was sealed in the killer's evil narrative as the 13-litre diesel engine erupted with a thunderous roar, breaking the silence and setting the stage for the tragic events. The deserted area was filled with the resonating rev of each engine, creating a reverberation that permeated the lonely night, save for a few stray souls.

As a drizzle replaced the earlier dampness, the killer's determination in their pursuit remained unwavering. Their cloaked hat heavenward, they inhaled deeply, taking in the intoxicating blend of falling rain and acrid diesel fumes—a mixture that carried the ominous promise of impending evil.

A commotion momentarily stole the killer's attention from a nearby side road. A couple, barely in their mid-twenties and intoxicated, carelessly stumbled along their raucous rendition of "We Will Rock You," disturbing the night's tranquillity. The innocence that clung to them spared them from the killer's cruel intentions. Tonight, all of their attention and focus were directed towards one man.

The killer watched patiently as the man's lorry careened recklessly through the car park, mowing down car mirrors and scraping by recklessly. Unless their prey left a trail of anguish and death in its wake, they knew exactly where it was headed. As the night unfolded, darkness and evil united in a shadowy tapestry, orchestrating a chilling reckoning.

The entrance to the haulage and recycling yard, marked by large spiked metal gates, had been violently smashed open. In the howling wind, the broken chain and padlock appeared to be beckoning the killer inside. The yard stretched out vulnerably and alluringly ahead as the killer crept toward a motionless truck. The engine hummed softly as the driver, deep in thought, took a moment to relieve himself by the front.

Wearily leaning against the truck's engine grill, the unsteady man struggled to coordinate, unaware of the killer's watchful gaze. The recent downpour had finally stopped, and if the killer had their way, the next few minutes of their prey's life would be equally fleeting. The darkness was filled with incoherent whistling that echoed while the guy lazily wobbled, and his head bobbed limply, showing no concern.

In the wake of a thoughtless journey, the street became a mess, with rubbish and the remnants of vehicles littering the area - broken wing mirrors, a mobile bin knocked over, and a motorcycle left in a mangled state, all abandoned at the curbside. Thankfully, no one else was hurt … at least not yet. As the trucker staggered away from the vehicle after answering nature's call, the wind carried showers of gravel dust that stung his eyes and coated his skin. He stood wistfully gazing at the line of trucks, trailers, and the imposing sorting shelters for recycling. From twenty feet, the killer watched as the wind gently ruffled the man's worn parka.

In the pale moonlight, their sinister black eyes glistened with an intense fury, sending shivers down the trucker's spine. Thoughts of murder and how to execute it swirled in the killer's mind. They noticed a nearby truck with a heavy-duty towing winch as their gaze shifted. The sight of its thick chains, coiled with lethal potential, ignited a sinister idea in the killer's imagination.

Both trucks had chains that glistened like ghostly Christmas lights, presenting a chilling surprise for their unsuspecting victim. The trucker, totally oblivious, finally turned around. He spun clumsily and stumbled again because he couldn't stay steady. His blurred vision made it even more remarkable that he found his way to the yard. The misty darkness slowly dissipated, unveiling an eerie and unsettling scene.

Fear gripped the trucker's throat tightly, causing unease to fill his stomach. In all his years, he had never come across anything like this. He entertained the thought of running, but fear held him steadfast. He stood face-to-face with his worst nightmares; every fear and dread he had ever harboured had manifested into this shadowed figure and had him firmly in its sights. His trembling hands were slick with clammy sweat, causing his cherished Michael Jackson T-shirt to cling uncomfortably to his skin. The patient and unrelenting killer could practically taste the fear of their helpless prey.

"L … look, I don't know what you want, but the yard is closed. Y … You are not supposed to be here," stammers the trucker, clinging to the faint hope that he was imagining the horrifying scene before him.

The eerie silence remained, broken only by the occasional rustle of leaves. The trucker attempted to flee, but his escape was thwarted as he lost his balance and landed with a loud thud on the ground.

"Look ... if it's money, there's a small safe in the office, petty cash mostly, but have at it," pleads the trucker, his efforts in vain. Gravel crunched beneath the weight of the killer's heavy boots, each grinding of stone against stone, sending a shiver down the trucker's spine. Every hair on his body stood on end, tingling with a deathly chill, as the killer continued to approach.

Little did the trucker know, chains with chunky red hooks were hanging ominously from the underbellies of the trucks, creating a haunting sight as they weaved through the gritty and moonlit landscape. Resembling, poised cobras ready to strike, they swayed with an eerie anticipation.

The killer, with a sinister silhouette that contrasted against the eerie glow of the moon in the backdrop, ominously stood over the unsuspecting trucker, who could only make out the menacing black eyes that gleamed with a terrifying and unnatural grey glow, piercing through the shadows of the killer's sinister mystique.

With a sudden, ghostly movement, the killer's arm slashed through the air, and the chains from both trucks came to life with ferocious intent. They lunged forward, their movements quick and calculated, wrapping themselves around the trucker's arms and legs like vipers on the hunt.

As the other truck roared to life, the helpless trucker was yanked away, suspended by his arms, creating a furious cloud of dust. He dangled like a grotesque piñata, his body slowly stretching, bones snapping, and cartilage tearing, all accompanied by a symphony of agonising sounds that filled the night air. The trucker's wails of pain, haunting and dreadful, echoed throughout the desolate yard, much to the killer's dark joy intensifying with each piercing cry. By their belief, revenge was a pleasure that carried both bitterness and sweetness, and they revelled in the suffering they had caused.

Amidst the heart-wrenching banshee wails, tears and saliva sprayed from the trucker's contorted face. Below the grinding wheels, the dusty earth quivered, and the chains groaned under the immense strain of the grotesque mess. Each agonising second brought fresh torment, bones snapping like brittle twigs, as the trucker's body was tormented and tortured.

Dripping with desperation, the trucker clung to life, his eyeballs popped, dangling by slender threads of optic nerves, swinging and flopping with each struggle, while his enormous belly flipped from beneath the torn T-shirt, revealing the gruesome tearing in his flesh. The horrifying sight compelled the killer to shift slightly, momentarily taken aback by the sheer brutality of their 'bloody' orchestra. Frothing cries for mercy echoed in the night, but went unanswered as the killer remained unrelenting.

Then, the last act of brutality unfolded with a sudden and violent whoosh. The trucker's torso was ruthlessly shredded from his lower body, releasing a gruesome torrent of blood and organs that showered the gritty yard. Each end of the severed body clapped against the fronts of the waiting trucks, creating a sickening and chaotic spectacle that the killer savoured in slow motion. The metallic scent of blood hung heavy in the air, whipped around by the wind beneath their hood and the hat's wide brim. A second victim was claimed, and as the torso flopped to its side, casting a spinal cord trail through the dirt, the killer saw the 'cross'. That fire behind the eyes burned bright with so much more to do, a question of who would be next.

With an air of mystery, the killer stepped back from the gruesome scene, their face completely obscured by a hood that concealed their menacing expression. Blood splatters painted their boots and clothes as they watched the grotesque aftermath of their brutal act. Now lifeless and mangled, the severed body lay sprawled on the ground like a grotesque work of art. The eerie glow of the moonlight showcased the macabre details, creating a chilling ambiance. The chains used as torture instruments now dangled ominously, still dripping with the trucker's blood.

The killer's heart raced with a mixture of exhilaration and satisfaction. They revelled in their power over life and death, relishing the fear they had instilled in their victims. The cross they had seen etched on the trucker's body symbolised their mission to prepare for what's coming.

Looking at the lifeless body one last time before fading into the darkness. Their brutal quest was far from over, and there was more blood to be spilled. The wind whispered their chilling laughter, creating an eerie atmosphere in the desolate yard and a chilling reminder of the horror that had unfolded. The village should sleep uneasily, their dreams haunted by the eerie 'whispers' in the night breeze.

Chapter 9

'Gerald-Library,'

Charlotte's eerie voice continues to occupy my thoughts, its echoes carrying, "Kill for me." And there seems no escape from the nursery rhyme, whether it's her or the crooked man. It triggered a vivid image from my school years when I'd endured religious education lessons. It was boring as hell, but now I wished I'd paid more attention. I remembered enough to recall some of the devil worship stuff. Thoughts that came with a wave of dread. The envelope's wax seal had a goat's head, supposedly linked to 'Baphomet'—a name messing with my mind.

The tape talked about a curse—a mysterious puzzle that made me think the library was a good place to learn more. It wasn't the curse itself, but theories about its links to the devil and other weird stuff. I'd also made plans to catch up with my buddy, Nathan Hartley, who was following his passion as a private investigator.

After we chatted about Colin, Nathan had been investigating father's hidden past. Not being related, his snooping wouldn't set off any alarm bells. We hoped he'd discover something to silence the gossip and protect Father's flawless reputation. I always saw Father as a perfect example of virtue, unable to do any wrong. However, Colin mentioned his fearful escape from the pub, intensifying concerns about the unsettling rumours.

Making my way up the imposing staircase, I cast a final, apprehensive look behind me, expecting something or someone to come from the shadows. As I entered the library, a gust of warm air brushed against my face, bringing the comforting aroma of old books. I couldn't help but appear like a fish out of water approaching the librarian's desk. Grace, a middle-aged woman with greying black hair tightly pulled into a bun, sat peering over her glasses with a serious expression.

"Excuse me," I began, hesitating, "could you guide me to the section on religious history, specifically regarding Baphomet?" I paused, grappling with how much information to divulge. Grace's response was swift, causing a tangible shift in the atmosphere. With suspicion etched in her narrowed eyes, she paused momentarily before uttering a word.

"Certainly," she replies, her voice tinged with caution. "You'll find what you're looking for on the first floor, row twelve."

I suppressed a reluctant groan, eyeing the endless flight of stairs ahead. The library's intimidating layout gave the impression of a whole other universe. The mahogany wood and blue-grey carpet drew me in deeper as I mutter, "Thank you," avoiding Grace's penetrating gaze. Heading up the creaky staircase, my unease mounted, and I felt I was being watched.

Eventually, at row twelve, the books looked even older than I'd expected. Their spines were all tattered and cracked. A cloud of dust and a choking, musty scent accompanied the sound of pulling out a crusty one. The book had the intriguing title "Occult Symbols and Their Origins." Not a terrible place to start, I thought.

The book opened, and bizarre symbols on brittle pages greeted me. I delved into the history of Baphomet, learning about its shady ties to secret cults and ancient orders and its mysterious role as the nemesis of the Knights Templar. Each word left me scratching my head.

Slumped against the foot of the bookcase, I grappled with conflicting emotions as I closed another old book. My anxiety heightened at the thought of my father's potential involvement with some twisted cult, real or otherwise, as it would mean the curse alluded to on the tape was about to bite me in the ass.

A sudden pale glow of flickering overhead lights gave the library an eerie feeling that toyed with my nerves. It was like watching a horror movie—you know it's all acting and makeup, but once it's finished, you're no less scared. That's how I felt after reading that book. The silence, interrupted only by the rustle of pages and the occasional cough from someone downstairs, didn't help.

From where I sat, I had the best view of everyone reading, except Grace. She couldn't stop staring at me, but now she was on the phone. Worry lines etched throughout her face emphasised the furrowed expression in her eyes. Her glances put me on edge. The car incident had me on guard, warranted or not.

Grace, who appeared elegant and composed earlier, now emitted an unsettling presence that clung to her like a bad smell. Her phone call seemed urgent, while the rest of the library remained calm.

That's when I spotted Nathan breezing through the library door, and paranoia tightened its grip. Nathan appeared visibly worried, his head swaying from side to side, his face turning red. As he glanced upwards, he met my eyes staring back at him from behind the metal bars. Nathan hurried past Grace without uttering a word.

Dressed in a casual brown suede jacket, blue jeans, and white trainers, his otherwise neatly crafted blonde hair had been battered by the same crosswinds I'd endured. With each stride, he cleared two steps at a time, his six-foot athletic frame gliding gracefully before pouncing to my side.

Grace, still glued to her phone, looked concerned and kept a close eye on me and Nathan, worried about what it could mean. Nathan leaned in close, his voice barely a whisper. "Gerald, we need to talk. I'm being followed."

My mouth dropped. "By who?" I ask, glancing at Grace.

With sweat on his forehead, Nathan looked toward the door and then back to me. "Two guys in black suits. I've seen them everywhere," he says, his voice trembling with worry.

I was spooked. As Nathan's worry grew, so did the sense of unease in the library, and my mind immediately turned to the words I'd read. The cool breeze from the air conditioning rippled against my skin as I anxiously checked around the library. The air was thick with the musty aroma of old books, and panic added an eerie undertone to the unfolding situation. Nathan's tormented look mirrored everything I was feeling.

"What do they want? Did they ever say anything?" I whisper back, my voice barely audible.

Nathan leaned in real close, murmuring, "I don't know, but they've been following me for days. They never get too close, but I can sense their presence. Ever since I began poking around in property records, looking for links to your father."

My mind was going crazy, trying to figure out another piece of this enormous mess of a puzzle. The connection between the symbol on the envelope, the mention of Baphomet, and the mysterious men in black suits became increasingly clear. I couldn't help but wonder how much my father was wrapped up in that creepy cult to have put us in danger.

Grace's voice crackled over the phone as she continued her conversation, her eyes darting between us. She wasn't leaving us alone, and that was unsettling.

"We need to get out of here," I say, eyes flicking toward the exit. The thought of confronting whoever was following Nathan in this crowded library filled me with dread. Nathan nodded in agreement, his face pale. "Agreed. But we can't let them know we're onto them."

As we slowly rose, Nathan glanced at Grace, who was still engrossed in her phone call. The two men in black suits had yet to enter the library, but Nathan's instincts told him they were getting closer.

We made our way toward the exit, acting as casually as we could, but purposefully. Every step could be a trap, and the weight of a potential curse hung heavily. I felt riddled with guilt for involving my friend.

Just as we reached halfway to the library's entrance, a shiver ran down my spine. I turned to steal one last glance at Grace, who was now off the phone and watching us intently. Her expression was a mixture of concern and something else, something that kept a constant icy breeze running through me.

With us caught in 'no-man's-land,' Grace stood up as if she was about to move and cut off any chance of retreating. The double brown doors swung open with intimidating menace. A looming shadow filled the doorway. Just as Nathan had anxiously explained, two men in black suits.

The once bright but windy outside suddenly became full of grey gloom, further enhancing their shadowed mystique. An occasional light from the library would glimpse the haunting twosome. Their paleness had me and Nathan shook, heads swivelling as we wrestled with our 'flight or fight' instincts, looking for another way out. After all, it's not like I knew them or what they could or couldn't do.

My clammy hands brushed across a heavyset, dark-stained table to guide us as we stepped back slowly, trying not to draw attention from anyone else. The two men stepped ominously forward; they appeared normal. If scarily worn could be called normal. The one on the left clutched a Bible close to his chest while their deathly black eyes narrowed on Nathan and me, as if penetrating our souls.

Meanwhile, Grace had manoeuvred herself from the desk to a huge bank of switches on the wall. I read what she intended—to put us in darkness and make it easier for the two in suits. My heart pounded as we fumbled backward; the library's lighting flickered ominously.

Nathan's voice quivered as he mutters, "We need to get out of here now, Gerald." I nodded in agreement, mind racing for an escape plan. The library was filled with unsuspecting patrons engrossed in their reading, still oblivious to the unfolding drama.

The two men in black suits continued their slow, deliberate approach, their eyes locked on Nathan and me as if we were prey.

I turned to Nathan, whispering urgently, "Follow me, but stay low and quiet." Nathan nodded, his face pale with fear. We crouched behind the table, shielded from view by the library's towering bookshelves. The dimming lights added to the tension, casting elongated shadows across the room.

Grace continued her deliberate approach to the wall of switches, aiding the two men whose menacing eyes seemed to glow, more so the darker it got. I knew we had to hurry, with a wave of worried heads perking up before reaching for their table lamp switches.

With Nathan close behind, I made a daring dash for the emergency exit to our left, just past the librarian's desk, my heart pounding with each step. The door was heavy, but I pushed it open just enough for us to slip through. The brisk wind outside was a welcome relief, and we stumbled into the library's back alley. It was a narrow, gloomy space cluttered with discarded, dirty old furniture and overgrown shrubs.

We kept low, our breaths coming in shallow gasps as we hid in the shadows. I watched as the library's lights flickered and went out completely, plunging the building into darkness.

The two men in black suits were moving quicker but momentarily lost sight, giving Nathan and me a chance to slip away. We needed to find answers and uncover the truth behind the supposed curse with two creepy guys chasing us.

Huddled in the alley, I wondered about Grace's role. Her actions were calculated, and her being on the phone while keeping me and Nathan in her view before the creeps arrived raised even more questions.

But for now, the priority was to stay hidden and evade the mysterious figures relentlessly pursuing us. The day was far from over, and the darkness would soon be upon us. Before then, safety was paramount, and I needed to find out what Nathan had uncovered to draw such dangerous attention. My world was unravelling quicker than I liked, and it seemed all roads led to the 'Bull and Barrow' for a well-earned pint. With the contents of the books still fresh in my mind, I had to decide which was fact or fiction because my life and others could depend on it.

Chapter 10

'Gerald,'

Nathan and I huddled closely in the dark of the pub corner, our senses acutely tuned to the unsettling aftermath of our recent ordeal. The library, a place that should have been safe and quiet, had turned into a nightmare.

Nathan absentmindedly traced the condensation on his beer glass, mirroring the sweat on his forehead. My family's secrets consumed his mind—or should I say my father's secrets—filled with uncertainty and a sense of foreboding. He had a hunch that something sinister was happening and that the danger was growing.

My hands wouldn't stop shaking as I held onto a whiskey glass, trying to calm the storm inside. The recent revelations had been one blow after another, and now I was losing my grip on reality. The unsettling figures in black suits had intersected my life. Thankfully, for now, they were nowhere to be seen. One of them held a Bible as a talisman and a damning puzzle piece.

We had solace, even if only for a moment. The other customers were busy chatting about sports, sex, and politics, which served as a raucous backdrop. I was in awe of their obliviousness while I sat, fearing something sinister was lurking nearby.

I was just about to take a sip of my drink when my attention was grabbed by a figure outside the window—a bloody raven. It looked strange, then it twitched, tipped its beak skyward nonchalantly, and let rip with a loud screech. The windows were thin, and the door was closing slowly, making the sound piercingly damning. I recalled from a passage in a book that it was a creature as ominous as the devil, looking equally haunting.

The raven's ebony plumage contrasted with the dull surroundings, and its beady eyes bored into my brain. Each tap of its beak against the windowpane reverberated through my bones. The bird's neck twitched in rhythm with its relentless pecking, intensifying the unease surrounding Nathan and me.

However, what had my spine quivering was the unnatural brilliance of the raven's eyes—a piercing blue that summed up our day, eyes that delved into the darkest corners of my mind. While the pub's patrons continued their fun-filled night, the intrusion of this looking creature consumed my senses.

Others soon joined in, descending upon the ledge with an eerie chorus. Their relentless tapping crescendoed into a deafening din, and I could picture the window shattering into a thousand jagged pieces.

Overwhelmed by the torment that built up much like everything else recently, I buried my head in my arms, seeking refuge from a high-pitched tinnitus—a maddening symphony I wasn't sure was real. Then...

'Hush, little baby, don't say a word. Mamma's gonna buy you a mockingbird, and if that mockingbird don't sing, Mamma's gonna buy you a diamond ring.'

An almost polyphonic sirenesque torment. High-pitched and squawky. Why the same one, over and over? To torment and weaken by Charlotte's memory and death?

Thankfully, my pain was finally broken. Nathan's low and uncertain voice dared to speak first. "Gerald," he began, eyes staring vacantly outside the window. "We've been through hell, and it's time we talk."

I turned to Nathan, still drawn to the unnerving ravens. "I'm sorry, Nathan," I say with resignation. Everything had happened quickly, and the last few days had spiralled. Yet I was no closer to understanding why.

Nathan mustered a reassuring smile, though his composure hung by a thread. "Well," he began, "what I've uncovered might add fuel to the fire. You know I've been digging into your father's past, into Henry's secrets. There's more to him than meets the eye, something a little on the dark side, tied to your family."

My dread deepened as I considered the implications of Nathan's words. With their eerie blue eyes, the ravens temporarily faded into the background of my thoughts.

Nathan continues, his voice strained: "There's a farm, Kingsley, I think. It isn't much on the surface, but it's jointly owned, and your family name, the Ackermans, is on the deeds alongside other family names, including mine. There are four lineages in total. It goes back bloody decades, perhaps even longer."

My scepticism surfaced. "How many generations are we talking about here? Did you find the farm's address?"

Nathan hesitated; his tone was heavy with uncertainty. "I can't say for sure, but it might span at least half a century or more. Here's the kicker—the documents are sealed with a strange wax emblem. Correct me if I'm mistaken, but didn't they stop using such seals with Henry the Eighth?"

Puzzled, my eyes narrowed, trying to understand the implications of what Nathan was saying. The trouble is, I don't remember my parents ever mentioning such a place. Yet, the strange wax seal ignited my curiosity, especially after the envelope at my mother's place. I had to know more, particularly about the other families involved. "After what I witnessed this morning," I whisper, barely audible above the relentless tapping of the ravens, "I can't ignore the bloody strange details. It can't be a coincidence, can it?"

Nathan's curiosity deepened. "I'm no fan of coincidences, so what else happened?" he inquired sharply.

I recounted the unsettling events of the day—the envelope with the cryptic wax symbol, the gruesome patch of my father's skin branded with a pentagram, and my mother's mysterious behaviour. Nathan's face paled as the gravity of our situation hit him.

Nathan finally spoke, his voice weighed down by mounting dread. "With everything that's gone on—the surveillance, the librarian — it's clear this is more than we ever imagined. When people go to such lengths to conceal history, it's seldom for innocent reasons. Gerald, this is a tangled web, and I fear it leads to something… Well. Something we wouldn't foresee in a million years. Common sense tells me to get the hell out of here, to run for the hills from this nightmare, but you're my best friend, and I can't leave you hanging. A part of me is inexplicably drawn to the mystery of it all. Whatever path we choose, we must be bloody careful, perhaps get some flipping bulletproof vests." Nathan's attempt at humour couldn't mask the gravity of our situation.

I nodded, Nathan's ominous words weighing heavily and not for the first time since I've heard those words recently. I had to protect myself and the girls from the rapidly consuming nightmare and this darkness I could feel growing inside me.

Later that night…

With a startling abruptness that made me jump, the library lights flickered and dimmed, casting a never-ending darkness. Panic surged within, clawing at my chest as I desperately sought a lifeline—a book, a shelf, anything to help pull myself from the floor. My trembling fingers groped at thin air, searching for purchase.

Moonlight pierced the night through the window, revealing Grace, the librarian, standing at the towering wooden doors. Her hesitant steps betrayed an overwhelming sense of suspicion.

The air grew cold, and an unnatural draft chilled the library and everything in it, including me. The remaining lights extinguished with a sinister hiss as power was severed. My heart thundered, and I watched in paralyzed horror as Grace was no longer alone. A towering figure appeared from the shadows, cloaked in a tattered, filthy hooded coat that billowed like a grim reaper. I recognised the figure with a sudden jolt.

The figure's face remained obscured beneath a wide-brimmed hat, but its intentions radiated intense terror that even scared me, and I wasn't as near as Grace. The air thickened, shrouded in wisps of ghostly white mist that slowly wove through the space, setting an eerie atmosphere. I could not move or utter a single word to warn Grace.

Her voice quivered as she stammers, "I... I tried. Please don't do this." Her pleas hung mournfully in the air, but they went unanswered, falling upon deaf ears that belonged to the sinister presence looming over her.

Then, in an instant, everything shifted. I was up close and looking at Grace's terrified face, my arm covered by the grimy black coat sleeve. With deliberate, evil intent and a gloved hand raised, I was now a passenger in the killer's mind or body; I didn't know, but it was as if I was an unwilling accomplice. Barbed wire, wickedly jagged and dripping with the sinister lure of blood, cruelly crashed through the fire exit door with unrelenting ferocity.

Much against my will or control, I drifted toward the trembling Grace, the barbed wire coiling through the air with horrifying menace. Agonised screams tore through the library, blood showering from the thick, fleshy, sliced wounds as the barbed wire tore through Grace, staining the floor in puddles of crimson.

I couldn't believe it, and fighting the urge to throw up, I lived every ounce of the killer's sadistic pleasure, an insatiable thirst for suffering and death that coursed through his very being. The killer manipulated the barbed wire with unnatural precision, moving with ruthless purpose. I could do nothing but bear witness to the horrors unfurling before me—Grace was being torn asunder, her life extinguished in a nightmarish onslaught of violence. As the barbed wire finally relented and Grace's life faded, my vision blurred, and the horrific view faded into darkness.

"AAARGGHH!"

I woke, bathed in a chilling sheen of cold sweat, the memory of the horrifying murder still fresh in my mind. It was an experience filled with brutality and evil that defied explanation and reason. It was almost a nightmare, yet it felt and looked so real I could still smell the metallic liner of blood, and I could taste the acid toxicity of bile swimming through my throat. Considering what we'd escaped, I understood why it may manifest in my mind, but this was different in so many ways.

I sat upright, shaken, as I replayed the details, trying to catch my breath. One thing was for sure: I'd been given an unholy glimpse into the darkness—an evil presence lurking in the shadows. Its insatiable appetite for violence and death resonated deep within my unwilling occupancy of the killer's body.

To compound my fear, it became apparent the killer was the same mysterious figure who had plagued my thoughts and haunted moments of my day-to-day life. The 'crooked man'. Not that Colin saw, but Mr tall and Creepy had changed the library into a theatre of horrors with terrifying ease, leaving me a trembling, sweat-soaked mess, clinging to the fragile hope that it was my overactive imagination.

Chapter 11

'Détective Reynolds,'

Exhausted, Dalton and I clung to our coffee, minds a mess, trying to make sense of the nightmare we'd been thrust into. That's two brutally murdered bodies now, one so soon after another. I should be used to it by now, especially after Scotland and the blood spilt there. Yet, here we were, facing another gruesome murder. Not even the Kanaima case in London seemed this busy so soon.

The absence of forensic evidence made it even more unsettling, leaving us with no leads. All it did was bring our awareness of the murders into a world we knew well. The only thing that could have killed Mr Eckleston was something supernatural. There was no other way to justify the scene. However, we needed another theory to sell to the locals if we didn't want to spread more fear than had already been circulating in the press.

Tight-knit communities like Willowbrook thrive on gossip; anything out of the ordinary would be rife by morning. Michael says it best, 'treat them like mushrooms,' at least for now. In other words, keep them in the bloody dark. Some days, I wish I could be the same, but that luxury is long gone.

The library stood eerily silent, its polished floors now stained with a thick river of blood that, even drying, still stirred the senses. The air was heavy with the overwhelming metallic scent of death. Eyes scanning the surroundings, I approached the uniformed officer who had the misfortune of maintaining the crime scene cordon. "What do we have here, Officer?"

The young officer looked visibly shaken, his pale face whipped by crosswinds, but he tried to maintain his composure as he explained, "It's... it's a real mess in there, detectives.

The victim, Grace, the librarian, she's… well, you'll see for yourselves. It's like something out of a nightmare." The officer didn't seem like he'd seen much death before. For us, it was just another day at the office.

Dalton nodded, his face grim, like always, at least until the caffeine kicked in. "Alright, we'll take it from here. Has anything been touched inside?"

The officer shook his head. "No, we've kept everyone out since we arrived. As instructed by the DI, he said you two have the experience of h… hundreds like this. I… I don't know how you handle it all, but the scene's all as we found it."

Michael sensed the officer's unease. "It's alright, matey. You'll develop a cast-iron stomach before long. It'll soon be water off a duck's back," he says, forcing a smile for the officer's sake.

We left him be, donned our cheap-looking latex gloves, and entered the library. The overhead lights were flickering ominously, catching my wandering eyes, prompting short flashbacks to some visions I'd experienced over the last year—the basement ones. We were greeted by a sight that was nothing short of horrifying. Grace's lifeless body lay sprawled across the floor, surrounded by a gruesome pool of blood and gore. Her once-neat bun was now matted with blood, and her glasses lay shattered beside her. I could picture how she would've looked beforehand. Sweet and wouldn't say 'boo to a goose' type of lady.

This one was on me. I lost the coin toss on the way to the scene, meaning I would take the lead. However, I still think Michael is trying to 'school' me, too, in his way of doing things. Don't get me wrong, he's a brilliant detective, and I've learned loads, but sometimes, the old git needs to relax. Anyway, we'll need to use our 'other' unique skills if we want to make any headway. I knelt beside the body, eyes narrowing to examine the scene."It's another weird one, Michael. Look at the precision of these wounds; they're too bloody, brutal, and deep. They had complete control and no remorse, hundreds of tears in her flesh, yet there was no sign of a struggle. How on earth does that happen?" I say, pointing out the wounds and noticing that they appear to have happened simultaneously.

Michael shuffled around, surveying the area, his attention drawn to the barbed wire covered in blood. "And this wire? How does it happen without the killer getting hurt, too? Rings a little too much like the flipping haulage yard."

I knew what he meant. "This doesn't sit right… Nothing about this is natural, Michael. The way the wire would've moved, it could've danced through the air like the chains… just as we saw on the CCTV from that place; I'm not reaching for straws here, we both saw. It's as if the killer had a supernatural ability; I'm going out on a limb to say the same happened here. The killer can end a life without laying a finger on the victim; how the hell do we manage that?" I fired off, frustrated and bewildered.

Michael frowned, eyes bulging like they do when his thoughts were racing. "We've been through this crap repeatedly. We always come out on top, especially in Scotland, but I agree with you; this is different. We must find out who or what could do something like this."

As we continued to examine the crime scene, I noticed something peculiar. "Look at this, Michael," I whisper, trying not to draw too much attention because of how weird these scenes have been. Clearly, they belong firmly in our secretive 'supernatural' wheelhouse. I gently parted Grace's clothing, revealing a gruesome branded cross, barely above her skirt's edge, carved into the flesh on her back, seared with precision and brutal intent. The surrounding skin was charred black and blistered, looking extremely painful.

I leaned in closer, my expression etched with grim determination. "Michael. It's the same symbol on the torso of the last scene. We need to get the hanging victim, Eckleston, re-examined, looking for the same, aside from him clawing the word 'B.O.O.K.' into his flesh; I fear this cross could be what connects the victims."

Dalton nodded, his eyes flickering a little yellow while keeping them hidden. Fixated on the branded cross, he tried to look closer. "Matey, it's got to be a mark of a cult or something weird. Just when we thought we'd got a handle on the weird."

I quickly sketched in my notebook, fearing this wouldn't be the last time we saw it. Or should I say, the last time we found it on a victim? It was a horrible reminder of just how dangerous the killer was and the nature of what was at play could be our worst case yet.

We continued to search, and our attention turned to the shattered bookshelf nearby. Books lay strewn about, their pages torn and their covers scorched. Michael quickly picked up one of the damaged ones, flipping through its pages. "Again, the sick bastard has staged the scene, ransacking the place in another attempt to confuse us."

I agree, eyes sweeping across the chaotic shelves. "We both know how easily you're confused, don't we, Michael? Seriously though, the killer wants to throw us off by desecrating places like this; they'll be in for a shock because we aren't buying it. What I don't get, considering the savagery of the murder with no evidence, why bother? On the one hand, showing off, and on the other, hiding. It's like they're conflicted, or someone is covering up," I attempted to sum up the mess, daring to delve into the killer's mind. Not a nice place to be, considering all I imagined there'd be was blood and anger.

The details led us deeper into the maze-like aisles of books and up the stairs, covering all bases, each step bringing us no closer to a truth that so far kept evading us. We were shuffling through when I spotted a dusty old book on the floor with nothing but a strange, faded symbol that looked a little familiar. At first, I was drawn in and went to open it until Michael grabbed my attention. I placed the book neatly on the shelf and walked away.

We neared the stairs, and I heard that familiar, unnerving rumble that we were being watched. That last murder had me paranoid, waiting for those two men in black suits to appear. The library had my wolf's senses going haywire. Something was off.

We returned to the library's entrance with the branded cross-lingering on our minds. The weight of the unknown and how dark it could get before we got close enough to stop the carnage niggled away at me. But unravelling these stories is what we do best.

Outside the library, the world remained oblivious to the horrors that had unfolded within its rustic walls. The streetlights continued to flicker, their distant glow finally going out as a new day began. We were entangled in a narrative different from what we'd experienced so far, and that's saying something considering our brush with vampires.

Michael looked unsettled, probably thinking over my comment about the victims being connected and cast an eye over the branded cross on Grace's back again; if any of my habits had rubbed off on him, it was that the details mattered. And there was a detail about the cross bothering him. Like I had, Dalton traced the charred lines with his gloved fingers, his mind racing to connect the dots, when a grim realisation washed over him. The symbol seared into Grace's flesh resembled the emblem he had seen on the cufflinks and pin badges worn by the two scary-looking men in black suits the other night.

"Georgie," Michael says, his voice low, "remember those blokes the other night? The symbol on Grace's back is like the one those men had."

I nodded solemnly. "It can't be a coincidence, Michael. We need to see if this dear lady was also one of their 'parishioners,' as they called it."

We exchanged a distressed, knowing to look, our thoughts intertwined in the mysteries surrounding them. Both dreading what might happen next while watching for the two haunting men in black suits.

Chapter 12

'Gerald,'

The shrill ringing of the house phone in my study jolted me awake, causing me to startle upright in bed. With tired, sore eyes, I jumped up, thinking it might be my mother calling about the girls. Considering everything, I thought it would be safer if they stayed with her, even if it was just for the night. My heart raced as I dashed for my desk, fumbling for the receiver, still dazed.

"Hello?" my voice wavered as I answer the call, my nerves still raw from the bloody nightmare. It was horrible and far too real for my liking, as if I were there.

"Gerald, it's me, Nathan," a familiar voice crackled through the line, bearing an urgency that cut through the early morning haze.

"Nathan?" I blinked, shaking off the remnants of the nightmare. "What's going on?"

I sat hunched over my desk, clutching the phone tightly, although my hand kept shaking.

"Listen, buddy," Nathan's voice crackled through the receiver, "you need to grab a copy of the morning newspaper. Something fucking awful has happened."

My curiosity mingled with dread as I glanced at the clock. It was far too early for a phone call like this, and the uneasy fear from the dream still clung to me.

"I don't understand. What's going on, Nathan?"

Nathan sighs heavily. His voice sounded scared, and he was holding back out of that fear. "It's about Grace, the crazy librarian from yesterday; well, Grace Lipton is her full name, but that's beside the point. She's dead, Gerald. Bloody murdered."

Nathan's damning words formed a dark cloud over my head, and my heart sank as my mind flashed back. I was going to be sick. Grace tried to mess with us, but she didn't deserve to die. I replayed every detail of what happened and didn't know whether or how to tell Nathan.

"Murdered?" I repeated, my mind struggling to process how it had gone from the dream to being real. "How? Why?"

Nathan's tone was sombre. "All I know is in the morning newspaper. They're calling it a brutal killing. It's plastered all over the headlines."

My surprised gaze darted to the side table beside the desk, where a newly folded newspaper lay untouched. My papers are delivered early, but I haven't been up yet, let alone gone to the front door—not that I remembered, anyway. Quickly, I snatched it and unfolded the pages to reveal the gruesome headline that confirmed Nathan's words. The image of Grace's serene face stared back at me, a stark contrast to the horror I'd seen.

"Police are investigating," Nathan continues. "They found her body at the library. It's fucking sick, buddy. Yeah, her motives yesterday were questionable, but this?"

I couldn't tear my eyes away from the article. The details of the murder were scarce, but the brutality described had my stomach churning. Hoping it had been a one-off.

"I can't believe it," my voice was raspy, not wanting to utter the words. "She was just... she was there yesterday. As you say, questionable, but..."

Nathan's voice softened. "I know, mate. It will shake the town, and we need to be careful. There's something crazy happening in this little place, and it looks like we've found ourselves in the middle of it."

As we spoke, one thing was on my mind: first seeing Grace and the looming figure, then becoming the killer's eyes. The murder of Grace Lipton was ominous because a pattern was forming. She was another person I'd crossed paths with, and now she's dead. It wouldn't take long for someone to find that detail and connect the dots.

With a heavy sigh, I finally gathered the courage to share the haunting details of last night with Nathan.

"There's something I have to tell you... I was in the library," I began, slow and deliberate. "I saw Grace... she was there, just as she always is, closing up for the night. But then, the lights went out, and I watched... I watched as she was murdered."

Nathan's silence on the other end of the line was deafening, and I understood the level of my friend's concern.

"It was like a nightmare, Nathan," I continue, a little paranoid, scanning around me. "I couldn't move, couldn't do anything to help her. And the killer... they were shrouded in the shadows, wearing a hooded cloak. It was the same figure I've been seeing in passing reflections or sitting in places, but nobody else can see them. It's like they've been haunting me. Then, the dream. The worst part is, at one point, I was viewing through the killer's sadistic fucking eyes."

Nathan finally spoke, his voice filled with unease. "Gerald, this is more than just a spooky coincidence. We must get a handle on what's happening with you because that shouldn't be possible unless you've developed some crazy psychic ability, bullshit, you lucky fucker. I suggest we keep quiet about it for now, but we need to tell someone if it happens again before people put two and two together and come up with you as the suspect. Besides, we will have our hands full uncovering the seedy secrets about this town and your father. I don't mean seedy for your father, but he's got some skeletons, that's for sure. Just tell me if any more weird stuff happens, okay?"

I nodded. It was weird, considering Nathan couldn't see me, but I struggled to reply. The past days' events rattled me badly, and I knew we were on the cusp of uncovering something we might wish we hadn't.

My paranoia wasn't letting up, eyes pinging back and forth, expecting to see that figure. Ironically, I could still smell Grace's blood and the killer's sick scent of death; the view of Grace's shredded flesh on the floor in a dark crimson 'bloody' swimming pool sent bile surging into my mouth. Leaving me with a genuine fear swooshing around in my head that more bodies would drop, and I hoped they wouldn't land at my feet. Yet, I got a horrible feeling...

I sat, reflecting in the silence of my study, my man cave, as Charlotte would call it. The antique clock on the wall ticked away the seconds, each in time with my heart. I didn't know what to do next, other than not going to work. My excuses were ready. The after-effects of the car crash were lingering. At least, that's what I'd say. Whiplash can linger a day or so, and the way I saw it, why the hell not?

Just as my thoughts drifted to the current boss and then the former, being my father, a thunderous banging echoed through my quiet, semi-detached home. Loud enough to make my heart leap into my throat and my blood run cold. The pounding on the front door was relentless, as if someone were breaking through.

Fear took over, sweat bubbling over my forehead as I slowly rose from the chair. My footsteps echoed in the peaceful hallway. Dread grew with each step toward the front door, and my imagination cooked up some nightmarish scenarios.

I reached the door, a shaky hand hovering over the doorknob. The pounding continued, growing louder and more urgent with each passing moment. With a deep breath, I summoned the courage to twist the knob and swing the door open.

What met me was not the nightmarish figure in the cloak I'd feared, but a postman standing on the doorstep, looking confused. The man held a parcel wrapped in a yellow jiffy package, contrasting with the ominous and needless thumping on my front door.

"Parcel for Mr Gerald Ackerman," the postman announced, his tired voice droning as he repeated himself with each delivery.

I sighed in relief, my heart still racing from the initial knock. I nodded and took the parcel from the postman's outstretched hand. The postman tipped his cap and departed, leaving me with the perhaps not-so-mysterious package, as I suspected it could be. It felt flat and solid, yet also light. The morning was about to take another turn, not for the best.

The door swung closed, and I carried the parcel back to the study, where the desk lamp lit a pool of light in the early morning gloom. Carefully, I unwrapped the yellow package, revealing what I feared: another VHS tape—much like the one I'd received before.

'Things you need to know—Tape Two,' the same red felt-tip handwriting, too.

It made me wonder, though. Why did Father have to resort to tapes? Why couldn't he say something? And why the hell did it have to be our family entrenched in this web of darkness that is on the verge of shaking the Willowbrook facade? If it hadn't already. Quiet on the outside, darkness underneath, is what I thought of the town now.

My hand hung in the air and paused. I didn't want to do it, but I had to. With the VHS stowed, the screen flickered to life, and grainy streaks covered my father's tired image, filling the screen. It was another recording, another glimpse into the past and what other bloody secrets my parents had. What did Henry have to say this time?

Chapter 13

'Gerald,'

The grainy image flickered to life, casting an eerie glow that seemed mesmerising. The video abruptly paused, freezing on an image that had tormented me since the first tape: Father, nestled in a darkened room.

I was fixated, searching for clues to tell me where these tapes were filmed. The man who had been my unwavering pillar of strength now resembled a shadow of his former self, haunted by a past I needed to uncover. His wrinkled, sweat-soaked pale blue shirt displayed the look of a man under pressure. The top button was left undone, and a navy blue and white striped tie encircled his neck like a noose waiting to be tugged tight.

Tears bubbled as I absorbed the image of my father. To see him struggling so badly and not letting on was a bitter pill to swallow. What had led to this harrowing decline? He looked burdened by guilt. Why didn't any of us notice Father's silent suffering? Unless Mother had, and she's holding back more than I thought. The symbol cruelly etched into Father's flesh left a physical and emotional scar, and many unanswered questions swirled in my fragile mind. Who could do such a sick thing? For what purpose? Was it a warning or an omen? Or something different altogether?

However, a familiar and haunting presence harshly interrupted my thoughts. The whispering man's faint, ominous outline lingered menacingly behind Father in the footage.

Pushing on, I pressed play again. Father's voice echoed from the speakers, each word full of sadness.

"Hey, Gerald, it's me, reaching out to you from beyond the grave." Father's voice quivered. "I'm sorry, but this is your reality now. I can only imagine the strange things you've experienced, perhaps even run-ins with certain individuals. Listen carefully; avoid the men in the black suits at all costs; they are linked to something called 'the knights templar' and far more dangerous than they appear. Deception lurks where you least expect it."

My jaw dropped as the words sank in. "Strange and unexplainable things will happen, tightening their grip on you," my father cautions. "Some will inflict unimaginable pain and if the worst happens, all hell could break loose. I mean, literally hell. I sought more information on this and ways of escape. Hunting for loopholes, but life kicked me in the balls. The answers exist, but I realised it was too late. My father, your grandfather, kept our family's darkest secrets from me; if only he'd been more forthcoming, we may have stood a chance."

This was a Pandora's box of nightmares. "Understand this, Gerald. Your world is changed forever," Father continues, urgency lacing his voice. "Our family name…"

Before Father could utter another word, his gaze snapped towards something in the room, and I followed his line of sight. The shadowy figure lurking behind him had shifted, raising a menacing arm to point ominously. Father's panicked reaction sent a jolt of dread coursing through me.

"Oh, damn it," Henry mutters, his voice tinged with fear. "I must go now. I will update you soon. Remember, I love you, my son. And above all, stay safe. Knowing you, you're probably already digging into this. If so, remember, a picture is worth a thousand words."

The recording abruptly ended, leaving me deciphering the cryptic message at the end. The figure in the shadows lingered on the screen; its presence plagued me. Scratching my chin inquisitively, I held off from swallowing a mouthful of saliva as I approached the TV screen. Slowly, I traced the outline of the shadow, feeling static beneath the tips, widening around the head area. "The bloody hat," I murmur, eyes widening, reflecting the frozen screen. My heart was beating two to the dozen after the last time the figure whacked against the screen, even though I hadn't rationalised an answer for everything happening.

"You… got…to…kill…them…all." Ice drifted down my back, my finger glued to the TV screen when I heard Father's voice again. This time, not from the TV and scarily high-pitched.

My head turned slowly as I heard his voice echoing from the hallway. **"There won't be peace until you kill them all,"** the voice continues. Each word made me shudder a little.

The footsteps that followed were heavy and deliberate, each step drawing closer. I was paralyzed, unable to comprehend what was happening. Father's voice and the ominous message were all too much to bear.

And then, as the shadow in the doorway became clear, my world unravelled completely. It was my father, but it couldn't be. It was impossible, yet he stood there, his eyes absent and ghostly.

"Do it, Gerald, end the bloodlines. End the cursed, collect them all and you will be free. There's no escaping your fate." Henry raised his hands, showing blood-covered palms. **"We all have blood on our hands in this family, but you can wash it away."**

My eyes bulged in shock, watching the blood drip from his hands, fixated as each drop fell, and then I noticed something that snaps me back to lucidity. The drops weren't showing on the floor, and there was no puddle, but I was no less scared.

The words kept repeating in my mind: **"Do it, Gerald. Kill them all."** How was it happening? I kept asking myself, thinking back to my mother in the kitchen, wondering if this was what my father meant about seeing things. I shook my head, hoping it would disappear, but Father remained. Suddenly, a series of thunderous booms resounded against the front door, each impact more menacing than the last. I wasn't expecting anyone or anything else. Then again, I wasn't expecting another tape, and the relentless pounding woke me up. I looked down the hallway, where the haunting image of my father had vanished, leaving behind a trail of unanswered questions. "Boom, Boom, Boom," the thumps echoed again, my neck hairs bouncing with worry.

I sprang to my feet as sweat trickled down my cheek. I glided silently to my bedroom, hastily dressed in jeans, and snatched the nearest T-shirt. As I slipped into my trainers, a low rumbling like distant thunder echoed from the front door. It didn't sound good.

I threw a load of bits in a holdall and got ready to leave via my study window. It would take me to the pathway at the side of the house, and from then on, it's a fifty-foot dash to the car. It seemed not even home was safe now.

"We know you're in there," a skin-grating voice called out, an accent, possibly Italian. "What the fuck? How could they?" I continue my hazy attempt at stealth, relieved not to have the girls with me just now.

"Come on now, give up, and we will spare the pain, and anyone else in your family, and your curse ends with you quickly. Don't, and all hell will rain down on you and everyone you know and love," an unfamiliar voice this time, much like the last, pitchy with a squeal of chalk grinding on a blackboard.

"Arrenditi traditore, abomination," sounded off in a language I didn't know, yet it was scary. I was desperate to understand why I was being hunted down with such ferocity and wondered how deep the trouble Father had got himself into.

I sneaked toward the hallway, hearing the vibrating louder. The front door knocker rattled against the wood. Their silhouettes loomed in the frosted glass. I was about to dash to the study when I saw the strangest thing: a black-suited arm passed through the door, and then, one by one, more limbs followed. I froze in awe and fear. Their heads drifted through, but they didn't look how I'd seen them at the library. Not in the beginning, anyway. Both appeared like 'death,' with skeletal faces littered with decay. They'd pass as zombies or similar if I didn't know better. Not that I believe in such things. At least, I didn't until this.

Both displayed menacing grins as their pitch-black eyes gleamed in the shower of daylight being cast through the windows. Finally, I returned to the task and ran to the study.

"Crap," the window stuck, doing its best to resist my efforts.

Their footsteps echoed through the hall. They were in. At this rate, I was going to need a pacemaker, the way my heart was being made to work. Pounding so loudly as I yanked with all my might, sliding the window a little.

The steps were closing. "Come out, come out, wherever you are," one shouts, sounding confident.

The window juddered a little more. "You have nowhere to go," they called again.

A loud squeak gave me away, but the window loosened more; with a final yank, it slid upward sharply. The haunting men were in the study doorway. I flung myself through in the nick of time as they lunged forward. My body hit the rough stone path hard, drawing blood across my palms and knees. Their horrifying faces drifted between the window gap.

With a deep breath, I dragged my body up and ran as fast as my legs could carry me to the car. All the while, their steps could be heard. My hand was shaking, unlocking my mother's car. The front door crashed open without them breaking stride. My car door flung open, and I dived in, bag in hand. Thankfully, the key slid into the barrel on the first try. The engine cranked to life, screeching away as the two angry men reached the door. There was no knowing where I was going or what to do next, as long as those monsters were fading in his rearview. It was a close shave. Far too close. The bigger question is, who the hell was hunting me? Other than two guys that look like they've been dug up from a cemetery.

Chapter 14

'Détective Reynolds - Morgue,'

Michael's footsteps echoed through the dark corridors of the morgue, each step reverberating ominously. His mind was elsewhere—no doubt cursing our luck. Angst harboured against A.D.I. Locke for trapping us in this nightmarish town. For a change, I was lagging after a hurried call to check on Ellena. Aside from the bloodshed, there had been moments of normalcy in Scotland, fleeting glimpses amidst the horrors we had now unravelled. Yet, the ominous presence of murder dragged me away, imposing its sinister interference in our lives.

The recent murder of Grace at the library had left us with more than just a chilling crime scene. It had planted a seed of unease in our minds, a cryptic symbol etched upon the victims' flesh. A cross, both intricate and ominous, had left an indelible mark upon two of the three bodies we'd encountered. Frank Eckleston, a hanging still full of mystery, loomed worryingly. I had my suspicions, and they were far from comforting.

We were headed for the autopsy room, where Frank's corpse awaited us, thanks to Michael calling ahead. The circumstances of the recent murder had left a bitter taste in old Micky boy's mouth. I was busy wrestling with the eerie discrepancies that defied the conventional more than we'd experienced so far. That speaks volumes, having been blindsided by a witch, gone toe-to-toe with vampires, and survived a Kanaima demon. We shared an aversion to returning favours that involved confronting horrendous corpses, and the prospect of a third had us uneasy.

The morgue's harsh fluorescent lights, casting menacing shadows across sterile tiles, exhaled a morbid ambiance. The scent of formaldehyde clung to the air, tainting our every breath. An unsettling, chilling, unforgiving atmosphere enveloped us as we entered.

Dr Emily Thornton, the morgue's resident pathologist, was already at work, her gloved hands busy with the grisly task of examining Frank's lifeless body. She looked up, her eyes reflecting curiosity and unease as we approached.

"Detectives Dalton and Reynolds," she murmurs, her voice bearing the weight of years spent alongside the dead. "I hadn't expected you so soon. I understand your desire to see this mess firsthand, but I had hoped to spare you the ordeal and offer you a report."

Michael's response was stoic, his sombre tone matching the unenviable task. "Thank you, Dr Thornton. However, we believe there might be more to Frank's death, just as there will be with the other two."

Dr Thornton nodded, shifting past us and viewing Frank's corpse. As she slid past Michael, the scent of Chanel No. 5 ruffled his senses, masking the otherwise morbid stink. Frank's lifeless body lay naked on the cold table, with a white sheet covering his modesty. His neck was distended and bruised, with dark purple swelling below the jugular. We looked on with apprehension; I hated this aspect of our investigation. We have seen enough death to last a lifetime, especially recently. I was still haunted by some things that went down and what I had to do, images of blood seeping over the pavement; now we're in another mess.

Leaning in, my eyes narrowed to focus before slowly drifting over the body as Dr Thornton manipulated Frank's dead limbs. As Thornton manoeuvred a tree trunk of a left leg, I glimpsed what we'd feared yet assumed would happen: the cross was etched into Frank's calf. The cross was vibrant, with most of the skin a cold, mottled white and purple, which seemed odd.

It matched exactly the one found on Grace's lifeless body and the dismembered body of Patrick Sheh in the haulage yard. The intricate design seemed to shimmer hauntingly, its meaning and purpose still a mystery to us, only that the two strange blokes had similar markings on their cufflinks and badges.

"Aside from that bloody thing, have you found anything else unusual? Is there any sign that he may have put up a fight after all?" Michael asks, a little distracted as he took in the cross's view, too.

Dr Thornton hesitated, her gaze shifting uneasily. "I've seen nothing like it, no pressure marks or bruising other than the carving in his arm. I swabbed the dried blood under his nails to be sure, but it was his; I don't understand who would have the mind to tear 'B.O.O.K.' into their flesh while hanging themselves?" she admitted with an air of confusion. "The 'cross' wound appears charred as if seared into the flesh. There's no sign of infection or external trauma. It's ... unsettling."

I shifted to face her, dreading what else the doctor would spill. "He didn't hang himself," I paused, glancing at Michael, who shook his head 'no'—not to tell her. He had help; we just don't know who, I finished reluctantly, holding back that it was supernaturally induced. That would make the Doctor's toes curl.

As we contemplated the cryptic cross, an eerie silence enveloped the room. The air seemed to thicken before a sudden faint whispering echoed hauntingly in the background. Michael and I stepped close to Dr Thornton and clenched our fists to hide our claws that had slid forward on guard.

A cold draft swept through the room, encompassing everything in its path. It extinguished the overhead lights with a frightening flicker and plunged us into darkness. With the look of 'not again,' Michael reached for his tiny flashlight, but the cross on Frank's calf glowed blood red before he could flick it on horrifyingly.

Frank's body suddenly writhed, and his dull eyes readily snapped open, glowing a haunting, ghostly grey. His fingers twitched at the sound of bones breaking. Each snap made me shudder, and a low, growling moan escaped his stern purple lips. It was a sound that skated a chill through us all. The Doc's scowl of distress spoke volumes.

"Frank?" I stammer in disbelief at what I was witnessing, unable to hide the shake in my voice. "Is that you?"

Frank's response was far from human. He sat up abruptly, his movements jerky and unnatural, his bones clicking and with more jarring snapping, only louder. His spooky, glazed eyes fixed on Michael and me with a venom that scared us, even with our unique abilities. I could hear all our heartbeats throttling like a Ferrari. We still held off, not wanting Dr Thornton to know what we could do. If the doctor knew I was a werewolf and Michael... well, let's say 'shifter' for now until we get to research more, she would run away screaming.

The room felt alive. Equipment rattled, and cabinets creaked open of their own accord, haunted house-like. Dr Thornton backed away; her fear resonated as her pale skin turned ghostly.

The reanimated corpse confronted us in the deathly cold ambiance of the morgue. We were in the middle of another weird twist in this web of mysteries that showed no sign of relenting. We stood frozen in the middle of the morgue, shielding the doctor. Our rapid breathing was visible with white clouds in the frigid air. Frank Eckleston was dead, now defied his brutal hanging and the laws of what I knew about life after death and all that jazz. Those ghostly eyes seemed to gleam, with a sinister smile twisting across his lips.

"What in the unholy hell is happening?" I gush. Fingers tensed as they fought their unnatural instincts, fighting back the claws.

Frank's voice, dripping with a ghastly cadence, slithered through the air, each word a chilling revelation. **"You seek answers, detectives, but answers have dangerous consequences for you and those you love. Answers your fragile minds aren't ready for."**

Frank hisses, the cross eerily shimmering brighter than before. "The blood-bathed reckoning is coming."

"We're not buying, I'm afraid. Tell your friends we don't need any visitors; the world is overpopulated enough already," I quip, putting up a front as I looked at Frank's overweight flesh. More symbols suddenly sliced their way through Frank's body until he looked more like a bloody patchwork quilt.

Frank's head juddered, twisting his broken neck, the bloated flesh stretching as the head circled around and around, blood drooling from his mouth as the head now faced backward, looking directly at me.

"You insignificant cockroach. I highly recommend you run home now. Kiss Miss Ellena Walker goodbye before it's too late. Mr Dalton, you and the doctor should get a room. You both want to; how better a way to spend your time seeing out the end of your world as the gates of hell burst open and the streets become rivers of red? The skies will smother you in eternal darkness, and the dead shall flock from their graves to embrace a new world and regime," Frank snarls, gargling blood through decaying teeth. I stood in shock, questioning how this dead thing could know of Ellena, let alone the dooming premonition.

"Piss off, you're not the first morbid doom bastard, and I'm sure you won't be the last," Michael fronted up, attempting to ease the doctor's visible fear.

"The knights are on the march, beacons of death, and there's nothing you can do," Frank cackled loudly, his shrills causing us to shuffle back a few steps.

The room shuddered as Frank spoke, and the morgue's lights flickered with fear-inducing regularity. A wild wind howled through the hallways, carrying Frank's words repeatedly, as shadows converged upon Frank's continuously deforming body, churning up symbols, swirling and merging into a nightmarish cloak of darkness.

"Is this guy for real, Georgie?" Michael hisses shakily. I didn't have an answer. It was real in the sense that it was happening before our eyes, but common sense told me it couldn't be.

I whisper in terror, "We need to get the fuck out of here now!" We looked to the doorway, bracing to run for it.

But it was too late. The room convulsed; the very walls pulsed. The morgue's cold steel tables and gleaming instruments rattled and clattered as if they, too, were being controlled. The fluorescent lights overhead flickered wildly, casting eerie, strobing shadows that danced across the white tiles now sprayed with blood.

Once a corpse, Frank's body was fast becoming a grotesque canvas upon which evil painted its horrific masterpiece. His limbs contorted and twisted in ways that defied the laws of anatomy. Bones snapped like brittle twigs, and his flesh rippled and writhed. The air thickened with the sickening stench of decay and burning sulphur; a foul aroma clung unnaturally to our senses.

As Frank continued changing, he filled the room with a morbid laugh that echoed around us, a haunting symphony reverberating deep within. It was a laughter devoid of any semblance of humanity. It was coming from all directions simultaneously, as if the walls and floors were mocking us.

Michael and I stumbled backward; our eyes locked on the freak show that had once been Frank Eckleston. His skin took on a sickly pallor, veins of oily blackness snaked beneath the mottled surface, and his eyes glowed with unholy light. Jagged, needle-like teeth protruded from his misshapen jaw, and a guttural, inhuman growl emanated from his twisted throat.

The room seemed to writhe in agony, leaving us, and the doctor trapped in a nightmare. The walls oozed a dark red that dripped and pooled on the floor, with Frank using everything around him to torment the life out of the doctor and us. Considering what we'd seen, that took some doing. The blood had a mind of its own, catching my attention, slithering across the sterile cream stone floor in grotesque patterns becoming strange sigils and a familiar symbol—the one Frank's corpse wore, as did the two men in black suits—blood-red crosses, whose lines curved ornately. The temperature had long since plummeted to bone-chilling depths, and the thick air was now heavier, making it harder for everyone to breathe.

Amid this dreadful nightmare, Frank's twisted body levitated hauntingly above the morgue table. He hung in mid-air, a scary marionette in a nightmare puppet show. The sinister cross upon his calf pulsed with an intensity that matched the frantic rhythm of our pounding hearts.

With growing horror, little Willowbrook was covered in a dangerous darkness that might be just the beginning. As we backed away, our footsteps echoed in the chamber of horrors. Evil hungered for death and chaos. In my mind, the sinister cross was the connection.

The morgue groaned in protest, and the ceiling above wept blood. Its once-sterile walls now bore the scars of unspeakable terror. The symbols on the floor and the cross had multiplied, forming a grotesque mosaic of evil. Their meanings remained a mystery, yet we could not tear our eyes away from the sinister sigils, whose lines curved, resembling ancient scripts or something similar, with Michael assuming them to be Latin.

Then, with a sudden, violent lurch, Frank's crazy contortions ceased, and the grotesque spectacle that had once been a man floated motionless at the centre of the morgue. His eyes remained fixed upon Michael and me with an unyielding, evil gaze that penetrated our souls.

Our breaths hung in the frigid air, visible puffs of fear and worry. The icy shadows that had crept across the floor now coiled around our legs, threatening to drag us into the nightmarish darkness that had consumed the morgue.

As we grappled with understanding the 'if's and how's,' Frank's voice began spouting strange words, an incantation that sounded like nothing we knew, perhaps from a film or a book, but nothing else. The eerie utterances lingered, a chilling torment that rattled our very being. Frank's twisted and grotesque corpse let loose a loud, piercing scream that echoed through the morgue, only to cease abruptly, leaving a disturbing silence in its wake.

The blood and shadows encircling Frank's body abruptly disappeared. The symbols on the floor faded, leaving the morgue in eerie stillness. Frank lay motionless on the metal table.

Reeling from the horrors we'd witnessed, our senses exchanged bewildered glances. Whatever evil had gripped the room, whatever irrational nightmare had unfolded, was gone, leaving us in disbelief.

Dr Thornton, who had watched the nightmarish events unfold with a mix of fascination and terror, cautiously approached Frank's lifeless body. She examined the cross on Frank's calf, which had once blazed unholy fervently, but now seemed inert and ordinary.

Her composed demeanour, shattered by the inexplicable events, could only shake her head in bewilderment. "What the hell just happened?" she asks, her mind grappling with the unexplainable. "It's as if ... as if that flipping dead body came back to life, possessed even."

Michael could only mutter in response, his voice bearing the weight of confusion and dread. "I do not know."

The room was now silent and unyielding, its walls and floor bearing the fading scars of a bizarre, evil, or other supernatural essence, which made me worry over who or what could be next. As we left, our minds were haunted, as the investigation had taken a sinister turn that could lead us deeper into the heart of darkness and the unknown.

Chapter 15

'Gerald,'

I needed to find somewhere safe to call Nathan first to ensure he was okay and then for help. Nathan was the one friend I could rely on in this search for hope and answers, consuming my thoughts. As I sped through the grim streets, my eyes desperately scanned for a phone far enough away. What else could they do if they could blow off a front door?

Finally, I spotted a phone booth just off the bend toward the end of the high street, tucked behind a wall by an alley. It was the perfect escape route if I needed it. With trembling hands, I screeched the car to a halt, leaving it looking abandoned with a small cloud of smoke from the engine that caused slight concern. I lurched from my seat, fumbling for change. The last thing I needed was to be without a vehicle right now; I'd be a sitting duck. With a fistful of coins, my fingers were clumsier than usual, uncooperative, as nervous energy coursed through me.

"Nathan, I need your help. I'm in trouble and being chased by those men in black suits again. They found my house; they're not flipping normal. They walked through my bloody door, for Christ's sake. We need to meet somewhere safe. I'm out of the way for now, but this shit has me paranoid. There's so much more to this than we realised," I say, twitching with nerves, my head on a swivel.

Nathan's voice surged with urgency as he responded, "Gerald, I've uncovered something too. It's about crosses. And a lot more. Meet me at the cabin, you know, the one my grandparents used. It's isolated and the only place I know that's safe for now. But for God's sake, be careful, Gerald."

With that, I hung up the payphone and returned to the car. I pulled away from the high street, my mind racing with fear and anticipation. The church ruins on the outskirts of town were a gloomy location for a meeting, but it seemed like our best option for now. I navigated the winding roads, eyes darting around, searching for any sign that I was being followed.

The pain in my back continued, a searing reminder that made me look in the mirror. Still there, I saw the whispering man again, as if I were the shadowy menace. As haunting as it was, it was the least of my worries. My hands tightened on the steering wheel as I drove toward the unknown, wondering what Nathan would tell me.

A run-down cabin stood in the heart of a spooky forest, nestled among an army of warped trees, concealed by tall, menacing oaks and elms. Their branches stretched across the meandering, gravelly road that led to what we hoped was safety for me and Nathan. Inside, a rustic fire blazed, providing the warmth and cosiness we desperately needed. The room was full of shadows cast by the flickering embers—shadows I couldn't escape but desperately wanted to avoid. This was a place nobody with cruel intentions should have known about, yet a sense of mystery and danger still had us on tenterhooks.

The logs in the fireplace crackled and popped, offering a semblance of comfort that had been sorely lacking recently. The firelight danced across the weathered walls, and the shifting shadows seemed to sway with a sinister life of their own, heightening my paranoia. Surrounding us were towering stacks of books, their spines faded and torn, but we hoped they might contain some semblance of answers. Their pages were filled with passages I struggled to understand. We delved deeper into the literary mountains, driven by the unsettling events that had shaken me earlier. It felt so real. I was powerless in my body and could've seriously hurt Nathan. Maybe even killed him.

Most of the books talked about dark rituals, occult practices, and evil entities lurking in the world's darkest corners. The pages seemed to throb as I stared, their words pulling me deeper into the unknown. Nathan was busy too, his fingers tracing cryptic symbols within the pages, his face etched with both fascination and apprehension.

The cabin, once a getaway for Nathan's grandparents, now offered temporary respite from the endless cycle of darkness that seemed to follow me wherever I went. Unable to escape the shadows, I felt marked by more than just a strange family curse. The voices have imitated Charlotte and, occasionally, my father hinted at a daunting agenda that seemed to have chosen me as its pawn in a dangerous game. And it scared me senseless.

Mother's hasty agreement to take the twins away for a few days left me with unanswered questions. It was as if she too expected trouble. Something ominous, something she likely knew more about than she was letting on. Perhaps she hoped that with Father's death, she wouldn't have to repeat the same terrifying past mistakes. But these questions would have to wait for another day as more pressing matters loomed.

The night outside was hauntingly dark, without a streetlamp in sight. My paranoia was getting worse by the minute, steadily feeling that we were not alone in this place after all. My eyes darted to the shifting shadows, dreading more whispers like earlier.

As Nathan and I continued exploring the books, a chilling pattern emerged. They were brimming with stories of dark rituals, occult practices, and the existence of evil entities that dwelled in the darkest recesses of the world, surprising Nathan, who had never imagined his family being involved in such matters. Not once had he got a clue that they'd been into that stuff. Every family has secrets, and Nathan dreaded what he might find next.

My fingers traced the words on the page, looking for anything related to symbols, particularly that incessant 'cross.' My back continues to ache with a burning sensation; as much as it was annoying and I should have seen what was causing it, there were too many bigger problems to handle, and I assumed it was stress-related. Like I get in my neck sometimes.

Nathan, his face etched with concern, looked up from his research. "Over the years, certain cultures and religious sects have sacrificed blood for spiritual wisdom. But what you told me about the knights templar and fears over the gates of hell being opened. It's as if we've stumbled upon something too dark for the typical library or bookstore shelf. There was a man I used to consult for information who delved into the strange and the dark. If you catch my drift, he might have some insight into this."

I shivered as a cold draft swept through the room, rustling the pages of the books like a chorus of eerie whispers. "A plan as good as any because other than that, I'm stumped about what direction we should take next," I say, my eyes fixed on the deepening shadows that filled the cabin, twitching nervously. "All I know is that we need to unravel this nightmare quickly. I saw Grace murdered in a dream as if I'd done it, which terrifies me. What's next? I try to kill you?"

Life would get worse before it could get better, and so far, it has involved mysteries surrounding my family. If I fail, if we fail, it could plunge me into a darkness from which there would be no return. Though disturbing, the voices from the shadows had forced our hand on what we had to face first. It was only a question of how.

As the night pressed on, Nathan's brow furrowed as he continued to research, his fingers tracing more cryptic symbols and incantations within the pages of the books. "Shit, Gerald," he says, his voice tinged with apprehension. "The gates of hell is one thing, but It's rumoured there is a book, a grimoire full of rituals and text created by 'Soloman' designed to release a specific army, 72 trapped souls or demons of the worst imaginable evil, designed to wreak havoc on earth, effectively paving the way for anything trapped there to escape and bring 'hell on earth'. As weird as it sounds, it makes the most sense. In some ten degrees of separation kind of way."

My heart raced as I ran that idea through my brain. What in God's name have we got ourselves into? More importantly, what the fuck have my parents done? The pain in my back, the nightmares, the whispering man—all of it was connected to a crazy plan that had 'doomed' written all over it.

The swirling storm brewing outside mirrored the turmoil within the cabin. It was as though the fabric of reality was unravelling, and we were caught in the storm's eye. But we were determined to uncover the truth and confront the darkness quickly becoming apparent.

"We need to find that guy you mentioned, the one who knows about this crap," I declare. "He may hold the key to understanding what we're up against and how to stop it. If not, we're screwed."

Nathan nodded in agreement, his gaze fixed on the flickering flames. "Agreed, Gerald. Maybe have a little faith, eh? We'll check out the guy and see where it leads us. And we'll cross the bridge for the rest when we come to it. Until then, try cheering the fuck up a little, will you? I don't want to deal with this crap and you being a 'mopey dick'—you daft sod. Oh, and forget any worry about roping me into this, please. I know it's not your fault. As long as I don't die, we're all good," Nathan chuckles, breaking the tension.

"Okay, okay. If you must, aim for an eye if you don't mind. Rather not lose a tooth or something," I say, breaking a brief smile in return.

If only it weren't fake. No amount of jokes or smiles can hide how bad things are. A question of how bad it's going to get and whether there will be more death.

Chapter 16

'Detective Reynolds,'

The relentless image of the vampire horde, the gut-wrenching sight of Michael sprawled lifeless on the floor before morphing into the elder, followed by finding Michael safely recovered at the B & B—it was a never-ending loop of nightmarish images that played in the circus of my mind.

I couldn't shake the lingering fear, a gnawing suspicion of the horror still to come from that one. Ruth's escape and the possibility of the elder's body-switching ability had me dreading them showing up in London and turning it into a bloodthirsty playground for evil.

The smoke-and-mirrors fight scenes while the vampires fled the supernatural onslaught only deepened my worries. But above all, my painful memory of taking a human life haunted me the most. It made me feel I must hold back the other side of me. Though the victims were not innocent by any stretch of the imagination, and desperate times called for desperate actions, our plunge from the window stained the pavement and my conscience. There was no making the bloodshed disappear. It's been keeping me awake at night.

As I lay in bed, dwelling on all this, most of the room was dwarfed by darkness, except for a slender sliver of moonlight sneaking through a gap in the curtains, casting a glow across my crisp white bedsheets. The Willowbrook constabulary had been gracious enough to provide lodging for me and Michael at a Holiday Inn hotel while we continued to work on this baffling case. At this rate, it seemed we might be stationed here for some time, especially since what had started as a single body had multiplied, with the unexplainable resurrection of one corpse still haunting my thoughts. In contrast, the symbols and the glowing cross had thrown us a curveball.

Was I cursed to keep landing all these horrific cases, or was it purely that we were best equipped to sift through the bullshit and handle the supernatural? My hotel room, although comfortable, provided little comfort for my troubled mind. The flickering of the muted television in the corner was distracting as I tried to calm the chaos.

Even with heavy eyelids, the eerie silence of the night had me on edge and restless. The soft rustle of curtains in the moonlit breeze and the distant hum of the town beyond were the only sounds that dared break the stillness.

A sudden chill made me shiver beneath the sheets as my eyes finally closed. I hoped to sleep and get some temporary respite from the relentless images that spun through my mind. The rustling curtains beat louder by the second. It wasn't long before my body was heavy, and I had given up for the night...

'Knock, knock, knock.'

A muffled tapping echoed through the room, and a dreadful, light rapping of knuckles vibrated against the wood. My eyes shot open, and my senses heightened as the wolf in me came alive. With a frustrated dash, I ripped open the door, heart pounding, but the hotel hallway remained empty. With my feet barely touching the ground, I returned to bed to try again.

'Knock, knock, knock.'

The tapping came again, growing more insistent and louder, as though someone urgently wanted my attention. I cautiously rose from my bed, footsteps soundless on the carpeted floor. With every step, the tension intensified. I reached out, hand trembling towards the doorknob. The hairs on my knuckles waved in a light breeze. Just as I grabbed a hold...

'Thump, thump, thump.' It came again, far harder... I dragged my hand sharply away.

Silence crept in; I counted five seconds before trying again. Finally, I twisted it slowly; the door creaking open, revealing the empty hallway again. The never-ending shadowed walkway stretched left and right. No one was there. I lingered in disturbing silence, confused and becoming slightly fearful, knowing nothing good usually happened next.

I peered into the uninviting hallway, grappling with what was happening. There was no normal reason for the persistent tapping, with no one to be seen. I was no stranger to horror films, where there'd usually be a ghost or the killer had somehow already got inside. Only me and Michael were on the second floor, which should make it difficult;

sadly, our world was drenched in things that seem to do the impossible.

I hesitated, deciding whether to wander for a look or return to bed and try again. The moonlight, now shaping eerie shadows along the hallway's walls, piqued my curiosity. I took a tentative step outside; the door closing softly behind me.

The hotel corridor seemed longer, with me fully immersed in its blandly stretched carpets and pale walls, decorated with nondescript artwork and poorly lit candle bulbs. There was something undeniably unsettling about the atmosphere. A subtle but intrusive odour lingered—a damp, earthy decay. And dare I think it, 'death.' The putrid stink rampantly swept through the imposing halls and worsened my fear.

Further down the corridor, my hackles rumbled, eyes were on me. Or, at least, felt that way... I couldn't tell where or why; my werewolf senses gave nothing. If I didn't know better, I would swear a young officer had been goaded into hazing their visitors. But then I would've heard them already. It was a frantic spin to look, and still nothing but space. The rumbling stayed strong enough to drag my claws forward. My pace quickened, footsteps echoing off the walls. There was intense silence, broken only by the distant, evocative hum of the hotel's ventilation system.

Then I glimpsed movement from the corner of my eye. It was a flicker, a shadow darting across the hallway, just beyond the reach of the dim overhead lights.

"Who's there?" I called out, a little rasp in my throat. There was no response, only the sound of my rapid and shallow breath, my pulse thumping beneath the skin. I took another step, eyes scanning the corridor for movement, my heightened hearing reaching far and wide. And then...

A soft, inaudible whisper carried on the swirling draft drifting through. The words were indistinct, but the tone was familiar—an eerie, haunting wail. The ghostly lament grew louder as I continued, reverberating through the dim hallway. Curiosity gripped me, driving me closer, seeking the source. My footsteps quickened. The shadows smothered the surrounding space until I could barely see my hand before my face; they shaped and danced at the edge of my vision. Unnerved, my throat tightened, and I remind myself, 'I'm a fucking werewolf; I shouldn't be afraid of anything,' but I also knew there was no fighting what I couldn't see. Common sense went out the window, and I kept walking.

Moving closer to where the haunting wails were coming from, the shadows writhed toward me. They twisted, reaching out with phantom hands. The mournful voices grew piercingly louder and more anguished, filling my ears until I felt ready to burst or bleed, whichever came first. I tried to slither away, to escape, but the corridor stretched endlessly in every direction. Panic set in as I realised they were suddenly coming from both ends; there was no way out, no escape from this nightmare.

Desperation forced me to race through the shadows to my room, my heart pounding like a drum in my chest. I dug deep into my tired supernatural reserves, moving fast, but the shadows pursued me relentlessly. Their ghostly fingers brushing my skin struck shivers through my body. I lunged into my hotel room, slamming the door behind me. Breathing heavily with relief, I scanned the room for more bizarre shadows that could've made their way in; the room was full of them, but none were moving. Until I saw a sliver of moonlight cast across the shadowed corner…

As if the night couldn't have been any stranger, creepily sat in a rickety brown wooden chair was one of the hauntingly gaunt men in black suits. The figure was draped in darkness, the bony contours of his face obscured. But I remembered enough from our first encounter.

Shaken, I locked eyes with the mysterious intruder. First, the shadows, and now this. "Who are you?" I demand, my voice shaky, riddled with fear and anger. The intruder remained silent, his gaze unwavering; gleaming black eyes pierced the night.

Eventually, the intruder spoke in a reverberating voice from the darkness, "You would do well to leave this be."

Threatening words. I stood in no-man's-land, questioning how the guy got in my room, let alone serving a warning. Cautiously, I stepped forward; my eyes stayed on the shadowy outline in the chair. Weary of what he could do, I held my claws out of sight, surrounded by an electrified tension smothering the air, a brewing storm; so far, I'd resisted my primal instincts.

"We are not your enemies, not right now, Detective Reynolds," the intruder continues, his voice a haunting rhythm vibrating within the walls. "But we will be; if you insist on pushing down this road, you won't like the horror that finds you. This is your watershed moment; do you stick or twist, be a thorn or step aside."

My voice struggled, my mind racing, to comprehend what was happening. Seeing ghosts was one thing. I didn't know what to label this other than weird. "What horror? What are you implying?" I finally found some courage. My words were barely more than a whisper.

The figure leaned forward slightly, a subtle shift in the shadows revealing a glimmer of piercing, haunting eyes. "There's a darkness coming, and you're getting in the way; you have a job to do, but I warn you, don't dig too far; you won't like what you find," he replies cryptically. "You have glimpsed but a fraction of the evil in this world, Detective Reynolds, and there is much more than history hid; it's time to let nature take its course or get swept aside. You don't want your friends, or dear, sweet Ellena, dragged along in the wake of the impending darkness, do you?"

I was a mixture of fear and fascination. The scarily calm intruder's words struck a chord with the unique events Michael and I had encountered recently; I knew there was more to the case than we'd seen so far. But the man in the shadows was there to hand out a warning, and no, I didn't want anyone else to get hurt or understand how they knew of Ellena. I also wasn't in the habit of heeding sinister warnings, especially ones in the middle of the fucking night after being chased by, of all things, a shadow. God, Michael will have a bloody field day when I tell him.

A small part of me urged going toe to toe right there and then, using my claws to peel the morbid flesh from the creepy bastard's gaunt bones and see what was underneath. At the crime scene, their faces shimmered to look different, and I wanted to know what they were. Regaining composure, thanks to the mystery man pushing my buttons, "Seeing as you know about Ellena, that tells me you know a fair bit about me; you should have gathered that I don't just stand aside and let creepy fuckers like you get your way, even if you appear to be men of God," I fired off, feeling the anger brewing.

At first, there was no response until the guy began laughing; he let out an evil, rumbling laugh that curdled my blood. "See, you don't even have that right," I nervously looked over my shoulder after hearing a rustling outside my door, a humming slowly growing louder. Wind whipping curtains back and forth, each slap louder in the chilly air...

'Knock, knock, knock.'

"Urgh, w...what the hell?" I bounced upright, the moon beaming through the window, my sweaty vest clung to me. With an erratic breath, I gradually got a grip on myself.

'Knock, knock, knock.'

"Georgie, you okay? I'm living every bloody ounce of your anxiety. What the hell is going on with you?" Michael shouts from the other side. I sat bewildered, questioning if I'd experienced a strange and haunting dream. It had to be.

I spun to face the chair, looking for my deathly guest from the dream. The seat was empty, as expected. Almost anyway, I was given another surprise...

A large burning cross blistered through the wooden seat, still smouldering a little. The stink of burnt varnish on wood got up my nose, leaving me questioning my sanity—and not for the first time. It wasn't a dream. Far worse, in fact. It was darker, and we were still on the back foot.

Chapter 17

'Dr Thornton,'

Dr Thornton hadn't given up, working long after everyone else had gone. She toiled endlessly in the cold dullness of the morgue, a chamber of secrets concealed behind rows of silver doors. Each door hid a cadaver with untold stories etched into their cold, lifeless bodies.

Her fingers moved rapidly, a ballpoint pen tracing an inquisitive path along her quivering lower lip. The autopsy notes sprawled across the steel table formed a haunting mosaic, revealing fragments of a tragic puzzle. The room carried an unrelenting chill, yet it was a frigidity that Dr Thornton embraced, mirroring the relentless curiosity that gripped her. This curiosity led her to question the very essence of the human soul and what happens to it once the flesh dies.

While the bizarre horror earlier in the day would have driven most to the brink of terror and flight, Dr Thornton remained dedicated to finishing her files for the detectives. However, her unyielding curiosity pushed her further into the unknown. How was it possible? Frank Eckleston's miraculous resurrection and horrifying suspension in mid-air had not only piqued her curiosity, but unleashed a torrent of questions in her mind.

She longed to confront Mr Eckleston, to glean answers from him, even though their encounter had been far from ordinary, marred by eerie symbols and malevolent taunts. However, the pragmatic sensibilities of her profession prevailed. She had agreed with the detectives to keep the details of the bizarre incident locked away from prying eyes, though few would be inclined to believe her account, regardless.

Outside, the world was already in darkness, the silence of which carried an eerie weight.

It was the ungodly hour of 2 AM. Thornton should've been at home with a glass of wine and her ginger tabby Jinx curled beside her. Instead, three lifeless bodies lay sprawled on cold, metal gurneys, waiting for her eager eyes, hoping to get the answers Dr Thornton ardently sought. Her nimble fingers drifted over the cool steel, gloved hands reaching out to compare the grotesque crosses etched into the flesh of the deceased.

Each cruciform sigil bore a disturbing resemblance to the others, yet Dr Thornton's perceptive eyes detected subtle divergences. The patch of skin encompassing the seared symbol pulsed with an eerie glow, and the flesh surrounding it appeared oddly preserved, if not entirely alive. The gruesome remnants of Patrick Sheh, severed and dismembered, elicited a queasy sensation in her stomach. However, being in charge has its perks; a discreet sip of whiskey concealed within her coffee gleefully provided a temporary respite.

Guided by her unwavering quest for truth, Dr Thornton allowed her limited artistic skills to manifest in the pages of her notebook. She sketched the intricate cross with meticulous penmanship, noting the distinct nuances that set it apart from the traditional ecclesiastical symbols she had previously encountered. As the ink flowed across the page, something was happening. Thornton's eyes were glued to the symbol in a hypnotic state, while the pen seemed to move with a mind of its own. Her hand lurched and scribbled relentlessly without Thornton doing anything, mirroring the disturbing nature of the symbols on the deceased.

Finally, she snatched her hand free from the pen, only to watch it continue dancing across the page. Thornton gasped, trying not to swallow as her confused, churned face soaked in what was unfolding. Before her clinical brain could rationalise the free-flowing pen as anything other than spooky, the morgue's sterile lights flickered, making Thornton jump, initially just once, as happened sometimes. Then it happened again ... and again... each time picking up speed, causing Thornton's heart to thump louder and louder... until that's all she heard between her ears. For a moment, Thornton was lost, struggling to pull herself together, when she realised the series of flashes appeared to be an unorthodox Morse code. She nearly dismissed it out of hand as too weird to be possible. But it continued forming patterns, so she attempted to decipher it. Finally, getting to prove 'Girl Scouts' wasn't a complete waste of her youth. The flashes had a particular sequence, 'like a short sentence,' she muttered, hastily grabbing a pencil and some scrap paper, partly eager, partly scared. 'Y ... O...U... W...I...L...L...D...I...E,'. By the time the words were complete, she was terrified.

Thornton dropped the pencil on the floor. The colour drained from her face, repeating what she wrote, 'You will die'. The lights danced, repeating the taunt before the room suddenly plunged into nerve-wracking darkness. Thornton shuddered, twisting and looking while overcome with turmoil. An icy breath whispered across the nape.

The hairs on her arms shot to attention, quivering. Dr Thornton's eyes strained to pierce the darkness, her mind reeling from the message. Thornton could sense someone nearby as the cloudy breaths persisted until she realised the looming presence behind her—a tall, intimidating figure clad in a deathly black suit, exuding a fearless aura of evil that penetrated the marrow of her bones.

With a sinister, blood-curdling grin catching the fluctuating light, the once-tranquil morgue transformed into a haunted theatre of horrors, orchestrated by the ghostly figure's bony hand.

Thornton lurched away, tumbling off her stool as she tried to put as much space between her and the uninvited guest as possible. The figure didn't need to move. Instead, he gruesomely summoned the corpses at the centre of Thornton's intrigue.

The dead bodies of Patrick Sheh, Frank Eckleston, and Grace Filton, who had been mere cadavers moments before, suddenly stirred. Their limbs flopped against the sturdy metal, then jerked and spasmed like morbid puppets, with their bones breaking and echoing around the room; their bodies were slowly being manipulated, as if being pulled by invisible strings. Dr Thornton was horrified yet slightly fascinated as their eyes, once dulled by death, flickered with an evil, ghostly glow.

The haunting figure in black masterfully orchestrated this dreadful nightmare. He wove his ghoulish tapestry with no apparent purpose or reason, not that Thornton could tell, transforming the dead into nightmarish marionettes, their movements grotesque and beyond understanding. Dr Thornton stood at the cusp of chilling torment, her unyielding curiosity luring her further into the heart of this supernatural darkness, even as the boundaries between life and death blurred ominously before her eyes.

Thornton's inner torment intensified as the haunting figure in black continued to commandeer the undead for his sinister pleasure. She, a rational scientist rooted in empirical evidence, found her world unravelling before her eyes. Cold beads of sweat formed on her forehead.

Her trembling fingers clung to the notebook bearing the sketch of the mysterious cross, symbolising her descent into realms that could lead to her death. She wanted to scream and flee from this unholy mess, but she couldn't move; whether the sinister puppeteer or her relentless curiosity, her body was stuck.

The undead puppets, now eerily animated, became instruments of madness, their bodies twisted and tormented. Every movement was a grotesque reminder 'that curiosity killed the cat,' and the signs were looking ominous for Thornton.

Her breath came in ragged gasps as she experienced their agony as if it were her own, their anguished yawning cries reverberating in the darkest recesses of her mind. The room seemed to constrict around her, its walls pulsating with evil.

The haunting figure in black, his predatory gaze now fixated on Dr Thornton with unnerving intensity, whispered words that sent shivers down her spine. "You, Dr Thornton, bear witness to but a glimpse of what will come. Your insatiable curiosity has led you to a path from which there is no return; you could've gone home to play with your pussy… Now, poor little Jinx will be motherless, all because those detectives piqued your interest. Unfortunately, we can't have people meddling with destiny."

Her rationality shattered like fragile glass, and the world around her blurred into a nightmarish phantasmagoria. Thornton realised she had reached a point of no return, consumed by the unravelling horror. She had become a prisoner of darkness in the cold, unforgiving confines of the morgue. "Please, I can help you; I can spread your message. If I'm spared, I will forget anything I saw."

"My dear, you will already help us. And your message will be resounding, although there is one last thing for you to do for us," he taunted. As the haunting figure in black continued to exert his sinister influence over the undead, their lifeless eyes flickered with an unholy gleam, and their movements became more purposeful, more horrifying.

The atmosphere grew thick with dread…

Dr Thornton, trapped in the suffocating embrace of the room, trembled with fear of the once-lifeless bodies…

Her heart raced, and her breath quickened, spreading cloudy white plumes as an icy hand of terror clutched her…

"What's that?" Thornton, her voice weak and raspy, finally asks, dreading the response.

"All you have to do is…die," he let out a curdling laugh and forced tears down Thornton's cheeks.

With uncanny coordination, the corpses lurched forward, their movements grotesque and unnatural. Patrick Sheh's pallid fingers reached out like elongated claws, Frank Eckleston's eyes glowed with insatiable hunger, and Grace Filton's lips curled into a wicked, sadistic smile. The toxic stink of mottled death filled the space between them and Thornton. Dr Thornton's mind screamed in fear as they closed in on her, their footsteps echoing with an eerie rhythm. She attempted to retreat, to find an escape route, but the room had become a nightmarish kill box, each path leading to a gruesome dead end.

Desperate to elude the advancing horrors, she stumbled backwards, inadvertently knocking over a metal tray with a resounding crash. The metallic clang reverberated through the morgue, an ear-splitting death knell.

The haunting figure in black, his looming presence unwavering, watched with sadistic delight as the undead descended upon Dr Thornton. Cold as the empty night, their hands tore into her flesh. Thornton's screams rippled through the air, and her lungs bulged to burst.

The dead, shredded piece after piece of flesh, flaying her body to reveal the glistening pinkish-red meat underneath, inflicting searing agony that had Thornton on the verge of passing out. Her anguished wailing relentlessly reverberated within the lifeless chamber, but nobody was around to hear her.

Dr Thornton's vision blurred as she fought to cling on, powering through the pain, and in her final, gasping moments, she mustered the strength to utter a hoarse, trembling question, "Who the fuck are you?"

The sinister figure leaned closer; his terrifying grin was barely visible in the darkness. With a voice that had her spilt blood bubbling, he whispers, "Gerald Ackerman."

Summoning the last ounce of her strength, Dr Thornton's trembling fingers dipped into the pool of her oozing blood, and, in an act of defiant desperation, she scrawled the word "Ackerman" onto the cold, unforgiving morgue floor. As darkness enveloped her and her life slipped away, the word remained—a chilling ending to the horror she had endured. A message was the only way she could. Hoping the right people found it. While evil had snuffed out Thornton's life and any possibility of meddling.

Chapter 18

'Détective Reynolds,'

It's 4 am, and we're back at the cold, unforgiving morgue. We got a call from Thornton's assistant, who'd been woken by a milkman doing his rounds. Mr Brian Lancaster drops off two pints of full-fat milk and a pint of fresh orange juice every morning around 3:30 am. Never in all his years delivering here had he come across it insecure. So, he called Miss Danielle Fenshaw in case of a mistake or something.

The Willowbrook control room called through to Michael just before my fucking night terrors fed through to him. I'm still not used to this 'pack' connection dynamics. Or, at least, I forget since we've been here. I put that down to what I've been going through since Scotland. Well, it's more about beating myself up over what and how things went down. All the holding back that I'm doing. Two baby steps forward and a huge leap backward.

This place, though, last time around, was eerie enough. I hoped we'd be coming back for a detailed report the doctor had been working on. Not this abstract work of 'blood art' covering the once sterile autopsy room and another statistic to the list.

I can't decide whether it's the early hour or the constant chill making it feel all the more hauntingly damning. I can't decide. But the nature of this murder is devastating.

As far as we knew, the doctor was innocent, trying to do her job like she's done it for the last ten years without a problem, according to my notes. So, why now? Was the doctor collateral damage, or was she a target to emphasise the point made by my creepy guest earlier?

Another crime scene and the fourth murder. Poor old Dr Emily Thornton. Looking at her flayed corpse, I was lost in a little daydream, picturing the story told by 'Skip' and what happened to his wife. Skin shredded from her body and mounted to the wall made me wonder. Did the Doc have a partner, a husband or wife, a boyfriend or girlfriend? I couldn't see a ring on her finger from where I stood, but that could've easily slipped off in the savage melee.

There was a lot of blood, too much for Michael and me. I could feel my claws edging forward, and now and then, the tips of my fangs caught my tongue. After a lot of hand-waving, huffing and frowning, and contorting his head in positions I didn't imagine possible, Michael's eyes flickered yellow, but I don't think he noticed. He was too busy with his notebook.

Thankfully, that meant the other officers were also too busy to notice our involuntary shifting. Sadly, that's one element I'm still struggling to get a grip on, the intoxicating lure of blood. It has been the case ever since I first discovered what I was.

Meanwhile, taking a few steps back and to the right by a row of corpse cupboards, Michael pulled his face from the book long enough to stand open-mouthed, surveying the carnage in its gruesome entirety.

Thornton's pinkish-white corpse glistened under the fluorescent lights that weren't flickering this time. She didn't have an inch of flesh left intact on her body. How? Even with the supernatural beings we've crossed paths with so far, such brutality would be too difficult for any of them, even the Kanaima. It was hard to tell what parts of her scattered, flayed flesh belonged where. Between that and the swamp of blood, it was truly horrifying. I watched in slight amusement as Michael attempted to sketch the scene in his notebook when a thought crossed my mind.

"Hey, Michael, without thinking, what's the first answer that springs to mind for this question?" I say, watching the cogs whirring to life. "Remember, without thinking. Should be easy for you, usually blank anyway." I jest, smirking, knowing I would piss him off.

Michael's hands drop to his sides, eyebrows raised with a straight-faced look of 'what the fuck did you say?' expression. "Fuck off, come on, I'm trying to work, in case you haven't noticed?"

I glance over the body and the copious amounts of torn flesh once more before facing back to Michael. "How many did this, and it's not one?" I ask, watching Michael's eyes ping wide. The open mouth look returns before a momentary glance. "Maybe three or more," Michael says, his voice pitchy, as if asking without fully committing to his answer.

He was on the right train of thought and exactly what I was thinking.

"I'm leaning to three. It's fucking brutal, and I can't see the slightest trace of flesh intact. Even her hair was stripped in one complete section." I say; no sooner had I responded, I look at the gurney tipped across the floor. There are three of them. Suddenly, a sickly cold sensation ripples in the pit of my stomach. I could almost feel the colour draining from my face and worrying enough to prompt Michael to breeze to my side. His ears were twitching, picking up on the quickening of my heart.

It was bizarre that I was even having this thought, and before today, it would go against anything I knew and had learned of our new world so far. Resting a tentative hand on my shoulder, Michael scans the area before me like I had. Each long silver gurney displays traces of bodily fluids and debris. It was Michael's turn to let the weird realisation sink in. I hear his heart speed up, too...

Michael's head slowly turns sideways to face me while his body stays forward, fists balled to hide the sudden appearance of his claws. A slight hiss of pain escapes his mouth, his palm flesh pierced, allowing thin trickles of blood to push out the creases between forefingers and thumbs. "Are you thinking what... what... I'm thinking?" Michael says again, and the yellow of his eyes sparkles briefly.

"If those tables had on them what I think they had, then that fucking circus freak show we witnessed come to life earlier pales compared to what went down for this murder," I say, thinking of my run-in with the Creep show that seemed a nightmare.

"All three murder victims were brought back to life, or the 'undead' to kill Dr Thornton. This begs the question." Michael says, pausing for me to fill in the blanks.

"Where the hell are they now?" I say, coming to terms with the notion that one creepy bastard occupied me while the other ran this morbid puppet show.

We're looking around. I'm watching Michael and his little changes when I notice a patch of pooled blood by Thornton's outstretched left arm. It's hard to see clearly with smears and parts of where her blood trickled. It looks like symbols, but I can't move close enough with how widespread the carnage is.

"Michael... Oi, you old git. I need you to block the view to me." I say, taking a second to register my words with him.

"Huh? What?" Michael Says, moving forward without thinking to block the line of sight from the doorway. "What's wrong?" Michael peers to the officer at the cordon tape and back to me, whispering.

"I need a better look at Thornton's hand. It might be nothing, but it could be something." I say, keeping my voice low in case it leads to something less in the remit of the normal local officers.

"Get on with it then and be quick. SOCO have just arrived and are already getting click-happy with their camera," Michael says, tilting his head as if to hear better. They were down the corridor by the main entrance, capturing the route and distance to the morgue, which tells the whole story, especially with no damage to the door.

My eyes flash wolf red, zooming in on her hand. It's not symbols, but Thornton scrawled an attempt at a message. One word only. I go to snap Michael back to tell him what I found when I feel a chill drift across my shoulders. I shudder and tuck my arms in tighter. There was no draft, although the morgue was already cold. This felt different. Enough to force my claws out. I quickly hid my hands in my pockets. My senses were going haywire. Suppose I were a betting man, which I'm not. I'd say we had company. My feet pivot on the spot as I soak up every detail and persons around us. No one stood out as different.

The chill came again; the breeze ruffling my hair. Michael is staring at me as if I'm going mad. Whatever this was, I didn't like it. Then I catch a scent. My nose twitches in disgust. It's almost a sickly 'off egg' stench. 'It's fucking sulphur', I mutter aloud. Michael catches on, inhaling deeply. His face screws up in disgust, and he searches like I had.

'Having fun there, detectives?'

A haunting voice snaps through the air with a scary cackle trailing. It sounded everywhere and yet nowhere. Michael and I stare at each other. Everyone else was still going about their business, for our ears only. They knew what we were or had half an idea. Even worse, I recognised the evil reverb within the shrill tones. It was one of those creepy fuckers in black suits.

'Is this your doing? You sick bastards,' I whisper back, assuming I'd be heard. Sure enough, I was.

'Well, as you like to say, 'the devil is in the details'. Have you found those details yet? I'm sure when you do, you'll find out who is responsible. Oh, in case you wonder what I know of you... Let's say... the file is extensive.' I look back at Dr Thornton's body and at what I was about to tell Michael. More worrying was the so-called 'extensive file' he goaded with that familiar cackling shrill trailing off.

"Michael, in the blood, Thornton wrote 'Ackerman', and that creepy fucker wants to push us down that line," I say, still twitching nervously, checking around us again. Michael had his usual puzzled expression; the cogs were turning, and I was waiting for the penny to drop. Or he would come up with an alternate theory.

"So, those fuckers manipulated the dead and gave that name to the doc, who in her last moments thought she was helping,' Michael says, with a sudden smug grin stretched across his face. He may have more police experience than me, but he's quickly catching on to the warped and crazy thinking of the sick supernatural. Trouble is, it's the idea of bringing the dead back to life and making them kill. More importantly, where was the 'undead' now? And who the hell is Ackerman?

Chapter 19

'Gerald,'

"Mmm, dark roast with a hint of hazelnut," I murmur as a warm waft teases my senses, making my nose twitch. My eyes reluctantly open. Sleep had been elusive, my mind overcrowded, and the howling winds outside straining against the chimney hadn't helped.

I had crashed out on a dusty sofa in front of the fire, an old book sprawled across my chest. Slowly, I hoist myself upright into the sofa's corner, each movement punctuated by clicks and squeaks from my aching body. Tucking the red tartan blanket around my waist, I see Nathan looking equally tired and unkempt. Despite his dishevelled appearance, his pale face, shadowed with stubble, is alight with excitement. He must have news, or perhaps he's already had too much coffee.

Nathan thrusts a steaming mug of rocket fuel under my chin. "Here, come on, take this," he says before darting over to the rustic round dining table and snatching up a small black phone book. "You won't believe this," he says, bouncing back before I sip my drink.

Before indulging Nathan's antics, I gulp a mouthful and take the book from his jittery hands. "You found a phone book. Congrats," I say, smirking in jest. Yet, Nathan stares as if expecting me to read his mind.

"Just flip it open, you idiot," Nathan urges, tapping the hardcover enthusiastically. I'm too tired for his puppy-like excitement; my eyes have barely cleared, and Nathan wants me to dive in cold turkey. I only hope it's worth the drama.

I part the pages between sips, and my finger catches a paper sticking out from the top. My eyes dart to Nathan, who looks even more bug-eyed than before, silently urging me.

A quick flick reveals yellowed pages and an old black-and-white photograph, weathered, creased, and, dare I say, haunting. I don't speak immediately.

"I know, crazy, right?" Nathan gushes, snatching his coffee from the table. I'm still digesting the sight of my young parents among a group of perhaps twelve others. I scrutinise the background, turning the picture in my hands—it was taken in this cabin. Coincidence? Maybe, but I've never been a fan of them.

"Yeah, that's my mum and dad," I finally respond as Nathan sits.

"And mine," Nathan blurts out. "My grandparents, too," he continues while I inspect the other faces.

"Who are the rest, and more importantly, what the fuck were they up to? Please tell me it wasn't some wife-swapping bullshit," I joke, lightening the mood and causing Nathan to choke on his drink.

"Well, I hope not, but you want to know what's even weirder? That's Colin's parents, maybe grandparents, and a few others that look familiar, but I can't place them," Nathan says, regaining his composure. Did Colin know more than he let on? "Wait until you turn it over," he adds while I'm lost in thought, uncovering more secrets my mother kept quiet about.

"You've got to be kidding," I say, inspecting the back of the photo as Nathan suggests. The idea of Colin's, mine, and Nathan's parents together in some secret group is unsettling.

"You know what that's meant to represent, right?" Nathan whispers, lowering his voice even though no neighbours are within a mile of the cabin. He nervously checks the front door.

My fingers trace the line work of a symbol on the back. "This was on the wax seal and the flesh my mother received," I whisper back, feeling a chill creep up my spine.

"Baphomet, right? You know, the devil, demons, and whatnot," Nathan says, eyeing the piles of books around us. The more I think about it, the more I realise we should've judged a book by its cover on this rare occasion.

"The goat's head and that cross symbol, yes. But there's something different about how the image is encircled—just a feeling," I say, my neck tingling with a foreboding sense that all is not right.

Nathan examines the picture again, his eyes narrowing. "I get what you mean. It's a bloody coin," he declares, a smile spreading across his face as he hands it back to me for another look.

He's right. The image, drawn long ago and faded like the photo, shows detailing around the edge that matches a coin, complete with a series of sigils within an inner ring, reminiscent of hieroglyphs but slightly different.

"You think it's a talisman of sorts? Maybe those creepy guys are after it?" Nathan muses. The cogs in his head are spinning. When they came after me at my home, it seemed they wanted more than just any old trinket. All they had to do was knock and say, 'Hey there, we might look like the Walking Dead but wondered if by any chance you had a weird-looking devil coin.' Then again, maybe not. Surely, there'd be simpler ways to handle the situation if that were the case. What about the guy who tried to ram me off the road? How did he factor into this? Were we being hounded by two different groups with a vested interest?

"Honestly, I don't know. But our parents are entwined with whatever this is. Except those creepy sods have a target on my back," I say, trying to piece together the clues.

"Our backs now. They followed me, remember," Nathan replies sharply, just as the wind hisses through the cracks in the cabin's wooden structure.

"Crap, look," I say, pointing rapidly at the image again after noticing another curious detail.

"Oh god, you're right. There are drawn cracks dividing the image—as if..."

"As if it's been split into four sections," I interrupt before rereading the photo to look at the group.

"Correct me if I'm wrong, buddy, but does that look like four families to you?" I ask, spotting my family, Nathan's, Colin's, and another set.

"What? And you think each family has a piece? How? Why? Surely, one of us would've known. Wouldn't we?" Nathan asks, his face reflecting my feelings of being left out of the loop, expected to handle it all on our own.

It makes sense, but to what end? And what did the coin or talisman belong to? How did it coincide with the expectation of filling a book with blood?

"Oh, Gerald... let me in, and we can find the key together. Let's paint those pages and open the gates," a sudden cold hisses by my ear. I twitch; the whispers are back, toying with my sanity. Nathan notices me shifting awkwardly.

"Fuck off... Leave me alone," I fire back, staring at the empty far corner. My body is boiling, sweat dripping, soaking my T-shirt, yet my face remains clammy and nauseous.

"Erm... Gerald, are you okay?" Nathan asks, hovering over my shoulder, not touching, just lingering there, shaking. His face is screwed up with worry. Our church incident has been more damaging than we'd realised.

"Let...Me...In... destiny demands it. You must let me in. Open the gates and set your family free," the whisper transforms into a more melancholic cry.

My body throbs and my hands slide over my thighs, balling into fists. I'm moving them; I have no control. It's surreal, something within me pulling me toward it.

"G...Gerald... block it out. Think about the girls. Think about Charlotte. We will break you free for them. Find peace for them. Remember, you are a father and still a husband; Charlotte will watch over you. Don't give in," Nathan's voice is softer, calmer. Every time he mentions Charlotte, I pull back. Whatever is going on inside feels powerful. Charlotte is my anchor, and Nathan is right; I must block out the noise.

"Leave me alone. Leave me be. Find someone else to be your puppet," I snap sharply, regaining control over my hands.

"Oh...Gerald, it was always going to come to you. You are bound. We are bound as one. Your ancestors made it so when they took the book. Your family line and their rebellious companions caused all of this. Now, it's your duty to set history right again. The chance of power, fame, and fortune could've laid the foundation for a prosperous future. Instead, conscience interrupted. Now you owe and it's time to pay... So... fucking... let... me... in," the voice persists.

Again, with the book and the past. Whatever my ancestors did has landed me in deep trouble, but I can't give in. I can't surrender. I feel Nathan's hand grip my shoulder reassuringly.

"Leave me be, leave all of us be," I say, venom in my words. Pulling away more and more until I regain control over my body. I turn to Nathan. A parting breeze whips past my ear.

"Gerald, thank God. You look like yourself again," Nathan says, allowing a small smile.

"What do you mean?"

"Your eyes. They turned black. It was bloody freaky." That would explain my lack of control. More worrying is just how much pull the whispers had. It's getting stronger and harder to resist. The church was a warning. I fear I may have inadvertently allowed them room to take over. I don't know how many more times it can happen before I lose. We need answers fast.

"I'm struggling, mate. Every time, it's worse. This time it mentioned my ancestors, power, and stealing a book being the causes of this," I say, quickly downing the rest of my drink to compose myself.

"Well, our next stop is that guy I mentioned. You know, the one who knows about this shit. But let's show him that symbol and see what he says," Nathan suggests, returning to his drink.

I sit and replay the weird conversation. I don't want to let the darkness in. I can't, but the struggle is real. I hope the guy Nathan knows can shed some light before it's too late.

Chapter 20

'Détective Reynolds,'

It barely resembled a door. What should've been a solid barrier was shattered into several pieces, with the bottom quarter just clinging to its hinge. We ran down a list of 'Ackermans' in the directory and known police databases. The first place was Merkfield Avenue, a quiet cul-de-sac—nobody home. It seemed we were on the right track with this one. 'There's no smoke without fire,' Michael liked to say, and my 'dots' weren't adding up. We stood at the doorstep, and I had issues—a feeling we were being led down the garden path.

First, the word 'Ackerman' was scrawled in blood at a crime scene, and then we found a front door obliterated. Voter records showed Mr Gerald Ackerman listed, while police reports indicated the family had been through wars lately. First, Henry Ackerman died after a freak scaffold collapse on the high street. Then Mrs Charlotte Ackerman was a victim of a 'fatal' traffic accident.

I don't know how the local constabulary works, but both reports contained no follow-ups or further investigation—just closed cases. And now we've followed the 'blood crumbs' to Gerald's home, a setup.

"Hello... anyone home?" Michael leans past the debris, calling through. There is no answer. My heightened hearing is in full flow, and all I can hear is a ticking clock.

"Michael, this doesn't feel right," I say, grabbing his shoulder as I step forward to catch up. Michael frowns. We both go to move when I feel it. Then I see Michael react. His eyes flickered yellow, and my hackles rumbled with a chill.

Another day, another bloody setup. My claws slid forward. Michael's did too. We made it to the hallway, and my senses were going haywire like no other time—not even in Scotland. I was feeling defensive and a little fearful. Whatever we were about to confront had us, particularly me, at a disadvantage. I wasn't ready to 'go there' again, to embrace all the werewolf part of me, not so soon.

Michael would joke about 'performance anxiety,' but this was more than that. Boundaries crossed in Scotland couldn't be washed away just yet. We shuffled along the wooden floors, relieved nobody else could see us part-shift. We'd reached the lounge doorway, my red eyes scanning the floor, able to see footprints. First, there were men's size ten or eleven. Then I caught a scent, just as a little trail of black smoke whispered on a breeze surrounding further prints.

"Michael, sulphur," I say, noticing Michael's nose twitch.

"Yeah, I caught it too, just like the morgue," Michael says, confirming my worst fears. Those sulphur-scented prints came in two sets—those creepy guys in suits.

'De... tec... tives. Ooh, detectives. Nice of you to join us,' a chilling voice hissed around us. Sounding everywhere yet nowhere.

"Show yourselves. And stop bloody interfering with our investigation," Michael growls with venom, fully on guard. I'm busy trying to catch a location.

'Oh now, now, you don't sound very grateful for the nudge in the right direction,' the voice chuckles at our expense—the cheek of the creepy bastard.

"A nudge? A misdirection more like," I say, pointing to the VCR, noticing a VHS ejected with the words 'Tape two' in red felt tip and another VHS on the coffee table saying 'Tape one.' Both were ringing all sorts of alarm bells. In my experience, and based on what we'd discovered so far, they were old family memories or messages. Then I noticed the padded envelope with the same handwriting on the sofa arm.

We had enough of these details in the 'Black Widow' case. God, I can still visualise how Inspector Bamford was murdered, drained, and mummified. That forked tongue. All in under an hour. Fucking awful.

'How so? We gave you a name, didn't we? You no doubt looked up the family enough to realise they've been through some trauma, and now revenge is sought.' The lack of conviction in the 'tale' was so telling, and my bullshit meter was getting overwhelmed. Michael was pissed, too. He needed a target to cut loose on.

"No, you want us to track the guy down for you, hoping to do the dirty work so you can swoop in. The revenge part is understandable, but from what we've seen, he's not the one doing it. And the theatrics at the morgue—I have a sneaky suspicion that's your handiwork," I say, waiting for a response, but nothing. It fell eerily silent.

Our senses were still going haywire, but it appeared I struck a nerve. We stepped further through, moving into the lounge. I wanted to check out the tapes. Something was telling me I should. A little niggle. We'd gone a few feet past the threshold, and everything darkened. Every instinct was screaming danger. Shadows crawled from the floor, encroaching on the walls, forming human-like shapes, flailing and writhing, painful screeches slowly building in time as the shadows moved until the dark smothered us.

There was no light through the window, nothing through the smashed front door. It was pitch black, except I was seeing in shades of red and grey. Michael was fully enveloped in that yellow aura as his eyes blazed. For a change, we were both stumped. What was once a door frame from the hallway gradually crumbled into dust. Anything normal was now gone, and I couldn't see a way out. My body was on fire with trepidation. Before long, the screeching became low sobbing. Strong, emotional sobs from a woman echoed around us.

'Why Gerald, why won't you leave it be? Why?'

"Helen?" Suddenly, the wind had been taken out of my sails. I was hearing the voice of my dead wife. It couldn't be so.

"That's not funny; pack it in," I say, firing back through gritted fangs and looking around us, hoping to see the creepy guys.

'What do you mean, Gerald? You missed me for so long, and now I'm here. If you leave everything alone, I can stay.' My head was spinning. I could hear Michael whispering to me, but I was too gone to understand. They were toying with my emotions, trying to hit me where it hurt.

"You're not real. Helen died years ago. This is bloody sick, stop it."

"Georgie, Georgie. Don't bite. It's a fucking game," Michael says, his words finally breaking through. It's easier said than done when it's pulling at the heartstrings and opening the old wounds created by Charlotte.

'What about me, Georgie? Will you stop for me? I don't want you to get hurt or worse... dead.'

I was rocked on my heels, panic-sweating to the tune of Ellena's voice. At least the imitation of her. Each time the creepy bastards spoke, they tried to get under my skin, pushing my buttons. More damning was the fact they knew who to use.

"Knock it on the head, will you? I don't understand what you're trying to do here, but you're in the way of our investigation," I say, attempting bravado with a lack of conviction in my voice. Which is quite hard considering I was part-shifted with fangs on show.

Ripples in the darkness, warped and writhed, the air stifled, my ears twitched sensing movement around us. Michael's yellow aura was frighteningly illuminating, and so were his eyes. I'm still not bloody used to it, to him like that. The glow really brings out the wrinkles below his eyes. (Not that I'd tell him.)

'Oh Detective, if you were half as intelligent as I thought you were, you'd understand the bigger picture here is far bigger than you could imagine. Far scarier... and let's say... unholier. Is that a word? Okay, let's say unholy. And someone of your standing should root for it. Instead, you're becoming a blip, a stain. A fucking inconvenience.' They cut the act momentarily, back to the usual sinister gravel travelled. (Think I preferred to hear it from Ellena's voice.)

My mind was stuck on two things, other than the horrible feeling the room was closing in on us. Michael felt it too. Shifting nearer to me. I digress... where was I, right, two things? My standing and the unholy. He sure as shit was referring to skin colour. Which brought me to my other affliction.

"So because I'm a werewolf, I should stand by and let people get murdered?"

'More so than you're part demon. Did you think we didn't sense that the first time we met? We're more alike than you think, and that's why I say unholy. Allow this story to unfold and we won't kill you and everyone you hold dear. Get out of the way and you will be rewarded.' their confidence was growing. A bone-jarring chuckle clung to the end of his words.

"Fuck off. And stop these theatrics. Getting tired of listening to your horseshit matey. Speaking of which, ever heard of mints? I get the impression you may be dead and all, but fuck me, your breath is mingling," Michael says, firing back. I glared at him, trying not to laugh. He shrugs as if to say... What? It's true.

The room fell silent, but our senses were going crazy. And then...'If you insist,' the darkness began deteriorating rapidly. Fading back to the lounge. Revealing a picture that stole my breath for all the wrong reasons.

'You see, detective, we figured you may need some motivation. A little incentive. So we brought you some.'

My eyes clenched, fighting back the anger. The pain. And the emotional hand grenade I'd been thrown, while I listened to a woman squirming with cries of pain. One creep had Ellena suspended mid-air by her throat.

His long honey fingers pierced the sides of Ellena's jugular, causing blood to trickle.

Her face was bright red, she couldn't breathe. Tears bubbled at the corners of her bulging eyes, building and building until they boiled over her puffy cheeks.

I edged forward, my brain racing, factoring in how fast I would need to move to make it in time before he suddenly ripped Ellena's throat out. Suddenly Scotland felt like a walk in the park compared to this.

'Uh uh uh.' the creep tossed Ellena around like a rag doll responding to my movement. Her squeals were higher pitched. I was so goddam helpless. I was fast, but they knew my every move and then some. In that vein, we couldn't stand by and let the world go to shit. Although, some may say, that horse bolted long ago.

"You bastards. There was no need. Supposedly men of god and you do this. It's sick."

'Once… maybe. Us? Sick? That's rich coming from a beast that needs flea treatment and crushed a man to death in Scotland.' again I was left stunned. How did they know all of this, all of that?

"Let her go."

'Not yet. She is our leverage. Bring us, Ackerman, and your Ellena will be released. All in time to witness greatness. Speaking of which, maybe you'll need to see the depths of darkness we're capable of, for yourselves.'

"What do you mean?"

"Now, now. You pesky werewolves aren't blessed with patience, are you? Okay, here's a clue…When is death not the end? Understand that and know what's coming, only a taster, might I add?"

This time, Michael dared to move. The room rumbled, electricity charged the air, and the two creeps disappeared with Ellena, crumbling into blankets of crows with bright blue eyes, hundreds of them, dissolving into a black cloud, leaving the room back to normal. Michael and I were stunned, traumatised, and did I say stunned? We've seen so many things in a short amount of time. Yet, anything supernatural like what they did in the smoke defied rational thought, even in my case, irrational.

"Georgie? Georgie? What just happened? How the hell did they get Ellena? Fuck… why does this keep happening? What on earth do we do now?"

I didn't respond, not immediately anyway. I was too busy reeling from being blindsided. A quick sweep around us. I saw the VHS tape again. We had to start somewhere other than angry.

"Get the fucking tapes. They have Ellena, but if they get this Ackerman, there'll be a shitstorm that my little lamb would tear us a new one for, and you know this all too well Mickey boy... There's something else too, when is death not the end? That's what he said."

"Don't I just... not the end? Fuck... When they come back to life. You don't think... like the morgue?"

Michael bent down to grab the tape from the recorder bus and accidentally knocked it in. The TV flicked on; the tape roared to life. An older guy in a pale blue shirt came into view, sitting on a chair in front of the camera. He looked stressed, sweating, and shaky.

'Hey Gerald, it's me, reaching out from beyond the grave. I'm sorry this is your reality now. I can only imagine the things you've experienced, perhaps even run-ins with certain individuals. Listen carefully, avoid the men in black suits at all costs. They are far more dangerous than they appear, and deception lurks where you least expect it.'

Michael tapped pause. I stared at the screen. There was more to see than just a guy who is Mr Henry Ackerman, a man who died in a scaffold accident. In the background, there's a shadow, an outline of something wearing a large trilby-style hat. Only a shadow, but hovered behind Henry. It's bloody weird, but perhaps our first proper clue. We needed to find Gerald Ackerman, and fast. If the creeps alluded to more of the dead coming back to life, we would have our hands full. For such a small village, I've seen at least three cemeteries already. The locals will be traumatised, and the dead cat will be out of the bag.

Chapter 21

'Gerald,'

"Hey... Mason... you there?" Nathan calls out. We had made it fifteen miles outside of Willowbrook, and I didn't have a nosebleed from leaving my comfort zone.

The small village of Melwood was much like Willowbrook, only smaller. Hard to imagine, considering our not-so-quaint place has a population of little over 2,000. Everything leading up to the shops screamed 'retirement,' the place to go when life has reached that point of needing calm. Much like mine now.

The place we wanted was called 'Kooky Comics & The Dark Side,' which was quite fitting, considering our situation. Hearing a flustered Nathan call out the guy's name, 'Mason,' was the first I'd heard of it since Nathan suggests it. Inside was quite basic and low-maintenance, decor-wise. Standard plywood flooring and the walls painted blood-red on the top half and purple-black on the bottom half.

Floor to eye level were rows and rows of comics in protected covers, some even in display cases, and tiny figurines. I quite liked comics as a kid and had a half-decent collection, too. Then, one year before senior school, we moved, and I think Mother was tired of the clutter and ditched the box. To this day, I'm sure I packed a big brown cardboard box full onto the moving truck, but they never arrived, and Mother claims I must've thrown them out by accident. Yeah, right, Mother? Pull the other one.

Seriously, though, the shop seemed quite cool, making me reminisce. Then, I noticed a few strange objects and symbolic statues on some shelves behind the counter. There was a dry muskiness to the place, perhaps to keep the comics in mint condition.

"Yo, Mason, you there?" Nathan calls again. I could see out to the back, and nobody was there. It was feeling like a wasted journey. Then I heard footsteps. Heavy ones on wooden, creaking steps, but I couldn't see where. Or how it was possible? There didn't appear to be another corridor, only a toilet and a tearoom by the looks of it.

I was fidgeting and getting antsy, but Nathan seemed more confident. Out of nowhere, a large bloke popped up from behind the counter, giving me a start. Similar age to us, six foot three, more on the overweight side of the scales, receding dark brown hair, a thick matching beard, and a pair of specs. I'm not sure what I was expecting, but Mason's face kind of fitted without being rude or slightly nerdy-looking.

Happy about that... or not. Maybe he was a walking encyclopaedia of all things dark and weird. We didn't have a choice or room to manoeuvre. Didn't stop my arse from puckering a little at the thought of us wasting time.

"Well, well, well, look what the cat dragged in. Been a minute, Nathan. What's up?" Mason says with a big grin as he gets comfortable on a stool-height chair.

"I know. Listen, we have a little issue. You're into all the freaky occult crap still, aren't you?" Nathan says, eyebrows raised, seeking confirmation.

"Freaky occult crap! Not quite how I'd put it, but yes. What's going on?" Mason asks, leaning toward the glass counter. His thick arms pressed over the view I had of some rare Superman editions.

"Gerald, show him," Nathan says, waving an arm and prompting me to get the picture out of my pocket.

I slid the photograph free, unfolding it before tentatively handing it to Mason with the faded drawing facing him. I didn't know Mason, and it's a big ask to trust someone I don't know. So, I was watching him closely. Nathan was too caught up in the moment to be careful.

Mason's eyes widened, and the smile vanished. I thought he recognised it, but with how our luck had been, Mason would no doubt lie. He went to speak, jaw flapping in the breeze, with no words coming.

Nathan shuffles forward. "Well, do you recognise it or what?" he says, waving his arm impatiently.

"I, er... Bloody hell, Nathan, what do you think I am? A bloody encyclopaedia?" Mason says, with a little fire in his tone. It was behind that I had reservations about. A little quiver. He knew it.

"What do you know?" I wasn't standing on ceremony, not with those scary blokes in black suits chasing us and so much more crap going on.

"I never said I knew anything. With respect, I know Nathan, but we aren't close. I sure as hell don't know you, so don't make assumptions," Mason says, shaky throughout. I was getting a bad feeling. The whole time, Mason's eyes drifted to the drawing.

"Come on, Mason, as you say, we aren't close, but I know you enough to tell when you're holding back. What gives?"

Mason stared at the drawing, panting. His hands kept fidgeting. After several gulps of saliva, Mason quickly turned tail and marched behind the counter. I heard keys jingling.

"Come on," Mason says gruffly before dropping low. Then, the thuds on wood we heard earlier. Nathan and I looked at each other, shrugged, and followed.

There was a large hatch on the floor. Mason was a big guy and looked thin compared to the hole and steps down. There was a rattle and a ping near Mason, a bit of the way down. A light flashed on, showing us dirty, damp lines of brick to either side, with rickety handrails. With each step Mason took, an echo grew. It must've been thirty feet down before we reached the bottom. Had me wondering if Mason made it or if he got lucky.

"What is this, Mason?" Nathan points to a large metal door, like those seen on walk-in safes.

"You'll see." Mason jammed the keys in the door with a loud clunk. Each twist made me jumpy. Ten seconds later, the door groaned open, releasing stale dust. Mason pings another light on, and I am blown away. We were still at the doorway, looking into a room at least fifteen by fifteen feet. Drawings and pictures covered the walls like wallpaper. Bookcases were rammed with old-looking books, older than what I'd seen at the library. More statues and ornaments, all quite bloody weird.

"What the hell, and this is related?" I'm scanning for similar images.

"Why don't you go look? Nathan, can I have a word?" Mason summons Nathan toward him.

I moved inside unthinkingly, a little overawed. So many symbols, 'crosses' that differed from the usual, seemed familiar. 'The Templar Knights' was scrawled below an image. Then, four feet to my left at eye-line height, I find an old page torn from a book. The paper was yellow-brown, almost leathery-looking. The image was something else, nothing I could imagine. The appearance of a puzzle box is shown in two forms: unfinished and complete. The completed one made me step back.

A large round symbol is in the middle, exactly like the coin in our photo. Four quarters moved and twisted until each part lined up. It reminded me of a Rubik's cube, and I bloody hate those. Beside it, there's a piece of pad paper with a handwritten paragraph.

'Believed to be Pandora's box. With many rumours circulating, that there's more than one. This one opens a secret hiding place of a long thought lost, Book of the Dead, which requires four sections of a stolen Baphomet coin. Centuries ago, a sect of four Templar knights split from the cause to forge their path. One filled with bloodshed and pain. They sought control and power, dividing the coin between them and knowing the true location of this Pandora's box. While another rumour is that it's simply the master key to unleash the gates of hell, and the book of the dead is used to summon the rarest and most dangerous demons or spirits, too terrifying and uncontrollable, they're banished to Pandora's void or the empty. A place only opened by a particular incantation whilst possessing the box configured as described in the book. At present, it's unknown if either ever used the book or where the box is, let alone the puzzle pieces. Suppose they fall into the wrong hands. Evil could be unleashed upon the world. Like with anything, there's always a counter method if the worst happens, a way to reverse it. Or so they say.'

"What the hell?" I mutter, wondering if Nathan's parents and mine knew about these boxes. The drawing from the cabin shows all four parts together. They had to have seen it.

"Hey Nathan..." I turn to call Nathan over, swivelling in time to see the door swinging shut with a resounding thump.

"Hey guys, this isn't funny." I dash to the door, banging loudly, but no one responds.

I'm paused, ear to the door, straining to listen. There's a loud hissing, but not from outside. I look back into the room. Fuck, there's gas. I see thick clouds of musky yellow gas streaming through vents near the ceiling. My heart thumps wildly. I'm trapped and don't know what's happened to Nathan. Only someone shut the door on me. Mason was a little sketchy when he called Nathan away, so the money was on him.

The room was filling quickly; I had nowhere to go and could already feel it in my lungs, burning. Every inhale caused it to tear deeper within. I was choking, struggling to breathe. After thirty seconds, I could barely keep my eyes open.

'Let me in, Gerald... Let me in. I will protect you.'

A cold whisper cuts through the cloud across my cheek. It was the last thing I needed, fighting on two fronts.

"N... Not... Now," I barely got my words out.

'Come now, Gerald, let me in. Everyone has abandoned you. I won't. I'm always with you, Gerald. So, let me in and we can rip out some fucking throats and get revenge.'

My willpower was at its weakest, and I was unsure if I could hold out much longer. It's taking everything I have to stay on my feet, and now the whispers feel their closest to taking over me. Heavy, ever so heavy. I stumble, legs turning to jelly. One step left, two steps to the right, legs tangled together. I couldn't keep upright. Until, finally… crash. A fallen tree in the woods. I crash hard. I couldn't move. I lost all feeling and control of my limbs. A final twitch, my eyes slam shut…

'Time to open the door, Gerald. All you have to do is say yes,' the whisper felt foggy through my eardrums. My head pressed against the cold stone floor.

"Y…Y… Ye,"

Chapter 22

'Détective Reynolds,'

The skies were already dark, being winter and all, but thick grey-black billowing smoke swarmed overhead, obscuring the incoming quarter moon. We hadn't even gotten out of the car yet and were gagging—charred human flesh, and if my senses were right, a fair amount of it. I was still licking my wounds, reeling from Ellena being swept up, like us, into someone else's problems and held captive to force my hand and flush out 'Ackerman.' Those creepy men in black were so much more than we had yet to figure out.

Those tapes seized from Gerald Ackerman's home were unsettling, to say the least. In Michael's words, "Fuck me, the guy looks like he's been put through the wringer, matey." He wasn't wrong. Whatever Henry knew or was into before he died scared him. Fear painted his face, and I suspect his death was covered up and written off as an accident. His demeanor and warnings suggested otherwise.

More unsettling was the shadow behind him, the figure in a hat. Then, the spooky silhouette thumped the screen. Michael nearly wet himself, and not much scared him. Even I jumped a little. Whether it could only be seen by the supernatural is anyone's guess. We haven't dared to show anyone else yet—not least the local plods. If this case shapes up how I think, then there's so much not to trust about Willowbrook and its people.

We were given 'Kooky Comics & The Darkside' after a sudden fire was put out. I didn't understand why a fire would concern us. After all, most arson cases involving business premises turn out to be insurance jobs. Yet, what we were smelling said otherwise. Michael and I benefit from heightened smell and hearing to distinguish the stench inside, making it doubtful whether a normal human would smell anything else. This brought me back to wondering why us?

We abandoned our car on Elk Street beside the shop's parade. The fire was in the second shop along and tearing through unabated. The firefighters were fighting hard. The blackening smoke didn't inspire confidence. Blue lights lit up the street, and hordes of people were escorted away from the buildings as a precaution. The last thing we needed was for it to spread through the parade.

Michael and I made our way toward it; the closer we got, the stronger the burnt flesh stunk. Pausing on the pavement at the corner, my hackles began rumbling. Michael shuddered. We exchanged knowing glances. This had all the fingerprints of something supernatural going down. Yeah, I get that. It sounds like a stab in the dark. After all, it could be a fire where some unfortunate soul got trapped inside. If I've learned anything by now other than to expect the unexpected, it's trusting my werewolf senses. They generally hit the mark when something was off.

Michael sifted a cigarette pack from his jacket, 'Bensons,' before flicking one into his mouth and turning to me. "How many?" he says without breaking his process, cupping the cigarette and a lighter to spark up.

I shook my head at the slightly poor timing, considering we were at a fire. "I don't know, but the stink is strong," I say, gazing at the bouncing flames. My mind wandered, momentarily mesmerized. I thought back to the stories of my childhood. The house fire at the foster home and how badly I was supposedly burnt. I say it like that because I still can't remember everything, relying on Skip to fill in the blanks. There's a lot of them.

Michael waved a hand before my face to snap me back to reality. "You okay, matey? Look, it was a real shit move on their part, but we'll get her back. Ellena is built differently from the standard woman. You know that," Michael says. He was right, of course. Ellena was probably already giving them grief, making the creeps rethink their life… or death choices.

"I know, mate. The trouble is, Scotland did a number on us all. We need to find how these evidence puzzle pieces fit together. Why did it have to be us here? The CAD sheet was vague, much like everything we've been told. Doesn't even mention who called it in."

"Perhaps it's what's sold inside, matey, not necessarily the comics. But any name that includes 'The Darkside' hints at something a little less than normal, matey. Now, I'm not counting my chickens, but I guess the locals know exactly how weird and felt it suited our current case." Valid points, and I hope he was right, something as straightforward. If only we didn't need to keep reading between the lines. It's like trying to box with one hand tied behind our backs. Or a game of chess wearing a blindfold.

We were getting carried away with ourselves without noticing the tide had turned. The fire was being pushed back, squeezed, and squeezed until it was on its last whimper. So much. I grabbed two sets of latex gloves from my pocket, handing one to Michael.

"Jumping the gun a little, aren't we?" Michael says, killing off the last of his cigarette beneath his rather expensive-looking, shiny black Italian shoes.

"Or just being prepared. You and I both know we're going in, regardless."

"What if the 'water boys' say it isn't safe?"

"What? For the overpriced leather? Just put some cover shoes on."

"Fuck off. You and I both know what these structures are like after a fire." No sooner had Michael says this, his eyes rolled, tilting his head to the sky, muttering 'fuck.' He assumed I'd take it wrong, but I knew what he actually meant.

"Relax, old man. And yes, but we both smell that shit, so we go in as detectives or sneak in as a werewolf and whatever the fuck you are. A were-Rat or something," I poked Michael's beer gut, messing with him. I didn't want him to think the worst. In truth, he was a mystery. So far, he appears a variant of a Kitsune, although he wasn't at the start; in the black widow case, they messed with his supernatural side. Judging by his yellow aura. A thunder type, too.

Near the first cordon, the officer looked fed up. Again, he was young, like the previous ones. I can relate, given how often I got stuck at a crime scene when I was new. His name badge said Officer Kirby.

We flashed our warrant cards, trying the good way first. "Hey lad, we're detectives working your murder spree in these parts and have been sent here. What's the crack? Any chance we can have a cursory once-over?" Michael says, waking the young officer up.

"Yeah, you've been expected. I'm surprised how quickly word spreads around here. How you two get to work all the spooky ones. Kinda envy you, to be honest. Instead, I have a scene log and a pen. But yeah, happy trails. Just be careful. We're lucky the floor is solid stone under ply boards," Kirby says, resignation in his voice. Yeah, it can be fun working on these weird ones, but with everything we've survived, I'm not sure he'd be so keen if he knew.

We dipped under the tape held aloft by Kirby and made short work of the pavement to the front door. All the glass was smeared black, and the dampness of burnt wood soaked in water was overpowering. It wasn't long before the stink changed. Around us, what had been comics and other items were nothing but burnt debris and melted plastic. The glass counter was blown out.

"Michael, take the left quarter. I'll take the right. Use your other eyes. This place feels all kinds of off," I say. With everything still smouldering and cloudy, it was hard to find the exact source of the burnt flesh, but any dead bodies would give off a unique signature under U.V. than the standard burnt crap.

There were footprints everywhere. A gasoline trail, too, spray marks up the walls, over the stands, and a long trail around the counter to the door behind us. My wolf's eyes worked the right-hand wall when I saw some odd symbols. Not the sort ordinarily visible, especially without the fire. These were meant only to be seen a certain way (black light) or by the supernaturally inclined.

I got so fixated on what I saw that I paid attention to where I stepped. Another 'goat's head in a star,' just like Scotland and anything linked to Satan or devil worship. The other symbols were more like the sigils at the morgue when 'Frank' first came back to life. While he was busy being 'living dead,' sigils formed from the shadows and in blood. I couldn't translate them, and sure as hell, Michael couldn't either.

My feet scuffed through the burnt plywood and puddles, still fixated on the walls, when I stubbed my toes. I jumped back in a panic. Not something I would've done had it been some wood or the counter. My heightened hearing heard a crunch. One all too sickeningly familiar. The fragile cracking of burnt flesh with fluids beneath the skin scorched away. Leaving behind a fragile burnt shell. The tips of my shoes must've gone an inch deep.

A full-grown adult male. I swiveled on the spot. There were three other corpses scattered nearby. My stomach flipped. It's okay; everything I had was not to spew my guts. Michael saw it, too.

'Three... two...one,' I counted, watching Michael dash to the far corner in time to spray the walls. Two bodies had the limbs ripped off, thrown wildly in the tragic aftermath.

"Not one word, you hear? Not one," Michael says, looking up and wiping his mouth.

"Who me? Never. If you're about done, princess, we need to connect these fucking 'dots'. In a comic store, of all places."

Michael tip-toed around the body parts with all the grace of a drunk ballerina. He was about to step past a chunky arm when he froze. His bright yellow eyes bulged wide, his mouth opened, but no words came. Not immediately, anyway.

"Fuck... fuck... fuck, matey, this isn't..." Michael looked shaken, and he's been good with most stuff like this, but he was rattled.

"What?"

"From where I am, I can see those cross things. You know, the glowing ones on the bodies in the morgue," Michael pivoted around the arm, face churning as he skipped across the puddles to where I stood.

The bodies where Michael was had a slight glow, getting brighter and bringing that symbol through the burnt shell. I checked the one near me. Or what there was. Upper right of what had to be the back began cracking and splitting. That glow fighting to push through.

"We can't let anyone else in, Michael. I have a bad feeling." I looked through the gap in the scorch marks across the glass. The numbers were growing. The only thing on our side was that it had gotten dark. I was doing the math, and it didn't work.

To handle what I feared would happen and stop outsiders from coming into the firing line, we'd have to split our attention. To do that, I'd have to unleash the wolf properly if the shit hit the fan.

"I know, matey. I'm still digesting what happened at the morgue."

Loud snapping in unison took us by surprise. A twitch here. A scuffle, crackle, and groan there. We had movement to bring that fear I mentioned to the forefront. All four corpses began crunching the char-grilled shells, slow robotic movements. Then, the inconceivable happened. Compared to the crap I've seen, that's saying a lot. If coming back from the dead was bad, watching in awe as torn limbs slowly slithered through the burnt debris.

Michael and I were gobsmacked, mouths hung open, stomachs flipped with bile surging through mine. Those limbs made a beeline to the relevant corpse. My wolf's eyes zoomed in to see them reattach themselves, crusty flesh sewing the pieces together.

Each corpse pulled itself upright. Puppets on strings, minus the strings. They appeared mindless and vacant, yet moved military-like. Loud, melancholic groans oozed through their burnt jaws, with scorched blood frothing over the edge. My heart was a runaway train. Michael's not much better.

"Michael, no matter what. Go to the door and don't leave it. Don't let anyone in or anything out."

"But."

"But nothing... If we don't and these things go out there, picture what was left of Doctor Thornton. I'm not saying that's what these want right now, but we have to prepare."

"What if they are being controlled and summoned back?" Michael says, making me think. For every argument, I had a counterargument.

"What if they had been normal before the fire? Once dead, thanks to those symbols, the corpses are reanimated." Michael had that rabbit-in-headlights look again. In fact, we both did because I just realized something, too. What if that's the plan? Anyone killed with a symbol becomes the living dead—an unstoppable army of death. We didn't know how many mindless followers had that symbol.

All four corpses were on their feet now. Staggering forward slowly. Their arms strained toward me. Whether they simply needed a target or were running off a memory beforehand, I couldn't take the risk.

I caught a glimmer of the moon through the window, enough to give a little boost, prompting a 'shift' not fully evolved but enough to scare the shit out of anyone coming in. I slowly backed away, sliding behind the counter. The corpses followed. There was a trapdoor open on the floor, steps going down. If I could lead them near, they'd fall.

The plan was working. I slid near the edge before the first step. I leapt backward just as they leaned forward. They'd be off balance and drop. I was rocking on my heels. Michael watching on with fear. All four groaned hauntingly loud. I didn't budge. It had to be the very last second. It was about to happen when a loud clap rang out. The shop filled with a thick black cloud that swarmed the dead, whipping a cloudy blanket around them and another loud clap. They were gone. The fuckers had been summoned back.

Breathing a sigh of relief, I was glad the dead were gone, but worried about what would be next. More importantly, what the bloody hell happened? Michael scooped an arm around my shoulder, happy it was over, too. Then he clocked the trap door, too.

"So, matey, the elephant in the room."

"Eh, your ex-wife isn't here."

"Oi, you cheeky twat! Although it is a fair point. Anyway, I meant, what do you think is down there?"

"Only one way to find out." Michael nodded before stepping down into the next unknown.

At the bottom, there was a large open metal door, a big safe one. I scanned with my wolf's eyes. There was drool on the stone floor within the room. Somebody had been down here. Aside from a little smoke damage, the fire hadn't touched its contents, and boy, oh boy, were we surprised.

Those sigils were nothing compared to this. More crosses were just like what we saw on the creepy guys. My attention went straight to an old parchment or an old page taken from a book. Leather appearance.

"Fuck... Pandora's box. This says they're gateways to hell."

"You're shitting me? Those things are real? I thought that was a myth," Michael says, shuffling beside me.

"This one is a puzzle that requires coin pieces. Once solved, it opens a gateway to where the 'Book of the Dead' is hidden. Oh god, a band of Templar knights split away, taking pieces of the coin with them. Four knights."

"Could those knights have bloodlines alive today, matey?" I was getting an eerie feeling. The kind that meant I was reaching for straws or going mad. A knot in my stomach made me think Gerald Ackerman's family could be a descendant. I know, quite the jump. The details made sense. Then there's the shadow on the TV screen. It's not quite the far-fetched theory, especially as the creeps had a similar link with those symbols. "Why else would they want Gerald? I guess so."

"Georgie, we both know I'm no genius in this stuff, but I have a hunch or a shot in the dark. But what if that Gerald guy was one of those knights? His family line. The creepy fucks suspect he has a coin piece, and they want it. For all we know, they've recovered the other three pieces. Then they discover the box wherever that may be."

"Then they get the Book of the Dead. Who knows what it could contain? Perhaps the key to bringing forth the big bad guy himself. Complete with an army of the living dead," I interrupt. Michael made a hell of a lot of sense. The question is, what actually happened here today?

Chapter 23

'Gerald - Melwood 8 PM,'

"Cuh, cuh. Where am I?" My eyes were slow to open. I could feel pressure on my wrists. Wait... my arms were above my head. I couldn't move them. God, my head was killing me. No hangover had ever kicked my ass this bad.

My brain was slow to catch up, trying to process what had happened. Why couldn't I move? Then I remembered the room below the floor in the shop. Hissing gas came through the vents. Bloody hell, I was locked in and knocked out by that gas.

Oh no, those whispers called to me when I was on the floor, telling me to let it in. I didn't, did I? Please tell me I didn't. Damn, where's Nathan? Where the hell am I? The pressure on my wrists gradually became apparent as metal shackles biting into my flesh. My eyes were open, but I still couldn't see.

Every breath felt warm and stifled. There was something over my head—a cloth hood or something similar. It smelled musky; I couldn't pick up on any other scents around me because of it. I tried moving my legs. The tips of my toes barely grazed the floor. I scraped some dirt, but beneath it felt solid. If I hedge my bets, it's straw over flooring. I was in a barn.

I could barely hear muffled moans. Sounded at least ten feet away. It could be Nathan, but if we're both trapped, then Mason screwed us over. I remembered him calling Nathan out of the room not long before I was shut in. Surely, Nathan wasn't in on the act. Fighting back a wave of sickly emotions, I needed to have a rational mind if I stood any chance of escaping.

"About bloody time you're awake." I heard a voice from the shop, abrupt but sounding a little like Mason.

"Who are you? Where am I? Where's Nathan?" I say, my throat still feeling the after-effects of the gas.

"Be bloody quiet. We'll ask the questions if you don't mind. More importantly, we want to know what you are. We have our suspicions, but we want to hear it from you. How you are a sick, killing machine." What? A killing machine. They must have their wires crossed, assuming I'm guilty when I've done nothing yet. Have I? Fuck, what if it is me?

"I'm not the one you want. It's not me; we're trying to find who too. They killed my father and wife. So who are you?"

"Oh, but you are. How about we start simple? Where's the puzzle piece?" What the hell is this guy on about? I knew even less than whoever this guy did, and yet he's asking me for some bloody piece of a puzzle. Had me thinking they were on about Pandora's box. The image on the wall. In the photo, it showed four sections, but I had none.

"Hey, come on, buddy, you really have the wrong guy. I didn't know what you're on about. Now where's my friend?"

"Nathan is fine. You two stroll into my shop, start inquiring about things only certain people will know of. My guess is you have a piece and want to know how to unite them to find the book. Well, newsflash, it's our destiny. Only those loyal to the cause of ushering in a new world. One where there's no pain or suffering. I witnessed the brutality because of your presence. The carnage you cause."

"What do you mean?" The guy was going off on a tangent while I was using the time to wiggle my wrists, hoping I could drag them free.

"Don't pretend, you sick bastard." His tone turned angry, stomping up close, whipping the hood off my head. True enough, there was Mason. We were in a large farm barn suspended from beams. Nathan was across the way and seemed out cold still.

Behind Mason, there were half a dozen blokes, only they're all wearing pointy black hoods with the Templar cross on the front. Mason had started some crazy cult. To what end? What did he think he would gain? His comment about ushering in a new world stuck with me. Did those creepy guys promise them power and riches or whatever the going rate is for stringing up two guys trying to prevent more death?

"Hey, I'm really not into whatever you and Brady bunch are, so how about you let us go and we'll leave you be."

"No way. All you bring is death. Now you have to make amends. We called others that are really interested in you, and we would've been in their good graces. I can't believe you don't remember. Perhaps this will jog your memory."

Mason balled his fist, drew back, and let rip with a punch to my left cheekbone. For a fat guy, he packs a whack. It bloody hurt. It worked though...

A quick burst of images, jumbled, trying to form a memory, then...

"Y...y...ye... No... I can't let you in."

My head was heavy. I could lift a little from the floor. I heard a loud groan, metal grinding against metal. I tilted my head on my chin in time to see the door drift open. I could hear banging from upstairs. The air was clearing. I could pull myself up, but I was so woozy. My eyes were bleary, like a sheet of fog in front of them, but I saw enough to stagger toward the door.

Then I lost the bloody trail...

"Wow, is that all you got, big boy? My kids can hit harder than that... Hate to crush your ego, they're two," I goaded, watching Mason's face turn bright red.

"F...f... For Christ's sake, Gerald, don't.... You don't know what you're doing... I mean, Mason is sensitive about his weight. He can't help being a fat double-crossing bastard," Nathan came around just in time. A little groggy but alive and with it enough to follow my lead.

"I know, right, Maid Mason and his merry band of six misfits?" It was my turn to return the favour and give Nathan the gist of what we were dealing with.

The barn was larger than I'd seen before. Enough to have a ground and first with ramps going up left and right to a big platform that has a hatch with a winch. The Bradys formed a loose semi-circle wall behind the main man, Mason. If we could get free of the shackles, we stood a chance. Although Nathan was groggy and I'm not much better. It's pitch black outside, and we didn't know where we were.

Our choices were slim. Play along, piss Mason off enough, so he slips up and gives us what we need to know. That starts by taking another hit, restarting that trail.

"You both think you're funny. Just because you killed those thugs, there's no way you're leaving here until we get what we want. As for the 'fat' comment. Have this, you arsehole."

'Thump.'

"Fuck... What was that, a wet fish?" My bravado was cashing cheques my body hated paying. He packed a punch, alright. But...

I was gripping the door frame. There's a commotion getting louder.

"Come on, Gerald, let me in. Your friend needs us. We can save him if you let me in."

The whisper came, but I hadn't let it in. I shook my head and continued up the steps. Okay, Gerald, if you're playing hard to get, how about an audition?

I didn't answer. If the darkness needed me to let it in, how could it do anything? At least that's how I thought. I'd made it halfway. There's nothing but darkness and suddenly a large outline of a man appears. He's moving quickly. There are others too. Nathan is on the floor already. The silhouette tears relentlessly through the group. I'm on the top step, then 'ouch' I feel a sharp pain in my neck. I turn to see Mason holding a needle. Then I crash to the floor.

I'm back in the present at the barn with memories intact. I didn't know whether to be scared or emboldened. Mason was half right, yet I didn't do it. Just the darkness trying to impress, and then Mason knocked me out.

"Cheers for that, you sneaky bastard. Skulking in the corner to inject me. You were wrong, by the way. I killed no one."

"Well, how about this, Gerald Ackerman? Yeah, I know your name thanks to this driver's license. You're the descendant of the late Frederick Ackerman, a traitorous knight of the Templar order. So, I know exactly who and what to expect. That's why I called these guys again."

Mason slipped a white business card from his pocket. Nothing but the same cross I saw in Mason's basement and the number '913. 0309.' Which was weird, not the usual numbers I'd seen, but I fear he called those creeps in suits. Whatever I was going to do, it had to be quick.

"So what, I have a famous relative, a bit like you're related to 'Jabba the Hut' and what's that? Your prostitute hotline?" I say, hearing Mason chuckle under the hood.

That was the straw that broke the camel's back. Mason stormed up close, kneeing me in my stomach, taking the wind from my sails. He leaned close, sweat streaming off his forehead, bright red and pissed. He leaned close.

"Where's the fucking puzzle piece?"

"Bloody hell, Mason, the breath. Would you kiss your mother with that mouth?" I say, feeling the singe on my stubble.

"Come now, Gerald... It's well known Mason has been kissing his Mother since he hit puberty... Congratulations, by the way. Last month, right... Now you're a real boy!" Nathan ripped into Mason. His words were a bit slurred and a struggle. Funny, though, and Mason was livid.

"So, now your secret is out, Mason. Get it in your thick head. I didn't know what you're talking about," I say, dropping the smile and glaring at Mason's fat, red face.

"They will make you talk. Funny really, I was so creeped out when they first came to the shop, but their vision for the future is exactly what this world needs. To think you're a Templar 'bloodline,' what a joke."

There was me digesting Mason's talk again about a new world and the creeps when I heard a 'click.' The shackle on my wrist felt loose. Mason stayed close, and somehow I could move.

'You're welcome,' a low hiss breezed down the bend of my neck. The darkness had auditioned for the second time. A compelling argument. Since when did something that could kill so ruthlessly ever turn out well?

Mason's head bobbed in front of my face. I took my chance. I yanked my hands free and swung an elbow square on the bridge of Mason's nose. Blood spurted across his face. I kicked him in the bollocks before snatching keys from Mason's belt loop. The Bradys were stunned, and Mason stumbled, struggling to regain composure. I unlatched Nathan's shackles, tearing the hood from his head.

We still had much to do. Nathan was a dead weight hanging from my shoulder. We shifted to the right. Nathan kept flinging his arm up, catching me in the face while trying to speak, but he was quite groggy still.

"G… Ger… Gerald…. The lantern. Get the blubby, I mean bloody lantern. No smoke without fire. He has the smoke coming out of his ears. Let's give them the fire. Look." Nathan threw his arm to point at the straw throughout the floor. I got what he was selling. And could be the perfect aid to our escape.

We scurried across to a lantern hanging from a support beam, knowing we should be lucky they're still using flame ones. Mason and his Brady bunch had regained their composure, darting toward us. With a quick flick of my free arm, I sent the lantern spinning through the air. I don't know why, but I was standing and watching, twisting through the air, seemingly in slow motion. Two of the Bradys dived, attempting to catch it. Others flung themselves in opposite directions.

A loud crash and 'whoosh' fire ripped through the shattering glass, across the straw. Within seconds, the entire section of open floor went up in flames. They couldn't get to us. I hoisted Nathan up higher and shuttled us to the doors. I couldn't hear anyone outside, but that didn't mean a thing. I'd be foolish to think there were only a handful of sycophant cultists deluded that evil would do anything for them. Which brings me to my issues. Why was this darkness, this strange whisper so hell-bent on being embraced that it helped us?

There's a dark panel van to the left with headlights on. We may have just got our first lucky break. We were definitely on a farm, a huge one, all in darkness. If we had time, it would be worth digging a little and seeing what else is here, but time wasn't on our side. I threw Nathan in the back. He was still very drugged, which puzzled me because I took the gas and an injection and was still more with it.

I dived into the driver's seat, thanking my lucky stars that the keys were there. First, turn... fuck... it didn't turn over... second... still nothing... third... it roared to life. With a quick rev, I chucked it into gear and was about to go when the night sky lit up with a flashing blue. An unmarked police car came tearing through the farm's muddy road, skidding to a halt in front of us.

My lights shone directly on their windshield, two guys in suits. Thankfully, not those creepy ones. An older, seasoned guy in the passenger seat, the driver much younger. I thought about fleeing, a quick reverse and spinning the van right. Until I caught sight of something weird... Considering how high my bat for that has gone lately, that speaks volumes.

Their eyes changed... one flashed red, the other yellow. I should have been scared. Oddly, my sixth sense was telling me they were going to help. I don't know why. We needed all the help we could get, even if I could be suspected of murder.

'Détective Reynolds,'

We flew through the farm, throwing our car to a halt just in time to stop a dark panel van from leaving. We discovered a house near the shop service road had CCTV that captured two guys bundled into the back. Both were limp and out cold. The van was registered to the shop but stupidly set off half a dozen speed cameras, tearing through red lights.

The bloody trail led us to Maplewood, thirty miles outside Melwood. We still had three farms to choose from, so it was a little potluck. The lights gave it away. Looking at the two in the van was like startled rabbits wrestling with flight or fight.

My senses tell me it was Ackerman and a friend. We couldn't take any chances. My ears were twitching to the tune of a commotion inside. We were reading all sorts of wrong, setting our eyes off. We were in a standoff. Michael grabs the mic for the loud hailer.

"Switch your engine off and step out of the vehicle slowly," Michael says, his dulcet tones screeching out of the speakers, jarring my nerves.

"It's not what you think," I hear the driver shout out the window. His heart remained steady, elevated from the situation—no blip during his words.

"Step out of the vehicle," Michael says again.

"We need to get out of here. What you want is there,"

My hearing drifts past the van, through the doors. There's a crackling from a fire and raised voices.

"Michael, he's telling the truth. And I think that's Ackerman,"

"Really?" Michael says, looking at me, puzzled.

"Yep, but there's trouble,"

We stepped out of the car. I watched the driver, still listening inside. The driver was on edge, and his foot tapped the accelerator. He wanted to go, but suddenly opened his door. His face was more of fear and worry. I didn't get a guilty vibe from him.

"Are you Gerald Ackerman?" I say, on guard as he steps in front of the van's headlights, projecting a silhouette over our car bonnet. That's when I noticed... The silhouette was the same on the tape, the one that loomed around Henry and smacked the TV screen.

"Y... Yes... Look, we were drugged and kidnapped. My buddy is in the back. In that barn is a bunch of weirdos into some strange cult."

Everything he said matched what we saw on the CCTV. There's still so many vague 'dots' to figure out, like why those creeps wanted him.

"We saw. We've been to your house, too. In fact, we know a little more than you'd expect. We're going to need you to fill in some blanks, though," I say, still listening for changes. I heard fire extinguishers being sprayed.

Ackerman raked his hands through his hair, gasping in distress. "You wouldn't believe me if I told you," Ackerman says, glancing nervously over his shoulder.

"We would. And now we have a vested interest. We know about the two in black suits,"

"Them creepy bastards. They blew my front door off, followed my friend Nathan, and chased us."

"What happened in the shop, the dead guys and the fire?" I ask. Ackerman pauses, thinking about what he should and shouldn't say.

"We went there looking for answers, was looking at some old papers when everything went wrong. I was gasses, but it wore off. I climbed from the basement to find Nathan passed out on the floor and some thugs in the shop. It was dark. Somebody attacked them. They ripped them apart. Before I could do anything, the owner of the shop jabbed a needle in my neck."

Most of what he said, but his heart jumped when spoke of the thugs being attacked. He knew more, but not in a way he was guilty.

"Well, if this little get-together is done, maybe we can get the fuck out of here?" Michael says, looking irritated. I sensed it, too. There was a change in the air. Nothing good.

"Right, you follow us. Do anything stupid, and everything you have said so far goes out the window," I say, checking for a flinch of uncertainty. Unfortunately, the lights were on, but nobody was home.

I stepped toward Ackerman, hands held up to show no harm intended. I needed him to get on board my train of thought and fast because something was brewing in the barn and the winds were sweeping in something far worse. My hackles were on fire. Michaels, too, I was loathed to show a mundane the other me unless push came to shove. The wolf prefers to do the shoving.

"It's okay, relax," I say. He wasn't relaxing, instead he kept looking toward the barn.

Wind hissed between the barn planks, whipping up an eerie frenzy. The extinguishers stopped. My hackles bounced, and then… 'chuh chuh' Michael and I looked at each other. He jumped beside me. Several shotguns just chambered.

I could feel it coming. Michael was watching me. "Mr Ackerman, I know there's more going on with you. But something bad is about to happen and what you'll see may scare you, but don't worry," I say. Ackerman stood open-mouthed at first.

"What do you mean??"

"Your shadow shows the hatted silhouette that's on your tapes. My guess is your father was cursed or afflicted. His death passed it on to you. Am I close," Ackerman nodded.

A stampede of footsteps rushed the barn doors. I was fifteen feet away with Ackerman in the way. Several thugs burst into the open. Fingers pressed triggers, I dug deep and powered forward. The muzzle flashes were in slow motion. For me, anyway, hurrying. I ditched. My jacket flared my claws and phased on the fly, pouncing over Ackerman onto all fours, fully shifted and without pain. Michael, using his speed, whipped Ackerman out of the firing line.

First guy went down easy, disarmed, and I didn't hurt him too badly. I didn't want to. Figured a good scare should be enough. Until I caught a stray bullet, one ripped through my thigh. Thankfully, it wasn't Wolfsbane. Hurt like hell, though, and really pissed me off. My claws tore through his stomach. As the guy fell, his finger stayed on the trigger, firing into his friends and taking down three others. I prowled upright, growling, teeth bared and claws dripping with that venom. I've never appreciated just how big I am until now, looking at my shadow on the barn. The rest of the gunmen fled into the vast, empty fields.

There were four dead on the floor, and I was bleeding. Only when the adrenaline eased did I appreciate just how bad. Slowing down, I phased back. Michael threw his coat over me. I was limping badly. The bullet grazed my femoral artery.

"Fuck matey, you pissing blood. You, okay?" Michael looked worried. Ackerman was too shell-shocked.

"Yeah, I'm okay. I can feel it trying to heal, but the artery is pinched. I need to cauterise it to speed up the process." I say, slumping against the van.

"Flares... yes, a flare. I saw some in the van," Ackerman says, running to the passenger side to grab one. Within seconds, he was back. A quick click, and it's lit up like a Roman candle.

"Do it!" I say through gritted fangs. My claws latched onto Michael's shoulder. With a swift move, Ackerman plunged the flare into my wound. My eyes bulged, searing heat tore through my leg and then my body. I let rip with a deep, bellowing roar that shook the barn to its foundations.

"Fucking hell, mate. I know it hurts, but do you mind leaving my shoulder attached?" I looked to see my claws were buried deep. Even worse, the venom was killing his flesh. I quickly retracted them and checked out the wound. Much to Ackerman's astonishment, it had completely healed.

"That is so cool," a voice blurts out from the van. Ackerman's friend was awake and had his head out the door. How much he saw was anyone's guess.

"I have to agree with Nathan. I should be scared shirtless, but that was awesome." Ackerman had finally settled and seemed confident and unafraid.

"Well, with that in mind, we need to make like a tree and leave. There's something else coming, and we're on the back foot," I say. The others nodded in agreement. Just as we were stepping away, me getting dressed on the move, I heard stirring. A familiar groan we'd heard earlier.

All four thugs were coming back to life. Each had that glow emanating under their clothing. Their eyes were jet black, skin a mottled grey-white. All back on their feet, moving as if riddled with rigour mortis. Not even a normal corpse sets that quickly. These stumbled like zombies.

"For fuck's sake, not bloody again," Michael gushes.

"As much as it would be great to go again, let's just go. Let these disappear like the others. I'm sure they'll come again." I say, ushering everyone to the car.

The living dead's numbers are growing. Those creepy church fuckers are hot BB on our heels, and they have Ellena captive. We have Gerald Ackerman now chalking a point in our win column for a change.

A storm is brewing, and it's threatening to rain blood. Before we know it, the streets will be swamped with the undead and their sadistic puppeteers. We need to punch their ticket permanently. All this rinse-and-repeat nonsense is wearing thin.

Chapter 24

'Gerald,'

I'm back at the farm. I don't know how. I'm headed to where we left off, in the driver's seat, but not in control. It's happened again. Dust kicks up along the muddy trail, every crunch under my feet too noisy compared to the stillness around. Tall grass lines the path left and right, bordered by weathered picket fencing. Not a streetlight in sight. Instead, there's a motion-detected halogen in front of a distant barn.

The air is icy cold, and white clouds billow in front of me. An owl hoots to the left, high in a tree showing all the ravages of winter. Shadows jostle, animated and full of rage, breaking from the fields toward the barn. One slightly bigger shadow burst through the doors.

I'm walking slowly. The air feels off, musky. I'm within twenty feet. Three guys and 'Mason' twist around, running towards me. I don't stop edging forward. Each has a shotgun, chambering loud enough to send my arm hairs to attention. Nothing. I'm moving without control.

"Who the fuck are you? What are you doing here? Did they send you?" Mason spits venom, not recognising me. Anger quickly becomes fear. Mason jumps back in line with the others. He snatches a gun from one of them, raising it, followed by the rest, but I continue forward. Shaky hands slide to the triggers and press. With a unified click, I dive forward.

Swooping beneath the first gunman, I lash upwards, gripping an arm. I hear a loud crunch of bone; I tear an arm clean off with the gun still held. Blood sprays skyward. Curdling screams fill the air. I'm not in control, but I don't stop.

The arm is tossed aside, and I notice my hands. They're long, thin, and clad in gloves. My arms are covered with black coat sleeves now dripping blood. I'm seeing through the eyes of the shadowy figure again—the one that haunts me. It's 'Grace' all over again.

My menacing, bony fist powers through another guy's chest, clutching his heart, smashing out of his back, squeezing it to splatter everywhere. The guy drops in a heap before I blur through the rest, limbs scattering across the ground, rapidly pooling with blood. Until the last man standing is Mason.

He staggers back, stumbling over a torso gushing a crimson river. Mason backs himself against the thick barn door. The halogen light above paints his frightened face—pale round flesh dripping with panic sweat and dribbles of his friend's blood. His mouth flaps open, but no words come. Until I reach out an arm.

"Please, don't," Mason begs. "Tell them I will make amends. I promise," Mason continues. I close him down like hunted prey, trapping Mason against the huge structure and a gruesome massacre mosaic.

My fingers puncture either side of Mason's windpipe. It's bony and squishy, toying with it like violin strings. Mason's eyes bulge, fit to burst from their sockets. Pale white blended with checking red. His body flails against my grip. A little pressure and I'm squeezing Mason off the floor, sliding his fat frame up the door. His chunky legs thrash wildly.

A little tug. A little flex and pull, a quick yank and my hand flies free from Mason's neck, his jugular still clutched between my blood-drenched fingers. With a loud gargle, Mason spurts a red fountain as he drops in a dead, bloody heap. A quick squeeze and I toss Mason's mess over my shoulder before soaking up my looming silhouette cast across the wooden doors to the sound of the owl hooting hauntingly once more.

"Oi, wake up."

"Huh, what?" My eyes jump open. I'm in the back of the police car, and Nathan is shaking my arm. My head is reeling from what I'd just seen. I'm drenched in sweat, my heart going two to the dozen.

Nathan stares at me as if I were the second coming of Christ. The car isn't moving, and from what I can tell, we're stopped in a layby. Both detectives are twisted in their seats, staring too. I quickly pat around my mouth, checking for drool. After all, why are they all boring holes in me with their eyes?

Maybe I was sleep-talking, I thought. Until I noticed both had bright red and yellow eyes. Their hands gripping the seat top had claws. Which brought me back to the farm and what I saw. It was fucking crazy.

How on earth had my life come to this? Knowing there are other things out there. Dead-looking blokes that can blow my door off with a wave of a hand. Coppers that can turn fully into werewolves, and a haunting whisper that somehow breaks me out of shackles. None of it was rational, and I'd call bullshit. But with the devil symbols popping up, me seeing murders happen in my sleep and those bodies… They bloody came back to life.

The only place I felt fit for was the loony bin. Now I had to break it to the others that Mason and his cronies were likely dead. I had the front-row seat. A place I wish for nobody.

"Gerald, you okay?" Nathan taps my arm to grab my attention.

"Er… yes and no," I say, watching in awe as the detectives' claws fade along with their eerie eye glow.

"We guessed, judging by the frantic muttering and the other weird," the driver, Reynolds I think, speaks up, sounding on edge. Who could blame him with the crazy going on?

I edge back in my seat, fully awake. "Other weird?" My head flicks between Nathan and the detectives.

"Gerald, it was nuts. I'm talking full-on out-of-body experience nuts. Only what came out of your body wasn't you. At least I don't think." Nathan is clawing at the flesh of his hands. He's on edge. Any shuffle from me has him flinching.

"I don't get you."

"Someone in all black, with a hat, long bony hands, gaunt, deathly features. Your eyes fluctuated from red to black. You had some upside-down Templar cross carved into the flesh of your forehead. And it floated like a cloud from your body, with ripples of black smoke." Nathan says, his tone trailing into one filled with worry, maybe even fear.

"Gerald, it was just like the silhouette at the barn and what we saw on the tapes," Reynolds speaks softly as if that would be reassuring. Nothing I've heard so far is settling me down at all.

I was dreading what my impending news flash would do to the atmosphere and the palpable tension I was picking up on. If they saw that projected from me, imagine their faces when I say, 'Oh hey guys, guess what, that thing you saw, I was it, in my sleep and I filleted Mason and Co.' No doubt those glowing eyes would come back quick. They had to know, though. I owed them the truth, considering the mess we were in.

"Well, I was dreaming. That thing you saw, I was it. A passenger of sorts, being carried along for a 'bloody' ride. I was back at the farm. And ran into Mason again." I paused, seeing just how spooked everyone was. Surprisingly, not that much.

"Come on, matey. Spill the beans before I reach pension age," the other detective speaks up, smiling in a weirdly unsettling way.

"Aren't you there already?" Reynolds pipes up, busting his friend's balls. Considering what they could do and see, they don't seem fazed, as if it's second nature to them. I dreaded to think what they'd seen in their careers to be so relaxed.

"I was just how you described, minus any control, as I ploughed through Mason and any remaining friends. I literally had Mason's jugular in the palm of my hand as his corpse dropped to the floor. Blood gushed everywhere. What was weird though, other than the obvious? Mason pleaded as though he thought my visage was sent from those creepy guys," I say without coming up for breath. I felt a little lighter sharing the load. Instead of shock, I saw the detectives facing each other, exchanging a knowing look.

I got the impression they'd experienced similar before. That I didn't envy. I can't wait for life to return to normal. Only, I had a feeling it wouldn't be the same again.

Silence fell between us, nothing but the low hum of some cheesy music on the radio and the sound of traffic whizzing past us. I was lost in a daydream, staring out the front windshield. Nathan had settled into his seat, half asleep. The detectives' mouths were moving, but I heard nothing. A perk of their condition? Super hearing maybe? God, how I dumbed that down, 'condition' like it was a sickness. Not that I knew what it was.

Sure, I'd seen the movies. The low-budget horror flicks. You know the ones, town folk with pitchforks and fires. Oh, and silver bullets being the one thing to kill one. I had so many questions I wanted to ask, but now didn't seem the right time. Although it was like an itch, I desperately wanted to scratch. Their faces spooked me a little.

Subtle twitches. I slid forward in my seat, watching their ears oddly changing. Something was wrong, and the detectives were picking up on it. Bloody weird but oddly fascinating. Out came the claws next. I can't lie. I was puzzled and Nathan was, luckily, oblivious.

Looking out the window again, a low glow the size of a pin caught my attention against the night sky. A star, I thought. It was getting bigger and brighter. The detectives swivelled their heads slowly to see it, too. The hair on their necks ruffled, like strange fur waving. How a dog's hackles would stand on end?

The glow was a bright blue, bolting me back to the pub after we escaped the library being chased by the creeps. Within seconds, the glow had landed on our car bonnet. A raven. Its freaky bright eyes peered directly at us, its neck twitching. The detectives were freaked out. One after the other, more came swooping down until the bonnet was full of them. Again, much like the pub. Hundreds of needy, haunting eyes glared through at us. I'm no fan of coincidences. By the looks of it, neither were the detectives.

Suddenly Reynolds speaks, but he's talking to the ravens. "What do you mean?"

"What's going on?" I ask the other guy, Michael, I think.

"It's fucking weird, mate. They keep saying, turn on the news, turn on the news. All in bloody unison. It's flipping spooky."

My jaw dropped, slumping in my seat. Just when I thought the night was crazy enough. Dreams and all. Reynolds twisted the dial on the radio. Silence was abruptly interrupted.

'Calls are flying in from the residents of Willowbrook. Talk of seeing the dead walking the streets. Wait, now neighbouring villages, Melwood and Tilling, are reporting the same sightings. Some are saying arms can be seen busting out of the ground in cemeteries. More to follow in an ever-changing situation,' the radio gets flicked off again.

All the ravens were tapping on the glass. "End it now, before anyone gets hurt," Reynolds was angry, growling even.

Then Detective Reynolds turned to me with a look of horror on his face, but said nothing.

Chapter 25

'Gerald,'

"What?" Detective Reynolds looked like a man wrestling with a problem—one that involved me.

"Well, aside from the dead coming back to life, they've threatened to resurrect your wife and father. Make them endure the pain of death all over again. That or... and I'm quoting here, 'We will bring back what he held dear, put them on display outside the village church surrounded by the living dead and news broadcasters, and have them torn to shreds by hellhounds under the watchful eyes of the world.'"

"W... what? Surely, that's not possible. Is it?" I felt the colour drain from my face as I sank into my seat. A wave of nausea churned in my stomach.

"I get the impression it is. They won't if you surrender yourself with the puzzle piece and the box."

I didn't have any puzzle pieces or the bloody box. I wish I had. It would give us some semblance of bargaining power. Why would supposed men of God want a 'Pandora's box'? And in particular, one that I can't believe I'm even saying this, is a gateway to the Book of the Dead?

Not once had my father mentioned it, nor had my mother, for that matter. Although, what she was keeping from me could fill a book of its own. I'm still a little slow on the uptake with all this weirdness, but I got the impression that Detective Reynolds was holding something back. His voice was riddled with emotion, and not just because of the threat to bring Charlotte and Father back from the dead.

That radio announcement was unsettling, but not what bothered Reynolds. I'm sure in his line of work, it would. This was different.

The ravens were still tapping away. "I don't know what they're on about. That's what drew us to the shop. The owner, Mason, who is now dead, was an expert in weird relics and the occult. We had this photo and wanted to know more," I say, handing the paper with a group picture on one side and a drawing of that coin in four pieces on the other to Reynolds.

Reynolds toyed with it, flicking from one side to the other and back again.

"Who are these people?" Reynolds asks, not taking his eyes off the group image, while the other guy was getting edgy over the haunting ravens.

"From what we could work out, mine and Nathan's immediate bloodlines. Parents and grandparents with the parents of Colin Milton. A friend of Nathan's."

"Hey, that weirdo isn't quite a friend. I just know him enough to ask for help." Nathan cracked his eyelids open enough to interrupt groggily.

"Okay. So that's this lot. What about the fourth cluster?" Reynolds tapped the picture. I didn't recognise them. Nathan didn't seem to when we first found it at the cabin.

Michael turned in his seat, smirking, raising his eyebrows at Reynolds. "Georgie, be gentle, will you? You can see they're fragile with all of this. Stop playing games and spill what you've figured out," Michael says, getting a slight smile from Reynolds in return. These two are quite the characters, and don't get me wrong, I'm glad they're on our side, but I wasn't in the mood for games.

"Okay, okay. Well, did you geniuses stop to do the math? How many bloodlines do you see here?"

"Er... four?" I say, sheepishly.

"Exactly. Why do you think there are pieces on the back of this photo?"

"But, Nathan? He's not going through what I am," I say, now looking closely at Nathan, second-guessing everything we've been through so far. Looking for inconsistencies.

"Well, I'd assume his father is still alive. For the time being, at least. The bigger issue is tracking down the other two bloodlines and seeing what they know about a box and coin pieces. Where's this in the picture?" Reynolds pointed out the cabin.

The tapping on the windshield was louder, a slight crack rippling just above the steering wheel. "I, erm, well, that's Nathan's grandparents' cabin. But shouldn't we, erm, do something about that before we're, er, I don't know, pecked to death or something?" I kept shuffling in my seat. Each peck was deafening, like what had happened at the pub.

"He's right, Georgie. Those demonic-looking fuckers will be in here shitting all over the place. Spray the screen wash or something. I read somewhere it's flammable."

Reynolds pressed the crap out of the stick by the wheel, pissing all over the little demons. They weren't budging. Instead, they began morphing, phasing into each other. Again, spooky yet fascinating. An outline of a man was forming, one of those creepy guys. I looked at the car roof, noticing the sunroof. Then to the armrest by my feet. There's a press-in lighter beside me, a newspaper. I quickly pushed the lighter, ripping several pages and wrapping them in a wad in time for the lighter to pop out.

I jammed the red-hot glowing end on the paper, sparking it to life. "Detective, roof," I pointed to the ceiling. Reynolds pressed a button, allowing a rush of icy wind to whip through. I shielded the flame, chucking my aversion to beady-eyed ravens to one side and stood up through the roof. Meanwhile, Reynolds threw the car into reverse. A finger pressed firmly on the screen wash, smothering the flying rats.

I faced hundreds of bright blue eyes fixed on me. 'If you just let me in, you wouldn't be afraid. Now just let me in.' A chill skated down my back. The darkness chose its moment, and I shuddered, shaking it off. The flame was barely alive. The ravens continued to merge. Soaked, I tossed the bundle down, engulfing the birds in the fire. I dropped back in time for the roof to close. Reynolds floored it, and the fire whipped and swirled. Feathers blistered to the wind. We watched the ravens fade to dust. Screeching tires set the tone as the flames blew out with the eerie.

'Detective Reynolds'

We were in the middle of nowhere, downright spooky. The entire journey I'd focused on the sky, waiting for more of those blue-eyed demons. Towering trees lined a gravel road, a little like the farm where we found Mr Ackerman.

I slowed us down, weary as we neared a really old cabin. Something out of a horror movie. Our headlights painted the weathered porch. No sooner had I clicked the handbrake on than I felt a familiar chill. A rumble through my hackles. Ackerman didn't tell me or Michael just how far back their families were connected to this place. That chill was telling me there was trouble. Or had been.

I was daydreaming, and without thinking, I rolled down my window. Instinct had my senses coming to life. Silence, nothing but the stirring of the woodland nocturnal. An eerie wind rode past us with haunting ease. It was carrying news. Not the good kind. Michael caught the trail, too. A giveaway is always his eyes, the little rumble of yellow. Death was here or had been.

Michael and I exchanged glances. Both on the same page. We had to be careful for the sake of Ackerman and Nathan. Playing it cool, we stepped out casually; I swept the right of the cabin, Michael the left. Then the chill came again. This time, more of an icy shudder from someone stepping on my grave. I knew what was coming next, and they'd been a little less lately. Ghosts, a man and woman in their late fifties, gave me a horrible, sickly feeling.

"Michael, I have a bad feeling before we go in," I whisper, looking into the woods and the never-ending darkness.

"Let me guess, ghosts," Michael hisses quietly.

"How?"

"Your eyes. They went black again."

"Well, I think something bad has happened." No sooner had those words left my mouth than we heard a slight shuffle inside. My claws flew forward. Michael's too. Keeping it from the others wasn't easy now. Ackerman seemed a little too keen on our 'shifting' side.

"Right, you two hang back a minute," I holler to Ackerman and Nathan, who looked puzzled until they saw the claws.

Slowly, we shuffled through the gravel. Michael stepped on the porch, and rotten boards creaked. Louder in the eerie silence. I flashed my red eyes toward the window. Thick grime festered around the pane. Carefully, I trod forward. At first glimpse, I thought it was a ripple. The dirty curtain moved. A draft, perhaps. No lights were on, and if it weren't for my supernatural vision, there'd be nothing but darkness.

"I think there's someone inside," I whisper, catching Michael with his face hovering millimetres from the other window. He was on edge. I noticed a tremor in his left hand. My ears strained to listen. There's a heartbeat. Very faint and slow. Far slower than I'd read from mundane humans. Vermin, possibly. The place was old and dirty enough.

I'd crept up close to the window, holding my breath. Everything was still... my heart pounded between my ears until...

Chapter 26

'Détective Reynolds,'

My attention snapped back to the window at the faintest tap—a nail rapping against the glass. The oval, head-shaped silhouette remained, fingers now elongating from its top, moving up and down as if counting or waving. I stared, perplexed by the silent show unfolding before me. My chest tightened with each breath I held.

The figure moved again, slightly but enough to make me jump at the sound of crunching, accompanied by a gelatinous, squelching noise that set every arm hair on end. I closed my eyes briefly, tilting my head skyward as I rode out the chill coursing through my body. I knew the sound all too well—a sad fact, but true, always in super high-definition thanks to my acute supernatural hearing.

Opening my eyes, I noticed again the absence of the moon against the purple-black sky. The tall trees and dense clouds thankfully obscured the half-lunar light; the full moon was still a few days away. Reluctantly, I looked back down at the window, digesting the realisation that I had just heard flesh and bone being severed. I caught Michael's grimace out of the corner of my eye; his eyes seemed unnaturally bright.

The oval head moved again, hauntingly slow, like a taunt, mocking our hesitation. In Scotland, we charged in, fangs blazing, achieving little—story of my life. Blood trickled down the other side of the window, dropping ominously into a puddle.

Now, the head had been ripped from a body. With a cautious glance to my right, the ghosts remained. Whether they belonged to the unfolding horror, I dared not guess. Instinct whispered the worst—they were Nathan's parents. The head rose higher on the window, fingers gripping a scruff of hair, tossing it around like a macabre ball. We had to act. The grotesque display was more than my stomach could bear.

"Michael, come quick," I called. His footsteps thundered towards me as we charged the door, smashing it against the wall. We landed in a large, musky, open-plan room lined with books. It was dark, but we used our other senses.

Over by the window stood a menacing figure, just a shadow, tall and imposing, silhouetted against the creaking, weathered walls. It let out an evil chuckle before hurling the head at us; the blood spraying wildly. Michael reluctantly caught it. The face belonged to a man in his late fifties, with short, greying hair and a patchy beard, his face contorted in pain and shock.

I had seen one ghost outside, and now my list of supernatural encounters was growing—more consistent than the U.K. weather, which varied from shades of dry, occasional sun, and frequent rain. The latter, I didn't mind; something was soothing about rain pounding against a window. Ghosts, however, were far less comforting. These had been dead for a while.

Either the freak show in front of us took their time, or they expected us to come. Michael placed the head respectfully on a table—it hardly seemed right to toss it aside like something insignificant. The body was slumped against the wall, oozing what blood remained. One might wonder how blood could 'die,' but it can. It carries a musky rot, distinct from its usual coppery scent. Then I saw the woman's corpse in all its grotesque glory.

We had been so distracted by the shadows and the head being thrown at us, that neither of us had looked by the fireplace. Hung by her ankles from a man-made deer antler chandelier was a woman matching the other ghost. She had been stripped to her underwear, drenched in blood. The amount of blood was too overwhelming to determine where the wounds were, though a dark line circling her throat suggested a fatal cut.

While grappling with the scene, I flicked my gaze between the menacing figure by the window and the horrific spectacle hanging near the fireplace. Michael stayed near the door, keen to avoid interruptions to our grim discovery. His mouth fell open, pointing at the lady. "Fuck, her eyes are so cloudy it's fucking spooky," he exclaims with a mix of horror and disgust.

As I turned to the gloom by the window, something dangled from the bony hand of the shadow—a string or something similar. "You're bloody sick," I spit out, grimacing at the sight. A slight clanking sound echoed faintly in the eerie silence.

"Two down, two to go," the figure declares with a sinister chuckle, sending a chill through my blood.

"Two what?" I demand, trying to discern what was on the string. The occasional glint under my U.V. light only revealed metal.

"Oh, you'll see soon enough. It'll probably be too late by then. Since when has that stopped you, Mr Reynolds?" the sinister voice snarls, its cockiness unnerving me. "That's right, I know who you are. And your little friend there. Not to mention your fondness for the full moon."

"Who are you, and what's all this for?" I ask, shifting cautiously closer to the body hung from the chandelier.

"To change history. Stop all the hiding and embrace the power that was so obvious to everyone who came before. All they had to do was open a gate," the figure replies, his voice echoing like a distant storm. We were like chess pieces, each taking turns moving around the board.

"And you think that responsibility falls on you? Where do you fit with the two church guys in suits?" I pressed, eyes darting to Michael, who had slithered inches from the door, blocking any potential escape route. I rocked on my heels, treading carefully to avoid any noisy floorboards. Unfortunately, I wasn't as stealthy as Michael. A creak from underfoot caused a stir in the shadow. The clinking sound came again.

In my head, I plotted a swift leap across the room to the window, possibly to grab the killer, though I was still unsure how dangerous they were. Odd, considering I'm a werewolf. It's the new, over-cautious me—thank Scotland and its gang brigade for that. That mess has a lot to answer for.

"Responsibility? Never. A calling. To finally step out of the shadows after being seen as a fragile weakling or undertaker and be noticed. Everyone else ran for so long when all they had to do was accept fate. I'm going one further. Call it reinventing the wheel," the figure boasted, his confidence knowing no bounds. The wheel? Really?

"What do you mean, 'everyone else'?"

"Bloodlines. And all it would take is to drop a few bodies, ready an army, and find the book. Instead, they hid behind secrets and wore the keys like jewellery. What a sacrilegious joke," he scoffs. It was what I saw in the basement—a Pandora's box needing four pieces of that coin, which Gerald had a drawing of. I heard the clanking once more. They had at least two already. I was next to the dead woman, my eyes blazing over her flesh under U.V. light, catching strange lines. Not tattoos, but something only visible under U.V.—a diagram... No, a map. At least part of one. Did the killer know?

"Have you found the book? What even is it?" I ask, ready to continue, when I heard movement outside. Footsteps trudging through the gravel. Gerald and his friend were approaching. Michael twitched his head, hearing it too. We couldn't let them in, not yet. Not with these being Nathan's parents.

"Soon enough. Right now, I'm enjoying myself. Leading everyone on a merry dance while, bit by bit, little by little, on this 'bloody' journey of discovery, I remove the obstacles that have held back change for centuries. All the while, others are too weak to embrace the darkness and become gods in a new world," he boasted.

I stood there, the sickly taste rising in my throat, déjà vu hitting hard. Another maniac, with a touch of the supernatural, wanted to rule the world or wield more power. It may sound weird, but reflecting on the simplicity of my past encounters—like with Charlie or Ethan, as he was actually known—felt almost nostalgic. Ethan's straightforward murderous rampage had been horrifying, yet he was undeniably human. This wasn't even our home soil; Locke had truly landed us in a mess, yet this village had an eerie charm. The demon within me sensed it, too—a dangerous darkness lurking, waiting to be unveiled. The population was sparse, and they certainly didn't need wannabe gods stirring chaos.

"You know that won't happen, so how about we end this little standoff, and you come down to the station? You can tell us more about your grand ideas there," I suggest, trying to sound more confident than I felt.

"Shame I have to disappoint. It's time darkness took over. After all, this village was made for this. Why do you think it's called 'Weeping Willow'? Not just because it sounds good. No, if only you knew the secrets. But you'll see. From what I gather, it's already begun," the figure retorted, shifting the man's dead body, likely searching for something I had seen on the woman.

The killer checked the flesh; his movements were meticulous. The radio reports of the Walking Dead echoed in my mind as we avoided the main routes to sneak here. I didn't doubt his words.

"Weeping Willow was an interesting choice for a nickname," I admitted, the huge, old tree on the outskirts of the churchyard giving the name some creepy validity.

We needed to take him down, and I was close enough to attempt it, but Michael seemed caught between decisions when a loud thumping at the front door interrupted our stalemate. Nathan and his friend were a dangerous distraction.

This was going to have to be on me. We couldn't afford for Michael to let collateral damage interfere. I felt a surge of supernatural PTSD—if there was such a thing. My senses were going haywire, and I had a dreadful feeling that this figure could be far more dangerous than any vampire. As the demon part of me picked up on the strange vibe, I slinked along the fireplace. The closer I got, the more menacing the killer appeared, the stench of blood almost overpowering—not just from the recent corpses, but splattered across his black cloak.

One final step forward, while the killer appeared distracted, searching the body. That step got his attention. A loud creak from one of the few loose boards I'd found making my hackles jump.

"Tut, tut, tut. I was happy to leave you be for now. Just finish what I came here for, then I'd be gone. You couldn't wait, could you?" Long, bony fingers drifted from the headless corpse, reaching toward his hip and beneath his cloak. I caught a glint amid the red haze—the hilt of a sword with a Templar cross. Its grip was bound in what seemed like leather—a quick inhale confirmed it was flesh, old, mixed with another substance.

One... two... three... four... Almost decay-like bony stems rippled around that grip. I heard the metal blade grate in its sheath as the killer drew the sword upward slowly. Only a few inches, enough to intimidate. For reasons I couldn't quite grasp yet, the killer wasn't looking for a face-off. We weren't on the menu for the time being, which unnerved me even more because it alluded to a grander plan.

I was fixed on the hand, watching for sudden movements. Everything was quiet except my heavy breathing and the thumping of my heart. The killer seemed cornered—I emphasise 'seemed.' Experience tells me he wouldn't allow himself to be trapped without an escape plan. The problem was that I couldn't shake the thought of what he was searching for and whether it was the markings I saw.

The silence was deafening, a fitting saying, until a pain-riddled groan unnervingly shattered the quiet. Michael and I exchanged worried looks. It seemed to be a theme lately. Only my ears had pinpointed exactly where it was coming from, and I was too scared to look—the crusty old table.

"You got that, Georgie?" Michael says with a sheepish smile, his eyes darting to the table as well.

The decapitated head began moving, its soulless grey eyes creaking open and oozing blood. Its jaw jutted with the groans, making the head wobble, gooey entrails squelching with each sway—a horrifying surround sound. The dead were coming back to life.

"Yeah, cheers, Michael," I responded, watching Michael shrug in resignation, as if to say, 'What can I do?'

I jumped, a shiver running through my legs. I felt a tapping on my thigh, a brush of my pocket. At first, I thought it was just the wind, or perhaps a draft from the howling fireplace. Then it happened again. Reluctantly, I glanced down and nearly choked on my saliva in shock. The lady's corpse was writhing in the air, her drooping arm not so droopy now, her hand twitching against my leg.

I scanned her face: vacant, ghostly grey, dead eyes. Her mouth wouldn't stop moving, twitching as if she was trying to speak but had been muted—the lights were on, but nobody was home.

"Fuck, Georgie, look," Michael says, pointing to the corpse near the killer. The headless torso lurched forward, its arms waving for anything tangible to grasp.

I looked at the killer, who slid the sword back into its sheath. His tall, deathly presence pivoted slowly, taking a step backwards. His shielded face swivelled menacingly, allowing me a glimpse of parts of his face. A surge of bile flew through my throat. Taut, bony contours, similar to the two church creeps. His face appeared rotten and dead. Before long, his eyes breezed through the haunting shadow—blood red set amidst endless black.

"And on that note, it's my cue to leave," the killer says, oozing with a confident menace.

"I don't think so, matey boy," Michael retorts, screeching from the door, slamming shut every time Gerald and Nathan tried to enter.

"Come now, detectives, this isn't the dance for us. Soon, though, that I promise. Until then, I have a puzzle to complete. The gates won't open themselves. Good luck with... all of this... well... death. I'll leave more for you to find," the killer taunted, waving at the moving corpses before my brain could engage to get my body moving. A black cloud smothered the floor around the killer's feet, consuming any vacant space, and in the blink of an eye, the killer faded into the cloud and then disappeared up the chimney. He had escaped, leaving us more on the back foot than ever. Gates... Not only did we have to stop more deaths. We had to stop the gates of hell from being opened.

Chapter 27

'Detective Reynolds,'

Michael let the door swing open, and Gerald and Nathan came rushing in, skidding to a stop. Nathan crashed into Gerald's back, who had already caught sight of the carnage. I remained by the fireplace, my thoughts consumed by the chilling theatrics that had just unfolded. The burning issue of Ellena being held somewhere dark and equally terrifying tormented my mind.

Gerald's jaw hung open, his gaze fixed on the head of Nathan's father, who groaned and yawned with all the grace of the undead. Christ, even to think it, 'the undead.' Not so different from vampires, I suppose, minus a brain, fangs, some aversion to sunlight (some of them, at least), and the raging bloodlust. Yeah, it's not much different at all. Gerald turned to me, visibly stunned, now confronting the sight of a dead woman hanging upside down from a chandelier. Her throat slashed. Like the other body parts, she writhed, unable to form words, a shell of a corpse waiting for a soul. Her eyes showed nothing at all.

I noticed a slight glow inward from her right side, that same creepy symbol. No coincidence there; it was symbolic to whoever brought these back. To what end? That's what I kept asking myself. The killer hinted at an army or something similar—could that have been some sadistic truth? With the dead marauding the streets as we hid in a cabin with two more, what would we do with these? We couldn't just cut them down; the head was proof the limbs would stay alive. Nathan looked shell-shocked, a trauma that would undoubtedly worsen. Did he even understand the connections?

I didn't have time or patience for sympathy. There was too much at stake. Michael put an arm over Nathan's shoulder, casually turning the stunned young man to head back out for some fresh air. Gerald didn't move. I was busy trying to get a closer look at the lines on the lady's back.

It was incomplete, half a map or a crude attempt at concealing a secret location. The lines warped and snaked. As I moved closer, avoiding the flailing hands, I noticed a familiar pattern, at least part of one. Then, even weirder, several small crosses appeared, looking similar to Templar crosses but too small to make out. I was distracted by raised voices outside while trying to find some rhyme or reason. Nathan was hysterical and understandably so, but not helpful right now.

"It's the village," I blurt out, finally realising the shape. I caught Gerald's attention.

"Sorry, what?" Gerald says, startled.

"I can see lines on her back and weird crosses. It's the village. Well, part of it and the surrounding area, leading to other parts of the country," I explain, recalling the A-Z I used to give Michael directions on our way to Willowbrook. God, I wished I could turn back time, take the first slip road off the motorway, turn around, and never take this case. That was going through my head, but I would never say it aloud.

"Crosses like the one in the photo, with the goat's head?" Gerald asks, eyebrows raised inquisitively.

"Could be. Hard to tell, really," I reply, looking again. The map outline was correct, yet I couldn't see more. As I drifted in thought, I heard a thump against the wall. It was the father's corpse, flopping around. Then it hit me: what if he had another part of the map? An undead tied up was one thing, but he was all over the place, and I certainly didn't want to get too close to his flailing neck cartilage.

"Do you think Nathan's dad has the same?" Gerald was surprisingly on the ball, considering the nightmare he was in the middle of.

"Possibly, but the way the body moves, we don't want to get caught in its clutches. God knows how strong an undead could be or if it can spread a disease to make others like it," I say, thinking like a normal person for a moment, forgetting I wasn't. While having that little epiphany. What if they could turn the normal living into the dead? Like a vampire bite, its toxin is injected into the bloodstream, all but killing the victim to resurrect as another bloodsucker. Or me turning others into werewolves with a bite. Christ, this supernatural world is crazy.

"Yeah, but aren't you some sort of super beast or something?" Gerald remarked, simplifying it quite a bit.

"Not exactly, but yeah, something along those lines," I reply, noticing more rope by the sofa.

"So, what do we do next? We can't leave them like this," Gerald wondered aloud, echoing my thoughts.

"Grab the rope and help me secure him," I instructed.

"Okay," Gerald responded, weaving past Nathan's mother to grab the rope. He threw one end to me. There was a cushioned armchair near the window line in the left corner. Using the rope, we could wrap around to secure the arms enough for me to get a look at his back. Then, we guided the walking corpse backward to the seat, where we hoped to tie him up, sparing Nathan any further emotional stress. It was all going to plan when we crossed paths on the wrap-around.

The corpse flailed an arm wildly at the wrong time, catching Gerald off guard. Gerald dodged and flipped the rope upwards, attempting to lasso the arm back down. But the corpse suddenly gripped Gerald's hand. Now, I'm used to weird stuff happening to me, all the conversations about my eyes changing different colours. To see it was something different altogether. Gerald froze, not out of fear or anything like that. His body went rigid, and his bloody eyes rolled backward in his head before turning a horrible, spooky grey. Gerald's jaw yanked open before letting loose with a high-pitched scream that had my hackles firing. Reality hit: Gerald had somehow been yanked into a fugue state, and there was nothing I could do. Gerald was on his own...

'Gerald,'

The bloody corpse snatched at my hand just as I thought I had the rope clear to yank down again. I felt a strange static shock, strong, a sudden jolt that had my body spasming. I couldn't stop twitching and convulsing. Then it all went dark. It had happened again, only this time I wasn't dreaming.

I'm sitting in the armchair, hiding in the shadows, waiting. The cabin is dark; only slithers of the night sky through the dirty window help give a view of the front door. I'm incredibly calm until I hear a car pulling up, wheels grinding through gravel before stopping.

My hands—I mean, the Killer's long, bony hands—rap impatiently against the arms of the chair. I can feel my heart speeding up. Shit… the Killer. I can't get used to seeing through the scary fucker's eyes. Grace's murder was hard; at least, I was dreaming. This felt every bit as though it were me. I was living with all the emotions, apprehension, and then impatience. Nathan's parents were excited and even happy. They laughed, making their way from their car; it sounded like a longer walk than ours; they must've parked to the side or around the back.

My left hand drops to my side; I feel the dirty, bloodstained material of the cloak, thick and coarse between my skeletal fingers. A little flick and the cloak is clear of a glinting metal 'butt-end.' A knife, possibly a sword. It feels weighty against my long, muscular, yet lean legs. It's a sword; I look down to see the grip, but it's hard to tell if it's wrapped in leather or flesh. One detail I notice is that even in such a dark, haunting environment, my vision is enhanced. Everything is clearer. I can home in on minute details with ease, and everything is a lighter black with shades of red. My heart is calm. The Killer feels calculated, and his beats jump slightly upon hearing their footsteps draw closer. Then, there was a loud creak of tired old wood; they stepped onto the porch; I now felt excitement—a small adrenaline rush.

'We' slid forward in the chair—yep, I say 'we.' It's easier to explain just how goddam strange this experience is. Simpler, I guess, although, let's get this clear, in no way, shape, or bloody form was I in control of anything. It was the complete sensory, unwilling passenger experience, and I couldn't wait for it to be over, as I knew what was coming next. Keys clunk heavily, unsteadily in the lock. They'd been drinking. Fuck, I could smell it. How is that possible? I'm on the other side of the door, and I can smell it, even a hint of asparagus and tomato soup. Holy hell, this was a new level of weirdness, and that's saying something. Then I wondered if this was how it feels for Detective Reynolds. Whatever that man is, I'm glad he's on our side; seeing him change like he did was scary but impressive. He must have super senses, too, like what I'm experiencing.

Oh god, my mind wanders; what if someone farts? I know, timing, right? I was about to experience the merciless massacre of Nathan's parents, and that's where my head went. Anyway, the lock finally turns, and with a chilling creak, the door yawns open. We don't move, not yet. The parents stumble over the threshold, and the loud creaking of the floor makes my teeth itch. The Killer's heart was pumping now; he couldn't wait to get going. Nathan's mother clumsily thrashes for the light switch to her right, connecting her third attempt... Nothing. They exchange confused looks; the father reaches and taps a nearby wall light, but nothing.

"I'll ch... check the fuse box," he says, slurring his words. The father could barely walk straight, crashing into the back of the sofa and the table.

"That won't do you any good," we say gruffly, with a bone-jarring gravel to the tone.

"Wh... who said that?" the mother says, her voice high-pitched and shaky. Slightly more coherent.

We reach inside the right pocket of the cloak, retrieving a lighter. A snappy flip, then a click sparks a flame. We hover it intimidatingly below our face. I can smell the light fluid strongly. Nathan's parents look on, shocked, mouths wide open. Even with the low light, I could see the colour draining from their faces. Neither looked capable of moving. Easy pickings, and the Killer was thriving because he had them right where he wanted them. Even if they ran, the Killer oozed confidence. It was a most dangerous game, and the Killer revelled in it.

"Wh... which one are you?" the father finally croaks up.

"The only one that matters, the only one willing to embrace what you all run from. To think all you had to do was let it in. The darkness can fulfil everything you wish, yet you squandered the opportunity and power. Even worse, you anger those who gave you this gift."

"It's not a gift. It's a bloody curse that tormented our bloodlines for centuries. And you think it's something to be happy about." The father became aggressive wearily; I could sense the tiredness in his voice. Not from a night out. No, this was a burden. There's more to Nathan's parents; that much is clear. They know more than I was told in the tapes so far or by my mother. Now they're dead. Well, not exactly now, you know what I mean.

"Oh, but it is; the world is fucked and needs a do-over. All these years, all the wars, death, hate and financial crisis. Now, it's time for someone to shake things up." I didn't like the sound of what the Killer was selling, nor were the parents. Their hands wouldn't stop shaking. They knew their fates were sealed. This was one last drunken stand. I hated every moment. Poor Nathan, how do I tell him what happened? I can't, surely?

"Humanity makes mistakes, sure. It doesn't need evil incarnate running the show."

"Oh, it's more than running. It will be hell on earth; I intend on opening all the gates, unleashing a demonic army and seeing how quickly countries want to go to war." The Killer said, unleashing a blood-stirring laugh while ever so slowly we're edging closer to falling off the chair. Now that would be embarrassing for the creepy fucker.

"You can't do that besides if you know anything about the occult and the devil. Demons need vessels. They can't drift aimlessly; they will burn out and die. No, returning to hell, they will be gone." Well, that's new, a little titbit for the group. Sick, but it's something we didn't know.

"That's where you one-dimensional cowards have been failing. You're afraid of destiny and can't see the bigger picture. Did you not know that everybody dropped by the darkness becomes a ready-made vessel in waiting? And believe me, I've been so fucking busy. It's great. Sometimes, all it takes is a wave of a hand to let it happen. You know, I picture it, and things happen. The best part is that the party has begun, and the undead are swarming the streets as we speak."

"Wait. What? You don't know what you've done. You're nothing but a puppet. Don't you understand the curse? It's because our ancestors rebelled and grassed up the locations of the Templars, who were executed without mercy. Suppose the rest of the knights are set free. There'll be no putting the genie back in the bottle, and you will be dispatched as soon as you've served your purpose." Nathan's father was so scared, reaching to grab his wife's hand and pulling her closer. They knew it would be soon but attempted a last go at reasoning in the thin hope of breaking through to the Killer. It wasn't happening; I could feel the Killer ready to move.

"I will be a god beside them. I've been told so. All the power and freedom to do what I want. No longer seen as a weakling, someone only useful for information when they're desperate. Speaking of which, it's time to cough up." For a moment, I was stunned by the need for the information part. Why did that feel familiar? Our hand dropped to the sword, slowly swirling the grip for extra menace.

"No. You can't, we won't. Anyway, did you think there wouldn't be a backup plan? We know there's one of us strong enough to break the curse, break what they're meant to become and will use it to stop your stupid, reckless and suicidal plan." Nathan's mother finally spoke up, leaving me more confused than I was. This vision, or whatever, had to have happened for a reason. No accident, but who could she mean?

"Makes no difference; I believe I have them on a string; in fact, I reckon so far I've led them perfectly on a nightmare trail; soon, they'll be too scared and traumatised to do anything. I can't wait to see his face when I tell him how many pawns have been moved through his life to get to this point. People willing to get their hands dirty for the promise of power. The trouble is, I share the limelight with nobody and have to do a little spring cleaning; call it a tale of two halves. Now give over the piece and tell me where the box is."

"Never." Nathan's father snaps back.

"Persuasion it is."

We dug down our left foot, ground into the floor, and spun on tiptoes; in what felt like a blur, we breezed over the sofa in a single stride, whooshed past the parents, drew the sword, and were back near the chair within seconds. We faced the corner as the room fell silent. Then, 'thud,' a loud crash sounded on the floor. We'd moved too quickly for me to see who it was. The Killer was ecstatic with himself, and then came the loud, guttural scream of pain and anguish... from Nathan's father.

We spun to face an emphatically crying father, who'd dropped to his knees and was now holding his wife's motionless body in his arms, blood spewing waterfall-like. There was no putting a band-aid on that.

"Sooo, about that puzzle piece and the box. Are your memories coming back to you? Feel like sharing now?" The Killer goaded. His laugh seemed to grow more menacing and evil, if that's possible. I can't truly describe how it was deeper, bellowing with a confident snarl. I could smell the intoxicating coppery aroma of blood—lots of it flooding the floor.

"Why... Why... Why, there was no... bloody... need." The father screamed at the top of his lungs, his face going a brighter red, flooded with tears. The Killer just laughed.

"Don't pretend you weren't expecting this. Now, how the rest plays out... Well, that's up to you. We have all night, we're in the middle of nowhere, and there's a million ways to make you scream in agony that I'm happy to explore. So, what's it to be? Easy, quick. Or a stubborn bastard, tortured until the end?" I needed to be sick. I was desperate. I couldn't take being a passenger anymore. It was downright inhumane. What's worse, it's another human being who succumbed to evil and allowed the darkness to take over. Everyone has a bit in them, some more than most. That doesn't mean you have to let it win.

"Here, take it. Useless without the rest, anyway. As for the box, I don't know; I didn't get entrusted with those details. Now, please, let me be. Let me bury my wife, and you'll never see me again." The father ripped a chain from his neck, tossing it to us before pleading through sobs for his life. I wish I could stop this; the whole no-control part of this adventure was awful, gut-wrenching, even.

"Aww, look who's pitiful and weak now, begging. Is that how you think this works? I appreciate the cooperation. I'm afraid it's too little too late. Besides, I may have been born at night, but I wasn't born last night. If I let you go, all you'll do is finally let it in and come after me. I can't be having that now, can I? Don't worry; when it passes on, your son will get the same treatment."

"No, you won't. You'll never find him; we made sure of that." The father allowed himself a brief chuckle, a slender one up on the Killer. I was impressed and confused because Nathan was their son.

"What little old Nathan, that's easy. I hardly call that hiding. Fuck, were you ever good at games in school? That's bloody awful." The Killer said, oozing smugness. I so wanted Nathan's father to turn the tables, let the darkness in and put up a bloody fight.

"You know the saying, don't put all your eggs in one basket? We didn't. Nathan is adopted; we desperately wanted a child and had one, but we knew the dangers. So we had our child safely adopted with a plan, set up for life and instructions for when the time comes. Nathan? Well, we had friends who'd just had a baby. Then one night, somebody broke into their home and murdered the parents while they slept—leaving the baby fast asleep. This happened just as we gave our baby over, so it was sad but perfect timing. We adopted Nathan, and he's none the wiser. So go ahead, do your fucking worst." Nathan's father laughs again, this time a full-on 'I don't give a shit,' laugh. The Killer became enraged, a quick shift of weight and boom, a blur up to and in, impaling the father's heart on the sword. He paused, drifting his head down to the father,

"Looks like I have the last laugh. I can't wait to see the look on their faces. Especially when you become an 'undead'. It looks like death becomes you, old man. Sweat dreams." The Killer slowly withdrew his sword, basking in his murderous mayhem. Until we heard a car, damn super hearing too, still a mile away; it was coming quickly.

We grabbed some old rope off the table and quickly stripped the mother before stringing her up by her ankles to the chandelier. Then we grabbed the father by his hair, dragging him to the window. In no time, we heard voices. It was us, as in Nathan and me, and the detectives. The Killer quickly smooshed the father's face against the wall. And then... I feel a surge of electricity... Before nothing... It's darkness.

Chapter 28

'Détective Reynolds,'

"Hey, wake the hell up. Come on, snap out of it." Nathan's voice cut through the groaning of the 'undead' and Michael's less-than-helpful attempts to assist. Gerald Ackerman began writhing as if on the verge of a seizure.

I dreaded to think what might have instigated that fugue state. His face contorted, jaw twisted, eyes remained fixed. The poor guy seemed to be enduring a lot of pain. Gerald had already mentioned seeing murders through the killer's eyes; my bets were that he was now witnessing the torture of his best friend's parents.

I've had my share of similar experiences, and let me tell you, it's no fun. I'm still reeling emotionally from all the bloodshed in Scotland. Experiencing it while helpless, as if you're committing the atrocities, is going to need a shit-tonne of therapy. I'll tell you a little secret: I have my first session booked for when we return to London. Michael doesn't know, nor does Locke. Only Ellena. She was the one who twisted my arm. I just don't know how to explain or talk about the trauma I've gone through, considering I can't tell them what I am or what we face.

For Gerald, though, it could be a little easier, although I don't know everything about him all too well. I've sensed that he's a good man, but that demonic element is really getting to him. We don't need another loose cannon. Bad enough, I had to carry a pensioner around. (Sorry, Michael). Jokes aside, this is one big cluster fuck of a mess I'm struggling to wrap my head around. Thank God, there are no nematons or telluric currents to worry about. I hope.

"What the hell is going on, matey?" Michael breezes in, the scent of his Armani aftershave softening the bloody stench, only slightly, but enough to quell my watering taste buds. Yeah, I forgot to mention I haven't kicked that craving yet. The longing for the taste was made worse by the vampires. I'm no savage or anything; it's just a bizarre apex predator issue, especially on a full moon, which is two days and sixteen hours away. If my math is right, it's quite possible it's not, but you get the gist. I hope we have Ellena back by then, but I don't want to fight to snatch her in the heat of the moment. Michael still needs to be chained up, so God knows how that will work.

"Honestly, I don't know."

"Well, fuck me sideways. The great Detective Reynolds doesn't know something. Only messing, but he looks like he's being given some hedonistic bondage shit."

"Piss off, Mickey boy, he doesn't have your proclivities or alternate personality."

"Hey, you leave Sharon out of this. That's only on the weekends. Anyway, seriously, what the hell?"

I went to speak, mouth poised and open, while looking at Michael, who'd been flitting his attention between Nathan, still outside, and us. Suddenly, the writhing stopped. Gerald lay flat on the floor; I had to lay him down when he fugues out; otherwise, he would have collapsed. Blood pooled around us and drifted tantalisingly close to Gerald's arm. My werewolf eyes blazed brighter. Everything was still. Nathan hung in the doorway, oozing pain and anger, but suddenly looked concerned for Gerald. All I could hear were our heartbeats thumping almost in unison, except for Gerald. His heart was racing, like a full-on V12 engine going for it.

I didn't say it. I wanted to. Only knew it would amplify the worry, especially for Nathan. I feared Gerald was in trouble. Some existential fugue crisis. Suppose there's such a thing. What does it matter? Not much of anything has a label these days. Except me. Lycanthrope. I mean, who sits around thinking of these things? What would they name the killer? The Grim Reaper's twisted cousin?

We all waited, expecting a sudden shock. Gerald didn't disappoint. He bolted upright, eyes pinged back to normal. "Hell, the gates." Gerald gasps, panting wildly, his head thrashing left to right, looking disoriented. I can imagine why, suddenly yanked back from seeing what would've been blood-riddled trauma. His heart continued rapidly, nearing dangerous levels. Gerald kept attempting speech, strands of saliva jetting free at each try.

"You okay there, matey? You had us a little worried."

"N... no, the gates. The killer wants to open the gates of hell. Demons will possess the dead." Gerald was frantic. Sweat dripped from his brow. I listened closely, especially when his eyes darted to Nathan, and he paused. It appeared Gerald had more to say. Then again, he'd just watched how Nathan's parents' murders went down and thought better of it.

Somehow, I didn't think so. The little wince and brisk judder by his Adam's apple there was something else and bad. Gerald caught me staring; he dropped his head meekly to avoid eye contact. I had to know.

"Did they suffer?" Nathan piped up, surprising me with his question. "That's what happened, right? What you were doing? You saw something. Like how you saw Grace killed. I mean, I get it wasn't nice, just look at them. But did he toy with them?" Nathan continues, looking solemnly toward his mother and father, moving in their 'undead,' way. Tears streamed down his cheeks.

Gerald didn't answer straight away, eyes searching the cabin for an escape he would never take before finally speaking. "It didn't seem so. He asked a few questions before anything, and then... Well, you can see." Gerald's voice was low and soft, hating what he was doing to his friend. A curse of this world, I'm afraid.

"Then why? ... Why the hell did they have to fucking die?" Nathan gushes with pain, his face red, eyes bulging fit to pop out of their sockets while tears rained down. That pain was rapidly turning to anger. I know what comes next. 'Hate.' I've been there, and watching Nathan now, I feel for the guy. Gerald has his battle scars, too. The VHS tapes tell part of the tale.

"In our line of work, matey, it's not nice at all, but bloody often these sick fuckers have no reason. At least none that makes sense to us sane people. Mostly, it's for the thrill or wrong place and wrong time." Michael says, shuffling calmly to Nathan, placing a reassuring hand on Nathan's shoulder.

I looked at Gerald while Michael spoke; he was uncomfortable. None of this was made easy by the 'undead' groaning and rocking in the background. Noticing Nathan's headless father, I still needed to check his back. My hunch was that he had another section of a U.V. map. I couldn't fathom why, though. What was the purpose?

Gerald shook his head, muttering to himself something like, 'For fuck's sake, why me? Why us? All it will cause is pain.' Then he raked his fingers through his hair, the whites of his knuckles beaming as he gripped clumps riding through the stress.

"It's Okay. Breathe. I will listen when you're ready," I say, facing Gerald down, my voice low enough to evade Nathan. Michael looked, though.

"I was him. Bloody him. I felt it all, but I couldn't move. Yet, everything was ramped up; I could hear our car coming from a mile away; yeah, that's right, he heard us well in advance. I could smell everything down to detecting the metallic essence of blood, and my eyesight, well, it was mixed shades of red and black but I could zoom in; everything was high definition. While that all felt good, I didn't like feeling helpless enough to stop it. All he wanted was some box and the puzzle piece." Gerald's voice crackled through waves of emotions. I could smell the salty texture of his brewing tears.

"Was there anything else? Even if it's small, it could be a detail that helps us," I say, carefully prising while cautious that the night was slipping away from us.

"He has two pieces of the coin puzzle. Doesn't have my father's yet, and I don't know where it could be. So that leaves one more. He knows you're on his case; he is letting us follow. We need to be careful of a trap. If the gates get opened, he boasted that he'd already killed quite many people. – Vessels, he called them…" Gerald paused, his eyes darting to the left. I could almost hear the cogs turning. He was grasping at a theory, a detail stuck with him. I get them a lot; call them my 'dots,'—the connections in a case that need to sync up. If any are out of line, it can really mess with your head.

Believe me, inside my head, that's not a pretty place to be. What Gerald is enduring. Being lured into the darkness. Haunted by whispers and having to sit within the killer. That's got to be tough right now. We needed everyone switched on, and Gerald had to open up sooner rather than later. Especially with the thought he was wrestling with.

"Gerald, just whisper, I'll hear," I say, hoping he'd feel at ease.

He looked at Nathan again. "The father boasted that the next in his bloodline was hidden away. Nathan was adopted after his real parents were murdered. Their baby was sent away to be safe, taking Nathan as their own." As Nathan breezed past his father's juddering, yawning head, Gerald paused. Nathan hovered his hands on either side of his cheeks. Nathan continued crying, his face churning with pain. That bombshell didn't need to drop right now.

The problem we had, there were now other elements we couldn't control. Would the killer take those words seriously and go hunting for the true bloodline heir? Or simply look to catch Nathan when he's distracted? Who may or may not begin experiencing the troubles Gerald is?

I left them alone. Nathan's father was pushing against the ropes, almost leaning forward, edging to the left of the chair along the window line. My werewolf eyes blazed. A flick of my claws, and I plucked the edge of his shirt loose and up. He had lines, too. A section connected to what I saw on the mother. More small crosses, a tree, and then three-quarters up his back, a small square with a badly drawn face.

Gripping the back of the chair, I shoved it across the wooden floor, grating loudly—enough to get all eyes on me. The chair was near the writhing mother. Arms were already bound. One hand on the piece by her midriff, the other I ripped a claw through what was tied to the light. Her body dropped quickly. Flipping her on her feet, still writhing against my grip, I had the backs side by side.

"Michael, get your book out and come here," I say, beckoning him to hurry.

"What?"

"Use your other eyes and just bloody draw. These undead are strong." If anything, I'd undersold it a bit. We didn't want to get tangled up with them. They may be empty shells, but what brought them back has given them an upgrade, supposed for the impending opening of gates.

"What the hell? Do you think the killer was looking for this? After all, it's bloody weird, ain't it?"

"Honestly, not even sure he knows it exists. Can only be seen under U.V. anyway."

"Next question, what's it about?"

"A map, I guess. Willowbrook and the surrounding villages, even further afield." Michael was busy sketching quickly, too. When he just stopped. His pen stayed pressed on the paper, causing a small bubble of ink. His expression was one of surprise.

"You ain't going to believe this," Michael says, which was surprising coming from him. He dragged the pen slowly, one line, then the next. Several lines later, I saw what had him startled. They formed a symbol. That star of 'Baphomet,' at least the pattern without the goat's head. Lo-and-behold, in the centre was that tree. They had to be gates with ley lines, but the tree was a mystery. And that square… I had a horrible gut feeling; that's where we needed to go next. Wherever 'there' might be. Once Michael had finished his masterpiece, we secured the mother in another chair. It was the only emotionally painless thing we could do until we discovered a way to enable them to find peace—a way to disconnect from the power that feeds the symbols on their backs.

Nathan, looking detached from reality, was busy wrapping them in quilts, tucking them in as if they'd be resting. The rabid, 'undead' groans gnawing at the air made him flinch now and then, but he still found it in him to stroke his mother's cheeks. He'd placed his father's head securely under an arm. A longing, sorrowful look drenched the air in pain. My heightened senses were reacting to it, and Michael's, too.

I sidestepped the morbid show, treading near the fireplace; I heard a creak—my foot wobbled. I looked down to see one wooden floor strip different from the rest. Lighter and less weathered. My claws were still out, so I jammed one into the thin crevice. There's a slight draft ruffling the hair on my wrist.

Eventually, the board came free, releasing a musky dampness and a shower of dust. A pit of black revealed nothing, so I reached inside. About a foot deep, I brushed a rough canvas bundle. I quickly retrieved it, unfurling the dirty green wrap across the floor. It was my turn to be surprised. An ancient dagger. Its blade was twenty centimetres darker than the typical silver. It had a strange smell to it, too, blood. Not old from being used, but infused with probably Damascus steel. There're symbols or sigils along the blade's edge. Some similar to what we saw at the morgue.

Its handle was a mix of ivory and brown deer antler wrapped in old-looking leather. My hand drifted close; I got a bizarre prickling sensation like static. My finger skimmed the blade; it glowed blood red through the edging. And each symbol was illuminated. Michael and I exchanged looks. Surprise mixed with a little shock. It didn't hurt me, instead more of a belonging or familiarity.

"Bloody hell, Georgie. Oh, look, there's a note," Michaels says, pointing to a small pocket beneath the blade. I slipped the leathery parchment free. It read…

'What you fear is always near. Light leads the way to keep the demons at bay. -The Demon Blade.'

No wonder it glowed; it was reacting to me. To my blood. I'm no genius, but I assumed that Nathan's parents had this in case the worst happened and what the killer was hellbent on doing. Only, I couldn't wield it. Trust is an issue for me, and if this were to be used for the battle ahead, I'd want Michael to wield it. His supernatural speed and strength would work well. The outside bet was Gerald. We know little about him but seem focussed on the task at hand. Michael and I have our shifter abilities to help us. At least the mundanes would be armed. Not that I wanted it to come to that point. Because that would mean we're royally fucked.

"Michael, take it, for now, it's reactive to me." Michael nodded; he'd read what I had. Now we pray. Cling to hope we won't need it. First, find a map to plot what Michael had drawn. How it looked, if all the gates opened at once, releasing all that evil, what's stopping those ley lines from ripping a demonic pathway through the country, tearing apart the earth's crust? There'd be so much death, more than just what demons possess. For reasons I couldn't understand, the tree at the heart of the symbol occupied my mind. How did these evil 'dots' connect?

Chapter 29

'Détective Reynolds,'

It was a war zone. Except the dead were the ones rampaging through the streets. We were driving painstakingly slow, zigzagging through hundreds of undead staggering across the middle of the road and sidewalks. We passed at least two cemeteries, where my stomach churned, watching decomposed bodies punching out of the ground. Some had flesh peeling from their bones, oozing black fluid, while others were a little fresher. None of it will leave me for a while.

I was in awe and terrified by how it had happened. Were those creeps in suits that powerful? In that vision, through the killer's eyes, he taunted Nathan's father about the gates of hell. George described those guys as demonic knights; could they tap into the underworld? Give the dead a little wake-up call? How else is it possible? The more I thought, the more my brain hurt. None of this should be possible, let alone be my reality. Did my father know how bad things could get? Nathan's father mentioned a Plan B. I hoped we would find it at this place marked by a little square on their flesh.

It makes me wish there was a 'do-over' button, rewind to before the accidents, and warn Charlotte and her father to avoid certain things. Maybe ask Father more questions and take an interest. Perhaps I'd be more prepared and, in exchange, warn him about what's coming. I know that's all pie in the sky, and I must start facing what's happening to me. My bloodline is cursed; if I let the darkness in, I'd be the same as the killer. Maybe even do exactly what he is. Was this what I had to come? The reason I keep seeing through his eyes. Or were we connected in some other way?

We neared the end of Wickham Street and exited the village of Billing, which, much like ours, Maplewood, Melwood, and Filton, were drenched in darkness. Not a light in sight. I'd be bold enough to say the power had been cut off on purpose, leaving these villages isolated. This game was getting old. Those fuckers knew what they were doing, creating distractions and vulnerability, letting the undead terrorise normal life.

This leaves me with the question: Can the undead turn humans? I get they can kill, but what if it's a scratch or a bite? Would that do? I still don't know how that happened when Nathan's father grabbed my wrist. It had to be the bloodlines; we're connected like in that photograph. All of them together. It must've been as we swung into another bend; I bumped against the armrest, and a thought came to me. A sickly, stomach-churning thought that I didn't know what to do with.

I'm back at the bar, the two polaroids slide out, and I see that symbol, the moment I'd absentmindedly carved into a coaster moments earlier. The devil star in a circle. Except this was blood on the sidewalk next to my father's body. It couldn't be, not when we'd asked for help. It's not like Nathan was in the right state or frame of mind for me to bother him on this. Besides, it made no sense anyway. Not that it stopped the tired cogs in my brain from turning.

Our wheels rumbled over another cattle grid into an even darker country lane. We continued slowly, not thinking there'd be any traffic, and I heard Gerald mention we could end up mowing down some of the dead if they'd made it this far. I could see the logic.

Nathan was slumped as far into the corner of his seat as possible. His expression was pale and vacant. Not the usual happy-go-lucky friend I was used to. Death does that. I would know. Detective Reynolds knew that, too. He didn't speak but empathised and helped while not pushing Nathan or me. I reckon he's been through some version of hell himself. Damn, that word, 'Hell', to think that's what we were trying to stop, the real thing. The detectives had mapped out that weird yet spooky diagram that was printed on Nathan's parents' backs. Fuck, I haven't even thought about how I'm going to handle that. Do I plead ignorance? What good was the truth right now, anyway?

Headlights beamed against a black-and-white sign as we swept around another bend, with the sore growing on my elbow feeling like the hundredth one we'd taken. 'Kingsley' was three miles out. Behind that sign, the view would otherwise look picturesque, with trees as far as the eyes could see and hilltops kissing a slightly lighter purple of the sky. Peaceful, that's how it looked, moments that have been few. Reminded me of the girls, praying to god they were safe.

Mother didn't tell me where they were headed; safer that way. It's not knowing if they're okay that worries me. I feel they are, though; I can't say why; it's just a flutter in my stomach when I think of them accompanied by that thought. Hoping they were obliviously sleeping while the world went to shit. This part of it, anyway. Mother would undoubtedly have heard the news; she has 'Radio Two' on twenty-four seven. No sooner had I been comforted by that image. Another came flying in like an express train, the father's head.

Before and after shots. The pleading and a final chuckle of defiance. Then, the yawning, chomping, mindless view rocking in a pool of blood on the table.

I'm looking at Nathan, worried as you'd expect. His world had been smooth sailing as far as he knew. He had a wealthy family, and he got to run around Willowbrook or wherever playing private investigator. Everything he knew had imploded, but that was without the truth. The look on his face now was a man in need of alcohol; boy, could I join him? All of this feels like a never-ending nightmare we can't wake from.

We're rolling into 'Kingsley' I'm wondering what's waiting. Nathan is twitching and seems edgy and aggravated. Perhaps his father was lying, hoping to throw the killer off balance. Soon, his father's bloodline will sink its claws in, and all of this dark stuff going on with me will take root. It seems odd he hasn't asked, 'When does this happen to me?'. Does he know something I don't?

I'm looking out the windshield into the darkness, like the black growing within. I see Detective Reynolds' hand change out of the corner of my eye. Dark fur grew thick and bushy; his hand doubled, maybe tripled in size, with his flesh becoming shades of brown. Seeing all this in a surreal, slow motion was scary and remarkable. Then came the claws. Menacingly long, thick, stretching to thin with sharp tips.

They were as black as the night around us and just as daunting. I wouldn't want to be on the wrong end of them. Why? That's what I asked myself. The little I knew of this world, I mean their world. It had to mean something, voluntarily changing like that. It feels weird, with the inclination to respect their job as detectives, but easier when it's less formal. So, I'll call it that way. After all, nothing about this felt 'Law' related. Not no more.

Michael did the same; his hair was lighter, longer, and thinner. No, so werewolf, but more akin to a feral animal. A fox. I'd say. Maybe it's more obvious to obvious, but these moments of the calm before the storm. I was learning as much as I could. Anything to take my mind off what's bothering me the most. Secrets. I don't like them; I was never good at keeping them, and in the last months, I've made it my job, much like Nathan, to uncover the reality behind them.

Look where it got us. George and Michael, though, were bothered right now. I was busy craning my neck and looking for the obvious when something weird happened to me. That bar is uniquely high for me, but this... I was propelled back through the eyes of the killer. Not literally, but those heightened feelings and senses. I could hear heartbeats. That might sound like my stress was getting to me, and it was my hearing. It wasn't. I could hear the double pacing of our supernatural friends in the front.

Nathan's was steady, low, almost a sleeping rhythm; he'd withdrawn far into himself and his dark thoughts. Just like I experienced in that vision, George rolled his window down; I watched his head tilt, inhaling to catch a scent. I hate to be rude, but I'd only seen that with a dog. Thank god these were no dogs. His ears twitched, too. My nose began going, too; I picked up on it all. Overwhelming in all its stinking glory. The toxic diesel spewed from our car, a dampness showing rain coming.

That shudder came again; I drifted back in my seat as I felt it. Death. That's what it was. The long, bony hand of death stroking my grave. Vibrant and deadly, it came in ferocious waves carried on the bitter breeze. Death blended with sulphur was travelling toward us, which had George alert. Michael was slower to it, I noticed. Again, why? I asked myself, why was I experiencing this? I shook off the chill in time for another wave. Chills, that is. This was different; I knew what came next. Seems the precursor to our dark standoff.

A finger-like brush of my cheek, then with the usual cold, melancholy, 'Are you ready, Gerald, ready to finally give in? Embrace it because what's coming? You'll need me. Now...Let...me...in. Let the darkness in and own your bloodline and its burden. No crosses need bearing. A curse doesn't need to mean a curse.'

"I can't; I'm not evil. I've seen evil, and that's not me if I let the darkness in. I become the one killing and looking to turn this world on its head." I whisper but caught George's eyes staring at me in the rearview. Not once have I said yes or embraced it. I came close in the basement, but I didn't. So why am I experiencing what I am? Why did the darkness help me at the farm and the basement, teasing me with all the heightened nonsense?

There's no manual for it, and my father ran from it. Nathan's parents, too. The more I dwelled on that puzzle and startling reality, with that melancholic calling hitching a ride with that ever-present terror bobbing on the tiny boat through my sanity. The river had become a tumultuous sea rife with monsters. All waiting to devour the boat, its passengers become captive to them, beasts.

A world of eat or be eaten. Kill or be killed. To compound my impossible choice in this 'most dangerous game', the boat had lost its steering rudder long ago. Broke loose when I watched Nathan's mother have her jugular cut through and his father, a sword clean through his heart. I guess what I'm saying is that at least two of the four bloodlines have run or attempted to hide from this, and they've ended up dead. Would doing the opposite have the same outcome? That's not me deciding to give in, more 'devil's advocate' playing blackjack with a losing hand, deciding whether to stick or twist.

I'm sure this all seems like the rambling of a man who's finally lost his mind, having skirted close for a while. Perhaps that's why the call came at this moment, when morale was low, heading into the unknown, surrounded by the 'undead' staggering through the streets, dripping their decomposing flesh all over the place.

'Why such one-dimensional thinking? If a mundane is inherently evil, it is in their nature that when the opportunity is within their grasp, they will become evil. If a mundane is inherently good, trod a righteous path all of their life, even when opportunities have presented themselves so willingly and that mundane still walks that righteous path. It will be their nature to be good.'

"So, what are you saying?" I say. It was probably my tired brain. I thought I understood the basics and the point, but then I kept looking for hidden meanings. When is evil ever truthful? I asked myself? Nathan continued twitching. I still heard his ultra-calm heart while Michael and George sounded as though readying for that deathly sulphur stench.

'If a mundane is naturally good, like yourself. Look at this crusade for the truth you've been on. I've watched it all; I hear your thoughts, and I know your doubts. I also tantalisingly know your potential. A mundane in pursuit of good. So, why would you think evil would be your path?'

Was I being reeled in? While something approached that I sensed was nothing good, the darkness whispered a sales pitch that made me think. "Are you implying that just because I embrace the darkness, that sounds very much hauntingly evil? I mean, the clue in the word 'darkness' speaks volumes. It doesn't mean I will become some crazed killer like the other guy. I mean, what the hell is he?"

'Finally, the penny drops. I knew mundanes were sometimes slow, but with you, I had hope. As for him, he has become one of the fallen knights; there are many other names or titles, but those like him have fallen from the cause, much like the two that hold your detective friend's girl. They were The Knights Templar at one point, until they became Baphomet chosen or the Eternal vigil because at anyone time there's two Knights watching over, creating chaos and evil in the world.-' I butted in as the last sentence hit me hard.

"What? What do you mean, watching over and creating chaos?" I say, forming a picture that these knights have been the spark for many a conflict that blights our world.

'You see, there's always been that hope, that quest to resurrect all the Knights slain centuries ago when their allegiance to Baphomet was leaked to the King of France. Who ordered them eradicated? Including their General Francois, Louis Philip the second. As evil as they come before embracing the devil. One day, the required relics would surface, and one day, a bloodline would give in to the power. Or they will go mad as so many over the years have. Now, there's a hungry killer playing puppet. While thinking he's playing chess. Mostly, in your life, he has. Suppose those Templars are broken out of hell with the demons? There will be an unstoppable army of undead led by some of the fiercest soldiers ever to walk your earth. To answer your question, the Knights need the right environment; they feed off it. You mundanes are easy to manipulate, and by them creating a world ripe with evil, it's like a drug. A highly intoxicating drug that fuels them.' I was stunned into silence. Although I had been whispering, I knew George was listening.

"What would that make me?" I ask. They say curiosity killed the cat. Well, I say better the devil, you know. Corny, right?

'That's one of life's mysteries, I told you; if you let me in, you will experience all the power you can imagine. But... that doesn't mean you have to fall, too. Could well be a true Knights Templar, one to restore faith and order.'

"But in the beginning, you made it seem you wanted me to kill and do bad. What happened?" I ask, thinking back to when the haunting began.

'What's one of those four-legged beasts in the wild? Oh, a LEOPARD. That's right. A leopard has spots. Those spots cannot change—you mundanes and your humanity, those inclinations, mostly to do bad. So, in general terms, you are all leopards, too. I thrived off your anger, pain, and hatred. So, to me, you were just another leopard with power within reach. There is no use in trying to make spots or stripes. Since then, I've watched and listened as you've strived against the pain and adversity. You can be what you want to be. Until then, I would be on guard; something is coming.'

The whispers stopped abruptly, and the chill was gone, but I could still feel that presence this time. I say darkness because it feels that way. If what it alluded to was true, I had hope, and the girls were swaying me. I could never forgive myself if it went wrong, and they came to harm. The reality is, I've been a kite dancing in a hurricane, and lighting was stoking the skies with all its terrifying, strobing might.

Those heightened senses had stayed, too; the nearer we got to Kingsley, the death felt. My ears twitched, which was odd. Getting a taste of what the detectives go through. For good reason, though.

'BOOM, BOOM, BOOM,'

My hand tingled; I looked, and I could see real close as the tiny black hairs ruffled to attention, like wind through fields of straw or a forest of trees. Tiny pimples popped across my flesh beneath; My heart was flying, causing my throat to tighten, and Fear was taking over to the tune of a beating drum. That's how loud and what I heard first before each one thinned out. They were wings flapping. Hundreds of them building to a deafening crescendo. Much like the layby, I saw the piercing blue next. It was bloody scary. A horizon was becoming a nightmare. Except for Nathan, who'd stayed oblivious, we all knew what was coming without uttering a word. More importantly, how? Were they following from afar, or did they know much more about this game than we realised?

With everything the darkness preached, I couldn't help but feel disheartened. The lengths to which these evil bastards go to. Manipulating us mundanes, as we're called. Stirring the pot, creating a world ready for them to enjoy. Sure, there's a lot of evil to go around in various forms. What scared me more was letting loose all those Templars and their general. Nowhere would be the same.

George rolls the car to a stop at least two hundred feet from the road sign 'Welcome to Kingsley'. The horde of deathly ravens swooped toward them, their beady eyes glowing brightly before they seamlessly moved, becoming one of those creepy knights. His face rippled in the moonlight, looking more like a walking corpse. Patches of flesh had long since decayed, allowing his skull bone to show through. I could feel the hatred dripping from him. Stepping slowly, the heavy heels of his shiny shoes clapping against the empty road, echoing a sinister tune.

"What are we doing, Georgie?" Michael says, glancing anxiously toward his friend.

"Fucked if I know. How did they even find us?" George says, thinking like I had while checking on us in the rearview.

'We can end this now. Hand him over with the puzzle piece and the box. He joins us and you lot can go on your merry way. The lovely Ellena included.' The creep spoke as though he were sitting with us in the car; his voice sounded that close. I shuddered again, shaking through the chill. Everything about this morbid Freakshow curdles my blood. I had no intention of going anywhere and hoped George was on the same page.

"I trust you can hear me, so hear this. No way in 'hell'." George says. I couldn't resist a chuckle—a poignant choice of words.

"Ooh, nice use of the word Georgie." Michael quips.

"Why, thank you. I thought you'd approve."

'You think you're so clever? This ends one way, with your death, and the same goes for everyone around you.' It may have been a trick of the moonlight or the car headlights capturing in front of us: the street sign, the scenic view of endless trees, and the creepy Knight. I could've sworn his eyes changed; pearlescent black became blood red.

"Hey guys, not to rush you or anything? But do you have a plan for dealing with something centuries hellbent on killing us?" I say, noticing George look at Michael as they exchanged smirks, as if sharing some inside joke I wasn't a part of.

"Well, we've had a little experience with old things. Michael experiences it every Saturday night down the YMCA chatting up the elderly."

"Hey, you dick. That was one night I volunteered to help run the bar for a friend." Michael says, laughing. I'm looking at these two, so calm and cracking jokes in the face of all this danger. How do they do it? It must be bloody hard on their families. The Knight widened his stance, braced to charge at us; what he thought he would achieve was anyone's guess. His right foot dug into the gravel, twisted, and he powered forward.

"Georgie... erm Georgie. In case you missed it, there's a scary-looking knight charging at us. Do something." Michael says, eyes raised, waiting for an answer.

George jammed the car into gear, and with the handbrake on, he throttled the life out of the engine. The car was rocking and vibrating; I shuffled backwards in my seat, feeling the rumbles beneath me; loud wheel spinning filled the air. His claws gripped the wheel tightly. "Fuck it," George says, "Let's go through him." Michael frantically grabbed at his seatbelt, checking he was strapped in. Still, Nathan was oblivious. The three-litre engine rocked the chassis some more. I toyed with being brave. There's nothing brave about crashing through a windshield if everything goes wrong.

I'm fighting against the tension to the best of my ability. My eyes dart to the front. The Knight is picking up speed, his coat flails wide, his deathly hand breezes to the butt of a sword. My eyes flick to my belt as I struggle, George unleashes the handbrake and hi BMW beast. The chassis twists and turns against the torque. Burnt rubber teases my senses. My eyes dart to the front again. We're flying, the Knight is too.

Finally, the tension releases, and I yank the belt into its lock. I'm looking on in fear and awe that this creepy Knight was taking on a car now doing fifty miles per hour. Bizarrely, the Knight seemed just as fast. Then... everything slowed. Or looked that way. The front of our car connects painfully with the Knight as he draws his sword. A loud banshee shriek rocks the air; thunder claps in the sky. What happened next scared the living daylights out of me? As we plough into the Knight, he crumbles, not into ravens, but more like decayed pieces of his body. Each part phases ghostly through our vehicle.

His horrifying face was full, gritted teeth, blood-red eyes, his sword comes through as the rest of his body was still in pieces. Then I feel it. The darkness rapidly forms a barrier around me, all those gruesome body parts ricochet off me. The sword whooshes past, and the scary part is that the Knight smiles as he blazes through, phasing through the rear of our vehicle. George slams on the brakes, screeching tires roar in the night, and the chassis sways side to side until we stop. My hands immediately pat over my body, checking for wounds while struggling to rationalise what had just happened. There's nothing. The detectives swivel in theirs, looking shocked; I look out the rear; the Knight was now fully formed, sliding his sword away. Everything went silent.

'Blood…'

I could smell blood—and death and sulphur. But the blood was closer, a lot closer.

"Cuh…Cuh." What just happened, Gerald, I hear beside me. I turned slowly, realising where the blood was coming from. Nathan had a puncture wound in his stomach, his white t-shirt swelling with red and then black. I didn't understand. Judging by their faces, the detectives didn't either. There was another smell, poison I assumed. It smelled rancidly toxic.

'Your friend has twenty-four hours before the poison reaches his heart. Find the box and surrender yourself to the puzzle piece and the box, and we'll let your friend live. You have my word as a knight.'

"What about your murdering friend?"

'That fool has another quest to fulfil. Don't worry; we'll allow you to uncover who they are. It's only fair to know who has tormented your family, after all. Tik Tok.' Before I got to respond, the Knight crumbled into the blanket of Ravens filling the sky. I'm staring at Nathan, watching black track lines spread through his skin as his wound wreaked of the toxin. Twenty-four hours, that's all we had to decide the world's fate. What do I do?

Chapter 30

'Gerald,'

When does this end? The same darkness blanketed the remaining road into Kingsley. I felt it growing, drifting in on all sides, choking out our headlights and hope. The air was thick with the stench of death and decay that wouldn't leave us. The Knight had left a greater imprint in our vehicle than Nathan's wound; black scorching marred the cream roof lining.

At first, all I saw were haphazard strips of burnt black. My eyes seemed to re-focus without trying to map the pattern and shape. It was the symbol of 'Baphomet,' ominously hanging over us. Pain-filled, yawning echoes of the undead still haunted the back of my mind, matching those carried on the chilly breeze from behind us. Nathan's condition was rapidly deteriorating, the poison spreading through his veins like wildfire. Those black tracks were thicker already. I couldn't let him die. Not here. Not now. He'd already suffered so much in a short amount of time—all because I asked him for help. That's where I was laying the blame squarely on my shoulders.

Michael and George were tense, their supernatural senses heightened to a razor's edge, and their claws stayed on display as we rolled from the asphalt of the country lane over the grilled metal of a cattle grid, squealing and creaking under our weight before churning through the gravel of a ghost town. Thick dust bucked and sprayed through the air; I was still getting used to the heightened sense of smell, wondering how long it would last. Every scent was vibrant and equally grotesque because of where we were.

Kingsley was eerie; the quiet was shattered by a flutter of wings that made me jump, looking around, fearing the Knight's sudden return for round two. Ahead, twenty feet to our left, set amongst what would've been thick green bushes once—the kind with sharp stabbing ends fortified like a wall, but now dead, with decaying flakes skittled to the winds. A looming tree, its fierce branched arms just as dead as the village, carried two bright blue eyes. We still had company.

"We need to get Nathan some help," I say, my voice strained with urgency. "We can't let him die. We need a bloody plan."

George nodded, his face grim. "We need to see what was so important about this place that it would be marked on Nathan's father's back. The Knight wasn't bluffing about the poison. It smells so strong."

Michael was already on it, looking at the map and tracing a finger through the darkened lanes. "There's an old church not too far into this place; maybe that's what that tiny cross meant in the square," he says. If there's any place to start, this could be as good as any. The Templars often used churches to hide their treasures, secret vaults, and whatnot.

"Look at you, the history buff," George quips, a little surprised.

"Well, you had a book just sitting there, and I was bored waiting while you were on the phone, so I got curious," Michael says, a little sheepishly.

The car continued through the deserted road; the surrounding landscape was bleak, full of shadows and shapes. The tension between us was palpable, each lost in our thoughts. I glanced back at Nathan, his breathing shallow, his skin pale. The black veins creeping across his body were a horrifying reminder of the ticking clock.

"Hang in there, Nathan," I whisper. "We're going to save you."

Further into the mouth of Kingsley, the outlines of the old church came into view, its gothic spires piercing the night sky. The place had an ominous aura.

We parked on a side road, which concealed our vehicle. My attention was being pulled away, and I was nervous about the 'stray' watching us. Its creepy head twitched left to right. The chill was cutting as we exited the car, jarring. The occasional rustle of leaves and the distant caw of that raven had us all on edge. Nathan hung from my shoulder, sobbing with pain. It was now I hated the heightened sense of smell I'd gained. Death—that's all I could inhale, seeping from his pores. So tangible I could taste it. Adopted or not, he didn't deserve this, all because of a bloodline curse. None of us did.

"Stay close," George mutters, his claws still out, his face part wolf, eyes scanning the darkness. We didn't know what we were walking into.

We moved as a unit, and every step was measured carefully. The church doors creaked open, echoing through the stillness, and we slipped inside, our flashlights cutting through the gloom. The interior was just as ominous as the exterior, filled with shadows that seemed to move and writhe. Panic sweat pooled around my brow, and all I could hear in my head were Father and Charlotte, their shadow versions that had me strangling Nathan. Which reminds me, why, if I could use the darkness for good, did it make me do that?

Currently, there are more cons than pros, and I don't like it. Details like that had me thinking it's all a ploy. Evil is coming at me from both sides. You know, good cop, bad cop. Something I'm sure Michael and George are well-versed in. And I reckon Michael is the mean bastard. Not that I don't think George has it in him. He's a werewolf, for Christ's sake. But he is full of empathy, as though he's trodden these painful paths many times before.

Straight in front were dusty pews, a cracked altar, and ancient stone walls. I couldn't shake the feeling we were being watched besides the raven. Hairs on the neck jumped on end. Every creak and groan of the old building punctured my spine.

"Look for anything out of the ordinary," Michael says, his voice calm. "Symbols, hidden compartments, anything that could lead us to the box or the puzzle piece."

"We don't know if this is the right place, and it could be a waste of time. Time, Nathan doesn't have," I say, coming across as flippant, but my friend was dying.

"AARRGGHHH." Nathan cries out loud and torturous.

"Georgie, come on, help him."

"How?"

"You know how, like you did for me." There was silence, and George looked troubled. "Come on, George, he's struggling. You can do it. George… George? Bloody hell, George, stop ignoring."

"QUIETTTTTT." Suddenly, George shouts a phonically loud 'Quiet' that rocked around the church. We were stunned to a standstill. What was more shocking was Michael's behaviour. He responded out of instinct, cowering on the spot. His eyes glowed bright yellow, and George's an even brighter red.

Eventually, Michael shook it off and stood upright. "Michael, it's not that I don't want to. I'm scared too. Like many things since Scotland, I don't know what is too far anymore," George says, moving to Michael's side.

Michael took George's arm and placed it on Nathan's. "You have a big heart but are so bloody stupid. I would never let it go too far, especially with that venom. The boy is struggling. Just try," Michael says, speaking ever so softly he'd broken through.

George's eyes changed, becoming a blend of black and red; his fangs seemed bolder, and then it happened. I was stunned. That black tracking began reversing, travelling down Nathan's arm and up George's like little black bubbles under his flesh, travelling up. Nathan was improving, seeming to be in less pain and less pale. George was feeling it all. Sweat was pouring from him, his skin, greying, and he looked in trouble, gasping for air. Michael lunged at his arm, yanking him free. Both landed in a heap on the hard grey stone floor. George was returning to normal, and Nathan seemed more comfortable... for now.

"Georgie, now's not the time for the wolf to go asleep," Michael says, pulling himself up. Nathan was breathing easier, but I was worried about how long it would last. I was grateful, of course. Michael got my attention with his comment, and he was right. George had fully turned normal.

George went to stand; his legs wobbled, and a foot slipped across the dusty floor. I heard a resounding 'clap' as he dropped, hands slapping against stone, trying to support himself. He was weak, really weak. I could hear his heart; it was going full tilt, and more worrying was the breathing. It was raspy, congested, almost filled with fluid, exactly like Nathan had been moments before.

"Georgie, are you okay?" Michael says, reaching to grab George's arm and help him up. I looked on, worried. I questioned how wise that move was. Michael shouldn't have pushed if George didn't feel right. I appreciated helping Nathan, but now we're down a weapon to help us.

With Nathan supporting more of his weight on his fight but still hanging around me, I walked over and saw if I could do anything. Not that I knew how this stuff worked and the supernatural. I was useless, but it's the natural thing to do, right? If I thought it would help or that George could do it, I'd offer to take the poison from George, or he could drain some of my energy.

"Micky, I'm fucked. I don't know what that poison is, but I'm tapping against the red, and it feels like I'm getting weaker," George says, trying to hoist up with the help of Michael, but he couldn't stand. His legs slid from beneath him.

We'd left the church doors open, and I could see right out to the tree, and the raven was still there, watching. Wind howled around us, hissing through the gaps in dilapidated timbers and boarded windows. Paranoia was taking root in my mind, knowing we were weaker by two now and stranded somewhere we didn't know, looking for things we didn't know where to start. Every rustle, creak, or rattle of wind chimes hanging at a house across the way had me jumpy. I could feel the goosebumps popping up one by one. Every second I looked into the shadows, I expected them to come alive. My heart bounced against my chest bone; I could see the flesh thrust out each time. Exaggerating, of course, but that's how it seemed.

Michael raked his claws anxiously through his hair; George was lying on the floor, propped up by his elbows. I felt a tickle at the back of my neck. Not from the darkness, a sixth sense overreacting, again thinking we were being watched. I was staring so hard into the darkened corner of the church that I swore I saw movement. Not the shadow, a slight glint of an eye or something. I don't know. Nothing felt right about being here; was it a trap? I asked myself. Then why would Nathan's father have it on his flesh? I countered. Then it happened again. More spookily exaggerated this time, like the outline of a person. I felt on the verge of freaking out when Michael piped up.

"WWED," Michael says aloud. George looked at him, screwing his face up, confused. "What?"

"What would Ellena do if she were here?"

George chuckles, his grey face looking sickly to overshadow his brief amusement. "She'd say, get the hell up, Wolfie, you got shit to do and people to save."

Michael grabbed a black wallet from his pocket. "She'd then give you this, her version of-"

George butted in. "A supernatural first aid kit." He caught a sweet or something. Seriously, candy? Right now? I selfishly grumbled. He smirked, looking at me and chewing away. My jaw dropped. It had to be steroids because his eyes blazed brighter than I'd seen them before. The wolf was back. I got to see his features change—another slow-motion moment. I had to savour something so awesome yet freaky. All the black track marks faded, and his claws came like a flick knife as they scraped through stone, levering himself up.

No one else would believe me if I told them. Okay, perhaps now, but pre-undead roaming around the village, I'd be sent straight to the looney bin. With George shaking off the last of the poison, he strolled over to me. My eyes closed, and I prayed he didn't come to have a go at me over the selfish comment he clearly heard. The shout and Michael cowering as he did, sod that for a laugh.

"It's okay, you weren't to know," George says, smiling, but looking where Michael was and whispering. "But we must talk."

"What for?" He had me confused.

"I can sense it, you know." I looked at him blankly, thinking, 'he must've bumped his head' before I forced a wry smile.

"What? My fear? Is it surprising?" I say, trying to bluff. I have never been good at cards. Ask Nathan.

"It's okay. You're a good person, and I don't think you have it in you to go bad." Now I was amazed, lost for words. For real. I went to speak, but nothing came. Mind reading another werewolf superpower? If so, I wanted in. A damn sight better than a crazed killer.

I'm really confused now. There's a demon in me? I thought, checking my backside.

"What?"

"That darkness you're fighting against. It's already taking root, infesting within you. It's sharpening your senses. I know the signs, such as head tilts and ear twitches. It began in the car. I think it could work for us." George was amazing; he didn't judge. He's just been through the wringer; He was trying to put me at ease. Didn't make me less confused though. Yeah, I realised my senses and figured it was a little 'suckup' trial run. But amalgamating with me, and it's a demon. Maybe the term 'darkness' should've been a giveaway. Hearing it sounded evil.

"How? How do you know the joining and demon?" I say. It probably sounded stupid, but I was distracted. There was another ripple, more than one outline.

"Because I'm part demon, too. And I'm not evil. So, maybe be prepared to embrace it in desperate times. I think it might surprise you. Now let's fucking keep moving. I believe we have company." George says, his eyes darting to the left corner. Where I saw the ripples, just under some pillars and crumbled walkway above. At least I wasn't seeing things.

"I thought I saw a couple of ripples in the shadows, but then thought it was me being paranoid."

"You need to trust your instincts. Whether you like it, you will join us in the supernatural. You'll have many changes and weird experiences. Don't worry; I will help where I can. As you can see, we're a bunch of misfits. We have three shapeshifters, a druid and maybe a witch, as part of our unit in London. So, you're not alone." I was blown away; what I was experiencing didn't seem so strange now. Then I caught a look at Nathan, knowing he wasn't a bloodline, and now he's dying. We're bragging about special skills and none of that... Nothing we have... Nothing... fuck, I can't even get the words. Right, I go again. There's nothing in all this fantastical world or abilities from shapeshifters and would-be demons which could save my friend if we're too late.

"What about Nathan? What if we run out of time? He doesn't deserve this, especially with what we know. Even that could shatter his world." I say; Nathan grumbled, stretched a little. I hoped he didn't hear. Michael joined us, slowly scouting the nearby walkway. My guess is that he was stalling. Sure as hell, if George can hear, he can, which was kind of nice, not to pile on the pressure. Meanwhile, the wind whistled through with haunting intent, hellbent on shaking us... Okay, me up. Michael looked at George, made a biting motion with his fangs, and pointed to himself. George raised his eyebrows as if to say, 'Oh, yeah, really?'

Much like cards, I'm crap at charades, but that didn't need interpreting. Suppose I've watched enough horror movies with werewolves. Usually, a bite or claws deep can make another. I think. What Michael imitated was a bite, whether he would do it or George bit him. I'm not sure. Maybe there's a backup plan after all.

Michael kept rocking his head around, bothered. He was sensing company, too. The how and why were details to bother us, but in the dead of night, carrying one wounded and Georgie barely fighting fit again as we traipse through this rundown church looking for a supernatural needle in a holy haystack.

"Michael, guard behind; I'll flank Gerald and Nathan. For all we know, it could be the 'homeless', but the read is off." George says, back to his werewolf form, head twisting anxiously. The initial boost Nathan had was already wearing off. I could feel him leaning on me more and more as we shuffled across the uneven stone. I'm looking, searching every crevice for something, without knowing what to look for. A bit backwards, right? Grey flagstones rested beneath our feet, at least a hundred years old. I was surprised they were still there. The type of things usually stripped for value. Then again, we don't know why the village is a ghost town.

It seemed a little purposeful, a rundown place, too dark and scary looking for anyone to go snooping. Maybe there is something for us to find here after all. Not necessarily this church, but somewhere in this god-forsaken place. If only Nathan were alert, with all his investigating, he could've come across a detail that seemed nothing. But now, it could be important. Dust was settled everywhere I looked, and there were no signs of anything major being disturbed by Nathan's parents or anyone they saw fit to help.

We're moving; the shadows hold the detectives' attention. Those ripples continued. Each time they moved, it appeared they were circling behind us toward the doors. All the surrounding architecture looked amazing, run down and left to rot, but I'm sure it was breathtaking in its heyday. Admiring glimpses with each pillar, we passed. I'm no architect, but these seemed wider than usual. I counted four on either side, a few holding nothing. One stood out. Aside from looking cleaner, it had a symbol partly carved, partly screwed in place. It's the 'Templar' cross. The original history book version. Except it was upside down.

I'm focusing as hard as possible, feeling whatever's in the shadows, waiting to make their move. We were more surprised that it was taking so long. They could've had a go while George was down. It was all too confusing. Nathan grew heavier by the minute. These track marks had grown again; they were thicker now. 'Inky' veins pulsated in the gloom. Even the supernatural didn't help him.

An icy breeze hissed towards me the closer I got; I checked the floor around the base, but nothing out of the ordinary. Thick with dust, like the rest of the stone floor. That 'hissing' continued. I was acting like a 'mundane' forgetting what the darkness was doing to me and my senses. My vision. I focused like a child playing with new toys. A faint line caught my eye; it rose from the ground, six feet up the pillar, curving the pillar before back down to the floor again. A hunch was forming, and I wasn't sure how I felt about it. I'd found either a concealed cupboard or a false door leading somewhere. The 'Cross' pointed down. It had to be a hint, yet as it's screwed in, I had a theory the cross needed turning. 'Righting' again. I was too drawn to figure out the logistics when a sudden 'whoosh' past made me jump.

That cursed raven flew through, landing on a rather damaged 'Jesus on a cross'. Its creepy blue eyes blazing on us. Every twitch gave me chills. I must look; the blue looks brighter, pulsating with an allure that scares me, yet I must stare it out. I'm not afraid... I'm not afraid. Those bastards can't get to me; there's nothing they can do that will sway or get under my skin. Look at it: nothing but a flying rat. Those eyes, though. I bet there are all manner of secrets behind them, the reasons for all this death and bloodshed. I can't look away... I feel so cold... So cold...

'Hush little baby, don't say a word. Mama's gonna buy you a mockingbird.'

"Charlotte?"

'And if that mockingbird don't sing. Mama's gonna buy you a diamond ring.'

"Charlotte? Is that you?"

'And if that diamond ring turns brass. Mama's gonna buy you a looking glass.'

"It can't be you. I know it can't be. Surely?"

'And if that looking glass gets broke. Mama's gonna buy you a billy goat.'

"What's going on? Why's this happening? Those blue eyes, it's you, isn't it? Where is everybody? Where's this fog come from?"

'And if that billy goat doesn't pull. Mama's gonna buy you a cart and bull.'

"I don't understand. This differs from last time, and the shadows are different. What the hell is going on? Christ, everything feels... so... heavy... Look at those blue eyes."

'And if that box and piece don't show. Mama's gonna make Nathan go.'

"What? That... that's ... not... how... how it goes."

'And if you just wanna give in. Mama's gonna show you what you win. Our new life will just begin.'

I can't see anything through the thick fog. It's freezing, every hair on my body is on end, but I can't keep my eyes open... Oh, those haunting blue eyes, are they doing this to me? I... I... I can't breathe, my throat feels tight. 'cuh... cuh' There's movement through the fog, several shadows moving, help... somebody help. I can't, I can't... Keep your eyes open...

"Hey, it's time to wake up now."

"Urgh, just five more minutes. It's too cosy. And you're so warm I don't want to move." My eyes reluctantly opened; I was so groggy. Wow, this hangover is kicking my arse.

"Well, you need to get up now, silly. We have the rest of our lives for cuddles, but the girls need to get to your mother's and get to work."

"Charlotte?"

"Of course it's me; who else would it be? Blimey, you and Nathan were hitting the bottle last night, weren't you?"

"I... I guess yeah," I say; my head was pounding, daylight beamed through the curtains, and I didn't want to move. Charlotte was so warm and soothing. Her smile made my heart pound harder. Yet, something was bothering me. A weird sensation... I didn't belong, but I can't remember why or what I did last night, for that matter. A sudden chill swept through everything felt close, too close. My neck hair bristled with a shiver. Out of nowhere, I was irrefutably consumed by fear. Why?

Chapter 31

'Gerald,'

Her hand felt warm, gently stroking my cheek. This moment was bliss, a sensation that had been missing for a lifetime. I couldn't even recall the soothing touch of loving fingertips drifting through my stubble. Yet, every glance, every admiring, lust-filled gaze of Charlotte's milky pale face and long blonde hair felt off. Why couldn't I remember yesterday, the day before, or even the day before that? Hangovers don't wipe out days, let alone weeks of memories, especially good ones.

The sound of the twins babbling warmed my heart, but it didn't shake loose any details I was desperate to recall. I lay in bed, not wanting to leave, ever. Something felt wrong, no matter how nice the moment. A nagging feeling told me I was supposed to be elsewhere.

"Charlotte, this might sound weird, but what did I do yesterday?" I ask, locking onto her beautiful green eyes.

"What do you mean, silly? You were with us; we had a great day," Charlotte replies, smiling.

"But what did we do? Exactly?"

"What do you mean, silly? You were with us; we had a great day." Charlotte repeated herself, and it seemed odd.

"I know that, but what things did we do?" I probed, hoping something would come to me. Charlotte twitched, tilting her head without saying a word. I waited, a slight chill hissing through the room. I pulled the covers up tight to shield myself.

"Every day is a great day with us; you know that," Charlotte finally spoke, but it was hardly convincing. Every word fed my doubts. I wanted this, but it didn't feel like mine.

"Of course it is, but I can't remember anything. So, I kind of need your help to fill in the blanks." Charlotte stared, her eyes tunnelling into my soul. Then something strange happened. Blood trickled from the corner of her right eye, blazing a scary streak down her perfect skin. The chill grew, cutting through the sheets.

"Honey, your eye is bleeding. Are you okay?" I ask, but Charlotte stayed still. Each whip of cold air felt stronger, and the smell of something rancid—death—filled the room. I didn't belong here, but I couldn't recall where.

"Every day is a great day. That's how it would've been." I shifted up against the headboard. Charlotte sat upright, her face becoming serious. I was unnerved and confused. Death and now sulphur grew stronger by the minute.

"What do you mean, darling?"

"Why is it so hard? Why is everything so hard for you? Life could be so simple if you left things be. Stop asking questions, stop prodding. Yet, you're a scared little mundane." Alarm bells were ringing; I carefully slid one leg out of the blankets to the floor as I slithered further away.

"I don't understand."

"Aww, poor little Gerald gets caught up looking for the truth, only to run when he doesn't like what he finds. All of this could've been quick and easy, and you'd get what your heart desires." Charlotte's voice slowly changed, becoming darker, scarier, with a deathly growl. She shifted onto her hands and knees, crawling across the bed. I was stunned into silence, nothing but the sound of wind filling the air.

'Bang!' The door flew shut, making me jump. I looked to see why and then back again, only to find Charlotte moving closer.

"Are you okay?" I ask shakily.

"We could've been. Now, all good things end. Have you ever noticed how uncomfortable skin can be?" Charlotte dragged her nails through her arm. "It feels so tight and restricting." Her nails dug deeper, raking, and blood flowed. I couldn't move. Strips of flesh tore effortlessly. "Ooh, now that feels so refreshing to just let the air in. You should try it, quite revealing." My stomach churned; I was desperate to puke, watching skin flap from her arms. Charlotte thrashed at her face. Nails flew deep into her forehead, and in one sickening move, she tore down her beautiful face to reveal glistening, gooey reddish-pink flesh. Sinews of muscle stretched across the curves of her cheekbones. The red gleamed grotesquely in the sunlight beaming through the window, making the whites of her eyes bulge brightly.

"Now that is so good. A shame to spoil this pretty face, don't you think? Then again, that's already happened, hasn't it? The recoil of my head from the steering wheel to the headrest. The sound of bone crunching between my ears. In case you wondered, that was my neck, teeth, and cheekbone. Oh, and a long crack through my skull. So, when you think about it, this is nothing." Horrifying, there was no other way to describe whatever this was. Charlotte's voice was long gone as she continued tearing strip after strip of flesh from her face. Blood poured profusely. I was desperate to escape, to be anywhere but here. Except I didn't know where to go.

"Why look so shocked, Gerald? Did you think this was real? You are deluded. If we can't have you, then there is no point. One… by… one, you little mundanes will fall, and all the king's horses and all the King's men will never pull your poor little world together again." Charlotte, or whatever this was, taunted with an evil chuckle that threw a chill down my back.

Breezing up close to my face, death oozed from her pores. I tried looking away, but her glistening flesh filled my view. There was no escaping the horror.

"What's the matter, cat got your tongue? Or has reality finally hit home? You've already lost, and you don't even know it. So, how about you run along like the good helpless soldier and find the 'FUCKING BOX'? Let evil nature take its course, and maybe, just maybe, we'll allow that poor little bitch, Charlotte's soul, to escape from hell too. Maybe that bastard of a father. In exchange, you go the other way and can spend eternity alone, scrubbing up the blood. Boy, there's a lot. Did you know souls bleed? It's a lot. I mean, it's like an endless amusement watching it piss out. So, that's your choice because we all know you're too spineless to become what's necessary. Too scared to acknowledge the darkness."

Charlotte continued, jarring the very fibre of my being, and everything began flooding back. Their deaths, everything. The bedroom slowly crumbled, darkening. Walls became pillars as I remembered where I was and what I was doing. Charlotte had torn all the flesh away, revealing the 'face of death'. It's an overpowering stink. I couldn't hold back the tears any longer. The thought of Charlotte and Father languishing in hell. Even accepting the idea scared me. The deterioration sped up, along with fake Charlotte, clawing more and more skin from her body as if to torment me. To make me feel the pain of losing her all over again.

'Gerald, snap out of it. Come on, Gerald.' I heard another voice breaking through the crumbling. George, I think, but I couldn't see anyone yet. Everything was too much, too quickly. My heart and brain were in pieces, and I didn't know how to mend them again. Not with fake Charlotte smiling in such an evil 'we just broke you' way. Daylight had faded to leave behind the dreary Christ on a cross again. Charlotte, oozing blood, was slowly becoming ash, scattering to the breeze that now rushed through.

"Hush, little baby, don't say a word. Mama's gonna buy you a mockingbird."

"And if that mockingbird don't sing. Mama's gonna buy you a diamond ring."

"And if that box Gerald doesn't bring. Mama's gonna kill you all."

"And if that doesn't scare you. We're gonna slay your mother, too."

That haunting nursery rhyme echoed through gargled mouthfuls of blood, spilling over just in time to see what remained of her scatter like decayed autumn leaves cast aside.

"Oi, Gerald, bloody snap out of it!" I heard again, closer now. I shook the last terrifying image from my mind as George appeared before me, his face a mask of worry.

My eyes darted over his shoulder; the raven was gone, but I heard a movement behind us. At least three, maybe four sets of cumbersome steps. They had to be 'undead,' the only explanation for such staggered movements.

"What the hell happened? You were out of it for a good five minutes," George says, checking over Nathan as I felt his weight across my shoulders again.

"I don't know. One minute I'm looking at the raven, mesmerised. The next, I hear Charlotte singing the nursery rhyme she sang to the twins. Then I woke up in bed beside her. Life was normal, and for a moment, I couldn't remember anything. Except there was a nagging feeling I didn't belong."

"Well, your eyes were wide open and pitch bloody black. I'm wondering what other colours they'll change to. It was freaky, and coming from someone well-versed in the strange, that speaks volumes."

"Right, now you've had the cosy catch-up, maybe we should find a fucking way out because it's about to kick off," Michael called out, his yellow eyes fixed on the front door, which was still open... until... 'boom'—it flew shut. Just like the bedroom door had in whatever the hell that moment was. We all jumped, and I nearly dropped Nathan, who stirred a little.

'Shuffle, stomp, shuffle, stomp.' The shadows came alive; their steps echoed around this cavern of ruins. Four figures slowly rocked their way into the limited light bearing down on us from the night sky, past the roofless timbers. They were 'undead,' flesh peeling and dropping from their bones with each step, dripping with that putrid sulphur stench.

Four of them against four of us. In a way, it was even, but not really. Two of us were mundane, and we were hindered by Nathan drifting further into death's eager clutches. Michael and George might be no strangers to this, but I got the impression facing things like this was a first for them. (Welcome to my world.) Up to a year ago, I was mindlessly treading water in Willowbrook, knowing that's as good as it would probably get. Wrestling with a cloud smothering my brain, revealing what this place really looked like.

As I've already explained, I've always known our village was different in one dark way or another, especially with nanna's tales. I saw some strange things throughout childhood that I thought were my imagination. Those faces that change—those remnants. Then Father passed, and it all went into overdrive. Never did I expect to see the 'undead' swarming the streets...

Fast forward to now, and that darkness feels ever so close to taking over. Yet I resist, scared. Rendering me useless at this moment, nothing but a 'crutch' to keep Nathan upright. For how much longer? The sands of time seemed to ebb quickly. Making it two vs. four, I didn't know how much fire that gum put in George's tank. If anything screams at me, it's his reluctance over whatever went down in Scotland. I'm not one to pry, but he needs to get back on the horse sooner rather than later.

"Are we doing this, Georgie?" Michael asks, looking at George, seeming apprehensive.

"I don't want to. What other choice do we have?" George replies. With each step forward, more of the wolf's features morphed into view. His claws grew longer, thickening and dripping fluid. Each drop scorched through the dust on the floor, burrowing into stone. I looked on, waiting for the face-off, then around us, for a Plan B—a way to avoid this. These might be 'undead,' mindless minions used to get at us. Doesn't mean they want to. 'Freewill' might not count for much in their condition. We still have it.

Those blue eyes sprang to my mind. More about what I was doing. The different pillars and the upside-down cross. I dragged Nathan across to it, keeping my senses open, listening and watching for surprises and the impending trouble with the 'undead.'

Sweat swam down my side. Nathan was pressed against me, and he was burning up. His flesh had gone a clammy greyish pale. Rain fell from his forehead. A quick hoist up, pulling Nathan further onto my shoulder so I could stretch for the cross. Its 'cold' metal was met with stubborn resistance, but it could move. I felt the draft 'hissing' through the cracks.

'Whooooooooooooooo,' a loud, hollow rush of air swirled within the pillar. My mind kicked into overdrive. This had to be what we were looking for—a good a sign as any.

I gripped the cross tight, yanking it hard; rusty screeches rattled my teeth until I finally 'righted' it to its proper position. There was some 'give,' a little movement. I could already see the outline on the pillar where it needed to go. A tentative push, dreading what might come next, and the cross slotted home nice and snug.

'Click.'

An unlocking noise or a spring releasing came next. That 'hissing' grew, and the panel jutted forward, allowing dust to break free. That hollow rush became a howl loud enough to get the detectives' attention. We had no time to stall. My fingers snuck around the panel's edge. Again, cold metal. A flick brought the panel wide open, revealing a darkness I envisioned matched what was inside me: murky black with all the allure of a rattlesnake.

Before long, it seemed to brighten, or my eyes adjusted. It's wider than it looks, always the way, right? Nothing is ever as it seems. There are steps, too, such as the outline of the first couple. It may not be what we're looking for or know where it heads, but it avoids confrontation.

I didn't need to call. Supernatural hearing and all. I must remember that in the future. Michael and George came running. Neither stopped for questions or second-guessing. Instead, Michael took Nathan, again, 'strength.' George led the way. Each step echoed, and by the time we'd hastily begun our descent, the pillar door creaked closed again. Once the first few steps were clear and we were past the pillar line, the ceiling opened up into a far more daunting darkness.

Damp and the persistent drip of water grew closer the further down we got. Until George found the floor first. I couldn't see a thing until he moved forward. One after the other, fluorescent lights flew on. Strips of them until a walkway well over a mile long lay before us. We stared in awe and confusion; it happened again. A tingle at the back of my neck.

George felt it too, then Michael. Enough to make us shudder. Something was about to happen. George's face told me it would be bad. Sure enough, a low 'hiss' began far ahead, growing. A plume of yellow smoke broke from the vanishing point, hurrying. We had nowhere to go, not with Nathan fading so quickly.

It was a wild, untameable beast, full of rage, hellbent on a feast, and our lungs were the main course. One minute—that's all it took to be on top of us. A relentless surge. It weaved between us, around us, and eventually through, until we all began choking. I felt it squeezing the oxygen out of my body; it had a rich fruitiness to it. At least it differed from the stink of death. We all went limp, my eyes bleary and so heavy. For the second time in a day, I was being put through the wringer. I watched Michael fall holding Nathan, George, and I fell next, a slow-motion descent to 'kiss concrete.' Time was ticking.

Chapter 32

'Détective Reynolds—Back to my worst moment,'

I find myself somewhere strange yet eerily familiar. Smoke clouds my senses, bringing me back to one of the worst moments of my life where it all began. There's no light I can feel, only the scrape of my hand against a flaking wall and the clutch of a wooden bannister. My nightmares replay in my mind, each creak of timber a haunting symphony before I discovered Chris. But this time, I'm not barefoot, and I'm not alone.

Listening past the whistling wind, I strain to catch heartbeats, hoping for sounds beyond ours. Skip and Michael are ahead, but someone is down there, and their heartbeat is faint. Michael sparks a lighter; the little yellow flame dances as we move, illuminating strange symbols—Latin, just like the box left in my car. The descent grows darker, and the rancid smell of burnt flesh intensifies.

Full of nerves, I bounce from one problem to another. I recall a giddy feeling that turns my legs to jelly, praying they won't give out as we hit the stone, dusty floor. Like my dreams, my feet kick through the dirt, sending a shower through the air.

"Oh my God, that's freaking vile. Can you smell that? Butcher's meat gone rotten," Michael says, retching, sickly saliva dribbling down his chin.

"Welcome to hell."

"What, Skip?"

"That Latin as we came down, it's a welcome to blooming hell."

All I see is a looming, flickering silhouette cast by the lighter. The space feels larger than I imagined. I stand in the same spot, spinning around in a daze, letting the smouldering air fill my lungs until the goosebump chill from my nightmare becomes real—a speaker. Heavy iron chains pound against the concrete, sending a metallic clang rippling through the air. Once... Twice... Three times... It's the ghost of my Christmas past.

"How does it feel, Georgie? Is anything coming back to you yet? I can always shed some light on you. Let you revel in the horror before the fun begins," the puppeteer's voice echoes around us, adding to my trepidation.

I step back, reaching for the bannister; burnt blood swirls through my lungs, and drool pools around my gums, feeling the lust build up. Loud clicking rocks around us before a dim light flickers on. We all gasp, staring in horror; Skip stumbles backward, falling into a craftsman's bench with a vice. Pinched within is a bony hand, rotten, more bone than anything else. Blood sprays chaotically throughout, enveloping the thick dust and grime.

Four adult-sized bodies are beheaded in kneeling positions. Hands and feet are bound in chains, with the remains of thick tape melted across their mouths; they couldn't move or call for help, even if they wanted to. They are more than decomposed and burnt, masking the clothing. The puppeteer has arranged the bodies around a circle, an old etching touched up to look new. Two triangles, one upright, the other inverted—devil worship. Just as Skip saw it twenty-five years ago.

My pulse pounds in my temple, throbbing in my ears; I'm lost in darkness, different from what we descended into. My arms are heavy, dragged down limply, feeling a tightness around my wrists. I look down to see thick, chained clamps. Only my arms aren't my own; they are smaller, covered in burnt red-black skin, bubbling and breaking. A pair of bolt cutters hover close and break the chains; I'm lifted like a rag doll before being covered in a sheet. I'm being carried; a haunting red glow in the corner is coming my way. It's a nightmare, and I have nowhere to go.

"You okay, Georgie lad?"

"Huh. Y... yeah, I think so."

Skip calls to me; my eyes clear, and I'm back, staring at the stranded heads, sockets exposed with eyes popping. I can barely see strands of hair on any of them. One, two, three, four, and five. No extra fingers this time; I'm not dreaming. This was Charlie, tormenting me over the past.

"Surely you remember now seeing my little masterpiece? Volunteers recreating what happened, showing you how my parents, my sister, and my grandmother died. How you were lucky to survive. The rest you'll get if you complete the game." The motive that drove that bastard was awful—murdering innocent people to make a point and push us around. I can feel the venom in his words thumping around. Chains rattle again on the far-right side, still in the shadows. I strain to look; all I see are dirty brown pillars made of solid wood that have weathered over time—Latin symbols carved into each one with slight differences. It's crazy.

"Skip, any ideas?" I point to the nearest pillar. Much like the strangeness of the box, a few resemble letters from the alphabet, only with extra squiggly lines.

"Well, it's old Latin, I think. I'm not that smart, lad: daemon, esto subjecto voluntati meae. Demon, submit yourself to my bidding. Something like that."

The puppeteer's family didn't mess around looking to summon demons. Not so long ago, I would've laughed that off as nonsense. Now, anything is fair game. The next pillar, ten feet to my right, has a similar inscription.

"What about this?"

"Ad ligandum eos pariter eos coram me. To likewise bind them before me. That's the gist; when the stupid sods delved into this shit, they created sigils. They wanted to trap whatever they summoned and use it. But remember, I told you about that big bloke at the hospital? He's something like that."

Another bump in the road: the newspaper clipping, Skip's bedtime story, and Charlie's tall tale that he gave him in the box. They all have different stories about this, and I was gullible, especially regarding Charlie.

While Michael is examining the shelves, I see another horrifying detail. Jars, row after row of wide, dusty glass three-quarters full, containing sickly body parts swimming in a dirty green liquid. Some are limbs from babies, including a head, only different—small fangs and two lumps on the forehead, beginning horns.

"Is this bastard for real? That looks bloody medieval. How the hell do we solve this one? More to the point, do we agree that this twisted wanker isn't working alone? How else would he do all of this?"

Michael is traumatised, and Skip isn't much better. That case was awful. It took me to where it all began. A child snatched from his parents and dumped into a seedy foster home that experimented on children. Except I was born a werewolf, and they made me something else. I got to relive it all and remember so much that I'd blocked out, including the fire that should've killed me. Look at me now, doing my best to ensure none of the same happens to anyone else, even if it involves stopping the gates of hell from being opened.

We have to do something. I stand looking at all the same devil trap markings and blood.

Skip and Michael freeze. The floor crumbled, fading, and changing. Everything around me was doing the same. In no time at all, I was back in the tunnel. Nathan, Michael, and Gerald were still knocked out. Confusing, I got to thinking about the Templar order; the original ones were prestigious knights and their secrets, until this day, are sought after. So, that could have been a test to see if I was worthy to carry on. All I can do now is hope that Michael's alternative life choices don't screw him up.

'*Michael,*'

Bloody hell, that was a trip and a half. One minute I'm in a tunnel, the next I'm back in time, reliving a moment I bloody don't want to remember—the time the Kanaima ripped out my throat, and I should've died. It was also the moment that changed my life for the better. I'm at the Spitalfields warehouse, watching the standoff unfold.

This killer and its master were deadly, leaving a trail of bodies in their wake. It was tough as hell. A twitch, eyes shifting between normal and Kanaima green. Claws coming and going. Georgie got into his head. Jack turned to Melanie, grimacing. Georgie thought he could save us all at once.

"Don't think about it. I control everything. Press this button, and toxins are released immediately. I know you won't control anything in a minute because of the blood."

Claws slid out; Georgie hid his hands, catching Ellena's eyes. He didn't want to freak her out, let alone let Locke find out. He watched helplessly, about to try his luck, but got hit by a thunderbolt of pain, dropping to his knees. His hands were in sawdust; they'd changed.

'It's okay, Georgie. Let it happen,' Ellena whispers, tears trickling. "I...I... I can't," Georgie struggled, bones breaking around us.

'It's okay, I know... I trust you,' she whispered. Locke nodded in approval. Did he know too? The pain had Georgie wanting to scream; instead, he roared as his fangs grew, shaking the warehouse. Melanie stepped back in fear.

He saw red until his vision settled—beads of sweat on Melanie's forehead. The Kanaima's eyes held black streaks in green. Jack was conflicted. The human side was scared for his life. Georgie was changing, but he had to hang on, halt it. The demon side was assimilating with the wolf; heightened wouldn't do justice.

Power surged, and Georgie sensed Melanie's fear for the first time. There was a vibration in her throat, and her pupils darted, seeking exits.

"Don't be stupid, Georgie," Melanie quivered. Jack worried, flaws fluctuating. Now was his time. Lights off again, darkness. He flew past, yanking drips out, landing on the platform, knocking Kanaima and me apart. The lights flicked back on. We'd landed feet apart; I'd forced Kanaima's claws into its abdomen, injecting its toxin, hoping the books were true.

Georgie dragged his angry self from the dust, looking up. Melanie stood over my body—blood pouring from my throat. The Kanaima ripped it out. I remember feeling so cold, so quickly. Shock mixed with the realisation I might have had my last day. I was choking on blood, trying to talk, trying to tell my friends that I regretted nothing about being wrapped in this new, dark world. I couldn't.

My body writhed as sawdust soaked the pool of blood. "Aww, you killed the 30 seconds, man. Tut tut. Another lesson I learned from the books. Always have a Plan B," she says, holding the remote. "Don't do it. The game is over."

"Not yet; it ain't. While you decide who to save, I'll take that key and be on my way," Melanie says. She pressed the button. A blast of wind; the Kanaima was still stricken. Who would've thought how much joy hearing four little words could bring?

'Hey-up Georgie, lad,'

Georgie turned toward the booming echo of his old Skipper and 'Beta' Andy Morris. "What the hell, how?" Georgie gushes.

"I heard you call, so I came. Now save them," he beamed.

My skin turned pale, lying in a pool of blood, slipping away. Behind me were two other drips rigged with toxin; Melanie assumed the obvious. Georgie ripped the needles out and flipped the tables flat, tearing through the straps. Returning to me, I was dying, and Georgie didn't know what to do. I'd lost so much blood we'd never reach the hospital in time.

"Skip. Please… tell me how," Georgie pleads. We stopped Melanie, but it's cost Michael his life. I was helpless and drowning.

"Bite him, lad; there's no other way," he says, gripping Melanie tight. I looked at her face, and the rage inside me wanted him to do it.

"I can't; what will everyone see of me?" Georgie screeched.

"You can save him, lad," Skip says.

"It's ok, Georgie," Ellena whispered. Locke stared. He was the unknown.

"Do it, George. Save him; we don't have long," Locke surprised Georgie.

He grabbed my arm; the pool grew, and my heart slowed to the last beat. 'Fuck it,' he thought before biting deep into my arm. His fangs pierced my skin and flesh, nicking a vein. A small spray of blood spurted over Georgie's face as he held on. His eyes blazed red, brighter than ever before. Every fibre in his body was alive with blood lust.

"That's enough, Georgie," Skip pleads. Instead, Georgie bit a little harder, causing me to squirm.

Air grazed past; Ellena came to our side, gently touching Georgie's neck. Her face breezed close, lips inches from his ear.

"That's enough, Georgie; let go now. I'm here for you," she cooed into his ear. Her words echoed, a bewitching effect. Georgie's jaw loosened, his eyes dimmed, and he slowly let go, falling backwards, feeling ashamed.

"I'm here for you," she whispers. Georgie tried to hide his face, but Ellena had none of it. She gripped his clawed hands, looking at him deeply with a caring smile. 'You don't need to hide anymore,' she whispered.

I groaned; my neck had healed. I could feel life ebbing back and then some. Colour seeped back into my skin. It was working. My veins were on fire, everything was repairing, and little knocks and issues I had endured through a long life were mending and getting stronger. I was getting stronger. I felt like a bloody kid again, from nearly dying to exhilaration.

"What the hell happened?" I croaked.

"You were all but dead. Now stop lying around; come arrest this bitch, will you?" Skip boomed, rocking me to my senses.

"What? Really?" I say, gathering myself.

"Yeah, Georgie saved you; he saved us all," Locke interrupts, lumbering up.

"So, you had to bite me? Does that mean I must be flea and wormed every month now?" I say, finding the energy to joke.

Staring at my blood on the floor, feeling lucky to be alive, everything began crumbling and changing. Before long, I was waking up in the tunnel with Georgie standing over me. Gerald was still out with Nathan.

'Gerald,'

Well, that wasn't in the brochure; that smoke or chemical cloud had us all out in seconds. I woke in darkness, smelling cigars. I'm in a house—my grandparents' house, full of the musk and staleness that comes with age. I ended up in a room. It's their spare bedroom from when I used to sleep over. A glimmer of moonlight ripples through the curtains, catching the far-right side of the room. There's me, the young version of me, at least. I'm no older than twelve. The clock on the wall shows a little after 1:30 a.m., and this scenario confuses me.

I remember little from then, and nothing jumps out. I look peacefully snuggled beneath my 'Batman' duvet cover. Most of the room is quite bland, except the walls are boyish blue. More posters pay homage to the same 'dark knight' that keeps me warm. A football and a cricket bat are in the corner, and a tiny television sits on the dresser. Still, I'm searching for answers, wondering why I was here and now. We were running out of time to save Nathan. Assuming we could. If that toxin overpowered a werewolf, my faith was being tested.

Any minute now, I muttered, hoping, then I saw the ripple of a shadow moving through the hallway. I barely caught it, thanks to a dim light at the bottom of the stairs. It was tall, like a man, unless I was seeing things, another hallucination, hoping to see something to end this situation. There's silence and then a crash caused by a lamp being knocked over and the bulb exploding. A loud scream from Nanna followed that drama, and then Grandad shouted, too inaudible to understand but loud enough to shake the young me awake.

My pale blonde hair swung across my bleary eyes and quickly brushed out of the way as another shout rang out. In matching Batman pyjamas, the young me jumped out of bed, dashing for the cricket bat and out of the door. I followed my little legs, still not remembering any of this. Their bedroom is at the end of the hallway, their light on, and I can see a shadow looming by the doorway. Young me had no fear. Charging headstrong into the bedroom, we barely broke stride over the threshold. I'm stunned. It's the 'whispering man.' He's stood over my grandparents, huddled in bed, facing down the sharp end of a sword. His deathly face had wisps of charcoal flesh peeling from his jawbone. How did this not terrify me back then? Perhaps that's why I couldn't remember.

The 'whispering man' turned to see young me, his demonic eyes piercing its deep, garish red through to my soul. His dirty trilby stank of dead blood, its peak casting a shadow across his haunting, menacing face. At least a metre long, a gleaming mix of metals. I smelled sulphur and then that potent toxin that was ripping through Nathan as I endured this 'trial or test.' What else could it be?

The 'whispering man' smiles before plunging the sword forward. Young me jumped through the air, landing on the bed. My little arms wielded that cricket bat as if it were a sword, too. It windmilled through the air, overhand, crashing down on the sword mid-plunge. The sword veered wide, burying into the headboard, but the bat followed through, and as the sword bounced and bowed before snapping, metal shards splintered through the air. Shocked, the 'whispering man' turned, retreating. "Death will come soon enough," he says, becoming a blur out the door.

Young me saved my grandparents and locked away the memory. The sword's tip still wobbled in the headboard before crumbling away, infecting everything it connected to. My grandparents, young me, and then the room all disappeared. I was back in the tunnels. Michael and George stood over me, waiting.

"About bloody time, matey," Michael says, looking at his watch.

"Sorry, but I didn't know what was going on."

"Well, we need to move. Since our little experiences, the twenty-four hours are nearly up." I was stunned, quickly hoisting Nathan to his feet. His body is on fire. We were losing him and any chance to stop what's coming. How the hell had we lost so much time? All the smoke and mirrors were gone, and a clear path awaited. We all experienced something, but none of us spoke of it. Instead, it weighed us down as we trudged toward destiny or hell. Now I know, when I first met the 'whispering man'. More fear-provoking for me, was not remembering or deep down, my brain made it into a nightmare, because the truth was too scary.

Chapter 33

'Gerald,'

A dead end. Thick grey stone loomed before us. Had we done this for nothing? Wasting time that could've been spent trying to save Nathan? By doing something, we stood a slim chance of succeeding. Michael and George searched every inch, hoping for another way. I listened, hearing only echoes, drips, and footsteps. The image of the 'whispering man' trying to kill my grandparents stuck in my mind. Thick moss was everywhere, but vine leaves only grew in one spot—the far-left wall beside the dead end.

If the smoke scenario taught me anything, these 'Templars' liked games and tests. Nothing is ever as it seems. Much like our grimy, bloody village. How the hell are we going to put all the 'undead' genies back in the bottle? How do we come back from this? Any ideas? If so, scribe it in blood somewhere; we'll stumble across it, eventually. Hell, be artistic and make it out-of-body parts; there's enough to go around.

I followed the vines, seeing where they led. They had to go somewhere, likely up. The damp swarmed the upper corner, swelling over a jagged cluster almost resembling an angry face. Who could blame it? Like a mushroom kept in the dark. Does that make us mushrooms, too? We're always surrounded by darkness.

The rocky pattern to the right grabbed my attention. A strip straight to the floor, much lighter and dryer, as if warmer. I nearly forgot my enhanced vision until a timely reminder.

'What you see isn't what is.' The chill still gets me, and so does the weepy tone; it wouldn't be so bad if he cheered up a bit. I hadn't dared to ask if it was the same one I saw in my grandparents' room. It couldn't be, could it? Perhaps a conversation for later, if we survive. How bloody cryptic, though.

It wasn't just the dry strip. My head lurched from side to side, doing some weird dance that got Michael's attention. He stared at me, confused. I wasn't losing my mind; that may have already happened. The rocks had a pattern along that strip, which was easily missed. I guess that's the point. When you look face-on, nothing. A little to either side, and you see steps. I couldn't tell how wide, but they went up, fading into black.

"Guys, check that wall; it looks like steps," I say, getting George's attention too. They both moved close with their glowing eyes. Another weird thing that gets to me. Will anything be normal again?

"He's right. It goes up, matey. A hatch of some kind made of stone," Michael says, glancing at George, who, judging by the constipated expression, was trying to work out the logistics.

"Right, Michael, you head up, open the hatch, then reach down to me, and I'll hoist Nathan up for you to drag through. Remember to go easy; he's fragile," George says, formulating as good a plan as any. That's the difference between us 'mundanes' and the supernatural. Fragile. Perhaps we should carry signs: 'careful we break easy'. The least we needed was Michael tossing Nathan around like a rag doll or smashing his head on the roof.

It was all going too well. The scared part of me was expecting trouble. For us to be blindsided. Like the 'young me,' only with less bravado. I wish I knew where all that went. I needed it in spades now. They were through; I dragged myself up slowly, cold stone scraping through palm flesh. My head finally popped through the hatch, thrashed by a wave of cold, dead air. No other way to put it: 'dead', stale, pungent swirls. It was dark; I heard footsteps pacing frantically. Judging by the short gait, it was Michael, looking for a light, I assumed.

With a flicker and a clicking of a lighter, Michael found a candle. Its warming aura adds a touch of 'spooky' lashing around an immense room. More a museum or art gallery. Wall to wall of stone, suits of armour, weapons, and statues. I looked but felt it was nothing more than a 'Templar' façade—a shell. I was expecting another twist. Finally, up amongst the relics and all the 'Templar' stuff. Nathan was resting on a bench; everything else looked ready to fall apart if they ever saw the light of day again. On another occasion, I might have even found it amazing. Instead, I expected one of those creepy knights to poke his 'dead' head out of the shadows.

There were more pillars, but no fake doors, no 'Christ' on a cross, and the floor was flagstone until I saw six man-sized and detailed tombs seamlessly blended four feet up.

They represented knights, dressed in armour with a 'Templar' symbol on their chests, hands clutching swords. With every second of information I took in, a sudden realisation hit me: another puzzle. Starting back at the pillars, there were only five or twelve statues, three suits of armour, and six tombs. There were so many more. What combination and where did they go? The altar to the far right had four-digit dials, all showing zero.

"It's a number game," I say. George breezed close, looking from my viewpoint.

"I see what you mean. Not what you think, though. It's too obvious and too many; the combination could be anything." George was right, of course. Who was I to think it would be that obvious?

"Look, on the tombs, there's a small number three on that one's chest," I say, pointing to the fourth knight in the bank of six. George spun on the spot, and Michael, too.

"There, the statues on the back wall, opposite the tombs, a seven down on an ankle," Michael says. That meant two digits out of four. In what order, though?

"One has a 'two' on it by the doors, the shields, the centre of the stack." George ran over to be sure. We had two, three, and seven.

"Quick, there, 3 o'clock, the flag mounted to the wall, a nine in the corner," Michael says. We had four digits, but in what order?

"Now what, play lucky dip?" George says in jest, but it felt...

"Wait, Michael, you said 3 o'clock. It's all a bloody clock. Look how it's all positioned." I noticed a grouping of artifacts at every clock point: conveniently, six tombs at 6 o'clock, statues at twelve, and so on.

"So we enter them clockwise, right? Two, seven, nine, three," George says, looking at me with raised eyebrows. I wasn't getting the impression they wanted me to test it. Bit of a joke, considering they can heal. I'm a bloody mundane, for Christ's sake.

Well, I may struggle with my fears and be haunted by the 'whispering man'. Come to think of it, I'm not a fan of the dark, eerie shadows, death, the Walking Dead, or those creepy knights. That's quite a list without thinking too deep. That little 'boat' weaving through the 'sanity river' feels more like a battleship with each passing hour—small steps, feeling the hard stone beneath me as if vibrating into my soles. I heard every heartbeat; Nathan was barely a blip.

Rodents scurried between limestone crevices, and the wind howled outside. A ferocious, intimidating beast on the rampage, looking for weaknesses and a way in. This room may be stone, and the doors reinforced iron; the surrounding cocoon whistled like timbers yawning and crying at the torture.

An unrelenting assault roared around us, fraying our nerves with each ticking second. I glanced at my watch. We had less than thirty minutes left to save Nathan, and we still didn't have the other piece, nor did we know where Father hid his. Step by tentative step, I daydreamed about the watch face, thinking of Father. I wondered what he would do in this situation or if he had any inkling this could be the future. The closer I got to the altar, the crazier the watch became. First, it stopped, and I shook it like a madman, thinking, 'Rolexes don't do that.' Then, the arms spun wildly in reverse before landing at the original time.

It made no sense, much like most of the horror that's unfolded or weaved through my life. Father told me on the tapes that our bloodlines were cursed. Is that why I could see death all these years, or was there more to me? Nathan's father alluded to a Plan B, someone strong enough to break free from these evil shackles. I can't shake what happened in the tunnels. I stalled near the altar, searching through Nanna's encyclopaedia of stories to see if any connected to that awful night.

"Did you know nobody moves on?" Nanna says. "They all stay behind the curtain, waiting to peek at us when we sleep. They hover over us with long, pointy fingers of wrath, hoping one of us can see and feel their torment." She'd say. "Our house has had a few. Yours too. I've seen them. I've seen a lot of things. My mother called it a 'gift,' able to see both sides of the curtain. Imagine walking into the bloomin bakery, only to see my great-aunt Agnes cutting bread. That silly woman tripped down some stairs at work and broke her neck twenty hundred years ago." Nanna always sounded like she was telling a few stories at once, her years a jumbled mess.

"Two." I spun the dial until it hit the magic number. I heard nothing, no click, nothing. I don't know what I was expecting, but surely something.

"Seven." The next one was done, but still no click.

"Nine." Again, nothing. I looked at the others; Michael was pacing, and George was raking his fingers through his hair, his face turning red. Nathan looked greyer, knocking on death's door with a sledgehammer. His breathing was erratic, sharp, struggling, and shallow. My hearing was laser-focused; his lungs were full of mucus, and I could hear the toxins ripping through every vein, artery, chamber, atrium, and God knows what else. A battle ensued within my best friend, and he was losing. His chest bounced like a vibrating bass drum; a curious little corded chain slipped from beneath his top, revealing an odd vial in an hourglass frame without split chambers. The fluid was bright red, akin to fresh blood, resting on it like oil on water.

Maybe it was something their family was into, carrying a piece of each other with them. Or it belonged to his actual parents if that last act of bravado from Nathan's father was true. Still, that trinket was mesmerising. "No. You can't, we won't. Did you think there wouldn't be a backup plan? We know there's one of us strong enough to break the curse, break what they're meant to become, and use it to stop your stupid, reckless, and suicidal plan."

I replayed the words again. They were two statements, not one speech—a backup plan. Then, we know there's one of us strong enough to break the curse, break what they're meant to become, and use it to stop your stupid, reckless, and suicidal plan. It was a two-pronged jab at the killer. Could that weird liquid be a backup plan and involve Nathan? How was my brain even making such drastic leaps? It could simply be a harmless trinket that caught Nathan's eye. The tiny remaining rational part of my grey matter was looking for bright silver linings within that near-constant haunted cloud. We needed a Hail Mary.

"Here goes nothing," I mutter, getting back to the task. "Three." I held my breath; my chest ached to the point of burning, tensing my stomach, expecting something, anything. I didn't know—like a statue coming to life or a tomb popping open to reveal what we seek. Then... A faint hiss in the background, not the wind outside, but from the pipes running throughout the perimeter. Then whoosh, air burst out, only it wasn't air, but another cloud, this time lilac, quickly filling the space above in a thick fog like a bitter-smelling cloud. We fell into a trap. It was a simple mistake; perhaps the sequence was too obvious. Michael and George were already detecting what it was, covering their mouths while throwing themselves as close to the floor as possible. Neither spoke, too scared to bother in case they inhaled the cloud.

I was stuck. Nathan would usually be my soundboard, but I sure as hell wasn't asking the voices in my head. I know that sounds equally crazy. Frantically, I ran the numbers again, the positioning going clockwise. It had to be the code. True to Templar puzzlement, it carried a sting. A rare lightbulb moment happened. I looked at my watch, moved it close, and it spun again in reverse.

"In reverse," I mutter, spinning the dials, "three, nine, seven, two." This time, a click. A loud reverberating click. The pipes closed immediately, and a vacuum kicked in, inhaling the cloud away within seconds. Michael and George scraped themselves off the floor, uncovering their faces. Both were shell-shocked, none more so than me. I pissed in the wind, and luckily, the winds had changed just in time—all thanks to Father's watch. I like to think he was with me at that moment. He sent the watch crazy, a hint at what to do, but it probably wasn't; I like my version better.

"Well?" Michael says impatiently. I understood the reasoning, but not the timing. That was all on me, and for want of a better phrase, I pulled a rabbit out of the hat. Obviously, not really a rabbit. Now, that would be rubbish timing. In all seriousness, I was flying by the seat of my scared pants, and they were turning fifty shades of brown at the minute. I'm still sitting by the altar, emotionally and mentally drained. I can hear cogs whirring—not the tired, rusty ones in my head. First, within the altar, then somewhere under the floor ten feet from me, a gap similar to the others. My sweaty face was inches from the dials, and I wished I could rest and catch a break.

"Pssssst." I heard it. It's ominously quiet, the noise a mundane uses to get another's attention without drawing attention. I looked slowly, doing just that, trying not to get attention or cause worry. It was close, that much I was certain. Dare I say it, from behind the dials. My gaze lingered on the dials momentarily. I saw dust peacefully drifting. A thin sheet of mist. However, it appeared to change direction. Another hallucination? I wondered. Nothing was off the table these days. There was something cosmic about it. Anyone who likes to read up on planets can see some have misty rings around them. Don't ask me which; I'm not one of those stargazers, but I've seen a few pictures. Anyway, it looked like that, and it was looping towards me.

There was plenty of time to move; I should have. Again, it's the little things that draw me in. The details other mundanes overlook. So I didn't move. It's almost a Schrödinger's cat moment. Leave the box closed and, in my case, move away. In my mind, the cat is alive, and this mist is nothing. Or open the box to see, likely knowing the cat is dead, and I allow the mist to come and see what makes it change direction for me. I opened the box, and the mist dazzled my eyes. I've never done drugs, but I imagined the sudden lightheaded, spaced-out feeling was what it could be like. (Step away from the drugs, kids. Drugs are bad.) Everything was hazy. Okay, it's like a mist wrapped around my eyeballs.

My foot slipped lazily across the stone floor; I heard gravel. I was relying on other senses as my eyes slowly cleared. Blood swam through the air, lots of it. My stomach turned; I dragged my foot back but knocked on something else. It rattled across the floor; it was long. I could almost see a faint white and black outline. It was bone. Beside it was a round object of the same colour. Oh my god, it's a skull. A mundane skull. I stood, shaky but stable enough when I could finally see...

Chapter 34

'Gerald'

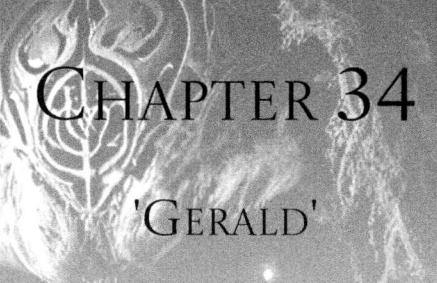

My eyes twitched. A deep, soul-disturbing burning began through my optic nerves. It pulsated behind my eyeballs. A fire sparked. None of that happy campfire stuff. This was a raging forest blaze engulfing the blood-red flesh lining around the sockets and lids. The whites bubbled and boiled until a bloody-white goo melted, oozing from my sockets until nothing but the nerve ends were left, swinging in the breeze. The horror before me was evocatively sickening.

As far as I dared to see, the once mundane village had become a terrifying swamp of blood. The 'Willen River' overflowed, drenching normality and transforming anything that resembled tragic, mundane life. A boat drifted through the blood-covered streets, crunching through a jumble of skeletons, stripped clean in a grotesque buffet.

Each step I took crunched beneath me, a horrific sound worming through my ears. In the distance, an army of 'undead' stumbled through intestines, bladders, and other organs, ripping apart any mundane that dared rebel. Army tanks lay impaled in shops and homes. A line of creepy knights flanked the dead, sitting atop equally horrific horses. Red eyes blazed from both horse and rider, piercing a brooding black sky lit by a blood-red moon. Their gaze fixed in my direction.

A heavy rumble roared through the soaked ground beneath me; I wobbled, barely keeping on my feet. There were no fault lines anywhere near here and none through the U.K. that I knew of. The first fracture was slight, tearing through the sidewalk on my right, allowing a luminescent purple-red glow to break free, throbbing. The ground was alive; the fracture grew, and the loud crunching of stone struggled to outstrip the haunting sound of bone ripping. That fracture destroyed phone booths, benches, and any street furniture in its path.

A shiver and a curdle of my blood drained my energy to my feet and rooted me to the spot. My life was tormented by the 'whispering man' and twisted by what Nanna called a 'gift,' able to see both sides of the curtain. Nothing prepared me for this. Out of that fracture slithered black clouds with red eyes: smoking, swirling clouds of evil. Demons were breaking out of hell, and with every one that tore loose, the fractures grew, gathering speed, splintering more and more like a menacing tree, shredding a path to bring hell on earth. I can't do this; I can't be a part of causing or being dragged into the middle of this if that's what's coming. My daughters already lost their mother; I lost my wife and father because someone thought it would be a great idea to 'shake things up a little.' So much death, so much evil. The sulphur is so strong that it's squeezing the life out of my lungs. All this blood before me, surely it can't be true.

What if it's a result of our meddling, not evil winning? We could surrender, and they'd spare most mundanes. That could work, right? I'm soaking in the horror, watched by the evil knights, streets littered with death and bones... Who am I kidding? Whether we want it or not, this is coming on the wings of fury. I may only be mundane, with no strength, speed, or anything like Michael or George, but if they're willing to face all this without a moment of thought, how can I turn and run? Even if I reached my girls safely, I'd never be able to look them in the eyes and say I did everything I could to save their future. Save everyone's future. Hell will come, and we will meet it head-on. That thought spun through my brain, watching in terror as the massacre unfolded. The whole time, it felt like a standoff.

Could they see me? Or was my fear making me paranoid? I nearly had the second option locked in when faint whistling travelled on the 'bloody breeze'; even that sounded fucking scary. Every hair on my body was on end, and I mean every hair. That torturing whistle soon took a turn for the worse. Tears swelled in the corners of my bleeding eyes, my heart throbbed, clutching my breath in my throat. It was Charlotte's voice again. Rippling in the wind, I could feel my heart breaking again.

'Hush, little baby, don't say a word. Mama's gonna buy you a mockingbird.'
'And if that mockingbird doesn't sing, Mama's gonna buy you a diamond ring.'
'And if that diamond ring turns brass, Mama's gonna buy you a looking glass.'
'And if that looking glass gets broke, Mama's gonna buy you a billy goat.'

By the time Charlotte sang the fourth verse, the knights kicked into the sides of their demonic horses, nothing but bone, flaking skin, and a blood-coloured fire acting as their lungs within decayed rib cages. Those sick bastards had to have seen me; they charged towards me with sinister intent, and I still couldn't move. I was stranded amidst a nightmarish crimson sea, and that 'tiny boat' was thriving in my turmoil. With nowhere to go, I felt like a 'mundane kite' twisting adrift in a hurricane of evil. Horse hooves blazed a path of hellfire, flying at me. The knights drew their swords, gleaming under the red moon.

Thunder savagely tore through the broken streets, the galloping pounding the brittle stone beneath, closing in. Was this it? Had I been fed to the demonic wolves, a last roll of the dice from the Templars, as a sacrificial lamb? Surely not. I tried summoning the darkness within. Nothing. I was all alone. Something I'd got used to, though this wasn't how I expected it to go down.

"Thump, thump, thump," came the gallops. My heart screamed for help, screamed for it to be quick. The deadly line of evil flew at me, deafened by the pounding. All I could do was close my eyes and hold them tight as their swords rampaged within a couple of inches. Wind tore through me, but that's all I felt. Daring to open my eyes, my gaze met a whirlwind of sulphur and pain. Not theirs. It was akin to a million screams at once, all melded within them. Moments like these are hard to describe as a mundane and not well-versed. I can only imagine and dread what the detectives have been through.

The nearest way to put it is that, as well as the screams and pain, I almost felt who and what they were, names being hollered, calling for help. Tormented souls unable to get to where they should be. If I guessed, over the centuries, these things would kill and would immediately absorb their essence. No doubt making the knights stronger. Every single one, all tearing through me. Victims ripped apart and swallowed up. Sick bastards—the mundanes' souls, all of their emotions. There was so much torment. It wasn't fair. No one deserves to suffer in life and after death.

No sooner had I felt the last pass through than everything changed, a lot quicker this time. I was crying, full-on sobbing; the pain lingered. Their fingerprints in life. Everything was back to normal, and I was with the others. And I couldn't stop, as if they were still travelling through me. Is that even possible? Each soul toyed with every fibre of my being. I haven't felt torture like this. I didn't speak; I couldn't. How could I put all that evil, blood, and death into words without destroying what fragile hope we had?

Not much had changed since I endured that premonition or glimpse of everything we feared could happen. I'm sitting in the same place, cold stone seeping a chill through my flesh. Another downside of being mundane, unlike George and those like him. They don't seem bothered by trivial details like that. I still felt the aftereffects of all those souls using me as a waypoint. So much blood and death. How was I going to break the news? Nathan had less than fifteen minutes now.

"We've dodged another bullet and completed this fancy puzzle. What happens next?" Michael says, yanking me from those gory thoughts. I'm getting sick of them using Charlotte to taunt me and that flipping nursery rhyme. The girls loved that, and Charlotte had it down to a nightly ritual—one of the few normal regularities in Willowbrook.

As if by magic or just the next phase in the cycle of the Templars dangling the carrot in front of us, the whole slab in the centre of the grouping rumbled. I saw a thin veil of dirt and dust jumping with each vibration. There's no cement lining the perimeter, unlike the rest—stone grated against stone. There's movement.

The slab is rising slowly, showering the air with pent-up nostalgia, history, and more dust that cuts a distinct feeling in the back of my throat. A little sickly for my liking, and for the others too. The price we pay to know still absolutely nothing about what to do next. An old and heavy-looking stone pedestal stuttered its way above ground.

"Is this some bloody joke, matey boy? Ten minutes to live and not a prostitute in sight for a 'happy ending'. There's dead roaming the streets, and some creepy fuckers want this guy for some reason. And this is what we get? A fucking fortune cookie riddle," Michael says, red-faced and pissed off. I get it. On top of the pedestal, there's an engraved plaque slotted within the surface. I see a slight glow, a gleam of light forcing its way out from the edges.

'Light will come from the dark. One less than whole possesses the 'might' to rise for the fight. The prize is granted to thee, with the fortitude to climb from the ashes of death and embrace the 'Knight'. What lurks as evil in the haunting black can shine against all in the white.'

George paced side to side, his eyes glowing bright red. He was checking every angle of the pedestal, clutching his chin, thinking. The cryptic verse had me as confused as ever. A constant state for me these days. All was quiet except Nathan's erratic, clammy breathing. He was close to gone. I saw the movie 'The Living Dead'. How quickly the assistant declined after inhaling the fumes from the 'dead guy' drum: the clammy 'dead' grey, the blackened mouth, thick black rings around sunken ghostly eyes. Every juddering breath produced white vapor plumes. His skin was shrinking, thinning as if bodily fluids like water beneath the flesh were rapidly evaporating.

"He hasn't got long," George says, glancing at me.

"I know, less than ten minutes."

"That's not what I meant. Use your enhanced sense. Focus on the surrounding smells; picture them like an IMAX cinema. So overwhelmingly strong but tangible, you can move through them like objects, shoving one after the other out of the way until you find your target. In this case, Nathan. You'll see what I mean," George says, whispering with a touch of resignation in his voice. He was only saying what I'd been too scared to acknowledge.

Closing my eyes, I did just that: focused, inhaled, and meandered through the vibrant jungle of aromas until Nathan. Rotting. Nathan was rotting from the inside out. His organs were slowly dying. I could hear each one tightening. Veins, fibres, ligaments, and stomach lining were all decaying. Suppose I was asked to describe the metamorphosis as a feeling or emotion? It was as if all the joy and colour had been sucked out of life. Everything is bland and tasteless, a million shades of grey: no fun, no happiness, just death.

"Fuck... Ere Gerald, that's got to be for you. You know, fate and all that malarkey. All the clues and talk of one from your bloodline nonsense, being strong enough to change things. Especially if you lot are descending from them Templar arseholes," Michael says, looking pleased with himself. My guess is George does most of the thinking for him. Not in a bad way, but he seems more clued up on all this dark stuff.

He was onto an idea, though, aside from being highly coincidental. Judging by the flagstones, nothing had been touched in a long while. How would they know? I moved closer, hovering my hand near. I'm staring at the words but not taking any of it in. Have you ever had that? Stare so long at something that your eyes get foggy. Except there was no fog. I was captivated. The nearer my hand moved, the glow around the edges pulsed. Getting quicker and quicker. All eyes were on me.

Cold metal sent a chill through my fingertips. Everything was silent. My head was in an empty black room... Nothing but the quick beating of my heart. Static rippled through my fingers. I could feel the tiny hairs on my arms buzz, trembling over the unknown. My fingers traced each letter, lighting it up like the pulsing glow—word after word. I looked at the detectives for reassurance, hoping they'd steady my nerves.

It's darkness...

Each breath was a flurry of white cloud... My brain citing each word off by heart, 'The prize is granted to thee, with the fortitude to climb from the ashes of death and embrace the 'Knight'.' Stood out, mulling over 'embrace the Knight' and that particular spelling.

'Hush, little Gerald, don't say a word. You'll never see mumma again to get that mockingbird.'

'And when that mockingbird don't sing. Death will come for everyone you're missing.' Charlotte's voice cut through the darkness and deep into my bones. Terrifyingly cold and gargled. My thoughts jumped to the girls, hoping by me not knowing the location. The evil knights couldn't find them either. My hand wouldn't stop shaking, searching for any hint there could be a secret button.

The door in the pillar has me questioning everything now. Still, nothing moves. I reached the last part, having gone over the rest. I trailed from the last letter, and there was a click. I felt the plate shudder against my hand. I jumped, and the plate lifted. There was a wooden box. Exquisitely carved with sigils that I recognised but can't place. The wood is dark, an 'Ash' of some kind, has a sweet smell, slightly floral, and is strong enough that Michael and George are backing away.

I grabbed the box. It's heavy, but in my haste, I didn't think about the true 'Templar' theatrics. Air whistled and cogs spun. First, the shields shook, and several fell, clattering to the floor, making Michael jump like a cat on a hot tin roof. Statues wobbled, and then the whole room shook. A loud squealing set the tone before we felt movement. We were on tracks—steel ground against steel. Michael and George displayed the worry I felt.

Chapter 35

'Gerald.'

The doors swung open, sounding like a strangled cat. (Disclaimer: I have never done that or seen it done, nor would I condone it.) But boy, have I heard them fight—high-pitched squealing loud enough to make my ears bleed. Great, we're mushrooms again. It's dark.

Twenty-four hours had nearly gone in the blink of an eye. We were still in Kingsley, by the looks of it, but a lot further in. For Christ's sake, another farm. The room we travelled in slotted neatly into a large rustic garage; anyone looking in would be none the wiser, and no doubt the room would travel back as soon as we exited. We were sitting ducks with too many run-down buildings and street debris to hide behind. For all we knew, the place was surrounded, waiting. Those creeps have been on our trail throughout, and that raven in the church did a number on me. I imagine they already knew of this place, but something stops them from getting access. This means I was the puppet on strings, and Nathan was paying with his life. The detectives were on edge, trying not to make me worry; they were ruffled. I'd rarely seen either of them knocked out of their stride, even when George endured the toxin. Michael remained calm, and the pair even joked. Now, though, they seemed to be 'touching cloth,' and that's not good.

A sudden change in the wind brought it howling our way, with it the unmistakable 'Eau de Death,' followed by the latest in 'Killer-Sheek,' 'Eau de Blood,' and for those special occasions, 'Eau de Sulphur.' Michael tilted his head, inhaling. George's eyes blazed a more blood red now, scanning the shadows. I could see further, but I didn't know how much longer. I wished mine were a bit fancier and would change colour like George's, maybe allow me to see different heat signatures. At least if mine went red or even yellow like Michael's, I could pretend to belong. Fake it until you make it, right? It's a bit like me feigning normalcy for years. You could say that ship has well and truly sailed. Likely on its way down the swollen 'Willen River' with my good friend 'the tiny boat,' AKA 'HMS Fear.'

Jokes aside, a lot of death is coming, and I feared how the cards would lay once the dust settled. That peek behind the curtain has me rattled. Even now, looking at the dry, muddy rubble stretch before us and the uneven track littered with creaking flared trees yawning their arm-like branches to the chaotic winds, there are flickers and sporadic flash images of blood. Bones, pungent blackened organs, and shredded flesh were used for nothing more than stepping stones amongst the crimson canvas. Intestines stretched purposefully from the lowest muscular 'oak' forearm, creating a swing with a seat from stretched torso flesh.

This is a nightmare view suited to any horror movie, bordered by a sky I didn't think could get any darker. How wrong was I? A blanket of wings, whipping the chilly air, swooped in from beyond the semi-peaceful horizon. That haunting, piercing blue set the ominous mood lighting of impending doom.

My throat squelched at the swell of saliva I hadn't dared to swallow out of fear of being heard. My heart set the anxiety rhythm throbbing between my ears. Nathan was now dead weight, flopped across my shoulders, his clammy flesh now a deathly cold. He was knocking on heaven's door.

'Hush, little baby, don't say a word; mamma's gonna make your screams heard.'

'And if those screams aren't loud enough, your mamma's gonna get torn up.'

A scarily hypnotic chorus of that tormenting rhyme chose the wrong moment to bellow through the skies. Charlotte's words were as menacing as those beady blue eyes. It grew louder, more piercing, and my ears throbbed painfully; the rhyme felt so close and smothering until my head felt like a needle was jabbed through my eardrums. I hung my head, finding it unbearable; the others were unaffected. George was looking at me like I was going mad. The torment was driving me close, and I found it odd that only I could hear it, especially with their super hearing. Then it halted.

"How far do you think it is to the car?" I ask naively, shaking off the ringing. If we could get Nathan and the box safe, there would be two fewer distractions from what I feared would happen. I assumed those ravens would let us move anywhere.

"By the looks of it, at least half a mile. Too far to try. Besides, I reckon they have other ideas," George says, pointing to the menacing flock in the sky. I glanced at Nathan's grey head, flopping forward. Life was all but drained from him, barely able to breathe. That corded vial swung into view as I shuffled him further on my shoulder for better support.

The cord had tiny black symbols throughout its edging. They were sigils. Not that I knew what any of it meant. We hardly had the time to pop into the library for reference. There were more on the wooden casing of the vial. I was about to return my focus ahead when I saw tiny letters etched on the thin lip, 'Plan B,' which made me think of Nathan's father and the backup plan. What was it, though? It had to concern Nathan. Otherwise, it could've been hidden with the blade in the cabin floor. We're all waiting, but nothing's happening except for the ravens looming.

"Might be wise to move along the path by the house there, with more shelter and obstacles between us and whatever comes our way. Nathan can rest on the metal bench on the porch," Michael says, pointing to the big farmhouse next door. The right side was shielded by the side of a tin barn, limiting access to us, and the porch was wide like a corridor, with the roof blocking that crap from above.

We shuffled along the dirt track; the detectives shielded Nathan and me. We only had to make it fifty feet, and Nathan would be safer. All I could hear were the wings whipping above us while the constant breeze ushered blood, death, and sulphur to follow us. The first step, 'crack,' Michael crashed his foot through the rotten timber, nearly sending him flying. Every movement had me thinking the house could fall. What happened to this bloody village for it to be deserted?

Nathan's safely laid out on the bench; Michael and George flared their claws sharply, looking ahead. I heard rustling by the bush line at the bottom of the path. I propped Nathan's head on the armrest, checking his breathing. I turned to join the others...

'Whoosh!' I heard a quick fizz through the air. George darted his claws in front of my face in a flash. He caught a long black arrow between his claws—an inch from between my eyes.

'Arrrgghh,' George growled, showing his right palm, which was bleeding. The sides of the arrow had been adapted with blades, and they were dripping a yellow fluid. The wound on his hand was infected, and yellow track marks weaved up his wrist. He weakened immediately, stumbling sideways into the crumbling railing, nearly falling through.

"Wolfsbane," Michael says, grumbling through gritted fangs. He tossed what could be a lighter but looked like a mini blowtorch. George caught it on the second attempt, fumbling—a quick click and a powerful blue flame jetted out. And I mean 'jetted,' like a fighter plane gearing up for takeoff. There was no messing around; George let it rip into the blood pooling in his palm. Much like the flare incident, he burned the wolfsbane out of him. Who shot the arrow and how they knew about wolfsbane? Yellow clouds drifted from his hand, the track marks receding in the nick of time, too.

"Hey Georgie, when you're done playing with fire, get over here." I didn't need to look. Painful yawning and churning filled the air. 'Undead' were approaching, and lots of them.

They swarmed from everywhere. Any point that could be a hiding place they came from. We were 'bottlenecked' as the farm's muddy road rapidly filled. Each one groaning, prickling my skin with goosebumps. So loud, so much pain. My mind flashed to the vision and how that felt—all those souls.

"Holy shit. Look at the front," George says, pointing with his now healed hand, looking lively again. I saw Grace, the librarian, staggering; her skin was peeling. All of those cuts from the barbed wire that I saw in my nightmare were pissing blackened blood. I glanced nervously at Nathan. There were only a couple of minutes left.

The beating wings above quickened. The blanket of ravens was now flying in circles, their spooky blue twirling in the sky. Like a tornado, they spiralled into a funnel, swooping down with a thunderous boom, quickly morphing into death; the two creepy Knights, without breaking stride, landed a fair bit ahead of the 'undead.' Both had the butts of their swords tipping past their dirty cloaks towards the night sky. Each nonchalant stride jettisoned black clouds of sulphur drifting from their feet. Every footprint made sizzled, blue fire rippled from the edges. Gone were the bony clear faces, no facades.

Chapter 36

'Gerald'

Their true selves were haunting—just bone. Old, grey remnants of flesh stretched thin like melted rubber across decaying bone. Their eyes gleamed a sinister blood-red, thirsting for pain, sunken deep into the bottomless, soulless black of their eye sockets. Their evil smiles chilled me to my core; no lips or gums, only rotted teeth. George looked worried. Glancing at Michael, I heard him whisper, "Where's Ellena?" No mundane woman was alive amongst the horde, and unless she was hidden behind their cloaks, Ellena wasn't here.

"Whatever you do, stay by your friend and that box," George says, looking me in the eye. I saw fear. I knew the feeling well, and George swam in it. He and Michael walked towards the creepy knights. My stomach tensed. I needed to pay attention to two places: Nathan's health and the horror at the front. Every wheeze Nathan forced out felt like it could be his last.

"Baby, is that you?"

Her voice was close, and it was... "Charlotte? Is that you?" I saw flowing blonde hair shimmering under the moonlight, a vibrant pale face, and rose-coloured pouting lips on the sweetest smile I'd missed for six months.

"It's me, baby. I'm free. I've been given a second chance." Charlotte looked alive and real. Tears were brimming in the corners of my eyes; an uneasy lightness nestled in my chest. It had to be her. Dressed in a fancy white blouse, a black pencil skirt, and a white porcelain coat. Exactly how she looked the day she died. Her tiny feet made the floorboards creak. It had to be her. The sweet scent of Chanel No.5 coasted through the air.

"How did you get a second chance?" Charlotte stopped in front of me. Her warm hand took mine. Her green eyes gleamed, but with a slight ripple—watery, maybe—a quiver that seemed to alter the retina. And then normal again. It had to be my fear playing havoc with my brain, translating the information wrong.

"How do you think, silly? Because of you, of course."

"What do you mean?"

"Being so brave to find the box. They wanted to reward you. They said you're a god amongst mundanes. Did you hear that, baby? They think you're a god. See, I always told you, baby, you're meant for more. You can do so much more. Don't quote me, but they want you to work for them." Everything Charlotte said felt confident. Her heart was beating and steady. It was what Charlotte said that made my balls twitch.

Charlotte drifted her hands up my arms, static rumbling over my skin. Her eyes, though, I couldn't take mine off them. Emerald green, tiny tree bark patterns throughout. The pattern seemed to spin. I didn't want to move. I couldn't.

"They want to reward me."

"Yes, baby, doesn't that sound exciting? Look what you've done to help make this mundane world better already." Charlotte's hands cupped my mesmerised face, turning it to face from the porch, slowly helping me get a better view, rocking my body closer to the steps to see nothing but wide open spaces, bounding green hills, horses running in a paddock, prancing happily. Our daughters are throwing a frisbee for our dog. Our cute Labrador mix is fast as shit off a shovel. Our girls are happy; everything looks peaceful.

"Did I do this?" I whisper.

"Hush, little baby, don't say a word. Mamma's gonna buy you a mockingbird. And if that mockingbird don't sing, Gerald is about to lose everything."

"And if that diamond ring turns brass, Mamma's gonna destroy Gerald's world and kill him last."

That rhyme came again. Charlotte was singing it. I was still mesmerised, staring at the tranquil green and the girls. Something was wrong. My eyes, whatever I was seeing, were glitching. The view shuddered, flicking between different images. There's green... no, it's dirty mud and rundown homes. No, wait, it's blood... it's lots of blood. It smells so strong and coppery and... and the pain... there's so much pain. The blood is everywhere.

No, it's green grass and hills. The girls are laughing. No, wait, it's muddy, there's sulphur and screams. Why is everyone screaming? It's so loud. My ears hurt; they want to bleed. It's all quick, unnerving and painful flashes. What's real? Is Charlotte real? Am I real? What if I'm hallucinating again? Oh god, the blood, there's too much. Can somebody stop it? Please... I can't breathe. My chest. My fucking chest is tight. It hurts. It fucking hurts. Sharp stabbing pain, my heart, it's... so... much... pressure. Something is squeezing my heart. I... I... can't take it anymore. My face is boiling... I... Can't breathe.... Please make it stop. Make the pain stop.

"Oh, baby... why would you want that? You'd miss all the fun. After all, you said I would have your heart forever. Fuck... It feels so squishy... I can feel blood trying to pump around your body... And if I put my finger on this little tube like so, you lose all feeling in the left side of your body. Colour and life is all forced to one side. Damn... you look like Two-Face."

Warm breath polluted by sulphur grazed my right earlobe with each word. The voice was hardened, raspy. There was so much pain, I couldn't feel my left side. I couldn't stand on that leg. I needed to fall over, but whatever was crushing my heart was also holding me upright. The flashes were quicker now; I felt so confused. It's a dream. No, it's a nightmare. Where am I? Who am I? Arrgghh, what's that piercing my back?

"How does that feel, a mundane meat puppet? A little flick of the nerves through the spine to your brain, and you don't know what day it is or if you still wear nappies? Damn, this is so much fun. If only I knew I could do this sooner. My dear, sweet Gerald, so kind of you to help. You remember helping, right? And you said for your reward, you'd like to know how it feels to be helpless and vulnerable, knowing your heart is literally in the palm of my hand."

"I remember helping."

'Gerald, let me in. Let me in now, before it's too late. That's not Charlotte. What you see is an illusion. A clever, evil illusion. Let me in, and the pain will stop.'

I heard weeping... Its cold, melancholic wails. It's familiar to me, but I can't think why. It sounded inside of me and all around. The flashing images were slowing....

"Oh, baby, you still have some fight in you. Let your dear Charlotte take that burden from you... Wait, what's going on? What is this sorcery? Let go of me. Gerald, help your Charlotte.... Stop that... So, it's like that. Let's leave a little mess to clear up; how's a broken rib, and a punctured lung sound?"

"AAARRRGGGHH!" Searing pain ripped through me; my brain was settling. My top right rib was snapped, and all air was ripped out of me as the rib tore into my lungs. Pressure ripped out of my back. I lost my balance, and my blood sprayed the floor as I fell.

I heard a familiar gravelly laugh. I hit the deck, drained and struggling to breathe. A tall, obscured shadow loomed over me, stepping forward from the moon's glare.

It was the 'whispering man'. It was the killer. The one who murdered Nathan's parents, Grace, and most likely the others... His gaunt, deathly face, wisps of charcoal flesh peeled from his jaw and cheekbones. Those demonic eyes pierced their deep, garish red vibrancy through my mind. That dirty, bloodstained trilby was covered in more blood now. While I struggled to breathe, blood pooling beneath me, I was locked onto his haunting aura, part terrified, reliving all those moments over the years.

All the glimpses, shadows and the black cloud breezing to stand over my grandparents. And my act of childish defiance. I was part curious. I don't know why, but I sensed something familiar and not haunting. I fell for it again, and now I was at the 'whispering man's' mercy. Blood seeped into my lungs, making me cough it up. Another nail in my coffin came quickly; his long, bony hand drifting inside his cloak, swiftly unhooking a large object before producing the proverbial rabbit from the hat. The 'whispering man' had the box.

A quick flick opened the lid, and a glowing Rubik's cube-sized artifact appeared. If it could be called that, an aura that looked more like a sliver of space, stolen and wrapped around its edges. Black with a white glow and a ton of tiny white speckles. Each side had tiles that slid to make up sigils, with one small space on four sides for our puzzle pieces. The 'whispering man' reached into his pocket, producing a third piece, covered in blood, which he wiped on his cloak.

'Click,' it slotted in.

I noticed the time: Nathan's twenty-four hours were up. I couldn't hear him breathing, and I had no strength or room to move so I could reach him and try that vial.

'I can help you... If you just let me in.' The darkness called again. I didn't respond. Not straight away. I looked at the thing that had plagued me, taunting me now that he had Pandora's box. I couldn't see what was going on with the Detectives. I turned to Nathan, remembering the farm and when we were trapped in shackles.

"Help him, and we'll see. The vial around his neck—tip the fluid down his throat," I say, clinging to the last of my hopes as I struggled to sit upright, slipping in my blood. Whatever happened with the undead, the Knights, and the Detectives, there was a lot of noise, the occasional bone-jarring roar. I was too limp and clammy to fight on. I felt it leave me, an odd thing to say considering I was swimming in blood and as near death as Nathan now. A branch-like spiral of black drifted unnoticed from my side. It snaked low until it reached the bench, coiling and twirling up the leg towards the armrest and Nathan's head.

The darkness lassoed the cord in a remarkable, yet spooky, performance. The vial hovered mindlessly, drifting towards Nathan's mouth, which hung slightly ajar. I cautiously looked at the 'whispering man', amazed at how inconsequential some deem the little things. My tormentor was busy gloating to notice. The darkness sizzled and struggled, trying to release the cap. I felt every ounce of the pain; I was burning up. It had to be the sigils; the darkness continued, gripping tight. If I wasn't in enough pain, this had me on the ropes and was dancing a jig on my grave.

Finally, the cap came off; the liquid glowed bright, and now that it was exposed to the air, the darkness tingled from it. Whether this thing that so desperately wanted to be a part of me was anything demonic, it had a connection to the essence of the fluid. Dripping freely into Nathan's mouth, all that was left was hope.

"So, now most of the fun has been used up. Where's the puzzle piece?" My attention snaps back, a wasted attempt because I didn't know.

"I wish I knew. Now fuck off."

"Still, a fighter to the end. I have to admit, it wasn't meant to happen like this. They had designs for you. What can I say? I got carried away. Trying a new trick, and I wanted to feel your life in my hands. Oops."

"Looks like you were premature; probably the story of your life. No doubt they'll make you pay." The 'whispering man' grabbed the butt of his sword and swung it wide before lunging forward. I caught the sword in my hands, the blade pushing through, tearing into my flesh, spilling more blood. Its tip pressed on my bony chest over my heart. I could feel it pushing and pushing. Having lost so much blood already, I was too weak and could feel it slipping, piercing my chest. The darkness had returned, and Nathan was in God's hands now.

Chapter 37

'Détective Reynolds,'

'Détective Reynolds,'

You've heard thunder clap. Now imagine that noise multiplied by a thousand, morphing into two sinister medieval Templar Knights, turned to the dark side. How they've survived for centuries and the changes they've witnessed, the carnage they've instigated, defies comprehension. Even if we overcome these two, we don't know how many more are waiting to be thawed.

It's not like they have some 'Templar test-tube baby production line,' do they? What if they do? In all seriousness, if we fail and the gates of hell open, there's no telling how many got slaughtered when the French king at the time declares the Templar order had grown too powerful and wanted them 'culled.' When I first heard the extent of this case was more than the typical serial killer, I was sceptical. Now, their history intrigues me, especially how dark the order has become. Even if we succeed, I don't think we'll escape soon. Some of us may not make it at all, and I will move heaven and earth to get Ellena back. Second chances like ours are rare. I can't let that be snatched away to be used as a pawn and collateral damage. I know Little Lamb is brave and mentally stronger than me most of the time. Watching these freaks enter without her was worrying unless she was hidden nearby.

I've tried locking onto the scent of her coconut shampoo, but nothing. In Scotland, I could filter out so much and find her from a distance just in time; otherwise, she would've gone off the cliff. The point is, I don't think she is anywhere near, and that scared me. The Knights had ditched their suits. Both had the butts of their swords tipping past dirty cloaks towards the night sky. Each nonchalant stride sprayed black clouds of sulphur from their feet. Every footprint sizzled, and blue fire rippled from the edges. Gone were the bony clear faces, no facades.

Their true selves were ugly as fuck. Just bone. Old, grey remnants of flesh stretched thin like melted rubber across decaying bone, their eyes blazing blood red, like mine. Only theirs looked hungry to inflict pain. Sunken deep into the bottomless, soulless black of their eye sockets. Their creepy smiles were something only a mother could love; as theirs kicked the bucket long ago, they were shit out of luck. No lips or gums. Only rotted teeth. It made Michael's look healthy.

All I could hear were the chilling, mindless yawns from the undead staggering slowly behind. There are hundreds of them. A cruel abuse of the natural process of things. These should be left to rest. I see Grace, the victim from the library; her body is ripped to shreds and oozing blackened blood. If she's here, the others will be somewhere, and that had me on edge because I couldn't see them. Translation: there's another plan afoot.

Michael and I stood our ground; the wound on my hand had finally fully healed, raising the question, who fired the air? It couldn't have been the Knights; they were too busy showboating in the sky. Unless the undead suddenly regained the use of their brains, then it couldn't be any of them.

"This was a fight you didn't have to join, Mr. Reynolds."

"Ah, well, we're here now. Besides, you kind of made it our business, letting your little pet run around killing people. Didn't you consider a little training, you know, to show a little restraint? He's like a stray dog humping anything that moves. Maybe that is your method, after all. To live vicariously through him? I imagine it's been a while, nothing but dust and a million therapy sessions. For the other party, of course."

"There you go again, hiding behind your mundane jokes. Failing to realise, the game is already over."

"If it's already over, why are you before us, flapping your… I guess you call those teeth? Either way, why all the theatrics, then?" I'm looking around, noticing the undead numbers had grown considerably. They'd gradually drifted around the space between the house, the dirt road, and the run-down shacks opposite. I was suddenly a 'B-List' movie star and had the leading role in a low-budget horror flick that could give 'The Return of the Living Dead' a run for its money. Everything about that movie mirrored our lives at the minute. Except for no army experiments gone wrong. Or calling out for 'brains'; instead, these are soulless, thoughtless, empty vessels.

I believe Gerald called it earlier... Nathan... He mirrors the young warehouse guy and the old man's boss when they bust the toxic waste drum with the zombie body in it. Nathan's decline mirrors, and by the look of these smug pricks in front of us, they have no intention of a cure. What I haven't told Gerald, in case I'm wrong, nor Michael for that matter, there's something different about Nathan. Unfortunately, I don't think he knows either. It's the demon part of me. I find it hard to explain the feeling, kind of like the rumble of my hackles when danger is near.

With the demon bit, there's a burning at the back of my eyes. The red glows brighter. Imagine the flashing of headlights to allow the driver opposite to pass or turn. My eyes react like headlights. It's involuntary, and no one notices. Took me a while to figure it out. But it was made all the clearer at the cabin when I was searching, and the standoff with the killer, or should I say Gerald's 'whispering man'. All nightmares get warped and changed, and as much as he's been plagued by the darkness calling to him. I fear the glimpses he had may have been the killer stalking him. It's clear he's one of the other bloodlines, dressed all dark and scary with the trilby hat. I reckon that's the universal 'designer chic' once they embrace the darkness. What a fucked-up dress code, eh?

The giveaway was Gerald's father on the VHS tapes. The shadow was his 'darkness' haunting him like what's going on with Gerald. So, these fuckers in front of us had the killer on Gerald's case for a long while. Probably crushed his father with the scaffolding, too.

"A few loose ends. Needed yourselves to retrieve the box. Only someone of Gerald's standing would've been allowed to retrieve it. All we need now is the puzzle piece, and judging by the looks of it, that won't take long." The Knight drifted with a bony, decaying hand, pointing to the house.

My eyes had to be deceiving me. I must've blinked eight or nine times before I saw the same. Gerald stood on the porch smiling his head off, holding his arms up around waist height. If I didn't know what I know, I'd say he finally snapped because he looked to be holding someone—hand in hand or arm in arm. Gerald alluded to hallucinations and whatnot. This looked personal, someone or something dear to him. I've been there, seen my share of ghosts, some so real it's hard to know what's going on. Thankfully, we didn't have Casper and his crew knocking around, too. There's plenty of dead to go around. Having ghosts would be the straw to break the camel's back.

Looking at 'happy' Gerald was unnerving, not least because these creeps seemed happy about it, too. And their smiles were giving me the 'ick'. Gerald was rocking side to side, almost dancing, tilting his head, listening. This went on for a good thirty seconds until Gerald was facing us on the mud track, again smiling his head off.

"Right, cut the crap, matey boy. What's going on? This circus is getting old, and I'm gagging for a pint," Michael says, firing shots across the creep's bow.

The Knights smiled, their red eyes gleaming. I could feel the undead closing in. "Keep watching," one says, his long, menacing fingers toying with the handle of his sword. The other did likewise. They were waiting for their moment to attack. Michael and I shuffled backward, kicking through the rocky mud, nearly tripping with our eyes trying to be in two places at once.

Gerald's face began changing, alternating between happy, sad, and then scared. It was spooky. All we could do was watch and listen to the undead yawning in sickly unison. Their stomps formed a chorus of impending doom, causing me to picture them as an army marauding the streets filled with blood, likely even now, while we're in no-man's-land. Gerald's face stretched, turning pale as his eyes widened until the 'whites' blazed bright. His mouth moved, making all the actions as though he was shouting, but nothing came out.

I shuffled my foot, ready to run to Gerald's aid. A knight wrenched his sword free. It glistened with that deadly toxin. I stayed, looking down the tip of the blade, wanting to send it where the sun doesn't shine. Even the slightest move now caused the undead to step closer.

"Nothing rash, George. You'll miss the best part."

Gerald grimaced, and in the blink of an eye, his body contorted, arching backward as if wounded in his back. A few seconds later, his upper body buckled sideways. He was in agony. Then, with no rational reason, Gerald was thrown backward in a heap. 'blood,' lots of it. I could see it spray across the porch floor. I was desperate to help him. The Knight knew this, pushing the sword inches from my chest.

Just when I thought I'd seen everything, or as much as any sane person can digest in such a short amount of time, I was blindsided by the 'whispering man' appearing. Dripping blood from his cloak, that haunting grey, menacing face breezed up to Gerald, ripping the box from Gerald's struggling grip. A blood river flowed. My eyes zoomed in to watch the crimson tide travel across the breadth of the crumbling wood, trickling over the steps, slowly at first. It soon became a bloody waterfall, one step after the other. Gerald clambered backward with his life depending on it, struggling to pull himself onto his elbows. The killer, as I prefer to call him, lifted a cube from the box. It glowed, encasing its edges with what appeared to resemble 'space' in all its twinkling glory. It was breathtaking and scary. I could feel the power emanating from it, all the endless darkness that didn't belong here, not in this world.

My anger simmered, waiting to explode. Michael too. The killer swiftly wielded his sword, thrusting it at Gerald's chest. Gerald caught the blade but couldn't hold it. The sword was tearing through his palms. I couldn't stand and watch this. How could we stand by and let Gerald be run down like this? If that wasn't enough…

"His heart just stopped?" I whisper to Michael, feeling helpless. I hate that feeling.

"Yeah, I just noticed. All of this is happening, and we're conveniently tied up. Gerald is pissing blood and facing down a sword. We're amongst this shit. Another move and that blade is in your chest. We run, they're probably as quick. Then there are these dead fuckers. I hate to say it, matey, but our backs are against the wall, and I don't know how this nightmare ends." Michael was right, of course. Every angle I looked at this mess from ended in bloodshed. Likely ours.

"Oooh, whispers, I like this game. How about I show you how this ends?" The Knight, not holding the sword, breezed beside me. He leaned in close. Never have I felt so powerless. In moments like this, he was more haunting up close, sulphur and death teased the tip of my ear as he whispered. I was so off guard by his sudden movement. I didn't expect what came next. Distracted by his nightmarish face, I wasn't watching his hand. Those creepy, long fingers whipped behind my neck. Deathly cold. His razor-sharp nails scythed into my flesh, penetrating deep into the nerves leading to my brain stem…

Electricity strobed through my body. My claws were full and thick. Searing heat burned through my brain, bright flashes and blood. It hurt, everything hurt, everyone was in pain. Their screams filled the air. Thousands of lost souls were in agony. I had to make it stop. It had to stop. No, don't do it… Don't do it. A sea of red covered the streets. I saw a knight with a mundane at his mercy, buckled to the floor. He was battered and bruised, but that wasn't enough. The Knight stared at me; he lifted his shiny, pointed shoe, hovering over the mundane's head. The Knight let rip with a bloodcurdling laugh, and then…

'Crunch.'

My eyes clenched tight, my fangs ground hard, pushing out the sadistic sound of the mundane's skull crushing. The pressure did not relent. His skull collapsed like a 'sinkhole,' his eyes exploded from the sockets. Their whites became dribbling mush mixed with the retinas. Two poached eggs popping, squelching as flesh ripped in half down the centre and through the nose. Its bony bridge splintered before the final few pounds of pressure shattered teeth, jaw, and gums. A gooey pancake littered with bone sank amongst a pool of blood. All the while, the mundane's body twitched and writhed for a few more seconds. A fish out of water, flopping around.

It was the same everywhere, streets ripped in half and glowing, air raid sirens echoing through the darkness. Oh, my god... There's Ellena... She's lashed to a giant tree in the centre of the village. Her head hangs limp, blood pours from open wounds, too many to count. She's guarded by undead, with others terrorizing fleeing mundanes. Any strays that are too fast get swept up by the Knights, dispatching them with the ease of that crushed head. I wanted to go to Ellena; I needed to. Every fibre in my being longed to save her from this nightmare, but I couldn't. I couldn't move forward. I was being held back by more than this vision or hellscape. A part of me thinks it's my mind too. Psychosomatic. Black smoke shaped like people poured from the glowing cracks in the street, screeching a piercing shrill that shook my hackles. They reeked of sulphur.

They were swarming the skies, weaving through the rain, looping past Ellena, lashing out, leaving claw marks in her flesh. Blood-rain fell from the sky. Hell had taken over. I need to stop this. It can't be allowed to happen. What if I hurt the wrong person? Scotland still has its claws in me, and I needed to remove them. My fear could cost me Ellena. If I don't stop, it could cost the world.

I had to embrace my nature again. The Knight scraped the remaining brain juice from his shoe, took another look at me, and bolted. He was a black blur with two red dots. He was nearly here. What do I do? His path was scorched with his footprints. He was getting close, too close. All this torment has to stop... NOW.

His blur slowed the more I focused. Within the ripples of black smoke, I saw him clearer. Wind caught his shirt, the middle button flapped loose under the pressure from his speed, revealing a bony, almost vampiric dead chest, and something else. It appeared mechanical, plunged deep into the area where his heart would be. Obsidian in color, with Baphomet's symbol on the surface, the goat's head too, except it's made from a blood-red stone. The gap closed. I stopped holding back. Feeling all that pain from those souls, all of my regret from Scotland, and I dropped my right fist with claws fully out. Still seeing the Knight within the blur, I ground my foot down and powered forward, punching my claws through the smoke and the red stone. His chest caved in, the stone shattered, and the Knight exploded into flames, quickly becoming ash, scattering to the wind.

The electricity rumbled again, and I was bolted back, the sword poised at my chest. I felt the knight's claws withdraw quickly. Something was different. I smelled it too—fear. His hand shook, nails catching my neck. He blurred back near the other knight, who had moved a few paces further back. Michael noticed it too and then looked at me. I felt different, lighter, almost freer. I checked my claws. There were shards of that red stone caught in my fur. How did I bring it with me?

"What happened?" Michael says, doing his best to whisper even lower.

"I don't know. I think it was a preview of what's coming. It was fucking awful. They had Ellena strapped to an enormous tree." I held back about the stone and the symbol in the chest. It had to be their weakness for that knight to combust the way he did. This knight that spiked my neck saw it too, and that's what has him worried. I believed I'd found the weakest link, the chink in the evil Templar armor.

"Oh... Th-that was exactly what's coming," the shaky knight spoke up, involuntarily reaching for his chest, checking. I had my mark. Yet, like all good ideas, especially ones by us, they never go according to plan. I was about to revel in my renewed confidence and give Michael the green light to cut loose and get bloody when I heard a loud scream coming from Gerald. The 'Whispering Man' was winning the battle, his sword impaling Gerald's chest little by little. I could feel Gerald's pain. Pure agony. A tear bubbled at the corner of my eye, watching. Michael too. It's crazy how pack dynamics work, feeling each other's pain... Wait... What did I just say?

Pack dynamics and feeling pain—we could feel Gerald's. How was that so? The only way that's possible was if he wasn't a mundane at all. More than the darkness within him. He's different. That's what could turn the darkness on his side. I bet he doesn't know, same with Nathan, yet also different. To me, a pack is more than being the same supernatural creature, the same color fur, or the same country the shapeshifter was formed. No, to me, it's family. It's friends that will drop everything at the first hint of danger. They look to protect one another from what may come.

It's also new friends that began on opposite sides of the law, with a common interest and will go toe to toe, side by side to stop 'Hell on Earth.' One thing is for sure, Gerald and Nathan were more than they know, and their parents hold the secrets. Some may have taken them to the grave. If there's any constant I've noticed in this world, nothing is truly dead. Gerald let loose with another loud scream. Something was happening to Nathan, too. His heart had stopped, but I sensed his core body temperature rising, and fast.

"Georgie? Georgie?... What are we doing? It's now or never."

A quick look around, weighing up the options. The undead, Gerald, and the Knights. "Now, fly right." Eyes glowed and claws flared. The undead swarmed us, closing the circle of death... For them... Again. I dodged Grace out of pity, shredding my claws straight through a line of the undead. Their bodies were brittle. I took their heads clean off. Black blood gushed through the air. This is what I call 'do or die,' with a liking for the first option. Gerald screamed again, weakening. I glimpsed his head dropping as the 'Whispering Man' buried the gleaming blade through his chest. Gerald's hands clung to the sword, the last trickle of life slipping away.

Chapter 38

'Gerald,'

Every scream was agony. I could barely breathe, with my rib using my lungs as a piñata. The 'whispering man' had me pinned. As if sadistic murderers needed added incentives, I was sure he enjoyed himself even more if he was the same one I had stopped from murdering my grandparents. The sword's blade slid deeper, cutting through flesh, muscle, tendons, and bone. I could feel the point dangerously close to the side of my heart. My saving grace was that he'd missed. I was sitting in a pool of my blood, trousers soaked through, and I could barely stop my hands from slipping off the blade.

Nathan's heart had stopped. As far as I could hear, anyway. I wanted to be angry. I wanted to explode into a fit of rage and seek revenge on those creepy bastards who poisoned him with no intention of coming through with the cure. There was no guarantee that one even existed. The darkness did what I asked of it, tipping the vial down his throat. For all I know, that was a joke, some inter-family thing, and Nathan had to wear it. Fuck, I can't even come up with an alternative story for it. My brain was all but done. My lungs swam in blood, and any attempt at bravado in the face of death led to me choking, spraying mouthfuls of it on my lap.

Everything we did or tried was for nothing. Michael and George were in the middle of some undead death match. I know that sounded better in my head. The undead swamped them, hundreds of them, all crawling from the termite-infested woodwork. Before the pit of doom swarmed, I caught glimpses of a standoff. One of those morbid, death-lukewarm freaks jabbed his nails in George's neck. What I found strange, in five degrees of distant cousins kind of way, I felt it. It bloody hurt. Not as much as being fooled by the image of my dead wife, my heart put in some kung-fu death grip, and then having a sword impale me. Still, I felt George's pain. With no reason. Me, a simple mundane.

'Ouch,' Again, Michael just had his flesh shredded through by nails or claws. If I wasn't in such a bad way and position, I'd be intrigued. Unfortunately, fate has other designs for me. Again, if I wasn't so weak, I'd be kicking myself for being fooled again. In my defense, the church was different. One of those bug-eyed ravens messed me up with hypnosis. Charlotte looked, sounded, and smelled real. Even dressed the same way as the day she died. All the details were too good. Even the sensation of her fingertips tracing my arms. I stared into her emerald green eyes and then... I don't know... I was lost. There were flashes of images, 'the good, the bad, and the ugly,' manipulating me into position to get blindsided. Now look at me. A stiff breeze short of flopping into hell. Perhaps I'll be scrubbing the toilets in hell. It's ironic when you think about it.

Baphomet and his minions want to get up here for some semi-fresh air and a tan. Okay, maybe not so much the tan. Not in these villages anyway, and their unlimited shades of grey. You're probably listening to me thinking, why is he so upbeat with what's going on? I'm not. It's more that I've slipped into a state of delirium. Everything is all sparkly in front of my eyes. It won't be long now if this is happening. Soon, it will be intermittent consciousness where I'll choke to death on my blood.

Through all this, the 'whispering man' is just staring, smiling in a 'nightmare on Elm Street' way. Yes, I quoted that movie again. But seriously, if you watch Freddy smile, you'll get it. What he hasn't grasped yet, with all the damage he's done, is that the fourth puzzle piece is still missing. Speaking of which, I wonder who had the third, who did he slay this time. That thought, though, the missing piece. I couldn't smile.

"What the hell do you have to be happy about? Have you not realized I'm in you?"

"Erm, no offense, and not even while I'm on my deathbed. That would never happen. Never ever. Not judging at all. If that floats your boat, good luck to you. Maybe one of those coffin dodgers will oblige or a coffin escapee. Just not me. Not even if you dress up as Charlotte again." I say, goading him through gargles of blood.

"Funny fucker, are you? Well, I'm surprised you even fell for that, to be honest. How gullible are you? Right, let's get back to business. Where's the piece?" I choked too soon. Still, he'll be disappointed.

"I told you before, and I'll tell you again. I don't know." I say, a little distracted by Nathan. No breathing or heartbeat, and everything was a struggle, feeling so drained. I heard his organs swell. Not in a bloated death way. Nor had he released his bowels after succumbing to the cruel blade of destiny. Don't ask, I read it somewhere. How true? I'd say 50/50. Not only were his insides deciding on a makeover, but I also felt warmth. I mean, yeah, I was colder, a numbing kind. That warmth was drifting from Nathan.

"See, I think you do. I didn't go through all this effort to get here and have you lie to me."

"All of what effort? I'm not lying. What would be the point?" I say, curious about the effort comment, mindful of the undead limbs being tossed through the air, their numbers falling rapidly. Blood flew from every angle imaginable. The two knights watched on, saving themselves. As much as I applaud the detective's efforts, it felt in vain.

Everything was a mess. My preview looked to be coming true, but there were still details that hadn't been lined up yet. If Grace was here, where were the others poignant to our dilemma? What was happening with George's Ellena? And who was the 'whispering man'? Their true self.

"See, I think you have it on you. I think you know exactly where, just being sentimental. The effort? Who do you think scared this shit out of your dear old dad and made the scaffolding collapse? I thought the polaroids were a nice touch. Smear a little of his blood, get photos taken, and job done. Fuck, you should've seen your face when they fell out of the file. Priceless. As for lovely Charlotte, tut tut, making her travel alone. All sorts of bad things happen on those big, nasty motorways. A reckless driver here, a nudge there. Next thing you know, she's kissing the windshield. It's great having people willing to do things for money. Sadly, it was getting awkward. You were quite the busy bee. So they had to go. Now, hand over the piece." He says, laying out his crimes. I was stunned. I felt a spark inside, finding the strength to feel angry. No, I was pissed. Yet, still, I could barely hold my head up.

"You sick bastard. If I weren't so dying, I would—"

"You'd do what exactly. Let's face it: even on your best day, it wouldn't happen. Always too scared. Now, I'll be taking that." He ripped my father's watch from my wrist. I didn't have the strength to fight. He was right; scared has been my second nature. Now, he was interrogating my father's watch with his free, garish, grey-skinned hand. They weren't claws, but the nails were long and fierce-looking. A little like talons. His black leather gloves covered very little, not least the grotesque peeling flesh. Deep enough to show bone. Definitely a point in the nightmare column. If the darkness meant my flesh would deteriorate like that, I didn't want it.

Michael and George were taking a beating, slowing down. They were still ripping through the undead, but their numbers were too great to sustain their energy. All those groaning yawns had me clenching. It was awful; they had to roam the streets like that, reduced to rotting punchbags. I replayed his bragging over and over. The anger had me clinging on. Then, the watch's underside got ripped off, and the puzzle piece fell, in slow motion, into the blood. I couldn't believe my eyes. I had it all the time. Father had to have known when he gave me the watch. Why didn't he tell me? Another question to add to the list of things Father neglected to share.

Chapter 39

'Detective Reynolds'

They kept coming, but I couldn't even see where from. My claws ripped through another undead throat. I had to remind myself they were already dead; it couldn't hurt them. Much like the vampires, a conscience is hard to water down or hide in a box. Every groaning, yawning face had already been through many things. Now, in death, they were the devil's playthings.

Whether they were vessels in waiting or a distraction, what we had to do was hard, and we were flagging badly. The killing circle had become a bloody free-for-all. Seeing Michael covered in blood and intestines was comical, yet sickening. While our batteries were being drained, the Knights were watching, and the one on the left was bothered by me. His jamming those girly nails into my neck hurt like—excuse the pun—hell. He knew what I saw, and it freaked him out. It was their weakness, and when the moment came, which we may only get one shot at, we had to aim there. I was intrigued, though; call it a detective's curiosity. Was that how they maintained such a long life?

Obviously, that was the most rational thought, as a wad of trachea goo splattered my face. The implosion was profound and exhilarating; I wished the others had seen it. The flames quickly turned to ash before scattering to the wind. They would've got a much-needed morale boost if we weren't so up the creek without a paddle.

The way his shirt flapped at the right moment revealed the mechanical thing in the Knight's chest,: made of obsidian, with Baphomet's symbol on the surface. He's a bit of a narcissist, if you ask me, making his prize toys wear such garish things with his symbol. Then again, it's the devil, Baphomet, the prince of darkness, or whatever ridiculous name he gave himself. Talk about being up one's arse: even the bling, a goat's head made from a blood-red stone.

I bet that wasn't cheap. It's not like they can walk into 'Warren James' and say, "Hey there, don't mind the just-dragged-out-of-a-coffin look. Can I have a dozen of your finest rubies carved in the shape of a goat's head? Oh, and it needs to be set in this devilish pacemaker right here. And I need it yesterday, or you'll spend an eternity in hell. Crap, do you take a Visa debit card? I left my Amex in the other 'bloody' cloak." Imagine the faces behind the counter. The nearest I've come to ruby is, as the Cockney prince calls it, a curry—a ruby Murray, me old mucker. Damn, where was I?

Grace kept coming at me; I know she's dead and all, but after being at her crime scene and seeing all of those cuts she endured, I can't bring myself to kick her while her coffin's re-opened. Oh, that's it. Just before I lashed out, I felt all that pain from those souls. What's with that? It's a new one for me. Perhaps it's what I've hinted at already about Gerald and being different. Even now, changes are happening to him with a sword in his chest. He will have to experience an ability to deal with lost or stranded souls. If my gut feeling is right, there will be much to sense soon.

At that moment, though, I unleashed all of my regret from Scotland, punching my claws through the smoke and the red stone. The way the Knight's chest caved in is no wonder Mr Close and Personal are worried. Not even Ellena has dug her nails into my flesh yet. The chance would be a fine thing. It seems we keep getting pulled apart by death, blood, kidnappings, and vampires.

I'm surprised she's willing to hang around when it's listed like that. Must be the hairy chest. Please tell me you get that, as my claws eviscerate another bladder and a pile of intestines that are now spewing over the mud that's rapidly becoming a crimson swamp. I shouldn't find it funny, but seeing the hundreds of limbs and heads still moving on the floor, I do. Taking any chance to find humour in this horror is a must. Everything is always so dark. My nightmares are relentless. Although they've come a long way since the demon's eyes in the burnt basement, they're wearing me down.

I haven't told Michael yet. Aside from the recent ones here, they were truly haunting. It's a chest-pounding fear... and involves London and the elder vampire. I keep seeing him. Not in a memory of what happened. Some of these are graphic, bloodthirsty attacks. Yep, there's a theme; no matter where we end up, there's blood. He genuinely scares me, which is hard to admit, but we won't see it coming if he could become anyone he chooses and is fixed on payback. The Knights evoke a different unnerving in me because they're unknown, yet we're about to get to know each other a little too well the way this carnage is unfolding.

I need to tell Michael that those stones I joked about will shatter if caught properly. The Knights have displayed super hearing, which takes whispering off the table, and we can't share our thoughts, you know, that inner voice thing. Okay, that's a little white lie. There was a brief situation in Scotland when I rescued that 'Alpha', and he jumped into my mind, and we spoke. I don't know how yet. There's so much I need to learn about being a werewolf, let alone an alpha. There's been no time to practise.

Michael and I spin, ripping through another couple of undead each. Blood gushes in my eyes, dripping down my face. I catch a bit in my mouth, too. It's rancid, blacker, dead blood, enough to make me gag. Ordinarily, I'm drooling at the scent of the fresh, coppery stuff, especially on a full moon. This, though, is awful. In our frenzy, Michael and I crash into each other, nearly ending up on the wrong side of some claws. We're panting and struggling. Michael's face told the story in all its vibrant gore. Back to back, shuffling in a circle as the remaining fifty undead close in. Gerald was still fighting; he was weak, but his emotions were everywhere. The 'Whispering Man' has Gerald's watch, the underbelly is off, and Gerald's face... fuck, he's shocked and angry. Oh shit, that can only mean one thing.

"Michael, did you see?" I say, again trying to keep my voice low.

Michael's panting wildly, wiping blood from below his eyes. "I, er, think so. Does that mean what I think it does?"

"Afraid so, detectives. I must applaud the valiant effort. But yes, it's game over. You've lost. There are no do-overs. We have the box and the final piece. Now, everything you previewed will come true, and then some."

"So, everything I saw is real?" I say, focusing on the stone, not thinking about Ellena strapped to a tree, but watching the Knight on the left shift uncomfortably. By the looks of it, it could be every knight for himself when the chips are down. That, right there, is a runner. It is also called Live to Fight Another Day. Something I would very much like to do.

"Everything. Now grab them."

A haunting chuckle follows his words as the undead lunges for us. The Knights draw their swords, breezing towards us. We dodge left and right, avoiding waves of rotten, fleshed arms flailing at us. We're almost cornered. I see a sword drive through a gap in the crowd at the last minute as it heads for Michael's throat, who is busy fending off two undead. I've gripped the blade, holding it off, but I'm weak, and the sword is pushed further.

There's nowhere to run or hide, all but tapped out. My hands slip, giving me a sense of Gerald's struggles. Blindsided, the other sword lunges through, tearing into my right rotator cuff. It's deep, and the knight keeps it in. My arm goes limp. I can't use it or move it. Absolute agony. Blood is pissing out. The muscles try to heal themselves, but the knight twists the sword. The other sword rips from my hand but thrusts back quickly. I try to fend it off, but it rips into my chest. Michael has three undead latched onto him as more pile on. The knights know what they're doing, driving down powerfully. My legs buckle. I'm forced to my knees, helpless. Everything is becoming muffled and foggy. I can hear the knights laughing. Michael is down, too.

They keep twisting and pushing the swords. Blood soaks through my top as I languish amongst the pool of guts and dismembered moving limbs. Everything felt lost. Tears filled the corners of my eyes. All I could picture was Ellena. Not her strapped to the tree. It's our first kiss by the canal. She'd accepted both sides of me without hesitation, and I never imagined finding love again. We've been through hell, but one thing is sure: we love each other. How can this be it? I die amongst other body parts at the hands of creepy knights? If she was here… If she…Oh god, I'm struggling. If she were here, she'd say, get the fuck up and show them who's boss. How? I'm picturing her smiling face. When I feel something weird, I can't describe it other than a small rumble of heat through my hackles. It's coming from Nathan. It's growing more intense. My red eyes suddenly become a brighter blood red.

My gut told me to roll the dice, trust my instinct and… Roar. I closed my eyes, took a deep breath to the pit of my stomach, and grabbed onto all the pain and suffering we've endured and still going through, all the sadness and loss. I pulled it up with as much venom and power as I could muster. Letting rip with an ear rocking, ground shaking, wood rumbling and bone-jarring… 'Rooooaaarrrrrr', emptying everything I had. Trees shook as I sent a mini shockwave rippling through the undead and the knights towards the house. Undead fell to the floor. Michael pulled himself free. His eyes were glowing bright yellow. My head flops forward, spent, but I feel a stirring at the house. That heat dialled up to a ten, and something was happening. Was it too little too late? Or me clutching at straws? There's silence except the groaning, then… 'der-dum, der-dum, der-dum'—a heartbeat.

'Gerald,'

Everything shook; the ground rumbled from George through to the house and beneath. I could feel the wet floorboards vibrating against my limp legs. It rocked the 'whispering man,' too. I felt the pressure on the sword ease slightly. My hands were fighting against the slipperiness of my blood, smearing the blade. Whatever that vial was doing to Nathan, George's roar kicked it up a notch. The heat grew and grew.

Watching the detectives struggle in the swamp of body parts and guts, I felt the swords plunge into them, just as this one did to me. Searing agony, even the numbness as my arm dropped, losing function. That roar, though, I felt it as a sudden shock. My eyes bolted open wide. Then, as if we hadn't navigated through enough twists and surprises, Nathan's heart restarted. Only small blips, but I could hear it getting stronger. Again, I can't believe I'm saying things like that. I'm at least ten feet away and hear shallow beats, as if my ear hovers over his chest.

With every struggle I put up, my strength drained some more. Looking at the smug, horrifying face in front of me was killing me more than the blade. I had the puzzle piece with me all along, and that stings. Because now they are on the verge of opening the gates of hell. A lot still bothered me. If I was dying, I had to know who the killer was—a little closure for the soul.

"Hey, thugly, when you ask for your pay rise or bonuses, perhaps you can ask for enhancements. Like attaching another set of arms, you may find it easier to pat yourself on the back. Maybe they'll throw in a personality for good measure," I say, getting the only reaction I expected. The sword twisted some more, and the blade grazed the right chamber, making me writhe in agony and taking the wind out of my sails.

"Why don't you die already? Your mouth is tiresome."

"Bet the Knights will say that to you soon, no matter how well you please them."

"What's that supposed to mean?"

"Exactly what I said. No matter how much wear you get out of those knees, you'll soon be dispatched." I wanted to laugh, but everything was a struggle. I glanced at Nathan.

It may have been my eyes weakening, but I could have sworn I saw a slight fiery glow assimilating through Nathan's body. The heat grew, too.

"You cheeky bastard! After everything that's been taken from you, there's no giving in."

"My life has been crazy from the get-go. Nothing has been normal, and you made it worse by snatching what's good from me. The difference between them and you is that they will live on in the lives they've touched. In the footprints in the sands of time. You're a footnote in a bad horror movie. Nothing more."

"I'll make history instead of being seen as the weakling everyone overlooks." Did I hear that right? It wasn't the first time, either. The way those photos were described from the folder. I thought it was said as the glimpse of the 'whispering man,' but my instinct caused a shiver that was more than another step closer to death.

"History is exactly that, the past full of people that weren't spoken about enough when they were alive. If you're a 'bloodline,' why don't you show your face? Your true face. Unless you're scared? You have us beat. Look, we're all on our last legs, and soon, the earth will be smothered by the dead in a sea of blood and hellfire. So, come on, a glimpse. For old times' sake. Or history, as you prefer it." I say, leaning into his need to feel wanted. I had to know the snake who destroyed my world and plagued my life. Everything about Charlotte kissing the windshield turned my stomach and boiled what little blood I had left.

George kept trying to stand against the blades. Each time, those creepy knights forced him back, blazing those evil red eyes. Every yawn of the dead was haunting, triggering flashes of that Red Sea and those bodies—a mundane skull. The crunches beneath every step, and that line of creepy knights flanking the dead. How could that be allowed to happen? The 'whispering man' smiles in a way that only a demented mother or a dead one could love. He gripped the sword, leaning into it, pushing the blade deeper. If hell had my number, I may as well fall with the face of the truth.

"Be careful what you wish for, Gerald. What was it?... Oh, that's right. Be bloody careful; this is just the beginning... See, I warned you, yet you failed to listen." There was another echo moment—everything I'd just pieced together.

Death and sulphur swirled on the winds of change, creaking the floorboards, rippling against the blade and beneath my fingers. The 'whispering man' drifted, his garish grey, decaying face close. To within inches of mine, his eyes were as red as the knights. In this moment, looking deep into them, all I saw was Charlotte's crash, the wreck of her car, fluttering like embers of her dying light in the depths of death incarnate, before me. Then the grey shimmered, and the decay faded, allowing the true visage of my tormenter to face me at long last.

Like nothing I've ever felt, rage rapidly grew within me, and so did the darkness. I allowed it to. Seeing the detectives struggle, the knights regained composure after the roar. Nathan was, against all odds, stirring, and I found the courage to look the real 'whispering man' in the eyes. Colin. The man we relied on for help with father's autopsy. He lied to my face. He slipped those horrifying photographs into the file. Fuck... and I bet he cut father's flesh to post to us.

"You sick bastard. How could you?"

"Spare me the melodrama. You couldn't care less who helped you and Nathan as long as you got what you wanted. My father was the same, bragging about how he felt like a king among mundanes and that it would be my turn one day. I didn't want to wait any longer, so I took it... The look on mother's face when she found me cutting through the last few fibres of muscle to remove his head. She too, asked how could I? So, I showed her by removing hers. Now, they sit together in the freezer, and I'm the one who is the king among mundanes. And you're the footnote. Now, it's your turn to die. Goodbye, Gerald, thanks for making it interesting."

'Let me in... before it's too late. They need you. I will bend to your will.'

Colin smiles, just as evil as the garish façade. He cupped my chin with those long, bony fingers, held my head facing him, and drove the sword deep with a final push. Blood spewed out my mouth, and everything went dark... and cold...

Chapter 40

'Gerald'

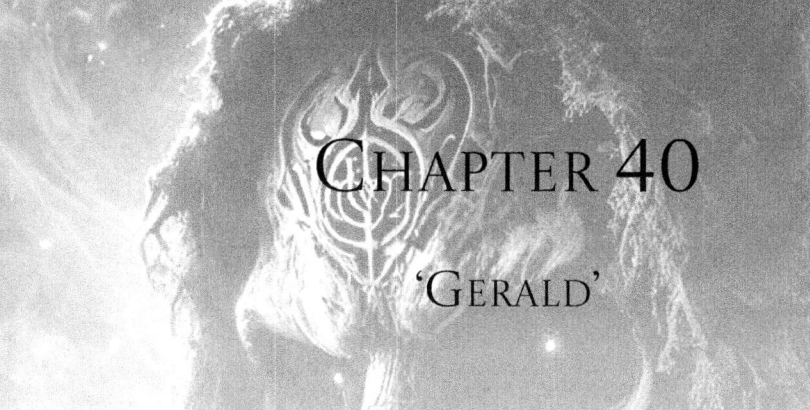

"Well, that was easy. I expected more, and I even hoped for it. It's been a blast terrorising your family and the other bloodlines. Now I'm the one. Finally, the curse means nothing."

Life is full of surprises and twists. Sometimes, it's the least expected that makes the biggest impact. Death is a relentless beast, devouring everything it touches. It lurks in the shadows, waiting until the last flicker of light fades, leaving behind nothing but darkness. Now and then, that flicker has the strength, the last trickle of fight, to spark back to life.

"Wait, what's happening? How are your fingers still moving?"

First came the spasms in my fingers, tapping against the sword and flicking blood. Spasms became a grip. Little by little, my hands pulled towards the handle. My eyes finally opened. It was surreal. Everything was vivid: shades of red, black, grey, and more. I could see the quiver in Colin's lip. His hands shook on the handle.

"How are you alive?" Colin's voice was missing the conviction of moments ago.

"Looks like I finally let the darkness in."

I had boundless strength and energy. I could feel my wounds healing. The blood beneath me was being drawn back into my body. My hands gripped the blade tight, pushing it out of my chest, dragging myself to my feet as the tip finally left. I was changing in ways I couldn't imagine. My hands grew wrapped in a grey protective covering over my arms. I caught my reflection in the blade just as a grey hood drifted over my head. My face was the same, except for piercing red eyes and perhaps slightly leaner. I was becoming the opposite of the 'crooked man,' in shades of grey with a two-tone Templar cross adorning my upper body. The real Templars, not the evil imitations. It felt profoundly euphoric.

And I had 'him'—Colin, or the 'crooked man'—at my mercy. I easily forced the sword up, turning the blade under Colin's chin and forcing him against the railings. Colin was powerless compared to me; anger burned bright, and I had revenge within reach. This moment was about more than that. If I let him go, he'd come again and again. I had to remove one evil bastard from the board.

The tip pierced his flesh; I felt him tremble. I gripped his jaw as he did to me. "Hey, Colin. Are you still with me? I have something important to say."

"Wh... What?"

"One sec... Okay, here goes... Hush, little Colin, don't say a word. Maybe Baphomet can buy you a mockingbird, but if that mockingbird doesn't sing, remember this: you were never a king, just a weakling desperate to be heard. All that will be is the screams from a lonely turd."

With a quick thrust, I tore the sword through Colin's chin, all the way through his skull. His mouth cranked open, feeling the blade's width rip through; blood gargled and spluttered, his tongue impaled too. I looked Colin in the eyes, feeling my pain slowly ebb as the life left his eyes. Tears filled mine, his body heavier on the sword, and capillaries burst, gushing down his cheeks. Revenge was bittersweet, even if it went against everything I stood for. That was then. This is now. I finally let the darkness in, and it's altered me in ways I don't have time to understand yet. The voice is still there, quieter at the back of my mind. One thing was for sure, I wasn't a mundane anymore.

I withdrew the sword, allowing a final spray of blood to paint the floor. Colin flopped limp, dropping. I hear two thuds. I go to see, remembering the box. A black cloud whips forward, sulphur and death. The cloud obscures everything in front. I hear 'yawns of the dead'; they're close.

The cloud vanishes as quickly as it came. In its place, a line of undead, including two that helped Colin, Patrick, Sheh, and Frank Ecklestone. These seemed different. Their eyes glowed a vibrant purple.

I counted at least ten while I was distracted by Nathan's sudden groan. I was right; that fiery glow had overtaken his body, but he was still out.

'How does it feel?' I hear in my head, forgetting the darkness for a moment.

"So far, so good. What exactly are we?"

'We are one. Your strength of character won me over, essentially a demon, the darkness everyone has but different. We are, I guess you could say, a demon Knight of the Templar order, a true heir to the original folklore that did so much good in the world. It's your turn now,' Hearing the voice like this was so weird, still as melancholy as it had been, but now we were one, and I liked the sound of a 'true heir.' Doing good had to start now—a quick check of Colin's cloak. The box was gone. That black cloud took it, meaning those bloody creeps had it.

We needed Nathan awake so we could help the detectives. And try getting the box back.

"Well, that sounds good, but you'll have to help me as I learn about this new world. First, there's these." I say, looking at Frank Ecklestone, his grey rotten flesh oozing that rancid black blood—the word 'Book' etched in his arm.

I surmised that the Book of the Dead may be a trail we must follow if that's the Knights' next step.

'Of course. First, allow me to wake your friend up. I have a feeling he will come in handy,' the darkness chuckles like it knows something. It's surreal to think both of us will be different now after being so close to death. Just what did our parents get involved in, and who were Nathan's parents?

That was another issue that needed to be handled with care. First, a farm drenched in blood, guts and everyone's worst nightmare, the dead roaming free. I feel it again, like when the vial was tipped down Nathan's throat. The darkness slithered from my side, wisps of black that were more grey now, spiralling particles drifting. A sight that will never settle in my mind, I don't think. It became a branch until it lingered over Nathan's face. The end morphed into a hand; I knew what was next. Nathan had an aura around him now, rippling fire, even the tips of his blonde hair.

'Smack,' The darkness let rip with a hard slap across Nathan's face. For a cloud or smoke, it packed a hit.

'ROOOOOAAAARRRRR.'

Nathan jolts upright, creaking the bench, and his eyes rip open wide. It was like seeing two balls of fire. No whites or anything, just fire, the same that quickly engulfed him but not burning. That aura was now a full, fiery bodysuit, as we saw Michael with that yellow fox. This was something else. I couldn't put my finger on it, but it was a kind of huge beastly hound. You've seen Ghostbusters, right, and the beasts that take over the geek and his love interest. The face was that. Nathan was bigger, too, muscular with a set of huge fucking fangs. This was awesome and so bloody scary. God had finally shone his light on us and gave us a helping hand. Maybe, just maybe, we could turn this around.

Nathan stood, moving quickly to face me, even more intimidating up close. While we had the perfect cannon fodder before us to test our training wheels. "Gerald, what happened? I died. I was in this big empty blackness; then suddenly, I was ripped back into my body, and now this. What am I? More the point, what are you?" Nathan's voice had a menacing growl, and I was so glad he was on our side.

"You could say I finally embraced my darkness. FYI, I died too. And guess who the killer was?"

"Who?"

"That fucking gimp, Colin."

"No way, but he was so nerdy."

"Exactly. But we'll have time to catch up. First, we must destroy this lot, save the detectives, retrieve Pandora's box, and stop an apocalypse."

"So, not much then." Nathan chuckles. It was so good to have my best friend back. And finally, we could make a difference.

Ecklestone and Sheh were first up. Sheh defied gravity and common sense; his torso was not connected to his legs, every move had the halves sliding in different directions. Nathan's fire aura glowed as the undead and their yawning groans approached. All it took was a raise of his hands, and fire flew, torching the undead. It was so hot their bodies were reduced to char-grilled black shells glued to the spot. I hear the cracking of crispy flesh. The putrid stink was almost unbearable. Yet, again, I was in awe. It was like watching the 'torch' from The Fantastic Four. I couldn't help but smile. What an upgrade. It kind of had me feeling a little underwhelmed now, which the darkness sensed. 'Don't worry, we have plenty of tricks. Those dead bastards aren't prepared for it. Take out your sword... The one on your hip!' I paused with a chuckle, drawing the sword. Heavier than Colin's. The metal was different, too, with thick leather wrapping around the handle. The butt had a thick round symbol of the Templar cross. There was a smell, too, not the toxin like the Knight's. A gasoline tinge, yet a strange added ingredient. Made me think of the church and its sterile holiness.

We carefully walked down the creaky steps and around the wall of crispy dead, hearing their rotten flesh sizzle. Burnt dead blood smelt even worse. No sooner were we clear.

'Ready.' The darkness says. A blue fire ripped through the sword from hilt to tip, searing heat. Yet it didn't bother me. Nathan was a walking wall of fire, his eyes blazing even brighter, growling as we trudged through the sloppy land of death. Heads yawned. Arms and legs twitched, with the occasional headless body stumbling in circles, their guts spilt like a conveyor belt of butcher's sausages.

From that moment on, everything felt in slow motion, weird all the time in the world, feeling as we moved, getting the knight's attention. The one on the left had let his sidekick impale both swords into George while he had Pandora's box, sliding the tiles around to move the coin pieces in place. Three were complete, and we didn't have long. Michael was still struggling against a mountain of undead—a raft of dripping, crumbling flesh staggered towards us. The moment reached within a few feet, George lifted his head, and his eyes flickered brighter. Michael's, too. The same happened to Nathan. I could feel their pain, particularly George's. Whatever our presence was doing, there was a shift. Both seemed to gain energy and renewed strength.

George let rip with another growl, which was not as loud as earlier, but still enough to shake the ground. With his eyes blazing, a hand gripped each sword, his fangs bared, he pushed the swords out of him. He'd overridden the loss of feeling in his arm to power through. The knight was shell-shocked. Before long, the undead were coming at us from all angles. I never wielded a sword, yet it seemed I'd held one for years. I moved fast and light, dodging and slicing; blood sprayed the air. Some hit my face. Nathan only had to touch one, and their body combusted.

Nathan ploughed through the pile on Michael, gradually breaking him free, who jumped to his feet, drenched in blood, roaring loud enough to give goosebumps. The blood-covered tide was turning, laying to waste anything that came at us, making up for lost time. I manoeuvred a path towards the knight with the swords. It was our turn to face off.

'Are you ready?' The darkness whispered between my ears.

"No time like the present."

'Don't worry, we've got this. Now let's slay this creepy freak.' It was surprising to hear that from something I'd run from for so long. Life is never a straight path. And this felt like a crossroads, a very gory crossroads. And by the time I ever get some sleep, I'm sure there'll be nightmares.

His peeling grey face grinning, spinning the swords, trying to impress. Every swoosh waved his cloak in the wind; every move filled the air with death. We mirrored each other's movements, wading through the bloody pool. I don't know how or why, but I felt a presence, two. A tingle to the back of my neck, a gentle touch on my shoulder. Charlotte and Father were with me. Not in the haunting ways that have tormented my life. I felt them in that moment and my heart. For the first time, it was full.

The knight breezes towards, swinging. I parry his strike, sparks in shades of blue and black, flew as the blades rattled. "Looks like someone got a makeover."

"Yeah, about that. You need additional help. Your guy doesn't have the chops for the dirty work, nor the brains, for that matter." Our swords ground against each other, slipping, and I dodged his next swing before ducking and swiping my blade across his chest. It hurt him, the blue fire was burning him, black smoke sizzled from the wound. I was getting quicker, to the point. The knight's next few attempts missed. I'm looking down through the end of the blade as it comes. With all the time in the world. Shocking, even myself.

I pivoted on the spot, turning and churning through the blood, my back mirroring the Knight before spinning out with my sword at the Knight's back. I drove it through, screaming with rage, then dragging my sword free again. Blue fire ripped through his back and abdomen. The Knight staggered, his sword buried into the bloody mud as a support to keep him on his feet. I turn to check on the others, each ripping through the remaining undead.

"The chest, Gerald, over his heart," George calls out, holding two detached arms without breaking stride or giving the Knight any rest. I spun around his hunched body. At that moment, the Knight pushes himself upright. I drag my sword, swinging and drawing back before impaling the Knight's chest. His face was shocked. Glass or a gem shattered, a fire sparked, and the Knight combusted and turned to ash. Scattering to the wind. Catching my breath, I'm looking for the other knight. The others finished the last of the dead. Nathan, Michael, and George stood covered in blood and guts, bewildered. The skies were changing, becoming a lighter purple as the first hint of sun rose. I could see the knight's ashes lingering.

Somehow, we survived and still failed. The other knight was nowhere to be seen. Then we felt it, a rumble of the floor. Soon after, the first crack appeared, splitting through the fight pit, and the blood poured into the ground. My preview was coming true. A light purple light boomed out of the ground. George's face looked in pain. He'd seen something, too. A new dawn was coming, and so was hell. We'd failed. George was in tears, talking to Michael. All I heard was about Ellena, still trapped with those evil fuckers. All four of us had an ability now, some newer than others, while Nathan and I fought back from the dead to slay some. The ground continued to shake; houses fell, not that it would take much. Without a word, a look did enough. We knew the fight had only begun. And we will drag our world from the ashes of hell if we have to. That knight ran scared. We could only hope the message filters down. We're coming.

Rachel: "Good morning, everyone. This is Rachel Cordwell reporting live for Sky News, coming to you in an emergency broadcast after reports of zombies roaming the streets. It's not even Halloween. My pilot, Lenny Chadwick, bless his soul, finally got it up. The helicopter, before all your deviant minds wander. Say hi, Lenny."

Lenny: "Hi, Lenny."

Rachel: "Wow, the old jokes are the best. Next to me, as loyal as ever, even at this ungodly hour, is my cameraman, Jack Casey. Give the viewers a glimpse of you on this bizarre and terrifying day, if true."

Jack: "Good morning."

Rachel: "That's great, Jack. Right, Lenny, where are we now?"

Lenny: "We're coming up on... What in God's name... It's Willowbrook, but not as you may know it. Quick look."

Rachel: "Oh my god, it's truly horrifying. The reports are true. If anything, they undersold it. The streets are lined with grotesque, dead walking. Zombies, for lack of a better term. Some are fresher than others; some are punching out of their graves as we speak. Oh god, one just lost an arm as it came through. I'm not mincing words or towing the P.R. line on this rare and monumental morning. It's fucking awful. Others are dripping black blood and shedding flesh. It's pure carnage, holy shit, that one is just an arm, a rib cage, a skull, and a spinal cord. It's dragging itself through a sea of red. Oh god, it was. Now, it's a stepping stone as a chunky one obliterated it. They have no coordination and little balance."

"With our side door open, even from up here, we can hear a horde of groans and yawns. No words, at least none we can pick up. Their eyes are cloudy and vacant; it's so goddamn spooky."

Lenny: "Quick, Rachel, look! As we head north of the Pennines, giant cracks are tearing through the streets."

Rachel: "As ever, Lenny is right. Holy cow... town after town, roads, gardens, and sidewalks are being destroyed, even farms, as fissures tear through like huge spider webs or branches. Now, if this doesn't evoke thoughts of 'hell' opening up, I don't know what will. Bright purple light beams out with intensity. These cracks are everywhere, getting longer and wider. There's no covering this up as an earthquake or reporting otherwise, CNN."

Rachel: "There's just so much blood as more and more is spilt. Oh no, people are fleeing their homes as the ground opens up and swallows them whole. They're not getting far, running straight into the zombies, who are savagely ripping these ordinary people to shreds. One is even waving a dismembered arm around like a bat. Oh crap, they just bit a chunk out of it. Damn, I think I'm going to be sick. It's fucking awful."

Rachel: "Remember, we are coming to you live. My word, this is a first for this reporter. Anyone at home watching this, do not leave your home or open any windows or doors. Keep the news on at all times for regular updates. This is unprecedented and an awful nightmare. I'm truly stunned and devastated."

Jack: "Crap, what's that?"

Rachel: "And it keeps getting terrifyingly weirder. This is no joke, no illusion. It's straight out of an IMAX-quality horror. Hundreds of body-shaped black clouds with blood-red eyes spewed from the ground. You heard that right: if Casper went to the Darkside and had millions of babies, this would be them. They're filling the air. Wow, some are flying into zombies, and they're changing. Just when you think it can't get any worse, these haunting bundles of smoke make the zombies more mobile and less rigid. Shit, one just ran and caught a human, ripping their head clean off. This is so tragically crazy, I'm almost at a loss for words."

Lenny: "Hang on, guys, it's going to get bumpy; several are flying directly toward us. Oh god, oh god. Duck, one's just flown inside. Aaarghhh, it... it's got me."

Rachel: "Did you hear that? Lenny just said one has flown in. This is Rachel Cordwell at the heart of the action, people. Wait, what's going on? Lenny just screamed out, that cloud has got him. Oh god. I'm going to be sick for real. We're in a tailspin, Jack, hold on. Shit, did you hear that? It's coming from Lenny. I can hear... It's loud, groaning, just like the zombies."

Rachel: "Shit, he's leaving the cockpit. Oh, no, wait, what are you doing? Lenny is staggering towards me and Jack; he looks dead, his skin has turned grey, and his eyes are jet black. EWWW, there's blood too. It's spewing from his mouth and eyes. Holy shit, no one is flying the helicopter. We're going down. Wait, what are you doing? He's grabbing at the camera. I guess Lenny wants his close-up. Oh, no, this has been reported by Rachel Cordwell and Jack Casey. Lenny has been turned into a zombie by one of those things that came out of the ground. It appears hell has opened its doors and is coming for us.

Blood drenches our streets, and we're overrun by the dead. If we don't survive this. Mum, dad, I love you. No, wait, let go, get your face away from Jack."

Dead Lenny: "We... kill... all. Arrgggh,"

Rachel: "You heard... it... here... first. They're looking to kill all. Oh shit, we're spinning out of control. Noooooo, we're going downnnn."

The End.

Acknowledgements

To the family and friends who sat through the countless drafts and listened to my crazy ideas. Even when my confidence wavered, at a crossroads of whether to give up. You inspire me to be better every day and with every novel I create. Especially with this one, and pushing me to let go, stop holding back. Thank you...

Printed in Great Britain
by Amazon